This book is dedicated to a dear friend

Latasha M. Barnes

I

PREFACE and
Acknowledgements

By Maudarica M. Lewis

In the spring of 2009, I began to have a reoccurring dream for about two months; I asked God what do these dreams mean? But He said nothing, until one morning in May of 2009; I was driving home after just dropping my daughter off at school.... He began to speak... I don't know about anybody else but sometimes God picks the oddest time to speak to me; most of the time when I'm least expected or minding my own business...However God began to speak and He said you're going to write a stage play. And you're going to name it Take up Your Bed and Walk. I grabbed the closet piece of paper that was near me in the car, which was a receipt paper. I began to write while still maintaining the wheel. He was giving me more information than I anticipated and spoke faster than I wrote so I grabbed an envelope and began to write on the back of it. I was overwhelmed because I had never thought of writing, let alone a Play. After three months of writing, and putting together a cast of 22 plus people it was time to perform. In June 2010, I successfully wrote, produced and directed "Take up Your Bed and Walk." We went on to do an Encore in July 2010.

In October 2010, I decided to go a little deeper in my writing and introduce the characters to a new medium—the novel. In October 2013, the novel was completed. Like the Play, part of the reason for the writing is to be informative, entertaining, draw laughter, and send a challenge to change.

I believe that "art imitates life," and that life is funny sometimes and the things that use to make us cry will eventually make us laugh... This book is a page turner, a cherry moon for the hopeless romantic, encouragement for all wayward children of God and a nonstop tickle to make your body jiggle!

First and foremost, I must pay homage to the Trinity; the Father, Son and Holy Spirit. I want to thank you for ordering my steps, enlarging my territory and giving me a creative mind. All the glory belongs to you.

To my three children: Dexter, De'Mariah, and Aaron; and special thanks to my baby girl De'Mariah for the cover design. Thanks Markia and Alexis for your services.

My friends Kawanna, Angela and Roman; thank you for taking the time out of your busy schedule to read the unedited version.

Thank you, Eric Sharper of (Dream Reality Records) and Dr. Lord Ajmer, for encouraging me and pushing me to go to the next level. I also want to thank Caterina Orr of (Get it write-consultant) for her editing service. To Pastor S. Knowles and Tony Allen, little means much, thanks you. And to everyone else if I have forgotten to mention your name, please charge it to my head and not my heart.

FORWARD

By Maudarica Lewis

See what viewers had to say about the hit stage play Take Up your Bed and Walk:

"The play was hilariously & thought provoking. One can change if they desire. Luv luv luv it

"Take Up your Bed and Walk" is a faith energizing dramedy."

Awesome!!! I was truly blessed by this play. The characters were awesome. I stayed on my feet. I laughed, I cried. I can't wait to see what comes next!

"This play was so real. The church scene had me on my feet...and yes I got my shout on in the theater. Lol"

"This play hit home with me. I seen the old me in one of the characters and I also saw my daughter as Brittney. It changed my sermon the next day. I was going to preach one message but ended up preaching Take Up your Bed and Walk. I enjoyed it,"

INTRODUCTION

By Maudarica Lewis

Living a Christian life can be difficult and in Take Up Your Bed and Walk, we can identify with how being in an unhealthy relationship, whether a friendship or courtship can cause you to lose focus. This fictitious dramedy is full of many characters and many personalities. Sit back and enjoy the ride as you partake in these one foot in one foot out church folk lives. As you take off with a smooth sailing don't forget to strap on your seat belt because on this journey you may hit a couple of pot holes; you may laugh, you may cry, you may even find yourself talking at the characters and you just might find yourself singing your old favorite Jam.

However this was written with no disrespect to anyone nor to bring harm but as stated before, to entertain, draw laughter, and provoke change. With this said let me introduce you to a few of my friends:

Kim is the owner of a small security firm known as "Jordan's Security," her business provides services such as body guard protection, crowd control, private investigating, and security guard. She is a native of Valdosta, Georgia and an active member of Friendly Freewill Macedonia Baptist Church where serves on the Praise Team. Kim is holding on to past hurt which leads to her promiscuous lifestyle; including one with Deacon Butray. She is currently in a relationship with **Keith**, a mild mannered truck driver who fails to give her the emotional attention she needs because of his past marriage. Can this four year relationship stand the test of time or will it dissolve like salt in water.

Brittney Renee is a native of Atlanta, Georgia. She currently resides in Valdosta, Georgia with her one son Jaylin. She is currently employed at local doctor's office as a RN. After five years of being a nurse, she is ready for a career change. Brittney is also a member of

F.F.M.B.C. where she serves on the Shout Committee. She is currently in a relationship with **Roosevelt Timothy Brinson** a.k.a. **Tim**; who grew up in the church but now wants nothing to do with it. Tim lives the lifestyle of a hustler one that Brittney would normally never take a second look at. But her love for him has caused her to compromise her relationship with God and she has now taken on his hard core, foul mouth characteristics ….Talking about being unequally yoked.

Monet is the owner of a small coffee shop known as the Café Latte'. She employs **LaZibra** a.k.a. 'Zi' and **Felicia** a.k.a. 'Lisa' who both adds flavor to the dramedy. Not only is Monet battling the early stages of MS but she can't seem to wipe off the married men magnet stamped on her forehead. Monet is also a member of F.F.M.B.C. She is one of great faith but will her physical limitations or the company she keeps cause her to waiver….

Dino is Kim's flamboyant next door neighbor. Dino has a gift; He is a dreamer and he is constantly getting on Kim's nerves with his colorful personality. Growing up Dino knew of God but a tragic incident cause him to have an internal nightmare. Will Dino ever wake up or will he continue to sleep walk.

Michael a.k.a. Mike, but to his childhood friends, Kim and Monet he is better known as **Donavan**, or **'Lil' Don**. This native of Valdosta recently came back to town to finish up some old business. Will this old business cause him to stay or will he move on to new business.

And last but certainly not the least **Pastor De'Angelo Downs** is the Pastor of (F.F.M.B.C) Friendly Freewill Macedonia Baptist Church. Will he live up to the name he was cursed with, Lo-Down? Hmmm I don't know but rumor has it his new name could be Down- Low.

Kim

"Kim, baby, let me holla at you for a second," Mike yelled as he ran across campus to catch up with her. He kissed her on the forehead. "How was your day?" he asked.

"It was good," she replied. "I passed my exam, so today is officially my last day of high school. I don't have to come tomorrow."

"Word! Me either," he said.

"I'm so excited about graduation tomorrow," said Kim.

"I am, too, but I'm also sad that I'll be leaving next week for college. I tried to convince Momma to let me start in the fall but she insists on me starting this summer." Kim drops her head. "Kim…" He called her name gently.

"Kim, look at me." She wouldn't look up. Mike took his hand and raised her chin.

"Kimberly, look at me please." She raised her eyelids to make eye contact with him.

"Listen," he said, "we've known each other since diapers girl." She gives him a half smile.

"I love you, you know that right?" She nods yes. "I'll be home every other weekend and holidays." He said.

"I know, It… It's just that I won't be able to see you every day like I'm used to," she mumbles as she drops her head again.

"I know baby, but guess what?"

"What?" she asked.

"I still have plans to come back and marry 'my boo' after I finish college," he answered smiling. She looked up at him and smiled. Just as she is about to give him a hug, she is interrupted by a soft spoken but authoritative voice in the distance.....

"KIMMM!!" Keith comes in the kitchen and finds her sitting at the table in a daze; smiling. "Kim!" He yells in her ear; she jumps.

"What the hell wrong with you, yelling in my ear like that!"

"I have been calling you for the last five minutes. What are you in here daydreaming about?"

"Nothing" she answers.

"Must be something or should I say someone cause you were caught up," he states with an inquisitive look.

"I was thinking about Brittney and Monet crazy tail."

"Oh yea, what about them?" he asks.

"The two of them were trying to out shout each other in church last night," she says smiling, knowing she's lying.

"For real?" He laughs.

"Umm Hmm," she says.

"Wow! Those two are a trip. How is Monet anyway?"

"She's ok; sometimes up sometimes down."

"Baby, I know I haven't been to church in a while but I do know she needs to start declaring God's Word over her life. She has to know within herself that God is a healer and by his stripes she is healed."

Kim is looking at him but not hearing a word he is saying; all she hears is Charlie Brown's teacher… "Wonk wawonk wonk wonk wonk."

She thinks to herself, *"I wish he shut the hell up; came in here interrupting my happy thoughts about Michael."* She snaps back to reality…

"You're right." She cuts him off and agrees with him quickly so he can shut up. "Monet just needs to declare the Word of God over her life," she says sarcastically.

"You 'bout to go to work?" she asks.

"Yeah, I have a short route today; I only have to go to Macon and back."

"Ok, well you be careful," she says as she walks out the kitchen. "I Love you. Lock the door behind you."

"Love you too Hon!" he says.

As he grabs his lunch out the refrigerator, he begins to talk to the Lord. *"Father I bless you, you are worthy, I praise your mighty name, I adore you, you are wonderful. Your love is like Campbell soup— "mmm, mmm good." Father, I ask you to forgive me for my sins known and unknown, renew in me a clean heart and right spirit on today. Lord, I ask that you encamp your angels all around my truck and them eighteen wheels in Jesus name. Take me to and from my destination safely. In….* Kim comes back in the kitchen just as he is walking out and interrupts his prayer.

"Who you talking to?" she asks.

"God!" he replies as he finishes, *"Jesus name, Amen.* See you later bay," he says as he walks out. She turns to give him a peck but he's in such a hurry he doesn't notice.

It's about 6:30 in the morning; Kim puts on a pot of coffee, turns the radio on and finds the Steve Harvey Morning Show, just in time to hear the second verse of *Fortunate* by Maxwell. She pauses and reminisces of the time she and Mike slow danced under the moonlight to that song…

"Where are we going?" Kim asked.

"Let's just go for a drive and talk," Mike replied as he closed the door behind her and walked around to the driver seat. When he sat down, he looked over at her and smiled. She smiled back. He put the key in the ignition and they began to ride and listen to R. Dub slow jams on 105.3. To her surprise seven minutes into the drive, she hears an oral expression over the air. *"This is Mike from Georgia, and I'd like to dedicate Fortunate by Maxwell to the love of my life, Kim. Kim, baby I want you to know that I love you and I am very "fortunate" to have you in my life."*

She looked over at him with her hands over her mouth; "I don't know if I should laugh or cry," she said with tears in her eyes but laughing at the same time. "Thank you baby."

He pulls up to Swan Lake; one of the biggest parks in South Georgia. It's located near the airport and surrounded by a beautiful crystal blue lake. Families picnic by day here and couples often times come at night to escape the cares of the world. Some may take a stroll around the lake admiring the moonlit lake; some may come to watch the planes take off or land, while some may even watch the sun rise or set.

Mike got out the car and walked around to open Kim's door. He reached for her hand. "Come on," he spoke softly.

"What?" She looked puzzled.

"Just get out. I want to do something different; we never danced before and I want to dance with you to this song, under the moon; this will be our song."

"In front of all these people?" she asked.

"Girl, you know anything is bound to happen at this park. Now come on before the song go off." She took his hand and they began to dance. "This is going to be our song," he repeated.

As they're swaying side to side holding each other tight he begins to sing in her ear…. ♪*"For- tun-ate, to have you girl….*

Rrrring …Rrrring the telephone interrupts her reminiscing.

"Hello?" she answers.

"Hey Kim!"

"Hey," she speaks back.

"Girl, you really tore the house down last night," Butray says sounding like Eddie Lavert. "I'm talkin' 'bout ushers needed ushers, nurses needed nurses and I could have sworn I seen Pastor doing the stanky leg!

Kim laughs. "Butray, you crazy."

"For real Kim, you know Pastor be tryin' to cut a rug, but seriously though, I really enjoyed your singing last night. You know praise and worship is one of the most important parts of the service."

"Umm hmm! And what about you, Hype Man? I hear you over there in the corner boosting Pastor up soundin' like Lil' Jon; YEAH!" she laughs.

"Hey Kim, lets hook up later," he interrupts.

"Ain't your wife back in town? Why you botherin' me?"

"Tricia, be tripping Kim, you know this. I don't know why we have to keep having this discussion. You know you need the extra money!" He exclaims with a little frustration.

"I don't even like you like that." Kim says.

"I know you don't, but you scratch my back and I'll scratch yours."

"Well, My –Back- Ain't –Itchin'!" she responds.

"Oh it's like that?" He says with unbelief.

Her doorbell rings. "I gotta go; somebody's at my door."

"Kim, it's not just about sex; I care a lot about you. Patricia is always gone outta town; she don't want to give me none no more. She don't cook for me anymore, or show me any attention. She changed on me Kim." The doorbell rings again.

"Tray, listen I got a lot going on in my life right now… have you talked to her?"

"She always says…" The doorbell rings again and Kim cuts him off.

"Let me call you back," she says. "Somebody's at my door."

"Ok." He hangs up.

"I'm coming!" Kim makes her way to the door.

"It's me BRITT—Ney!" She says as Kim flings open the door. "What took you so long? Who's in here?" she asks looking around being nosey.

[6]

"Ain't nobody in here. I was just on the phone with that Butray." She answers in a low tone.

"What he want now?" Brittney asks.

"He wants to hook up later."

"Sounds like Mr. BUTRAY wants some BOOTAY!" She smiles.

"Child boo! Not tonight 'cause Keith will be back in a little bit; he only had to go to Macon today and, besides, that thing with Tray is gettin' old. Do you know he had the nerve to tell me he care a lot about me? I almost thought he was going to say he love me."

"Hell! He probably does, Kim. Patricia ass ain't never 'round no more." Kim looks at her

"What? Don't be lookin' at me with your nose all tooted up!"

"You've been around Tim too long." Kim says. "Now that cussin' demon on you."

"I know girl; pray for me. I'm still a building under construction. Like Steve Harvey saying: *Don't trip He ain't through with me yet.*"

"Your building was complete until you decided to renovate and go get a new architect." Kim says with an attitude.

"Why do you always have to criticize my man, Kim?"

"I just think you can do a whole lot better."

"So what's up with you and Keith?" Britt changes the subject "It's been about four years now. When are you two getting married?

"I'm not quite sure yet, we talk about it but that's about it. I think he still has some ill feelings about his ex-wife, Sonya." Kim says.

"What that got to do with you!?" Brittney asks.

"He mentioned something about not wanting to go through another

[7]

divorce."

"DAMN THAT!" Kim looks at her with disbelief.

"I'm sorry girl, but he can't make you pay for her mistakes; and quit looking at me crazy every time I say a little curse word. Hell, you sleep around! Both of us got a little dirt around our front door, but it's all the same in God's eyes; ain't one sin greater than the other. I just need a little Listerine for this mouth and you need a little Vin-e-gar for that one!" She points in between Kim legs.

"Brittney, girl, you are Crazy." Kim says laughing hysterically. "That man has really changed you."

"Girl, I had to change. I'm dealing with a hustler; he'll run all over me. Don't get me wrong; I haven't lost myself completely. I'm still humble, and I still love God. I just got a little boldness about me and picked up a little cus-sing spirit." She says, bashfully.

"I see." They start laughing.

"And I don't tolerate foolishness." Brittney adds. "One of Tim's baby's momma tried me like a shawty one day. We went to go pick up his son, Devin. Tim gets out the car and stands by the driver door; she comes out the house and yells: *I know you didn't bring this 'B' over here!*" Mannn, Kim I jumped out that car so fast; 'B' *I got yo' such in such, 'B',*" I scream.

"Tim snatched me just as I made it to the back of the car." Kim is laughing her butt off.

"See, I didn't curse either." Brittney says.

"I see that. So what has Tim been talkin' 'bout these days?" Kim asks.

"Girl, he's been singin' that same tired ol' song," Brittney says.

[8]

"What?" Kim starts singing and bouncing: ♫*"Everyday I'm hustling, Everyday I'm hustling, Everyday I'm hustling.*♫ Nawl here it go... ♫ *I put on for my city, put on for city, put on for my city."*♫ The two of them snigger. "No this the one, Brit."

Kim starts to bounce again and as she starts to sing, Brittney throws her hand in the air and sings along with her: ♫*Stacks on deck, patron on ice we can pop bottle all night baby you can have whatever you like, you can have whatever you like."*♫

"Kim, you are crazy girl, you gonna stop clowning my man but, on the real, in his defense I must say he is very good to me. He's always buying me flowers, he's attentive to my needs he listens to me, and he's my best friend. He said he's not ready to marry me just yet because he wants to be able to provide for me and Jaylin."

"Seems to me he being a good provider for them crack heads," Kim whispers under her breath.

"Excuse me!?"

"I didn't say nothing. Where's Jaylin?" Kim changes the subject as she walks in the kitchen to fix herself a drink and Brittney follows behind her.

"We went by my parent's house after church last night and he wanted to spend the night so I left him there. I went home and went straight to sleep."

"Have some?" Kim asks.

"No thanks." She sits down at the island.

"Kim, girl, I got to find me another committee to work on."

"Why? What's wrong with the one you on?"

"The Shout Committee?" Brittney answers with her nose turned up. "Girl please! Sister Shirley will wear you out with all those shouts." Kim starts laughing. "Wait a minute, wait a minute. Does she tell yall how to shout?"

"Yes! You're gonna get your shout on and you gonna shout on point." Kim continues to laugh. "And does she come up with all those shouts?"

"YES! And if you're not shouting right she comes up behind you and taps you on your shoulder to let you know you're off beat."

"Why doesn't she ever shout?" Kim leans on the island.

"Because she says she's graduated from shouting." Mocking her in a foreign accent, "'that's why Pastor put me over the shout committee.' She says, 'This is a committee of excellence.'"

Kim chokes on her drink, "a committee of excellence? I think pastor was creating something for her to do."

"UHH *yeah*!" Brittney sarcastically agrees.

"He got tired of her interrupting him every time he trying to preach," she says laughing. "She be saying stuff that don't make no sense: 'Amen, Pastor! Come on, Pastor! You betta ride that white horse!'" Kim is rolling on the floor laughing her butt off.

"Britt…" Kim calls her name trying to catch her breath; "Britt…she be saying what? You betta ride that white horse? Oh my God! You sound just like her. Please stop! I can't take it no more." Kim continues to laugh.

"For real, Kim; you know I'm telling the truth. But I got to give props to you right now, girl; you were off the chain last night. You really worked us. People were falling out everywhere. And Pastor was up there doing the Stan-ky Leg; HEEY!" She mimics pastor doing the dance. "You were awesome!"

"To God be the glory!" Kim replies.

"See, God know what He be doing." Brittney stands up. "He knows just who to give what gift to. 'Cause if he would have blessed me with a voice like yours…hmm, it would be all flesh" raising her right hand in the air with her eyes closed, "Straight entertainment," moving her hand from head to toe. "Super star!" holding her hand as if she were holding a microphone.

"Brittney girl, you are crazy," Kim says.

"And you see how you always be giving God his glory? This flesh would have been like 'glory to who?' See, God don't make no mistakes. He gave you a gift."

"And He gave you a gift of motherhood." Kim says.

"Girl, please! That was not God. That was me being grown and fast and disobedient to my parents. Had I held that pill between my knees like my doctor told me, I wouldn't have been a mom. But I thank God for my son Jaylin; he's my booga bear," she smiles. "He keeps me humble and he's one of the reasons I gave my life to God at an early age…. I never wanted any kids."

Kim looking confused, "Hold up! I'm still stuck on this pill; what pill, Brit?"

"My birth control pill." Brittney smiles. "My mom took me to get on the pill when I was thirteen and the doctor told me to hold this little pill between my knees; and if I ever let it fall, I was going to get pregnant," Brittney smiles.

Kim starts laughing, "Brittney you know what… you need help girl. Guess you dropped the pill, huh?"

"Guess I did." Brittney begins to laugh with her. But Kim is laughing a little too hard. "That Sh…I meant mess ain't that funny, Kim."

"Let me get my oil so we can pray," Kim says.

"I know… I know, I'm working on it," Brit says.

"Do you want any more children?" Kim asks.

"Hell No! Didn't I just tell you I didn't want any to begin with? Besides, Tim already has four."

"Who says you going to be with him forever? Brittney, if he's telling you he wants to be a provider first, that's bull. Let me tell you this; as long as he out there hustling, you will never be number one. He's gonna always be chasing that paper. You need to get yourself a saved man!"

"He is saved, Kim! He's just in a Backslidden state." Brittney says.

"BACKFLIPPING!" Kim says sarcastically.

"Look we all have our issues and I'm not giving up on my man because I know he's gonna be delivered soon," Brittney says with confidence.

"Yeah! When pigs fly."

Brittney starts shouting, "Heeeey! Halleluuuujah, Halleluujah; that's confirmation right there. Thank you Jesus! Glory to God! I know deliverance is coming soon!" She sits back down on the couch and Kim looks at her like she's crazy, "Brit why you say that?"

"'Cause they got this swine flu going around," she replies with a serious look.

"Are you bi-polar?" Kim asks.

"Is yo momma bi-polar?"

"She is," Kim answers. They both laugh. "But girl, that man is not going to change."

"Yes he will, Kim. You never know how God will bring you the answer you been praying for. If he can use an Ass…" looking at Kim; "to speak, and bless this negative vessel in front of me, surely he can save my man. God says He's married to the backslider, but I'm not mad at you girl. I know that's just a spirit in you."

"Brittney, I'm not negative!"

"Yes, you are, Kim. For the past few years I've known you, you been negative, judgmental; you sleep around with married men…and the deacon, Kim? You two are going straight to…"

Knock, knock, knock. Brittney is interrupted.

"Come in!" Kim yells.

Kim's next door neighbor Dino walks in, "What up, Kim? Brittney?" He speaks as he comes in.

"What you want, Dino?"

"I came over to tell you about this dream I had."

"Dream, huh?" Kim says.

Before he mentions the dream, he gets side track and asks her about their church. "What happened to yall building? Why are yall having church here now?"

"The Pastor ran off with our building fund money," she replies.

Dino puts both his hands to his mouth. "See that's messed up, Kim.

You want me to call my cousin C- low and them? They'll find his ass! Oops, excuse me Brittney."

It's okay; she already brought that spirit up in here this morning," Kim interrupts.

"I meant they'll find his tail and bring that money back!" Dino says with frustration. "That don't make no damn sense; see, that's why people don't want to go to church now. Hell! I think sinners stand a better chance of making it to heaven than some of these so call Church folk." Kim and Brittney look at each other, surprised to hear him talking like this. "Ah well, I guess that's the answer to my dream," he says.

"What dream, Dino?" Kim asks.

"I saw a tornado headed towards your church…" He pauses "Wow! I guess it did tear up some stuff and cause a division too, huh?"

"I wish he would just shut up and leave, matter fact I wish the both of them would leave; I need to get ready for work." Kim says to herself.

"Yeah, I see some members go over to Bro. Brinson house." Dino carry on. "Who is the Pastor now?"

"De'Angelo Downs," Kim answers quickly.

"Not Lo-down, I know," Dino yells.

"They don't call him that any more, Dino." Kim says.

"Oh- I- know- what they call him." He says rolling his head. "Lo-Down; his momma cursed him when she gave him that name, you know that right? You got to be careful what you name your kids. And now I hear some people call him down low." Dino continues to ramble on. "He ain't gone never get ahead in life with a name like

[14]

that."

"DINO!" Kim interrupts. "You ain't gone keep talking about my pastor in my face!"

"Oh I see," Dino says slowly, "so you got one of them kind, huh?"

"One of what kind?" Kim asks.

"One of them kind taught to fight for their pastor…. NEWS FLASH KIM," he gestures his hands to mimic a flashing light, "they talked about Jesus too."

"It ain't that! I'm just not gone let you dog the man out like that when I know he's change." Kim retorts.

"Sorry, girl. Dang! But he wuzz cute in school. Girl, I had the biggest crush on…"

"Get out!" Kim interrupts, and points to the door. "I've heard enough; you just rambling."

"I'm sorry," he responds sadly.

"Get out before you make me cuss." She gets up and walks him to the door.

"Alright, dang, but I'm coming over here to yall bible study… Tuesday right?"

"Un um, Wednesday." She lies as she opens the door to let him out.

"Bye Brittney," he says walking out the door; Kim slams the door behind him.

"That Dino, always talking about 'God said,' or 'I had a vision.' If I didn't know any better, I swear he is Martin Luther King reincarnated."

"There you go again, talking negative; what if God really did speak to him this time?"

"Child boo, God ain't said nothing to him with all that sin going on up in his place. You know him and his boyfriend was fightin' last night." Kim says whispering.

"For real?" Brittney asks.

"Yes! They were throwing down next door. He swung at Dino and punched a damn whole in the wall, then threw his ass out in the hallway. See how you done brought that cussin' demon up in here?"

"No baby, that was already there; what's in you gonna come out; you were just waiting to get some license to cuss," Brittney says with an attitude. "What else happened?"

"I heard Dino, hollering like a punk." Kim says.

"He *is* a punk!" Brittney responds enthusiastically. "Now your negativity is rubbing off on me."

"Anyway, Dino, must have told him he had a vision about him 'cause I heard his partner say, "I'mma put both your eyes out." Kim laughs.

"Hey, the bible does say, gift and callings come without repentance." Brittney laughs.

Girl, let me get out of here so I can get to work."

"Alright girl; lock the door behind you." Kim looks at her watch and gets ready for work.

On her way to work, she turns on the radio to her favorite station 105.3: ♫*"He saw the best in me, when everyone else around, could only see the worst in me."*♫ Kim sings along: ♫*"He saw the best in me…"*♫ "That was Marvin Sapp with The Best in me." Coming up we have the birthdays with Butterfly Eugene and phone prank with Uncle Tommy."

Kim's cell phone rings, "Hello?"

"Morning lady."

"Hey Moni."

"What are you doing for lunch today?" Monet asks.

"Nothing. Why? What's up?"

"You wanna have lunch?" Monet asks.

"Yeah, that's cool. What do you have a taste for?"

"Let's do a buffet or something. Maybe O'Ryan's?"

"Ok, I'll meet you there around 11:45." Kim says.

"Alright, talk with you later."

"Bye," Kim says.

Brittney

Brittany, an RN at a private practice, stands at the front desk talking to Donna, one of the medical assistants, about a patient when a floral delivery guy comes in. "Awww! They are so beautiful," Maria, another assistant, says.

Brittney glances at the flowers and continues her conversation with Donna.

"They're for you, Brittney," Maria says. Brittney looks up and walks over to admire them.

She smells them. "They are beautiful!" Brittney exclaims.

"Tim always sends the most beautiful arrangements," says Maria.

Brittney looks at the card: Meet me for lunch at the spot. I love you, Tim."

O'Ryans

Kim is in her car listening to the radio, on her way to go meet Monet for lunch. *"Coming up this hour we got Alicia Keys-Unthinkable, a little bit of Maxwell, Chrisette Michelle, A brand new one by El DeBarge, but first we gone kick this off with, Deborah Cox; yall remember this one?"* The Dj asks. "Oh, Lord," Kim states, "Are you trying to tell me something today? I get up this morning; *Fortunate* was on the radio which was me and Mike's favorite song and now, our break up song: ♫*"Weee can't be friends, 'Cause I'm still in love with you"*♫ as the song continues on. She pulls up in the parking lot of O'Ryans and reminisces about the day when she first heard that song:

Rrrring rring! Her cell phone rings. "Hello?" Kim answers.

"Kim, baby we need to talk," Mike says.

"What's up? What's wrong? You don't sound too good," Kim responds.

"Baby, you know, I love you right?"

[18]

"Yes, what's going on Mike? You're scaring me."

"Baby...Kim. I will always love you. We've known each other so long, and I do want to marry you Kim, I do baby....." Mike can hardly get the words out because of the tears.

"Mike, I'm not liking this; WHAT'S GOING ON!?" she yelled and tears began to roll down her face.

There became a brief moment of silence. "Whatever it is we can work through it." Kim cried.

"She pregnant!" He blurted out and began to cry even more.

"She what? Who pregnant, Michael?" Kim said with a stern voice as the tears came to a halt. Michael Jarrod Johnson, please don't tell me you got some girl pregnant.... Please! Please! Please don't tell me!" She yells to the top of her lungs. "Oh God!" She started crying again. "Why? Why you do me like this?!" she shouted.

"Baby, I'm sorry!"

"I can't even talk to you right now," she faintly spoke and hung up the phone. A few weeks later she learned of Mike marrying the young lady that was pregnant. He would call but she wouldn't answer. He would even make special trips home just to see her only to be disappointed. Kim began to slip into depression. She became numb to her emotions and food became her best friend. One day while sitting in her room and she heard this new song by Deborah Cox come on the radio. The chorus caught her attention. ♫*"We can't be friends, 'cause I'm still in love with you."*♫ When the song went off she googled the song to listen to the lyrics again; her intentions were to call him at a time when she knew he wouldn't answer, so she could let the song play on his voice mail, but instead he answered.

"Hello?" Mike answered. Just as he was about to hang up he heard music playing; he listened to the words:

♫ *"I went by Mother's, saw your car there*
To her you're still family, and it don't seem fair
For everyone to just go on
And I've tried and I can't do it
'Cause I'm still torn…" ♫

Her thoughts are interrupted by a tap on the glass. "Kim!" Monet taps her window. "Get out this car! What are you over here day dreaming about? I was standing over there waving for you to come on for the last two minutes."

"I'm sorry," she says getting out the car. "I….there…" She stutters. "Lord, I can't even talk."

"You okay?" Monet asks.

"All these songs keep playing on the radio today that reminds me of Donavan." She says getting out of the car.

"This morning , I turn to the Steve Harvey Morning show and *Fortunate* was on and on my way over here *We Can't Be Friends* by Deborah Cox comes on. And what's crazy is' I've been thinking about him all day."

"Familiar Spirits have a way of finding you especially if you entertain them, Kim."

"How many? Two?" The hostess asks.

"Yes," Monet answers.

"Follow me," the hostess says.

As they sit down, Kim continues; "That's true, but if I had to be honest with myself, I never let go; I suppressed a lot of my feelings. Monet, he was my first love, and I put my all into him. I don't like feeling this way. I know it's been about seven years now and I have a good man…"

"That doesn't want to commit," Monet interrupts.

"That's true, too, but I think we both holding on to past hurt."

"Maybe you need closure," Monet says.

"I thought I closed that chapter of my life when I gave it to God."

"But you went and picked it back up." Monet answers with sarcasm.

"Why do you keep doing this to yourself? Why do you keep rehashing the past? ... Look, I know Don loved you, I was there. You two use to make me sick with all that lovey dovey mess…

"What can I get you to drink?" The waitress asks.

"Water," Kim answers.

"I'll have water also and we'll take the bar," Monet says.

"But honey, you've have got to move past this; Keith is a good man and the only problem I see between you two is communication. And part of communicating requires you to LISTEN because you talk too much, Kim. You think you know it all. And you can't expect this man to read your mind; men aren't mind readers. As much as we want them to just look at us and gravitate to our thoughts….Sorry it's just not going to happen. Now you do have some men, very little though, that are in tuned with their partners and they can look right at them and tell something is wrong. But that comes with being in tune with

[21]

one another.

"But we've been together four years now," Kim says.

"So what does that mean?" Monet asks.

"He should know me. He should be in tune with me!"

"Which one of you? Because your mind so tied up in, Donavan, Butray, Tony, and Keith. That's why you're so discombobulated now. You have too many people in your space… Kim imma say this and I mean no disrespect at all but you need to get saved for real. Don't you know every time you lay with a man, he is imparting a part of him in you? That's what you call soul ties, and that's why God designed sex for marriage to prevent situations like this."

"Why you so quiet?"

"Didn't you just say I need to listen? I'm just soaking it all in….. To be honest, it's tight but its right." She smiles.

"And that's why yall can't really come together because he doesn't have room to receive you and you don't have room to receive him. He needs to get over Sonya, and you need to go get your body parts back."

"What do you mean?" Kim asks.

"Where is Mike?" Monet says.

"Don't know," Kim answers.

"Tony?"

"Texas," Kim answers.

"James?

"Tampa," Kim says.

"Cody?"

"Cali."

"Drell?"

"Jail," she answers.

"You've been with all these people, right?" Kim looks at her with no response. "Right, Kim? Come on we're girls; tell the truth shame the devil. You got pieces of you everywhere, spread out all over this country. You need to go get your body parts back. See a lot of them still holding your parts because they don't know the new you. And the reason they keep calling because in their mind they see the old Kim, not the saved Kim. And how long has this been since you rededicated your life? About six years now? Child, tell them heathens you changed your life and you saved now! Some might get mad and stop talking to you while others will respect you and no longer look at you that way. Shoot, you don't even have to answer your phone. Do you understand what I'm saying?"

"It's tight, but it's right," Kim says again as they both get up from the table and go to the bar. "Now my turn; what's going on with you, Lady? Have you been feeling okay?"

"I've been okay, sometimes up, sometimes down…"

"Is that Brittney and Tim walking in?" Kim cuts her off.

Monet looks around the bar… "Yeah, that's them."

"How many; Two?" the waitress asks.

"Yes two," Tim answers.

"Okay, follow me." The waitress says "Would you guys like a booth or high table?" She asks. Brittney looks at Tim for an answer.

"It's whatever you want hon." He answers.

"We'll take a booth." Britt says.

Just as Brittney was about to sit down, "Brit, honey, go ahead and order for us; I left my phone in the car. I'll be right back."

"Hi, my name is Nicki, and I'll be your server for today; can I start you out with a drink?"

"Yes, let me get two waters and a coke." She answers.

"And will you two be ordering from the menu or will you be having the Bar today?"

"We both will be having the Red beans and rice combo." She answers. "Okay, well you know it comes with a salad so you guys can just help yourself; again my name is Nicki and I'll be right back with those drinks; Enjoy!"

"Thanks." Brittney smiles.

"Well, Well, Well. I see Mr. Man decided to take a breather and spend a little time with you," Kim says as her and Monet stops at Brittney's booth on the way back to their table. Brittney's smile quickly dropped, "See this is why we always have a problem, Kim this is an ongoing thing with you; you need to stop sweating my man and sweep around your on front door." She says as she stands up to go to the bar. She turns to Monet, "You do realize misery loves company?"

"Your momma!" Kim retorts.

Tim walks up behind Brittney and put both of his hands on her shoulders. Over hearing Kim's smart remark, he gives her a stern look.

[24]

"You don't scare me," Kim tells him.

Ignoring her, he put his arm around Brittney's waist and they walk over to the Bar.

"What's going on, hon?" Tim whispers in his low raspy voice.

"Nothing. Kim just gets on my nerves sometimes." She says in an aggravated tone.

"Kim gets on everybody nerves," Tim says. "I don't see how Ol' boy put up with that every day. People like that you just have to pray for." Brittney looks at him with disbelief.

"What!" Tim asks, "I know what you about to say. And don't start with me today."

"I'm just saying…."

"Saying what Brit? ….. Look, I got God! You know I grew up in church…"

"Then why you act like you so mad at Him?" she cuts him off.

"I'm not… any more. Look you got to understand, when I was growing up, we were in the church every time the doors opened. We were deep off in that thang. My momma was the chief prayer warrior, and my father despised sin like Superman to kryptonite. I was laying hands at two, speaking in tongues at eight. I was seeing miracles…."

"So what happened?" she asks with frustration.

"You know that saying, don't let the devil ride?"

She nods.

"Well, at some point my parents gave him a ride, then he began to drive." Both of them started doing drugs--crack was their choice. We went from riches to rags in a blink of an eye." He says as they sit back

[25]

down.

"Baby, you can't blame God for the choices that your parents made."

"You right! But for a loooong time hon, I was maad at God. I started hustling and right now it's paying the bills, keeping a roof over my head, your head and keeping them white folks off my back with this child support."

"Why they got to be white?"

"You right!" He takes a bite of his salad.

"Ain't no telling these days since we have a black president. But all I ever dealt with was the white ones."

"And don't include me in your drug reign, you know I make enough to handle my own."

"True, but you my lady and I like taking care of you."

"You know, eventually you're gonna have to trust that God will make a way. I know it sounds easier said than done; truth is, we all face adversity every day. The bible tells us we can't get to heaven without trials and tribul…"

"I KNOW BRIT!" Tim raises his voice in frustration.

"That's why I told you I didn't want to talk about this shit," he takes a bite of his red beans and rice and spits it out; "WHAT THE FUCK?"

"Tim!"

"This shit is sour! Oh my God! Excuse me Miss," the waitress walks over to the table." This here ain't right," Tim says.

"What's wrong?" the waitress asks.

"This shit nasty! It taste sour."

"I'm sorry about that. Would you like something else?"

"Nawl, We'll just eat whatever on the bar."

"Ok." The waitress answers.

"Here you might as well take hers, too," he remarks sarcastically.

Tim continues, "See that's why I didn't want to get into this conversation. It gets me all worked up. I love God and I do have my relationship with him. Believe me he whoops me when I'm doing wrong."

Every day, Brittney remarks sarcastically to herself.

"Look can we change the subject please? I just wanted to spend time with my baby and see you. I missed you."

"Umm Hmm. Thank you for the flowers," she smiles with her eyes.

"You know them eyes do something to me when you look at me like that."

"I know," she says seductively.

"I'm really not that hungry anymore," Tim says.

"Me either."

"Come on, let's get out of here, so you can get back to work on time."

"Work! Eeww," she sighs.

"What's wrong?"

"I like what I do babe, I'm just not passionate about it anymore."

"Why not?"

"I've been thinking about having a business of my own."

"Really? When did this come about?"

"I always had it in the back of my mind, but lately I been thinking a lot about it."

"Well what do you want to do?"

"Hair."

"Hair?"

"Yes."

His phone rings; "Yep yep," he answers.

"Give me fifteen minutes.......Yep." He hangs up the phone.

"Baby," he says getting up from the table and helping her up as well. "You gonna have to finish telling me more about this hair business later; I never knew you had another interest. I'll give you a call later; I gotta go handle some business right now. Love you, Hon." He kisses her on the lips, and Brittany heads back to work.

Kim

"Another day's work," Kim says as she cranks up the car.

"It's the Doug Banks Show, don't touch that dial."

♫ *Who- who- whowhoo."* Just as she starts singing to Jennifer Hudson's song *Spotlight*; her cell phone rings, "Hello?"

"Hey Cody.... I've been thinking about you too.... Of course I miss you.... Do you miss me?.... Nothing much, just working.... Yes I remember..... Can't wait to see you too!.... So when you coming back to the states?.... Oh so we counting down days now not months; alriiight! Are you still going to be stationed in California?..... Georgia?.... You coming back here?..... Oh Snap. Hey somebody is beeping in, give me a holla when you get in town..... Ok bye."

[28]

"Coming up Dee Dee's five things you need to know right now." She turns the radio down and dials the number back from the call just missed and she uses her Bluetooth that's programmed into her car to talk.

"Hello, did anyone just call Kim?"

"Yeah, it's me Tony."

"Tony, what's up?"

"I wanted to know if you would do me-- I meant do me the honors of having dinner with me tonight, then maybe dessert at my place afterwards."

"Sounds good; …… Wait! Nooo I can't. I'll get back with you. Let me see what I have going on at the house later."

"Alright."

"Bye." She pulls up in her parking lot; before she can get out the car, Dino yells out his window.

"Hey Girl!"

"Hey Dino," She replies nonchalantly.

"How was your day?" He asks.

"It was good; I hope you're not about to tell me about a vision."

"Nope, but I would like to come up and talk to you about something."

"You want to talk? Give me a minute; let me get myself together and gather my thoughts and I'll meet you downstairs somewhere."

"Ok, I may be at the pool," Dino says.

Kim continues on up to her apartment; as she's walking in the door, her house phone rings. Just as she's about to answer, she looks down at the caller ID and because she doesn't recognize the number she turns to walk away. The phone stops ringing but immediately rings again. "Who is this calling me from an 813 area code?"

She answers with a Jamaican accent, "McCullen Baker Funeral Homes. You stab 'em; we grab 'em!"

"Hello, may I speak with Kim?"

"Kim not here at the moment but if you leave your name and numba, she be sure to call ya back at her convenience."

"Kim?" the voice on the other end asks.

She pauses....."Mike?"

"Yeah, it's me. We need to talk."

"Mike, I haven't seen you in God knows when. Where are you? How are you?"

"I'm in town. Can we meet somewhere?"

"Where's your wife?"

"We divorced and she took our son and left town."

Kim begins to do a happy dance when Keith comes up behind her....

"Hey Baby." She jumps and hangs up the phone.

"What are you doing here? I wasn't expecting to see you till later tonight.

"I told you I had a short route today."

"Yeah but I thought you were going to chill at your place or something."

"You want me to leave?"

"No, you cool."

"Then why are you acting so nervous? And who was that on the phone got you pop locking and gyrating?"

"Nobody."

"So who were you asking, 'where your wife is?'"

"I didn't say: *where's your wife!*"

"Yes you did, Kim!"

"I was talking to my friend, Kierra. You remember my friend Kierra?"

Keith shakes his head no.

"You know Kierra married to Anthony!" she exclaims.

"No I don't." He shakes his head slowly trying to remember.

"Well, anyway he use to beat on her and I was asking her how- was – her- life. I'm glad she finally got the sense God gave her to leave that joker. Anyway bay, I know you must be tired so I'm going to go meet Dino downstairs while you get some rest."

"Dino?" Keith asks.

"Yeah, he says he needs to talk."

She shrugs her shoulders and walks into the room to change. The house phone rings and Keith answers it. "Hello?"….

"Sorry, no Peaches here," Keith says. "You have the wrong number." The phone rings again. "Hello…… Oh what's up Dee?..... The Community room?   Alright I'll let her know."

"I'll be back in a few." Kim tells Keith as she walks past him.

"Oh. Dino called when you were in the room; he said to meet him in the community room."

"Ok, thanks. See you in a bit."

Kim / Dino

"What's up?" Kim speaks entering the room.

"Thank you for meeting me. I don't have too many people I can talk to."

"Dino, what's going on with you?" she asks sarcastically.

"Kim, I had a vision."

"Ahh, here we go."

"No Kim, listen. You're always brushing me off when I come to you like this; just hear me out. I can't help that God has given me this gift. And just because my life is a little colorful right now doesn't mean God doesn't speak to me; so don't judge me because I'm in a relationship with a guy."

"I know the word say gifts come without repentance, but what is it profiting if you're not living right?" Kim asks.

"I know what I'm doing is not right in God's sight. Some of the stuff you do ain't right either, Kim. Oh if the walls could talk. Oops! Wait a minute.....they do talk and I hear everything that go on over there. I just never say anything 'cause you're my girl and who am I to judge?

"Well Mr. Spiritual man, The bible also say if you see your brother or sister overtaken in a fault...hold up let me break this down for you. If you see your brother or sister in sin, you who live by the Spirit should restore that person gently, but watch yourself, be careful not to fall into that same temptation."

"Don't do that!"

"Do what?" Kim asks sarcastically.

"Trying to act like I'm so deep. And you know I'm not even like that. However, I do have a scripture for you. Many are the affliction…hold up, let-me-break-it-down-for-*you*….The righteous person faces many troubles, trials, issues but guess what….The LORD DELIVERS him from them all."

"So what is it that you want to talk about, Dino?"

"Why the attitude? You act like I just get on your nerves."

"Well Dino, you do! Every time I turn around, it's always, 'I had a dream,' 'I had vision' or 'God said this' or 'God said that.' Hell, He ain't told you to stop sleeping with that man?"

"I get enough people turning their noses up at me out there; I don't need that from you, Kim. Whatever happened to people loving one another? I was taught you should hate the sin but love the person. My granddaddy use to say: *you need to love the hell out of people.*" They both laugh…. "I'm serious Kim. Sometimes that's all people need. They have all types of spirits up in them and they just need people to love the *hell* out of them."

"You right," Kim agrees. "Love does cover a multitude of sin."

"I know what I'm doing is wrong. I grew up in church so I know the Lord and His word. But what a lot of people don't know, I was sexual abused by my pastor and family members for a couple of years. I can remember the first time it happened; I was eight years old. I felt so dirty I went home to take a bath; I tried to wash the dirtiness and filthiness and unclean sensation off me. I must have bathed about ten times or more with a brillo pad. The tub was full of blood; I don't

[33]

know if it was from the abuse or me scrubbing my skin off. My mom came in the bathroom seen all the blood and went ballistic. Needless to say, that pastor isn't pastoring anymore. Then after that, it was two close family members. I went through a series of identity crisis. I hung with the blacks, the whites, the skateboarders, the Goths, started messing around with an Ouija board, didn't know if I wanted to be gay or straight. Girrrl, I pray every day that God gives me the strength to walk away from this lifestyle."

"Have you ever been with a girl?"

"Yes child! Was in love with one; but this spirit became a strong hold and overpowered that natural feeling of wanting to be with women. This thing ain't no joke! It's hard to break free from. But I do know greater is He that is in me than he that is in the world."

"Dino, I didn't realize…

"It's okay." He cuts her off. "Nobody ever knows the story; they just tend to prejudge. Like we poison or something. But I want you to know… when I walk away from this… from this lifestyle, I'll probably move back home for a little while until I get my own place."

"I'll be praying for you. So tell me about the dream," she changes the subject.

"Ok… I was walking in this dark forest and I couldn't see no light or where the forest ends. I kept walking for miles and miles; then, all of sudden I heard something snap! I looked down and realized I had stepped on this stick; the moment the stick broke, a light appeared and I was at the end of the forest."

"Wow! That's powerful," Kim says. "Tell you the truth I don't see you staying around here too much longer; I can see Him tugging on you."

"Well yeah, it's about that time; I been running long enough," Dino agrees.

Kim laughs. "Tell me this; why do most gay guys talk so dramatic? They be doing the most!"

"Child, that be that feminine spirit showing itself strong, girl. I know how to turn it on and off; I can go deep, or use my regular voice." He's switching up his voice to show Kim how it's done. Kim is laughing her butt off. *"And of course this is my gay voice."*

"Wait! Wait! Do the regular voice again." She can't stop laughing.

"Dino," he says.

Kim continues to laugh. "Now do the deep voice."

"**Dino.**" Both of them are laughing nonstop….

"Now the gay? Kim asks.

"Dino," he says dramatically.

"Dino, you are crazy!"

Keith

After Keith wakes up from his nap, he goes down to Bruce's Deli to get something to eat. When he walks in, he notices Mr. Gabriel at the bar. "Hey Mr. Gabriel."

"Hey Keith, what's going on man?"

"Nothing much; just got up from a nap and had a taste for a cold cut."

"Yeah, Bruce does have the best tasting sandwiches in the area."

"What are you doing here man?" Keith asks.

"Working."

"You work here now?" Keith asks.

"No man, a different kind of work!"

"Oh I see, whatever that supposes to mean," he mumbles under his breath.

"So how are things going with you? Anything new since the last time we talked?" Gabriel asks.

"Everything is pretty much the same. My job is keeping me busy, so I haven't been going to church like I use to."

"And your relationship with Kim?"

"We're still hanging in there."

"You still haven't asked her yet, huh?"

"Asked her what?"

"Come on Keith man; to marry you?"

"I will one day."

"What you waiting on? You said she's everything you wanted in a wife."

"I don't know man. I been down that road before with Sonya and I don't want to go through another divorce."

"Kim is a good woman that's lacking the emotional attention she needs."

"Oh yeah and how do you know this?" Keith looks curious.

"Any man can recognize she's a diamond in the rough and if you don't take care of her and polish her up, somebody else will."

"So what you saying, old man!?" He jumps up in his face.

"Sit down, son!" Mr. Gabriel said in an authoritative voice. "That's what's wrong with you young folks today; you won't listen! I'm just trying to give you a little advice."

"I hear you; now hear me....Stay away from my Girl!"

Keith leaves out the restaurant without ordering.

As Gabriel sits at the bar staring up towards the heavens he begins to think to himself: *Lord I've been here three years now. These people are set in their ways; Stiffnecks is what they are. You sent me here on an assignment and now I think it's about time to wrap this up.* He then reflects back three years prior when he was sent on this assignment: *"GABRIEL!"* A voice of power calls out.

"Yes Lord?"

"Willie Mae Jones has been praying for her grandson since birth. She has been faithful and because she honors me, I shall honor her. I have an assignment for you."

"Yes Lord."

"Pastor De Angelo Downs is the pastor of Friendly Freewill Macedonia Baptist church. The church has become corrupted and I am not pleased with Mr. Downs, but because of his grandmother, Ms. Jones, praying for him, I will not take my spirit away from it just yet. I need for you to convince him and his followers to turn from their wicked ways, but do not impose on their free will."

"Yes Lord."

Meanwhile, Kim and Monet are sitting in the living room

talking when Keith comes in with a disturbed look on his face; he sits down on the love seat. Kim looks at Monet as she gets up to go console him.

"Keith, honey, is everything okay?"

"Are you sleeping with him?" He looks up at her. Monet drops her head and puts her hand over her forehead.

"Huh? Who? I meant, No I'm not sleeping with nobody; what are you talking about?"

"Gabriel!" Keith yells. Kim and Monet sigh with relief.

"Heck nawl, boy! Where you get an idea like that from?"

"I saw him over at Bruce's Deli;… don't…don't worry about it, I'm trippin."

"Yeah you are," she agrees.

"Do you still want to go out later?" she asks.

"I was thinking we could just watch movies here tonight," he states as he walks toward the bedroom.

Kim sits back down next to Monet. "See that's what pisses me off about him. We use to have so much fun when we first met. Now this joker doesn't want to do anything. He used to buy me flowers, tell me he loved me, open doors for me, and he used to make me feel like every word I said was important."

"Have you told him this? Where is my purse?" She looks around.

"I tried throwing him some hints."

"Girl, you got to talk to that man! Didn't I tell you men aren't mind readers? That's you and a lot of other women problem, expecting a man to know what's on your twisted mind."

"Twisted? And you're not?"

"I didn't say I was exempt but I'm talking from experience. Go ahead and talk to the man; I left my purse at O'Ryans; I'll talk to you later.

"Keith, honey, we need to talk," Kim yells.

"What's up baby?" He answers walking into the living room.

"Keith I'm not happy."

"What's the problem?"

"We never go anywhere anymore; you never compliment me. The things we used to do when we first got together, we don't do any more. Hell Keith, you don't even go to church like you use to. And I'm tired of just talking about getting married. When are we gonna set a date; better yet when are you going to ask me to marry you?"

"Hold up! Where is all this coming from? You know I love you, baby. And I don't come to church like I use to because of my job."

"And what about us getting married? Because you can't keep spending the night over here, that's not pleasing God."

"How is it that not pleasing God? It's not like we having sex, so where's the sin? I tell you what He's not pleased with……" Keith pauses at the words of Gabriel replaying in his head: *Kim is a good woman that is lacking the emotional attention she needs…if you don't take care of her, polish her up, somebody else will.*

"Say it! Say it!" she demands.

"Don't worry 'bout it. I shouldn't have even…."

"Well you did!" She cuts him off.

"And since you did Boo Boo, say what's on your mind," she responds clapping her hands.

"Man, Kim, gone with all that; it was nothing! Aiight? I didn't mean to say that."

"What Keith? What about me God isn't pleased with? I wanna hear you say it!" Still clapping her hands to every word that she speaks.

"Look I'm out! I'm going in the room to watch the game."

"No! What you can do is go to your room at 5212 Hopper Lane and watch the game!"

"So you want me to leave because I'm trying to spare your feelings?!"

"Say what's on your mind, Mutha Fucka!"

Keith is now flabbergasted. Out of the four years they have been together, he can't recall one time Kim has ever spoken to him in this manner. In fact he doesn't even recall her ever using a negative four letter word. Not knowing how to respond, he grabs his keys and wallet and proceeds to the door.

"Where are you going?" She grabs his hand. "I want you to talk to me."

"Where do you get off talking to me like that? I have never once disrespected you, lied to you, nor cheated on you, I have been nothing but good to you."

"I wanna hear what's on your mind!" She demands.

"You walk around here, pretending you have it all together. You get up on that praise team, jumping, shouting and exalting the crowd when you're not living what you singing. You want to hear what's on my mind? Well here it goes; God is not pleased with you, with all your lies, and your promiscuous lifestyle. You think I don't know about all the men you have in your life? You actually think I'm that

[40]

gullible to believe that I'm the only man in your life? You think I don't know about you going to meet them, or they coming in and out of this apartment into the guest room? You think I don't know, Kimberly? I put up with your crap for the last year and half, praying that you would change, you know why? Because I love you! I genuinely love your behind! I know how bad that Donavan dude hurt you. Hell, I was hurt, too. You know what Sonya did to me; that's why I would have never done you wrong. And the sad part is, as much as I tried to fill that void, I thought to myself: *if God can't fill it; who am I?*"

 Kim is holding his arm with tears in her eyes. Clinching her teeth, she tries to bring herself to apologize, but the words just couldn't form.

"Look at you! You have so much pride in you; you can't even say you're sorry." He makes eye contact with her one more time and walks out the door.

She sadly walks towards her bedroom crying and just before she gets there, she hears a soft knock at the door. She turns around, runs to the door wiping her face; "Keith?" she says as she opens the door and to her surprise Mike is standing on the other side of it. They both pause and look at one another.

"What are you doing here?" she asks as she pulls him into the apartment, looking around in the hallway trying to make sure Keith wasn't anywhere in sight.

"I had to come see you," he comments admiring her place.

"You can't be popping up here; I got a man," She says with attitude.

[41]

"If you're talking 'bout dude I just seen leave up out of here, I think it's a rap; dude looked pissed!"

Kim takes a deep sigh. "Have a seat."

"Is everything okay? Did I come at a bad time?" he asks still standing.

"Yes, you did!" she answers…. "How did you find me?"

"I went by your mothers' house."

"Snitch….. Well, since you're here, you might as well have a seat."

"So how have you been? You look nice. Can I have a hug? He looks her in her eyes and notice they are red. "Have you been crying?" he asks.

"No, allergies."

"Kim, honey, what's wrong?"

"I don't want to talk about it." She starts to tear up.

"Maybe you should just go; this is not a good time right now."

He stands up and puts his arms around her to comfort her and she begins to cry out loud.

"Shhh; it's okay," he whispers as he consoles her.

"I'm here now." She cries even the more. Just as she is calming down.. "Where's your bathroom?" he asks.

"Down the hall, first door on your right," she answers.

As he goes to the restroom to get her some tissue, Keith comes back in the door. Kim jumps at the sound of the door opening; she turns around, and Keith is walking past her without saying a word, heading towards the bathroom.   He stops at the sight of this 6'2 man in his path. He turns to look at Kim.

"I thought you had at least an ounce of love for me." Keith says with disappointment.

"It's not what you think," she comments.

"I wasn't even out of the parking lot and already you got some cat up in here."

"Look man, No disrespect but she didn't even know I was coming by. I'm Mike."

He extends his hand but Keith doesn't accept.

"Mike, huh?"

"This is Donavan," Kim reiterates.

Keith sizes him up.

"So this is what the root of the problem look like?" He turns to Kim. "What a coincidence or shall I say how convenient it is that your ex shows up right after you…." He thinks for a second. "It makes sense now. You purposely picked a fight with me so I would leave and he could come over."

"That's not true…

"Look, she didn't even know I was in town; I went by her mom's house and she gave me the address." Mike interrupts Kim.

"So you decided to just show up? Keith asks sarcastically. "No phone call or….." He pause again and reflects back on the phone call earlier. "Didn't you call here earlier asking for Peaches?"

"I didn't know what the situation was… look I'mma let you two finish this conversation; Kim I'll be in touch," Mike says.

"No! You stay!" Keith demands.

"Correct me if I'm wrong but you're saying you didn't know what the situation was and yet you still bought your 6'2 happy ass over here not knowing if the guy that answered the phone was her man or not?"

"Pretty much, but it wasn't my intentions to cause any trouble. I figured, if she has moved on maybe she'll be more prone to talk to me now rather than run and hide like she used to."

He looks at Kim, "This is who you were on the phone with dancing and carrying on, when I walked in the room; I knew I heard you say: *where's your wife!* You straight up lied to me, gone try and feed me that crap bout some chick name Kierra. What were yall doing? Making plans? *Let me piss him off so he'll go home tonight.* You know what Dawg, You stay. I'm out."

He goes to the bathroom and gets his shaving bag and leaves.

"Kim I am so sorry." Mike apologizes.

"It's not your fault." She walks around to sit on the couch.

"What did he mean by, 'so this is what the root of the problem look like?'"

"He seems to think because you hurt me, that I'm still holding on to the past. And my actions have affected our relationship. And in a sense he's right."

She begins to weep again. "I been holding on to you for so long, I couldn't see what was in front of me. You didn't love me. But he did."

"Kim, that's not true Baby. I loved you with every breath I took. Life for me was not easy without you. I was miserable and angry. I was hurt because there would be times when I wanted to speak with my

[44]

best friend and you wouldn't answer my calls. Sometimes it would be the little things that I know only you would understand or a joke that only you would get….. I messed that up. I messed us up, and I'm sorry."

Kim drops her head and he raises it back up by cuffing his hand under her chin.

"I remember that one time when you called and I was in class, I was so excited I ran out the classroom just to take your call only to answer and hear Deborah Cox on the other end singing: *We can't be friends.* I CAN'T STAND THAT SONG 'TIL THIS DAY because it reminds me of how bad I hurt you. Let me tell you a little bit about that two minute marriage….I was miserable, I wanted to do the right thing and marry her because I didn't want my child growing up fatherless."

"But there are a lot of parents co-parenting," Kim intervenes.

"I know that now, but I wasn't thinking like that then. I wanted to be in the same house and raise my baby and be there for it like my dad was for me."

"But what about me? I was your baby. You didn't even consider me!"

"I did sweetheart. Come on Kim, I know you're not questioning my love for you! I thought long and hard and probably cried just as much as you did. But after you kept refusing to see me and not answering my calls, I made a sacrifice. I sacrificed our love for the love of my child. That marriage lasted about a year and a half. I was miserable; I lost sight of who I was. I became angry, bitter and at the same time I was pretending to be something I was not. I pretended until I couldn't

[45]

pretend anymore; the angriness started seeping out and I became a little abusive."

"Abusive?"

"Not so much physical--I mean I shoved her twice, but for the most part it was verbal. I was just being plain mean and I wouldn't allow her in. I felt like she was an intruder, invading your space. I would be lying in bed at night wishing my son was our son. She would be so nice to me and I would lash out at her like she the enemy. The second time I shoved her out my way, she hit the floor and she looked at me and asked, *"Why are you so angry?"*

It was like somebody turned on the lights and I just began to cry and I opened up to her. I told her all about you and how I felt about you. And believe it or not, I felt a huge weight lifted off me. I began to see how loving and caring she was, how great of a mother she was and an awesome wife. We tried to work it out but eventually we separated then divorced. I had some issues I had to work out within myself. And it wasn't fair to her or my son."

"So what did you do after the divorce?"

"I left the country. I had a scholarship to play ball overseas, so I took it. And in doing that I went through a spiritual cleansing and received Christ in my life."

Kim takes a deep sigh, "So where is your son now?"

"Don't know. I've been looking for them since I've been gone. I heard she moved shortly after I did."

"What about her parents, relatives or somebody?"

[46]

"Her parents moved as well. I'll find them eventually, even if I have to hire a P.I. I miss my boy."

Kim gives him a half smile, "Let me know when you're ready; I know a good investigator."

"So what about you? What's been going on with you; are you married? I'm sorry again, 'bout today."

"Don't worry 'bout it. It's not your fault; I must admit I have some issues I need to work out within myself. But as you can see, I gained a little weight."

"You still look good girl. Stand up and give me a hug."

"Thanks." She blushes a little. Well, I have my own business."

"You do?"

"Yep, I graduated from college with a MBA, started work for this security company for a few years; and after learning the business, I started my own."

"I'm so proud of you. What are you doing for the rest of the day?"

"Nothing much," she answers.

"Would you like to finish this conversation over dinner?"

"Welllllll!" she says hesitantly.

"I won't take no for an answer. Let's go someplace nice and quiet. I want to hear all about what was, what is and what's to be in your life and what led up to this confrontation today. Go get dress and I'll come back in… let's say about an hour?"

"That's fine." Kim agrees.

Monet

Monet enters into O'Ryans; "Excuse me, did you see a black purse around here?" she asks the hostess.

"Oh yeah," she replies. "I found it after you guys left; let me get it for you."

"Monet!" A voice in the distant calls; she turns around and Mr. Gabriel is sitting at the bar.

"Oh hi, Mr. Gabriel, How are you?"

"Good." He replies. Is everything alright with you?"

"Yes, I'm blessed and highly favored."

"Come on Monet, you don't have to pretend with me."

"Who's pretending? I am blessed and highly favored."

"That may be true, but talk to me and tell me how you really feel; so many people hide behind that *"I'm blessed and highly flavored."*
You'll feel a whole lot better if you just say how you really feel; come on have a seat and talk to Gabby," he says smiling.

"It's that obvious, huh?" She sits down next to him. Just as she begins to speak, the hostess brings her purse and she drops her keys in it.

"Thank you," Monet says. "Well, I've been sick for some time now," she begins. "At times I wonder if the Lord even hear my prayers; It feels like he has left me but I know He hasn't because his word said He'll never leave me nor forsake me.

"You right about that, Monet. So many times people tend to equate

God with their emotions or feelings; but God is not a feeling; he is always there when we need him. Let me share something with you. A good teacher does all the talking before the exam. He gives you everything you need before the test. So it's not that He's ignoring you or He doesn't hear you, He's just quiet during the exam. What does Hebrew 11:6 say?"

She pulls out her phone to Google the answer. "But without faith it is impossible to please him," she answers.

"And Isaiah 53:5?" he asks.

"Oh I know this one by heart: "BY HIS STRIPES I AM HEALED!""

"And doesn't Isaiah 43:26 say to put him in remembrance?"

She looked that up as well. "It sure does, Mr. Gabriel."

"This journey that you are on is not easy but God trusts you; he has equipped you and just know, Greater is He that is in you…." She looks up at him and gives him a half smile and finishes the rest of the verse.

"…. than he that is in the world. Thank you so much Pastor."

"Oh No; I'm no Pastor," he corrects her.

"Well you should be."

"Not my calling."

"Again it should be," she responds with sarcasm and a smile. "Well let me get out of here."

She stands up, "and if it be the Lords will, I mean….Thank you Lord for my healing and Lord you might want to consider letting Mr. Gabby be a pastor." She adds with a smile. "Did you see how I just slid that last part in there?"

"Yes, I caught that." He smiles.

"I'll see you later."

"Take care," he says.

She turns to leave. While making an exit towards the door, she looks down in her purse for her keys; at the same time two gentlemen are approaching the door to come in. The first guy is turned around talking to his friend so he is unaware of Monet coming out. Before the second gentleman can say *Watch out! The* two of them bump into each other.

"Excuse me; I'm sorry I wasn't paying attention," Monet says.

"No, Excuse me," he says.

She continues on out the door to her car and the two gentlemen proceed to come on in. The second gentleman continues to talk while the first one keeps watch on Monet.

"Excuse me one second man," the first gentleman states. He walks back out the door to say something to Monet. "Excuse me Miss. She turns around and stops by her car door.

"I just couldn't let you go without saying something to you. I might not have this opportunity again." Being captivated by her beauty, he pause as he approach her vehicle.

"Well?" she asks smiling.

"My apologies for staring; you are so beautiful. My name is Mitchell."

"Nice to meet you, I'm Monet."

"So, did you come here alone?"

"Actually, me and my girlfriend were here earlier and I left my purse."

"Girlfriend?" he asks with curiosity.

She laughs, "No not that kind of girlfriend."

"I'm sorry, now days you can't be too sure about that."

"You right," she agrees. "What about you?"

"What about me?"

"Is that your boyfriend you're with?"

"Nope," he answers.

"Do you have a boyfriend? Do you like men? Are you down low?"

"Nope, Nope, and Nope," he answers. Both of them laugh.

"What a way to start a conversation," Mitchell says.

"You came out here harassing me," Monet replies sarcastically.

"Oh I'm harassing you…. I see. Well do you think your boyfriend or husband mind if I take you out to lunch sometime?"

"Only if your wife or your girlfriend doesn't mind."

"Sounds like a plan; take my number." She programs his number into her droid and dials his number.

"Shoot my phone doesn't have a signal." She holds it up in the air and waves it around until she gets one.

He looks at his phone, "Is this you?" She nods her head. "Alright sweetheart, I'll lock you in; it was a pleasure meeting you."

"Nice meeting you as well."

"Let me get back in here with my partner…. I meant my friend." They smile at each other "and I'll talk with you later."

"Ok Bye!" Monet says.

As she pulls out of the parking lot, her phone regains full signal; voicemails and text messages begin to pour into her phone. She opens up the first text; it's from Brittney: Hey girl, where are you? Call me.

The second one is from Kim: CallMe. Just as she is about to call her voicemail to check her messages a third text pops up;

Thinking about you. She smiles; it's from Mitchell.

She then dials her voicemail. *"Hey Moni girl call me, its Brittney. I need to talk."*

Press seven to delete this message; press nine to save this message… Message deleted.

New message: *"Monet, this Darryl. I need somebody to talk to; when you get a minute holla at me." Message deleted.*

New message: Monet this Adrian. Just calling to check on you, love ya girl.

Although Monet is single, she holds the record of still being able to maintain a friendship with all her ex-boyfriends.

She calls Brittney back first. "Hey girl, what's up?"

"Girl, I'm in the bed now… but Tim and his baby mama drama is getting on my nerves, bad enough I'm compromising myself for him."

"What happened now?"

"I had to pop off in his lil girl mama ass, talking all that smack."

"What happened?"

"She so damn simple! Why she called over here trying to go off on me because I did her daughter hair; talking 'bout '*how I send her with her daddy is how I want her to come back.*' "I cussed her tail out and hung up the phone in her face; ain't nobody got time for that shit…I meant mess. Excuse me girl; I done got mad all over again!"

"It's okay. I don't see why she would get mad." Monet says.

"Thank you! You know that girl got that Haitian hair."

"Hold on. Kim is calling; I'm gonna click her in." Monet says.

"Hello, Kim."

"Hey girl.

"Hey, Brittney is on the line too… Brit you there?" Monet asks.

"Yeah, I'm here."

"What are you two gossiping about?" Kim asks.

"I was just telling her how I had to go off on Tim's baby momma Renee; she got mad 'cause I did Di'jonae's hair."

"So what! I hope you put a relaxer in it; you know she got Jesus DNA…….hair made of wool." Kim says sarcastically.

Brittney and Monet laughs. "For real, yall know I'm telling the truth; that's why you laughing."

"What's going on with you, Kim? Did you talk with Keith and not at Keith? Monet asks.

"Yeah we talked and I put his ass out…. Damn! I forgot Brittney on this phone."

"You need to stop trying to blame me for you cussing," Brittney retorts.

"I don't ever cuss until you come around and spirits do travel through phones you know; bow your head right now; we finna pray," Kim says sarcastically.

"Is your head bowed, eyes closed? Monet you keep your eyes open. We need a watchman…..Father we loose all telecommutative…"

"Communication!" Brittney interrupts.

"You wanna pray?" Kim smartly asks.

"You need to stop playing. You play too much," Britt says.

Kim starts laughing. Monet pulls up in her garage and goes in the house.

"Why did you put Keith out?" she asks as she kicks off her shoes and put her purse down on the sofa.

"I didn't actually. He left on his own."

"What did you do Kim?"

"Monet we been together four years and he still holding on to what Sonya did to him. Why should I have to pay for her mistakes? She the one stepped outside their marriage; I will never cheat on him with another woman like she did."

"Dang, Kim, another woman?" Brittney laughs.

"But you will cheat on him with another man."

"Shut up, Brit," Kim snaps.

"Kim, what did you say to make him leave?" Monet asks again.

"I was simply telling him that I wasn't happy with our relationship and I was ready to get married…

"Seriously Kim," Monet interjects.

"Do you wanna know or not?"

"I'm just saying; you know darn well you're not ready for marriage."

"Will you be quiet and listen! So I was telling him we been together four years and it's time to set a date, and that God wasn't pleased with him spending the night or me spending the night at his place and let me tell you….He blew up from there."

"What he say?" Monet asks.

"He said '*why wouldn't God be pleased? It's not like were having sex! Where's the sin?*'"

"Weell!" Britt butts in.

"Then he goes on to say that God isn't pleased with me."

"God ain't pleased with you about what girl?" Monet asks.

"He wouldn't tell me at first. I had to get straight hood with him; I got in his face and called him a M.F."

"OH MY GOD!" Brittney is astonished.

"KIM!" Monet shouts.

"I know I was dead wrong but listen to this; he went on to say how I was perpetrating in the church--I'm not living what I sing and God is not pleased with all my lies and my promiscuous lifestyle…."

"Oh my God, how did he find out?" Britt asks.

"Listen, I'm not done; then he says*: You think I don't know about all the men you have in your life? You actually think I'm that gullible to believe that I'm the only man in your life? You think I don't know about you going to meet them, or they coming in and out of this apartment into the guest room? You think I don't know Kimberly?*"

"Not the government name!" Brittney says being comical.

"Hold on, I ain't done; my feelings were really hurt; He goes on to say *I put up with your crap for the last year and half, praying that you would change, you know why? I know how bad that Donavan dude hurt you, hell I was hurt too; that's why I would have never done you*

[55]

wrong. And the sad part is, as much as I tried to fill that void, I realize if God can't fill it; who am I?"

"What were you doing when he was saying all this?" Monet asks.

"Girl, I was fighting back the tears." My mind was like WHAT IN THE WORLD!"

"So what happened after he said that?" Monet asks.

"He left; then I bust out crying."

"Dude got you under surveillance," Brittney comments.

"How in the world do you think he know all this?"

"I have the slightest idea. But then right after he left, I hear a knock at the door. I'm thinking it's him so I run to the door wiping my face and guess who it is?"

"Who?" They ask at the same time.

"Lil Don," Kim answers.

"Lil Don?" Monet says shockingly.

"Lil Don, Lil Don, Lil Don." Brittney is thinking out loud.

"Who is Lil Don?"

"Michael," answers Monet.

"Talking about the guy you dated from your momma's womb till the time you graduated from high school?"

"Yes," Kim answers.

"Why yall call him Lil Don?"

"That was a nickname we gave him when we were younger," Monet answers. His daddy name is Donavan so we just started calling him Donavan or Lil Don

"I can't believe he just showed up at your door. How did he find you?" Monet asks.

"My mom."

"Snitch!" Monet says.

Kim started laughing… "Same thing I said."

"Well what did he want?" Monet asks as she goes in the bathroom to pee.

"He said he had been miserable and he had to see me. We talked about a lot of stuff and he apologized for hurting me; which that helped a whole lot! I had been crying before he got there so he held me until I stopped, then he went in my bathroom to get me some tissue and guess who comes back in the door?"

"Girl please don't tell me Keith came back!" Monet states as she flushes the toilet.

"He did and to make a long story tolerable he thought I purposely picked a fight with him so I could hook up with Don."

"Well what did he come back for?" Monet asks.

"His shaving bag."

"You think it's over?" Monet asks.

"Yall, I have never seen him so angry. Normally he's so patient, kind, meek, loving, joyful….."

"Don't forget self- control 'cause you show ain't been giving that man none!" Brittney intervenes.

"I mean even though he doesn't attend service like he used to, he never lost his relationship with God; I mean he's always walking around the house talking to God and I notice he picks up his bible to read more often than me. I mean… he has his faults but I'm tripping on the small stuff."

"It took this to happen in order for you to recognize that?" Monet asks.

"I guess so," Kim answers.

"I know with his trust issues, if we ever did get back together, I can forget about getting married. That joker probably won't ever commit."

"Brittney, why you so quiet?" Kim asks.

"Girl, I'm in my bed 'bout sleep."

"Well, I'mma let you guys go 'cause somebody is beeping in on my line," Monet says.

"Alright; yall good night," Brittney says.

"Bye Brit," Kim says.

Monet

"Hello?"

"Hey, Monet; this is Mitchell."

"I know who it is," she responds.

"I just wanted to hear your voice before I head in for the evening."

"Aww!" She smiles.

"Hey but listen I want to be completely honest with you about me and I would like to sit down and talk with you more but please don't shut me down with what I'm about to say. Okay?"

"I'm listening," she says as if she knows what he is about to say.

"You got to promise me."

"I don't make promises."

"Come on," he says.

"I'm listening!" she exclaims.

"Ok, I'm in the military, and I'm married… Monet didn't say a word because he said exactly what she anticipated.

Heelloooo?" Mitchell says.

"I'm here," she answers.

"Listen, I know you may be thinking I'm a jerk, or I got some nerves, but it's nothing like that. I just want you to know up front and I would like to sit down and explain the situation to you if you allow me to. Will you?"

Against her better judgment she was willing to hear what he had to say.

"Well, will you?" he asks again.

"No," she answers

"Monet please don't make me beg. Just five minutes of your time."

Hesitantly, she answers, "Yes, I will listen."

Mitchell breathes a sigh of relief.

"So listen, I'm gonna let you get some rest; I'm pulling up at the house. You have yourself a good night, okay?"

"You too." She hangs the phone up; "Another one--I knew it! God, do I have a marriage magnet on my forehead? Where are the single guys?"

Just as she finished her sentence, her phone rings. *"Mitchell--what he want now?"* She thinks to herself.

"Hello?"

"Hey, I'm back, so where do you work at?"

"At the Café Latte on the corner of Arlington and Statenville."

"My favorite," he says.

Oh really?"

"Yeah I've been there quite a few times, but I never saw you. Did you just start?"

"Nope, I've been there since ninety-two."

"Really? What time do you normally go in?"

"About nine thirtyish."

"Really, I should have seen you at some point."

"I'm normally in the back office doing paperwork when I come in."

"Oh so you manage the place."

"You can say that. I thought you were in for the night; sound like you back in your car."

"Truck," he corrects her.

"Excuse me--TRUCK!" she mocks him.

He chuckles, "I forgot to pick something up from the store. So when will I see you again?"

"Why would you want to? You're married."

"My marriage is complicated," he says as he is getting out of the truck at the store.

"Does your wife know it's complicated?"

"Look when I see you again I promise I will tell you what's up."

"Mmm hmmm," she says.

"You don't believe me?"

"$2.14," the store attendant says.

"I really don't," she responds.

"Hold on a second baby; how much?"

"$2.14" the cashier repeats.

He gives the cashier the exact change. "Thank you. Okay, I'm back." He gets in the truck and heads home. "So you said you don't believe me?"

"Ummm Hmm."

"Well I guess I'll just have to prove it to you then, well let me let you get some rest," he says as he pulls up in his driveway.

"I'm about to go in this house and take a shower and get ready for work tomorrow."

She hangs up the phone without saying bye. "The one thing that irks me is when a nigga gotta hang up the phone with me to go be with his wife. Who do he think I am!? "He got the game twisted. I will not play second to anyone anymore."

Brittney

The next morning Brittney is awakened by the aroma of coffee, pancakes, eggs, and sausages. She gets out of bed and tip toes toward the kitchen. As she peeps around the corner, she doesn't see anyone so she stands in the kitchen looking around; then Tim comes up from behind and puts his arms around her waist; she is startled. He kisses her on her neck and whispers in her ear, "I love you."

"I thought you were doing business out of town last night?" she asks.

"I did, baby, but I finished up early so I could get back to you; I know Renee pissed you off yesterday and I'm sorry 'bout that, you know I don't like to see my baby upset, right?"

He kisses her neck again.

"You need to put her in her place," she states.

"I did and I will again. And just to let you know, you did a beautiful job on Di'Jonae's hair."

"Thank you baby," she turns around and kiss him on his lips. They continue to converse holding one another.

"So tell me about this new interest of yours that you been keeping a secret," Tim asks.

"What interest, babe?"

"The hair interest."

"Ooh that!"

"Yes, that. Or is there something else I need to know about?" He asks, kissing her on her forehead.

"No," she answers.

"I'm kidding baby, I know you love me."

"Oh yeah, and how do you know that?" she asks.

♫*"Because the bible tells me so;"*♫ he sings. She looks at him with a disturbed look and laughs.

"Oh you got jokes?" Brittney says.

"I'm kidding baby. I know you love me because I see the way you look at me, and when you miss me, your smile light up the room when you see me; you respect me and you put up with my shit. I see a lot of me in you; the good and the bad has rubbed off on you, but baby don't change who you are. I can see you have compromised yourself for me over the years and that's not you. I know who you are--a strong woman of God, just like my mom. You don't judge me and I appreciate you girl."

She looks into his eyes.

"I do," he assures.

"That's why I love you babe; underneath this hard shell is soft chocolate. You're like my big M&M."

"Oh yeah, what color?" He teases.

"Brown!" They squeeze each other hard and laugh.

"I thought you were going to say green. You know what they use to say about the green ones...."

"Yeah, they make you horny."

"You are so old school!" Tim laughs.

"So tell me more about this hair thing? I noticed you have skills but I didn't know you were into that."

"Man, I love doing hair," she answers with excitement.

"I think it's been a thing of mind since I was about three or four when my grandmother use to ask me to grease her scalp…….. Wait a minute."

She looks at the clock on the stove. "Jaylin! I got to get him up for school."

She starts to walk away and he grabs her by one hand.

"He's already up."

She looks at him. "Yeah, I woke him up to shower, got his clothes out, ironed them, and I came to start breakfast."

She steps back towards him. "He's in his room playing the game right now. When we're done with breakfast I'll drop him off for you."

"Mmuah," he kisses her on the forehead.

"Now sit up here."

He pats the stool next to the island, "and tell me more about what's-going- on- with- you."

He walks around the counter and begins fixing Jaylin's plate.

"Well, I went to school to be a nurse for the money, but after five years of doing this, I can't stand this job."

"What's wrong with it? JAY-LYN!" He calls him to come eat.

"Nothing really, it's not for me anymore. I just want to do something I enjoy doing. My grandmother once told me: *if you do something you enjoy, you'll never work.*"

"Your grandmother was a wise woman. Here you go buddy."

He sits Jaylin's plate on the table. "You want milk or orange juice?"

"Orange juice please." He pours the orange juice. "Thank you."

"You want milk, right baby?"

"That's fine, hon," Brittney answers.

"So what do you need to do to make it happen?"

"Honestly, the first step I need to do is go take the state board exam."

"State board? Uh baby, don't you have to take some kind of class first?" he asks sarcastically.

"I actually been to school already and got my diploma; I just never went and took the exam."

"I was about to say; they must've started counting your hours when you were greasing your grandmothers scalp."

Both of them started laughing. "Shhit you good girl!" They giggle. He gives Brittney her food and both of them join Jaylin at the table. Tim blesses the food, "Lord, we thank you for this food we're about to receive for the nourishing of our body. We ask that you bless it and sanctify it in Jesus name. Amen."

"Amen."

"Amen."

"So honey, are you gonna make arrangements to go take the exam?"

"I am."

"You done, buddy? Go get your book bag so I can take you to school."

"Ok. Thanks for breakfast, Mr. Tim."

"You welcome, Buddy." Tim finishes eating and kisses Brittney on her cheek.

"I'mma drop Jay off and I'll see you when I get back. Hey, if you leave before I get back, do you want to do lunch today?"

"Yeah," Brittney answers.

"Call me and let me know what you have a taste for," he says.

"Alright. Love you, hon… we gone."

"Love you too!" H.e shuts the door

After Brittney finishes eating, she loads the dishes in the dishwasher, and gets dressed for work. Just as she is walking out the door, she gets a text message from her job: **Brittney we need you to come in early today.** "Let me call this school, 'cause I'm tired of this mess. Where's my phonebook? Oh there it is."

"Langston's Beauty Academy, how may I help you?"

"Yes, may I speak to Miss Bobbie please?"

"Hold one second."

"Bobbie, how may I help you?"

"Miss Bobbie, this is Brittney; I'm ready now."

"I'm already on it darling. It's about time Brittney; I've been telling you you're too gifted to let all that creativity go to waste. I just need you to bring a hundred dollars so I can send it in with your paperwork."

"A hundred dollars? It used to be fifty!"

"Yes ma'am, it went up a couple years ago."

"Ok, I'll stop by on my way to work."

"All right Brit, I'll see ya shortly."

Kim

"Thanks for letting me stay over," Mike says as he walks in the kitchen and kisses Kim on the cheek.

"Thank you for getting me out the house and for taking my mind off Keith. And I must admit, it felt good having you here holding me all night."

[66]

They look at each other and smile.

"I see you haven't forgotten I don't eat pork."

"I know everything about you," Kim says as she puts him a piece of turkey sausage and turkey bacon on his plate.

"So what's on your agenda when you get off work?" he asks.

"I thought I'd take the day off and hang out with you today."

"Well, what do you have in mind?"

"May-be we can ride over to Swan Lake, and then grab something to eat."

"Swan Lake," Mike remembers.

"Do you remember we shared our first dance together at Swan Lake?"

"Yes, I was just thinking about that earlier today as a matter of fact."

"That will be great; what time do you want to leave out?"

"This morning sometime, perhaps?" she answers.

"Well, let me go shower and put on some clothes. I'll meet you back here say… about an hour and a half?"

"Okay, sounds good."

Kim walks Mike to the door and closes it behind him. She stands with her back to the door with a smile on her face… then she starts dancing and singing, ♫ *"I got my maan back.. I got my maan back!"* ♫

Her cell phone rings. "Hello?"

"Kim, you can stop dancing." The two of them start laughing.

"How did you know I was dancing?"

"I know everything about you," he says smiling.

"Touché, my nigga, Touché!"

They couldn't stop laughing.

"Alright, I'll see you when you get back."

Just as she is about to hang up, she notices a miss call from Keith. *Hmm, my phone didn't ring.* After taking a shower, she picks up her phone to check for any missed calls; she did notice she has a voicemail and just as she was about to check it, she is interrupted by an incoming call.

"Hello?" she answers.

"Kim, what's up?" What you doing later?"

"Not you!"

"You ain't even got to act like that. I just wanted to see you."

"Sorry, not interested, I have company in town."

"Come on Kim, man!"

"Chile, lose my number."

"Oh it's like tha..."

She hangs up the phone before he can finish.

About an hour later Mike comes back over. "You ready?"

"Yeah let me grab my purse. Are we taking my car or yours?"

"I'll drive," Mike says.

As they are leaving out, Kim spots Keith's car headed towards the complex.

"Slight change of plans," Mike says.

"So where are we going?"

"I thought we should be a little spontaneous."

"Okay."

He gets on interstate 75 heading south. "Don, where are we going?"

she asks again.

"To the beach." He looks at her with a smile.

"I hope its St. Augustine and not Jacksonville," she comments.

"Why? What's wrong with Jacksonville?"

"That water is dirty."

"All beach water is dirty Kim."

"I mean it just looks dirty."

"I got you; just sit back and enjoy the ride. He puts in an ole' school cd that took them back to when they were in middle school and high school.

Kim's phone rings.

"Hello?"

"Where you at?" Monet asks with frustration in her voice.

"Me and Don are headed to the beach."

"The beach? Yall could have asked me if I wanted to go."

"We don't need a third wheel; threes a crowd."

"He's my friend too, helfa. That's why Keith looking for you!"

She starts laughing.

"For real?"

"Yeah, he's been blowing my phone up. He said he called your job to see if you got the flowers he sent and they said you weren't there and he said he called you and left you a voice message then he said he went by your house."

"What did you say?"

"What was I supposed to say, Kim? I haven't seen you today."

"Good."

"He doesn't sound like he's mad, more like he's anxious to see you to apologize or something." Quite frankly, I don't know why he feel he should apologize when he was speaking the truth."

"Affirmative!"

"Affirmative? Girl don't go talking that *Lost in Space* crap. I think you owe him an apology."

"That may be true," she answers.

"When yall coming back, 'cause I can't take all this robot talk?"

" Sometime today."

"Tell, Don I said, what's up?"

"Monet said hey."

"Tell her what's up."

"Well, I'll holla at you when I get back."

"Alright girl."

"Bye."

"Hey Kim, remember this one?"

Mike turns up the volume and her phone rings again; she hits ignore because it's Keith. She looks at Mike and smiles.

"Yes, I remember this song; this is the song we had our first dance to."

She starts swaying side to side singing. ♫*"For tu nate to have you girl…"*♫

Mike pulls over at a rest area and gets out of the car. He walks over to Kim's door and opens it.

"What you doing?" she asks.

"Come on let's dance."

"Right here?"

"Come on Kim, get out."

"You crazy, Lil Don," she laughs as she gets out the car.

"Hit the back button so it can start over."

She takes his hand and the two of them begin to relive their first dance at Swan Lake. When the song ended, they continued on their journey to the beach.

"Ooo oo, this the jam right here," Kim says. "You sang Eric's part and I'll sang Chante's part." She directs Mike: "Okay, your turn."

Mike looks into her eyes and begins to sing: ♫*Now baby the days, and weeks and the years would roll by, but nothing would change the love inside you and I.*♫

She looks Mike in the eye and makes her verse personal as well: ♫*And baby, I'll never find the words that could explain, just how much heart, my life, my soul you chaaange.....when no one else understand.... You're my man... how much I love you.....*♫

They look at each other and sing the next verse together: ♫*Can I just spend my life with you?*♫

"Man Kim, that was the junk back then. I miss you girl. And you still have that gift."

"You didn't sound too bad yourself either. Sound like you meant what you were singing."

"I did," he answers. "And sound like you meant what you were singing."

"I did," she answers as she sits back in her seat smiling.

Kim looks up and sees Welcome to Daytona Beach.

"Daytona?" She asks surprisingly.

"I wouldn't dare take you to, as you say dirty water." He smiles.

After walking, running and playing on the beach like two little kids they make their way to the mall where they windowed shop.

"Ooo I like that!"

She notices a mannequin dressed in a mauve colored halter top with a pair of black crop pants and a charcoal colored necklace with a mauve colored rose attached to it.

"I like this," she says admiring the whole assemble.

"Try it on," He suggests.

"Excuse me Miss; can I get this? All of it; I want the necklace and all."

"You sure can," the sales lady says.

"It's right over here. Do you need to try it on?"

"Yes," Kim answers.

"Follow me."

She leads Kim to the fitting room.

"I'll be right back with the necklace," the attendant says.

Kim comes out the fitting room.

"Baby, that's you all the way; you look good in that!" Mike compliments.

"You think so? Thank you!"

"I think the pants are a little big," Kim comments.

"Do you want me to get you another size?"

" No this is the last one."

"You can get it taken up," he suggests.

"You right. Anna can do that for me."

"Anna?"

Kim nods her head. "Oh she's not just Anna any more she's Simply Anna. Lady is bad I'm telling you. She be doing fashion shows and all. I'm talking 'bout from making dresses from Target plastic bags to making the baddest Maxi dress out of a curtain...

"She be doing it like that?" Mike asks.

"Hello World!" she smiles...Man I didn't know a trash bag can look that good when wearing it."

"Ole Anna, I need to get by there and holla at her."

"She'll be glad to hear from you."

"That will be $37.42," the cashier states as Kim pulls out her debit card.

"Um uum, no ma'am. I got this," Mike says.

After leaving from that store, they grab something to eat from the food court and head back home.

"Here I got you something." Mike pulls out a small box and Kim is stunned.

"When did you have time to get me something?"

"When you told me you were going to the bathroom," he answers.

She opens the box and finds a pair of earrings she admired when they were in Kenzie's Jewelry.

"Mike! How did you know...?"

"I saw how you kept looking at them," he interrupts, "and I thought they would look good with the new outfit you got."

"Thanks babe," she says as she continues to smile. "I have a confession to make."

"What?"

" When I told you I was going to the bathroom, I really didn't go. Here I got something for you, too." Mike's eyes stretch big.

"Girl... now this is...I'm shocked; I don't know what to say."

He opens the box and there is a watch with a card underneath it: *Thanks for a good Time today.* "You are so welcome baby, but the pleasure was all mine. You really surprised me! But you know what they say about buying somebody a watch?"

"I don't believe that crap....don't buy your mate a watch cause your time might run out. Or don't buy your mate any shoes cause they'll walk out on you... I guess we should return these clothes as well..."

"Why you say that?"

"Cause when these clothes wear out, then the relationship will."

"Guess we'll have to put those in the cleaners," Mike says laughing.

"I never heard that one before."

"I made it up," Kim says.

"Oh okay, I'm only kidding about the watch. Our time will never run out," Mike says.

"So where are you staying, Don? And how long are you here for?"

"I'm staying in an extended stay hotel. I'm not sure how long."

"You can save that money and stay at my place until you figure out what you want to do."

"I don't want to impose on you, Kim."

"You're not," she says as she rejects Keith's call again.

"What would your boyfriend think? Just because you two had a heated discussion doesn't mean the relationship is over. I know you love him and he loves you, too, obviously." He looks at her phone. "I insist that you stay."

"Did you just hear what I said?"

"Did you hear what he said to me? Dude is done with me."

"How do you know that? He probably wants to apologize, but you've been rejecting his calls all day."

"Mike, we haven't seen each other in about seven years; I just need time to think and I can't talk to him right now. So will you stay?"

"What would your Pastor say about you shacking up?"

"Hey, it's only a sin if we give in." He looks at her and laughs.

"For real I know the older folks be saying it's a sin to shack but the sin is actually in the sexual escapades."

"I wouldn't want to tempt you."

"I have a spare bedroom."

"Alright, if you insist but I don't want to cause any problems."

"You good," she assures.

"Well, I think I'll take you up on that, at least for tonight. I'm kinda tired." He says as he pulls into the complex.

"That's fine. I'll show you where you will be sleeping."

Keith watches from across the street as they go upstairs.

"This is where you will be sleeping." She points to the guest room, "and this is where I will be sleeping. Let me get you a rag and towel to wash up."

She goes in her room and sits on her bed while Mike takes a shower. Just as she begins to think about Keith, he calls and she hits the reject button once again. She takes a deep sigh and thinks to herself as she go in her bathroom to shower, *I love you Keith but I need think and I need time to heal from past hurt. And I need to see if this is thing with me and Don is going anywhere.* When she gets out the shower, she notices Mike is passed out in his new bed. She closes his door and go lay in her own bed. "Dang! What am I gonna do? I really miss Don, but to be honest, things are not feeling the same and I'm not sure if I'm ready to let go Keith yet... Can you send me a sign or something God? I can really use your help right now." She dozed off in a fetal position waiting for an answer. She begins to toss and turn in her sleep; pushing backwards trying to feel for Keith's stomach to rest her butt in. Then she begins to reach for his hand to wrap around her waist.

Keith enters the room but to his surprise Donavan is not in the bed with Kim; he notices that he is asleep in the guess room. When he leaves out the apartment, the sound of the door closing awakes Kim. She sits still in her bed with her eyes barely open, "Is that you Lord?" she asks. "I'm still waiting for an answer." She reminds God and dozes right back off to sleep. Longing for a man's touch, she begins to toss and turn again. "I can't take this," she says as she leaves her room to climb in the bed with Mike. There she gets into her fetal position and takes Mike's arm and wraps it around her and sleeps like a baby.

Brittney

"Good morning baby," Tim says as he greets Brittney with a kiss when she enters the kitchen.

"Morning hon."

"How did you sleep?" he asks.

"I slept well."

"I already made breakfast and blessed the food; Jay has already eaten and is getting dress. We have to leave a little early cause I got to go by and get Devin and Di'jonae and drop them off at school."

"Oh. Okay. Thanks for making breakfast."

"Anything for my poo poo." He kisses her on her forehead. "So what's on your agenda today?"

"Work, home, bible study. You want to come?"

"I'm like Madea; not till they get a smoking section."

"We have one," she says sarcastically.

"Stop playing."

"Pastor roped a section off just for Madea; she has her own Amen corner," she laughs.

"You play too much Britt." He smiles.

"Naw but seriously you ought to come with me one day."

"For what; to see the preview of the coming attraction of hell? Number one: God said judgment is gonna start in the house of God and I'd rather be out here doing my thang 'cause some of yall Church folk aint right! Nawl, I'm straight. Number two: you already told me the last Pastor ran off with the building fund money. And Number three: yall having church at Kim's house where the sex demon and all his cousins hang out; lust, fornication, adultery, and miserable. And now you telling me yall have a smoking section! Why would I want any part of that?" he asks smiling.

"I ain't fixin' to be like them other cats and say 'God know my heart'; but I will say Me and the Big Man have an understanding."

"Boy, I was just playing about that smoking section."

"I know…. but listen church ain't like it used to be; it's all about the business now. They always want money; don't get me wrong I know it takes money to run a church, but you don't have to be putting that burden on people; especially if they ain't been taught the principals behind giving. Every time I look around, they taking up money for a building fund; look what happened to yall money. You got the love offering, pastor appreciation, sacrificial offering, Founders day, Founders week, pastor anniversary, and church anniversary. Now they got this first fruit thing, oh and get this… I saw a bucket on the pulpit labeled "Just Because." Just Because, Brit? Come on. I believe the church is putting their faith in the people instead of God. Don't get me wrong, I do believe in tithes and offering, sowing and reaping and a little sacrificing, but some of that stuff is a little extra. I was in this church one time and the pastor said, 'its five people in here, God told to give five hundred dollars,' then he gone say, 'we ain't leaving here 'til we get it'…. Come on that wasn't God, I saw all through that; he was trying to get his bills paid for the month. I done been in church where they had the money lines… This line for tithers, this one for offering… The pastor trying to pinpoint who is who. I grew up in church I know the business. And get this… We used to go to this church, a well-known church, and my sister was doing a fund raiser to be in this pageant. She had to collect three hundred and seventy three dollars; she went to the church and asked for a donation, 'anything you can give will be appreciated' and you know what they told her?"

"What?" Brittney asks with curiosity.

"We don't have it. We're trying to build another church."

"Wow!" Brittney says.

"Yeah, they were the same people that taught us to give, the same people that said God can't bless you if you got your hand closed… So guess what I did?"

"What's that?"

"I stop giving my money to the church; I just started blessing people outside the church. My sister was disappointed and started going to church with her friend. My mom was hurt at first but what she did was had a big fish fry and asked some of her friends that wasn't even saved for a donation and guess what; some of them old friends use to sell dope. She got the whole three hundred and seventy three dollars in one day. I looked at my momma and said *'the wealth of the wicked is stored up for the righteous.'*"

She laughed and said, *"Well that mean the church should have been….let me leave that alone."*

Wow, your momma a trip but I can understand why you feel the way you do….."

"I mean don't get me wrong, there are some good pastors out there…"

[79]

Tim interrupts.

"I'm ready Mr. Tim."

"Okay Buddy, go wait in the car, I'm right behind you."

"Okay. Bye mommy. I love you." He gives her a hug and kiss.

"Love you too, baby."

"One more thing before I go; another thing I don't agree with about the Pastors pressuring the people for money is because Jesus told Peter *Upon this Rock I will build my church.* I don't know how you interpret that but to me that says, if God called me to be a Pastor then He will build the church.....I don't know something to think about; or how the bible say...Selah." He smiles and kisses her good-bye.

"Oh, bay... let me tell you this right quick before I forget. I went by the school yesterday to pay for my test. I take my state board on the twenty-eighth of next month."

"That's what's up. See that's why we make a good team; you don't waste no time."

She smiles, "Love you baby."

"Alright love you too. Bye. Talk with you later," Tim says.

Kim

"Good morning," Kim says as she rolls over.

"Good morning," Mike replies. "Now you know that's not fair Kim!"

"What?"

"You slept with gum in your mouth," he says and she laughs.

"I almost wasn't a gentleman last night; you come in here putting your butt all in my stomach."

Kim continues laughing, "I wish you wasn't."

"So it would have been okay if I touched you here?"

"Umm hmm."

"What about here?"

"That tickles," she laughs.

"Oh yeah!" He tickles her even the more.

"Stop it! Quit it!" She laughing so hard she can barely talk. "Mike stop….."

Monet

"Good morning LaZibra," Felicia speaks as she goes over to the register to clock in.

"Morning Felicia," LaZibra speaks back. "You're glowing this morning."

"Girl, let me tell you."

"Hold on before you get started; I just about have everything ready. Can you hit the espresso machine behind you and grab some hazelnut and vanilla cream from the back?"

"Yeah... girl, wait 'til you hear this…."

[81]

Felicia walks to the back to get the creamer; when she comes back, LaZibra takes it out of her hands and puts it on the counter. They both are putting the condiments in the containers as Felicia begins to tell her story. "Girl how 'bout I met...

"Excuse me I have a delivery for…" Felicia is interrupted by a guy holding an edible fruit arrangement.

"You didn't lock the door behind you?" LaZibra asks Felicia.

"Sir, were not open yet," Felicia tells the guy.

"I have a delivery for a Mo Net Johnson." LaZibra and Felicia look at one another surprised.

"It's Mone't and I'll take it. Thank you," Felicia says.

"You ladies have a nice day."

"You- too," Felicia responds slowly looking at the arrangements.

"This is nice," LaZibra says admiring the arrangements and taking it from Felicia's hand. "She has pineapples, chocolate covered strawberries.... well don't just stare at it open the card."

Felicia opens the card and it reads: *Thinking of you... Mitchell.*

"Boss lady done got a man," LaZibra says laughing as Felicia takes the arrangements back from her to take it in the office.

"So but anyway Felicia continues; I met this guy over at the Starbucks on Piedmont. Girl he is PHINE! Pretty-Hot-In-Emmaculate!"

"Uhhh Lisa honey, Imma need you to get off the Porsha train; Immaculate starts with an 'I'. And what you doing at Starbucks?"

"Girl please, I like my job, but I love me some Starbucks. It's like crack to me."

"Anyway, did you get his number?"

"Not yet, but my girlfriend Erica say he comes in there faithfully. She said he always gets the same thing and that he seems to be really nice and she said she never saw him come in with a girl."

"Must be gay then," LaZibra comments.

"I don't know but I would like to be the one to make him HAPPY!" Felicia replies as she twirks.

"Girl you stupid," LaZibra says laughing. "It's time to unlock the door now….."

"Dr. Carlisle office how may I help you?"

"Hi, may I speak to Brittney please."

"Hold one moment."

"Brittney speaking."

"Hey girl, what are you doing for lunch?"

"I'm not sure. What's up?"

"I wanted to see if you want to have lunch today."

"Ok, hold on let me see if Tim wants to do anything."

"Okay."

She places the caller on hold and calls Tim. "Hey, babe are we doing anything for lunch today."

"Why? What's up?"

"Monet asked me to lunch."

"Oh well, go ahead, I have some other stuff I can be working on."

"Alright babe, love you talk to you later." She switch back over.

"Monet?"

"Yes?"

"Where do you want to meet at?"

"O'Ryans," Monet answers.

"Is that the only place you know?"

"We can go somewhere else if you like."

"Na. I'm cool with that; I was just messing with you. Is Kim coming?"

"I tried calling her phone but I didn't get an answer. Wait… here she is beeping in now."

"Go ahead and talk to her; I'll meet you there."

"Hello?" Monet answers.

"Yeah what's up?"

"Where you been? I been calling you all morning. Where is 'lil Don?"

"He right here."

"Don't tell me he spent the night."

"Okay I won't."

"Kim!"

"Mind your business… What you want?"

"Details! Details! Yes ma'am….. Listen, me and Britt are meeting for lunch at O'Ryans and you needs to be there."

"Maybe I will, maybe I won't," Kim responds with a smile.

"Don't play with me Kim."

"Alright, I'll see you." She laughs lightly.

"Bye," Monet says hanging up the phone. "Let me see what Mitchell is up to this morning." Despite her declaration of never being second again, she has found herself attached just by conversation.

"You have reached the Sprint voicemail box of 2-2-9 6-3-0- 0-6-8-8. To leave a voice message press one."

She hangs up the phone just as she's pulling up to work.

"Good morning ladies," she speaks walking in the door; not noticing the look they have on their faces.

"Morning Boss lady," they reply at the same time. The tone of their voices cause her stop and look them in the face.

"Why yall looking at me like that? Zi why are you looking like something stank; and Lisa, why do you have that smirk on your face?" She looks at them with curiosity. "Let me go put my purse in the office and when I come back you girls better start talking." As she's walking towards her office, they tip toe behind her. When she makes it to the door, she notices the fruit arrangement on her desk; she stops at the door and looks back. The two of them are pretending to be working. "Awe you guys, you shouldn't have," Monet says.

"We didn't," LaZibra replies. "Mitchell did."

"How yall know?" She notices the card partially closed. "Yall some nosey heifers."

"So who is Mitchell?" Felicia asks.

"Somebody I met the other day at O'Ryans."

"The other day?" Felicia asks. "Dang boss lady you give up the booty quick."

"I just met the guy and we exchanged numbers and talked little on the phone that's all.

"Oh I know his type," LaZibra replies.

"And what type is that?" Monet asks.

[85]

"He likes to invest in the product, get you to fall in love, sell you a dream then disappear on you."

"So what makes you an expert?"

"Life."

"So what does he do? Felicia asks.

"Military" Monet answers.

"Alcoholic," LaZibra remarks sarcastically. "And either he's married or a hoe. Or he could be both--a married hoe."

"Stop planting them bad seeds in boss lady head," Felicia intervenes.

"I'm planting real seeds. The bible say be wise as a serpent."

"How you know what the bible says, you don't even go to church?" Felicia says.

"That's what the devil want you to think," she says with a smirk.

"LaZibra you go to church?" Monet asks.

"Yes I do."

"What church do you attend?" Monet asks.

"Right now I go to Hold My Mule Down by the River Missionary Baptist Church."

"You playing girl, ain't no church name Hold my Mule Down by no damn River Missionary Baptist church," Lisa remarks.

"Yes it is. I grew up in that church, it's one of them traditional religious church." We have church on second and fourth Sundays."

"Second and Fourth? You go to a pau-lay church, maan," Felicia replies.

"What church do you go to Lisa; Bedside Baptist?"

"Yes ma'am. I'm in my bed faithfully every Sunday morning."

[86]

"Where do you go boss lady?"

"I attend Friendly Freewill Macedonia Baptist church."

"Yall killing me with these names," Felicia responds.

"Maybe on the days you don't have church you can come visit our service," Monet says to LaZibra.

"I will 'cause I'm on the Search Committee right now. I've been looking for another church to visit. I read a lot on my own because they don't do a lot of teaching."

"And you too missy," she says to Felicia.

"Oh I reads my word boss lady."

"Then both of you failed to read the part about meddling in my business."

"My bad boss lady, I'm just nosy," LaZibra replies.

"My point exactly; ladies front counter, customers just walked in the door."

"Welcome to Cafe' Latte' how may I help you?" Felicia asks.

Meanwhile Monet tries to call Mitchell again. *You have reached the sprint voice mailbox of 229-6-3-0-0-6-8-8 to leave a message press one." to enter a call back number press two. Your call back number is 2-2-9-3-0-0-7-4-4-7.*

"How many?" the hostess asks.

"Two" Brittney replies. Just as she was getting ready to be seated Monet walks in the door.

"Brit Brit," Monet calls.

Brittney turns around. "What's up lady? Is Kim coming?"

"She said she'll be here."

"Make that three" Brittney says to the hostess.

"So how you doing?" Brittney asks.

"All is well, hon. I'm doing great."

"You sound like it."

"Yeah, I was talking with Mr. Gabriel yesterday and he really encouraged me. And I got to thinking. My God is bigger than this MS, and for me to walk around here talking about *playing the hand I was dealt*…. Brittney this is not a game! I realize the devil is not playing with us so guess what I'm not playing with him. I went home and began to declare the word of God and I spoke to this thing, I began to sang the Oil of God, I said ♫*"Sickness..... you can't hold me*♫ then I said ♫*"MS... you can't hold" me.*♫ Girl I went to telling God his word back to Him, then I started telling my problem about my God; not God about my problem. *Shonda he comin in a honda.* Girl you got me speaking in tongues. I feel good Brit... I feel good!"

"I'm glad to hear that Moni; a merry heart doeth good like medicine."

"That's a healing scripture within itself right there; A merry heart, laughter, all that is good for the spirit. Many people don't realize that positive energy can help heal the body and negative energy can cause your body to be at dis-ease that's where disease comes from."

"You better say that... girl don't start nothing up in here," Britt comments.

"Nawl we will save that for church tonight," Monet says.

"What yall talking about? And why yall looking so deep?" Kim asks approaching the table.

"Child we were about to have some church up in here....hey hey," Monet says.

"You know I'm always down with a little church." Kim starts singing and moving to her own beat. ♫ *Somebody ought to testify... Oh oh oh somebody ought tes-tify. Say for God I live For God I die.. Somebody ought to tes-tify..... Can I get a witness?"♫*

"Alright, alright! Let's save this for tonight cause yall know, I'm gonna tear the church up. I got to get at least three laps in," Monet says.

"Hey I'll run one with you girl," Brittney comments.

"New business." Monet changes the subject.

"So Kim, how did Donavan end up at your house last night?"

"He spent the night?" Brittney asks.

"How you go from heaven to hell just like that? We were just having church, then you shut it off like a faucet." Kim says

"What will you ladies be drinking today?" the waitress asks.

"Water," Brittney orders.

"Me too," Monet says.

"And for you?" she asks Kim.

"Let me get a Margarita."

"Kim!" Monet yells.

"What? The lady asked what I wanted."

"Bring her water," Monet tells the server.

"No, you can bring me the Margarita like I asked, thank you," she states as she gives Monet an intense stare. "And a water," she adds.

"Okay, I'll be right back," the waitress says.

"You need to be shame of yourself, Kim," Monet says.

"And it's a church night," Brittney comments.

"Oh shit, I meant shoot. Damn Brittney…"

"Don't blame me for your demons ... I ain't said one cuss word today," Brittney says as she gets up from the table to go to the salad bar.

"Oh well, I guess she sick and told me," Kim says laughing, getting up going to the bar.

"I guess she did," Monet agrees.

As they were sitting back down, Kim says, "I'll bless the food."

"No I will bless the food," Monet intervenes.

"Quit acting so damn holy, Monet. You act like I can't pray 'cause I said a lil' cuss word and ordered a margarita; hell I forgot we have bible study today. And besides Brittney cuss all the time and you don't say nothing to her. Matter of fact, I didn't start cussing 'til this heifer came around."

I'm just saying Kim."

"Saying what Monet?"

"Bless your own damn food, okay?" Monet says.

"Al-right, that's enough of that shit; god-lee," Brittney interrupts.

"Lord, we thank you for this food we about to receive for the nourishment of our body. We ask that you bless it and sanctify it in Jesus name. Amen!!!"

"Both of yall cussed," Kim says laughingly.

"You play too much," Brittney says.

"Monet started it; she act like I can't pray. She act like I'm on God's reject list.

"Call block," Monet answers.

"Yeah, right before the letter **M**onet, but after the letter **B**rittney," she responds sarcastically.

They all laugh.

"If He blocked me, then He blocked yall too durn it." Britt and Monet continue to laugh.

"Yall heifers love me. I make you laugh; that's why yall keep fooling with me."

"So what's up with you and Donavan? And why was he at your house last night?" Monet asks.

"Here are your drinks ladies."

Kim grabs the salt and starts shaking it in her margarita as she begins to answer....

"Wait! Who is Donavan?" Brittney asks.

"Mike," Monet says.

"Thought you guys said his name was Lil Don?"

"Lil Don, Donavan, it's all the same. But his government name is Mike," Monet answers.

"When we got in high school, he didn't want to be called Lil Don any more but since we grew up with him every now and then we will still call him Lil Don or Donavan."

"Anyway before I was rudely interrupted; on our way back from Daytona, I asked him where he was staying and he said at the extended stay hotel but I insisted that he stay with me until he finds out what he wants to do. So there it is!"

"No- it's- not! I want details. How long is he here for? Did you two sleep in the same bed? Did you have sex?" Monet interrogates.

"Don't know, No and Yes," Kim answers.

"What do you mean No, and yes? How can you not sleep in the same bed but have sex?"

"She did it on the couch!" Brittney remarks.

"EWW! Which one? Remind me not to sit on it," Monet says.

"Too late!" Kim starts laughing.

"Kim, you nasty!" Brittney exclaims.

"But, no we did not have sex on the couch. I slept in my room and he is staying in the guest room. I woke up in the middle of the night and got in the bed with him. He was a gentleman all night; but this morning…."

"THAT'S why your tail didn't answer the phone," Monet says.

"And THAT'S why your tail smell like sex," Brittney says sarcastically.

"I took a shower," Kim declares.

"And?" Brittney asks.

"And I don't stink."

"I didn't say you stink. I said you smell like sex."

"Same difference," Kim says.

"You can smell me for real?"

"UH yeah…especially when you came in here testifying and carrying on, swaying back in forth, perfuming our booth with your sex on the beach scent. Smell like you bathe with musty balls." Everybody starts laughing.

"Monet did you smell it?"

Monet shook her head no.

"Well honey I have a nose of a hound dog, it picks up on everything. Shoot I know how it can be sometimes. I don't care how much you bathe or scrub, sometimes that's a twenty-four hour scent." Kim and Monet continue to laugh.

"So he's staying with you?" Monet asks.

"Yes," Kim answers.

"What about Keith?" Monet asks.

"What about Keith? What about Keith? What about Keith? What about Kim? Damn! Can I be happy? I'm so sick of hearing about his ass."

"I'm just saying, Kim, you been with him for the last four years, and I know you still love him."

"All I want to know is did you get the key back from him?" Britt asks.

"Daang, No I DID NOT!" She thinks back to last night.

"Why you looking like that?" Monet asks her.

"Cause last night, I thought I heard my front door close, but when I got up and looked in the living room the door was locked."

"Ahh man! You think he came in and saw yall?"

"Will this be on one check or separate?" the waitress asks.

"Separate," they answer in unison.

"No, I don't think he came in, but even if he did, I didn't go get in the bed with Don until after I thought I heard the door close."

"Serious talk, Kim, I hear you say you want to be happy, but you and Keith been together too long to just let it go like that," Monet explains.

"Moni, I'm tired of paying for what Sonya did to him."

"And I'm sure he's tired of paying for what Donavan did to you."

"What exactly did she do other than cheat with a woman?" Brittney asks.

"Nothing that I know of," Kim answers.

"Well that in itself is enough to mess with a guy's manhood."

"I'm sure it did, but he got to get over that."

"How are you ladies doing?"

"We're fine Mr. Gabriel," Kim answers quickly to shoo him away.

"Monet, you looking good girl."

"Thanks Mr. Gabriel. I feel good too," she remarks.

"Kim, I know you are a wise person, so I have a riddle for you: God tells us to put on this suit of armor, right? He tells us to put on a belt, a chest plate, shoes, helmet, a shield and a sword, but why do you think he didn't give you anything for your back? And why do you think he places your feet in front of you?"

[94]

Kim thinks for a moment and answers smartly, "I don't know Mr. Gabriel; why didn't he give us a shield for our back and placed our feet in front of us?"

"Because He has your back and He intended for you to keep moving forward. Your past is just what it is. Learn from it and keep moving. You ladies enjoy the rest of your day."

As he walks off, Brittney faintly hears a voice say, *"No man can serve two masters."*

"Did yall hear that?" Brittney asks.

"What Mr. Gabriel said? Yeah that was deep, I never….."

"NO Kim!" She cuts her off; ***No man can serve two masters***; did you guys just hear that?"

"You tripping," Kim answers.

"No I'm not. I heard it loud and clear. It's something about that man. I'm telling yall," Brittney says.

"I know, right? That analogy he just gave about God having my back and me to leave the past in the past--that was real," Kim answers.

"Umm um, it's something else…something different about him," Brittney remarks with paranoia.

"Yall 'bout ready? I need to get back to work," Monet says.

"Why? You don't do nothing!" Kim says.

"Whatever! I'll see you guys tonight. As she heads out, she picks up her phone to call Mitchell again…. *you have reached the…* she hangs up.

"That's the last time I'm calling him," she says.

"Calling who?" Brittney asks.

"Nobody," she answers.

"Looks like Nobody disappointed you."

"I'm alright. I'll see you tonight."

"Alright sis, have a blessed day."

Kim

After work Kim goes home to take a nap before church. Just as she's enters her apartment the phone rings.

"Hello?"

"Hey Kim, how was your day?"

"It was good," she answers in a nonchalant tone.

"Okay, do you still need that money to pay a bill?"

"Yes."

"Alright I'll bring it to bible study tonight."

"What's wrong you don't sound too good?"

"I'm tired," he says, "and I'm leaving Patricia."

"Look Tray, don't leave just yet; have you tried counseling?"

"She don't want counsel; talking 'bout she don't want people in our business, but at the same time she won't even talk to me. She talks to everybody else and put our business out on Facebook but she won't talk to her own husband. She won't cook or have sex with me anymore. When was the last time you seen her in church? She constantly want to put me down telling me I ain't shit, and 'F' you.

She talks to me like we go together, like I'm her boyfriend or some nigga off the street. What kind of mess is that? Kim I have always worked two jobs to make sure she was happy. I don't deserve this foolishness. Nineteen years Kim! Nineteen years and I have never cheated on her 'til me and you started kicking it. I love that woman but ever since she got that new job, she ain't been the same."

"Are you ready to walk away from nineteen years?"

"I'm done; she can kick rocks."

"Whoa! You talking out of anger. Chill out!"

"I'm good; I know what I'm saying." As of how I feel right now, it's a rap."

"Tray, I'm gonna get some rest before bible study. We'll finish this later."

"That's what's up," Butray says.

"Tray, trying to be hip, *that's what's up,*" she mocks him after they hung up.

She fix her a sandwich and watch a little TV right before she doze off on the couch. About thirty minutes into her sleeping she begins to dream...

A man dressed in an all-black suit ties her down to a chair and begins to speak as he walks around her: "I got you just where I want you: In your mind, your body, and your finances. You gave me the power to control you. Why do you think I wake you up for church? I want you to go to church because I know you can do more damage inside the church than outside the

[97]

church." He begins to laugh in a subtle and obscure tone.
"Go ahead; sing your dirty corrupt heart out." He laughs
again. "Taint the people in the church; this is what I live for,
to kill steal and destroy."

Mike walks in the living room and notice her tossing and turning, He realize she is having a bad dream.

"Kim, Kim honey wake up!"

"Noooo!"

She jumps up frantically, trying to free her hands.

"Are you okay? You looked like something was holding you down."

She is holding her chest, breathing hard.

"I'm okay," she says as she looks at her hands.

"What were you dreaming about?"

"The devil," she says sarcastically.

"Huh?" he asks.

"Nothing," she remarks.

"What time is it?"

"A quarter to six," he answers.

"Let me get up from here; Sister Shirley will be here shortly."

"Sister Shirley?" he asks.

"Yeah, tonight is our bible study."

"You can stay if you like."

"Thanks, but I think I'm going down to the sports bar to watch the game."

The doorbell rings.

"Who is it?" Kim asks standing in the doorway of the kitchen.

"It's me. Sista Shirley."

"Will you let her in for me?" she asks Mike.

When Mike opens the door to leave out, Sister Shirley gives him a stare down and Kim interrupts, "You here early."

"Yeah, I wanted to come by early and pray. I felt something last time I was in here."

"What arrogance!"

"You felt it too?"

"Every time I'm in your presence," Kim says sarcastically, leaving Sister Shirley to look puzzled. "Hey, but you get started praying for yourself…I meant praying and I'm going use the bathroom."

"Funny, every time I'm in your presence, I want to do the nasty," Sister Shirley whispers.

"Excuse me, did you say something?" Kim asks.

"No sweetie, I'm praying," Shirley answers.

As she begins to pray, in comes Brother Roger, Pastor, Butray, two crack heads, Keith and the rest of the congregation. As Kim comes out the bathroom, Butray passes her in the hallway, slips her the money in an envelope and enters the bathroom. She puts the envelope in her bra. "What was that?" Keith asks her.

"What was what?" Kim answers.

"That envelope he just gave you."

"That was his tithes," she answers agitated.

"Then why did you put it in your bra?"

"Because I'm about to go do praise and worship. What you doing here?"

"I came to study the bible. This is bible study night, right?"

"Keith you haven't been to bible…."

"Look Kim…" he cuts her off, "I've been calling you and I want to work this out."

"This is not the time or place for this," she says as she walks pass him to go on in the living room.

"Who let Lilo and Stitch in here?" Kim asks, referring to the two crack heads.

"I found them in the alley and invited them up," Monet responds.

"Watch them; make sure they don't go no further than this living room," Kim says.

"Sister Kim, you're going to be our new praise and worship leader," Pastor says.

"Where is Ciara? Is she not coming back 'cause she done missed, one, two, five, four services?" Kim says counting on her hands.

"She will be back soon. Now can you lead us with three songs this evening?"

Kim begins to sing: *What a mighty God we serve, I'm a Soldier in the army of the Lord, and the Lord is blessing me.* The congregation starts shouting; Pastor is praising and Kim, being stuck on herself, is enjoying the fact of them cheering her on. After exalting the congregation, she begins to slow it down. "How many worshippers do we have in the house tonight? If you don't mind let's lift our hands to reverence the Lord. The song says, ♫ *Here I am to worship, here I am to bow down, here I am to* say that you're my God…".♫

Monet kneels down in front of the couch and begins to worship……

Before service ended Kim orders pizza for everyone and after service, everyone sticks around for a slice.

"Deacon Butray, where is Tricia?"

"She is…I don't know Pastor. I don't know what's been going on with her. Ever since she got this new job she just been… I don't know, she won't talk to me. I asked her to come to counseling and she looks at me like 'boy please! I'm tired.' God himself gonna have to fix this."

"Pray about it…."

"I'm tired of praying," Tray interrupts.

"One thing I do know, Tray; after you done all you can…You just Stand!"

When Michelle left me, I prayed and cried, prayed and cried, prayed and cried. Then God began to speak; only time could heal my hurt. This too shall pass, you be encouraged. Hey everybody, I'm gonna get out of here. You guys have a good night."

"Good night Pastor," they all reply.

"I overheard you and Pastor talking ….his wife left him?" Kim asks being nosy.

"Dang, nosy! You heard the man. Why you asking me?"

"Okay, let me rephrase the question. Why she left him?"

"Don't know, don't care. I have my own problems to deal with," Tray answers.

Excuse me! is the look Kim has on her face.

"Yall have a good night," Tray says.

"Yeah, I'm about to get out of here myself," somebody else says.
Shortly after that everybody leaves.

"What's going on with you and the deacon?" Keith asks as he approaches Kim.

She turns around. "Why are you still here?"

"Can we talk?" he asks.

"Look, I can't do this and I won't do this tonight."

"Why? Because you doing your new boyfriend?"

She pauses to look at him, "I have spent the last four years of my life patiently waiting for you to ask me to marry you."

"PATIENTLY? PATIENTLY? You call doing every Tom, Dick, and Harry patiently waiting?"

"So you starting that again? Well maybe I wouldn't had to see every Tom, Dick and Harry if I had a man that would commit and stop holding on to what his ex-wife did to him."

"Forget Sonya, man… That chick don't mean nothing to me," he yells with anger.

"I gave her everything she wanted. She had the house, car, money; she didn't have to want for nothing. Then how does she pay me back? She starts spooning."

"Guess you wasn't man enough for her?"

"That was low, Kim."

"Get the hell up out of my house! I told you, you wasn't over that bitch. And give me my key," holding her hand out.

He looks at her with disappointment in his eyes, hands her the key and walks out the door.

She sits on the couch and thinks about the last comment she made: "Man that was a low blow. I shouldn't have said that. Forgive me Lord."

"Don't ask me to forgive you, you didn't offend Me," she hears in her spirit.

"You right Lord."

She picks up the phone to call him to apologize.

"You have reached the T- Mobile voicemail box of 2-2-9-4-4-4-4-0-0-1; at the tone please leave a message."

"Aye it's me, look I'm sorry for that last comment I made. It was a low blow and I was talking out of anger. Forgive me, and I'm sorry again." She hangs up the phone to gather her thoughts. A short time later she goes over to her book shelf to get a bible.

"Naw I think I'll read some more of this one," she states. About two hours later Mike comes in and notices she has dozed off on the couch. He walks over to the hall closet to get a blanket and comes back to cover her, she wakes up…

"Who won?" she asks.

"The Heat," he states.

"What's this you're reading?" He picks the book up off the floor to look at it, *Take up Your Bed and Walk,*" he reads. Hmm, interesting title, what is it about?" he asks as he hands the book to her.

"Church folks and their issues."

"Go figure," he says as he sits down in the chair beside her.

"Why you say that?"

"Because the title is biblical and everybody that came to that pool had issues. So how was service?" He changes the subject.

"It was nice."

"What was the message?"

"A better me."

"I like that, sounds like it was good."

"It was. My pastor also talked about looking at this building he saw not too far from here."

"Oh really, Well you know if it needs any work done, I can do it. I'm thinking about either relocating my business here or starting up another one."

"Lil Don's Construction; Yeah I can see that," Kim says smiling.

"Don't play. Yall gonna stop calling me Lil Don; I'm too old for that crap. "

"Okay, okay. I'm sorry, Mike Johnson," she says as she continues to laugh.

"I'm going to bed; you coming?"

"In a minute," Kim replies.

……..Two Weeks later……..

"Good morning ladies!" Monet speaks as she walks into the Café'

"Hey Boss lady," LaZibra and Felicia speak back.

"Y'all, doing alright today?" She asks as she heads towards her office.

"Yeah," Felicia answers.

"Oh boss lady," LaZibra calls. "Here." She hands her a message.

"This Mitchell guy has been calling you all morning. He said for you to give him a call whenever you got in." She takes the message and throws it in the trash.

"If this Mitchell person calls back, I'm not in today." She continues to walk to her office.

The phone rings no sooner than she closes her door.

"Café Latte' Felicia speaking. Oh she told me to tell you she not here today. And apparently you're not one of her favorite people anymore."

"Give me that phone! Hi Mr. Mitchell, excuse her manners, but Monet will not be available today."

"Well, will you please tell her I will not be going anywhere until she come out and talk to me," he says as he walks in the door and stands at the counter. LaZibra drops the phone from her ear a little and turns around. She has this cheap grin on her face…..

"I suppose you are Mitchell?" she asks.

"You are correct," he answers. Felicia exits from the front counter to the back office.

"Hold on one second; I'll let her know you're here." LaZibra scurries to the back as well.

"Move. I'll tell her," Felicia says as she shoves LaZibra.

"No, I'll tell her," LaZibra says as she grabs Felicia's arm and pushes her out the way.

"Tell me what? What is going on out here?" Monet says as she slings open the door.

"Boss lady, there is a guy in uniform who wants to see you," Felicia says out of breath.

"Mitchell?" She asks with curiosity. Both girls nod their heads 'yes.'

"Mitchell is at the front counter?" she asks again with a smile.

"Yes, boss lady and HE-IS- P-H-I-N-E—FINE! Get your butt up here." Lisa grabs her by the arm.

"No!" She snatches her arm back. "Tell him I'm busy." She shuts her door.

LaZibra walks back to the front counter while Felicia stands at the door and tries to convince her to come out.

"She's busy right now," LaZibra tells Mitchell.

"Do you mind?" he asks.

"Um um." She shakes her head. "Go on back."

"Monet, listen. I'm sure there is a perfectly good explanation; just here the man out.

"GO AWAY, Felicia!"

"Monet that man is too fine for you not..."

Mitchell taps Felicia on the shoulder and Shhh's her. She walks off quietly back to the front counter. Mitchell slowly opens the door.

"Felicia, you know darn well when my door is closed I am not to be distur…. What do you want?"

"Listen to me please," Mitchell pleads.

"I listened to your voicemail enough," she remarks.

"I'm sorry. Give me two minutes."

"One," she replies.

"You know my situation; I'm trying to get her packed and situated by Wednesday. She has duty in Afghanistan."

"She's in the military, too?"

"Yeah."

Monet takes a deep breath and rolls her eyes. "Look just give me 'til Wednesday."

"You can leave now," Monet retorts.

"Monet?…..Monet?"

"Mitchell, get out my office."

"Monet, don't be like that."

"Be like what Mitchell? Let me recap this for you…. You bump into me at O'Ryans….

"No, you bumped into me. You're the one that was looking down in your purse," he interrupts.

"Ok whatever. I bumped into you but *you* came after *me* to my car, then *you* called *me* more than a few times, *you* invited *me* to Niecy's sports bar; with your wife there, then *you* sent this fruit bouquet to my job, but you never answered my phone calls. I have been calling you

[107]

for two and a half weeks and now you want to show up at my place of business?"

"I just told you I had some things going on at my house. Can I see you on Wednesday night?"

"Mitchell get out of my office!"

"I'll call you," he says as he walks out.

"I won't answer!" she remarks.

As Mitchell walks back towards the front, he could hear Felicia and LaZibra talking.

"You ladies enjoy the rest of your day," he says as he walks past the counter going out the door.

"Ummm hmm; you as well," Felicia replies.

"Yeah he's married," LaZibra says.

"And a hoe," Felicia adds.

"Ummm hmmm," LaZibra agrees.

Mitchell stops at the door, turns around and looks at the two of them; he smirks at their appearances and decides to save his breath, so he turns back around and continues back out the door and chuckles.

Got to keep it on the
Down-Low

A few hours later Kim walks into the Café, "Hey Lisa, hey Z."

"Hey!!" they speak in unison.

"Is Monet back here?" she asks as she walks past them going to the office.

"Yeah," Felicia answers.

"Knock, knock." She knocks and opens the door at the same time.

"What you doing?"

"Nothing much at the moment."

"You want to do lunch?" Kim asks.

"Sure. Where you want to go?"

"I don't know. We'll figure it out; let's ride."

"You want to drive or me?' Monet asks.

"You drive 'cause I don't have any gas."

"You never have any gas." Monet laughs. "Let's go."

As they begin to pull off, Kim says, "Hey make a right at this next light, I want to see something."

"Who you spying on? Keith?" Monet asks.

"Nawl, I thought I seen pastor car over here."

"Annnd?" Monet inquires.

"And, look-- he's coming out that apartment door right there!"

"Right where?"

"The blue one!" Kim yells.

"Where he at?"

"He just stepped back in; slow down a lil' bit. There he is--the second apartment on top."

"He might be praying for somebody, Kim."

"No Ma'am! Did you see him just give whoever that was a kiss? Drive girl! Here he comes."

"That might be his wife, Kim."

"Or that might be the reason him and his wife ain't together. Let's go I'm hungry."

"What do you have a taste for?" Monet asks.

"I feel like having some pasta, let's go to GiGi's."

"That sounds good…. How are you and Mike doing?"

"We're alright. He's thinking about relocating back here."

"I know you're excited."

"Hmmm," Kim sighs.

"What do you mean hmmm; you're excited right?" Kim continues to look forward without answering. "Kim?"

"What?" she answers as if Monet never asked her a question.

"What? You heard me. What's going on?"

"Right now, I don't know. Mike was the love of my life at one time; and I use to pray for another chance to be with him. But honestly, I'm not feeling him like that anymore. I mean we are so cool together as friends and I think he knows this as well. I heard a preacher say one time *"sometimes God will give you what you want, only for you to see it's not really what you want at all."* And I see what he means."

"What about Keith?"

"Keith mad at me. I haven't spoken with him since that night he came to bible study."

"Did you two talk?"

"Yeah. He accused me of seeing other people again."

"He ain't lying," Monet smiles.

"Shut up. Anyway he accused me of seeing other people and I told him he accusing me because he still holding on to what Sonya did to him. He ain't over her, Monet!   Girl he got irate and started venting. I could tell he had been holding that in. So I told him to give me my key and get the hell out of my house."

"So he got mad because you told him, that he was only accusing you because of her cheating on him?"

"Nope, he got mad because I told him maybe he wasn't man enough for her."

"NO YOU DIDN'T KIM? WHY DID YOU…?"

"I know but he pissed me off, and I felt so bad afterwards. I called to apologize but he didn't answer."

"Girl you 'bout done damaged that man ego; I wouldn't talk to your butt either."

They walk in the restaurant….."Auhh man I forgot they be having the lights dimmed in this joint," Monet comments.

"What's wrong with that? Kim asks.

"Hell, I don't want to be sitting up in here with you, with no lights."

"Well, you ain't got No man, and I want some pasta with stuffed meatballs!"

"Your butt need a salad."

"How many?" the hostess asks.

"Two," Monet answers.

"Follow me."

"You think I'm getting big?"

"Have you seen your butt? That thing is a monster!" she responds strongly.

Kim stops, looks back at her butt, and gets her Beyoncé on *"uh oh, uh oh, uh oh, uh oh,"* she sings. "I'm about to start going to the gym, just to keep it up you know?"

"I hear you."

"Are you still talking to that guy you were telling me about, Mitchell?"

"Not really, girl he's so full of it. As a matter of fact he came by the store today… Let's talk about something else. So how long will Mike be staying with you?"

"I'm not sure."

"Brittney never met him, has she?" Monet asks.

"Come to think of it she hasn't," Kim says.

"We're gonna have to have a barbecue slash game night one night at your house so they can meet. Would you have a problem if she brought Tim?"

"Oooh Jesus! Let me pray about that one….. I guess I can put my feelings aside for a few hours."

"Are you ordering from the menu?" Monet asks as she gets up goes to the bar.

"Let me go with you to see what they got first."

As they are looking around the bar, the sunlight from the outside catches Kim's attention. She looks toward the door but the beams are too bright to distinguish who is entering the door. As the door closes, the light decreases and she is able to make out a guy. Her eyes follow him as he walks to the back of the room to a corner table.

"KIM...KIM," Monet calls.

Kim looks towards Monet.

"Quit being nosy," Monet says.

"But that look like Pastor," Kim states.

Monet turns to look in the direction in which Kim is looking; she notices a man standing at the back corner table. "He does favor Pastor."

"That's because he is Pastor," Kim replies.

Monet tilts her head forward a little... "O.M.G."

"What you O.M.Ging for? The man is just back there talking."

"YOU? Kim is actually giving somebody the benefit of the doubt? I don't believe this," Monet says sarcastically.

"Well, you can't precipitate until you investigate."

"Huh?" Monet looks dumb founded.

"What are you about to do?"

"We- are- about to- sit down- and eat and mind- his business," Kim says in a choppy dialect as she begins to fix her plate and watch the pastor take a seat across from the unknown person

"Oh lord, I'm not getting in this with you Kim; I'm minding my own business," Monet claims.

"That's cool. You got a spot on the back of your pants."

Monet turns around to see if she can see the spot on her pants. "I'll be back; I'm going to the restroom."

"Umm hmm," Kim replies.

As Monet walks to the restroom she didn't have to pass the table where Pastor was sitting, nor did she think to look over that way; she is too concerned about something being on the back of her pants. *My period just went off last week she thinks to herself.* As she makes it in the restroom, she turns to look in the mirror over the sink to see if she could see anything on the back of her pants. "I don't see anything." She bends over and looks down between her legs. "What is Kim talking about a spot on my pants?" She goes in the bathroom stall and pulls her pants down to see if there were something in the seat of her pants…. "Nothing! What is Kim up to?" She pulls up her pants and walks out of the bathroom; this time she has to walk pass the table where Pastor Down is sitting. She didn't think about how Kim had deceived her until she approaches the corner table and looks into Patricia, Butray's wife face. But the two of them are so engaged in a conversation neither one notice when she passes by. When Monet makes it back to her seat, Kim is already sitting and eating.

"Who is she?" Kim asks.

"You play too much, Kim. I'm all in the bathroom bent over looking between my legs and stuff."

Kim starts laughing. "Well how else were we gonna find out? They would have noticed my big ass if I walked by." They snort.

"That's why I aint telling you. You play too much. But that was a good one though." She continues to laugh. "Let me go fix my food."

"Tell me before you go."

"Nope and you will freak out if you know who it is."

"Monet, I will follow you up there and dash your head in that bowl of lettuce."

"OOOOOh I'm scared!"

"Monet come on." Kim starts whining like a baby.

Monet smiles at her and goes to the bar. Kim raises up and looks back towards the corner to see if she could see anything. "Dang I can't see nothing. Wait a minute where is he going? Oh my, he's changing seats."

"Kim quit being so darn nosy," Monet says when she comes back to the table.

"He switched sides."

"What you mean?" Monet asks.

"He's sitting next to her now!"

"I never said it was a She," Monet says sarcastically while smiling.

Kim spits out all the food that is in her mouth; barely catching her breath she says as she gets up, "I'm going over there."

"NO!" Monet grabs her by her arm. "Sit down Country! Imma tell you who over there."

Kim starts laughing, "You know I was going, right?"

"Hey Monet," a voice from behind speaks.

"Oh lord." She says under her breath as she recognize the voice. She sits up. "Hey Mitchell," she speaks in a low tone.

"Mitchell?" Kim asks Monet.

"Yes," he says, "and you are?"

"Kim," she answers. "Nice to meet you, I learned so little about you."

Mitchell chuckles. "This is my friend James. Chris James. James this is Monet and Kim."

"Nice to meet you, "Kim says.

"Likewise," Chris responds.

"Monet, I hope to see you soon," Mitchell remarks.

Monet didn't feel the need to respond.

"Nice to meet you Kim," Mitchell says as he walks off.

"You too; take care," she replies. "So that's Mitchell," she says to Monet. "He's cute. And Chris looks damn good in that uniform."

"Yeah whatever," Monet comments.

"Why are you so mad at that man? Did you sleep with him?"

"Nope; he's just full of it."

"Let's get out of here," Monet says.

As they stand up to leave, Kim looks back to the corner table. She sees Pastor Downs stand and extend his hand to assist the mystery person getting up from the table. Kim's eyes lock on the two making sure she doesn't miss anything.

"Sit down Pearl!" Monet snatches her down. "You're being too obvious."

Before she stands completely up from the booth, Pastor reaches behind her from the left side to get her clutch; she turns towards him and from what Kim can make out, the two embrace in a kiss. As she makes her way to the restroom door Kim says, "Is that…"

"Yes! Now let's go." Before Kim can get another word in, Monet grabs Kim's hand and leads her out the restaurant.

"I can't believe this! How can he….How can she…? Poor Butray," she says as she open the passenger door.

"Poor Butray? He alright; you been doing him--I meant taking care of him," Monet says smiling.

"Shut up! I'm trying to think. What are we going to do?"

"I tell you what we ain't gonna do; we ain't about to take this pass the two of us," Monet responds.

"Well, what do you think we should do?"

"Pray."

"For what?" Kim asks.

"Healing, Restoration, something, Kim... The word says if you see your brother overtaken in a fault we need to pray that he be restored and healed and stuff."

"Pray? You want to pray at a time like this? Come on Monet, we just saw Pastor… Our Pastor having lunch--an intimate lunch--with Patricia, Butray's wife, not to mention he kissed her… Pray? Do you pray for me?" Kim asks.

"All the time; I mean come on Kim," she says as she cranks up the car. "…what if it was you? What if your dirty laundry was exposed?"

"I wash mine before I air it," Kim responds sarcastically.

"What do you mean you wash it before you air it?"

"I mean I've already done it and repented before it gets to you guys."

"What you mean repented? You still involved with Butray and Mike."

"You doing stuff, too, Monet."

"But I'm not trying to be judgmental, Kim. Besides that could have very well been an innocent lunch date."

[117]

"Innocent?!" Now you know better than that. You saw them kiss."

"No *you* saw them kiss, I saw him helping her up."

"Whatever! Why you always have to be so optimistic?"

Monet stops and looks at her as the car comes to a halt in front of her café.

"Is there something wrong with being optimistic?"

"I'm just saying, I'm a realist... I call those things that I see... to be."

"Well maybe you should be a little more spiritual," Monet says as she gets out the car. Kim opens her door to get out as well.

They part ways; Monet walks back towards the café and Kim to her car.

"I'll call you later," Kim says. She sits down in her car and recalls the conversation between her and Butray:

"What's wrong? You don't sound too good?"

"I'm tired. I'm leaving Patricia."

"Have you tried counseling?"

"She don't won't counsel; talking 'bout she don't want people in our business, but at the same time she won't talk to me. She talks to everybody else and put our business out on Facebook but she won't talk to her own husband. She won't cook, or have sex with me anymore. When the last time you seen her in church? She constantly want to put me down telling me I ain't shit, and 'F' you. She talks to me like we go together; I'm her boyfriend or some nigga off the street. What kind of mess is that? Kim I have always worked two jobs to make sure she was happy. I don't deserve this foolishness. Nineteen

[118]

years Kim! Nineteen years, I have never cheated on her. I love that woman but ever since she got that new job she ain't been the same."

"Are you ready to walk away from nineteen years?

"I'm done, she can kick rocks."

Kim cranks up her car and heads back to work.

Brittney

(Two months later)

"Hey honey, what's going on?" Tim answers.

"Nothing much. Where are you?"

"I'm getting coffee, Hon; you want anything?"

"I'm at the Café Latte' getting coffee, where are you?

"Starbucks, Hon."

When are you coming to the house?"

"Awe... I'll be there when I finish working. Everything okay?"

"Yeah, I just miss you. Will that be tonight?" she asks in her lonely voice.

"Na, probably in the morning. What my lil man up to?"

"He's with Nina and Papa."

"DAMN!" Tim yells. "You okay?" He asks the young lady standing behind him.

"Yeah I'm fine," the young lady answers.

"My bad; I didn't know anybody was behind me. Let me get some napkins."

"What happened?" Brittney asks.

"Some crazy ass bitch was standing right up on me, so when I turned around, my coffee spilled on her." Tim whispers in the phone as he walks away to go get napkins.

"Alright honey, let me take care of this and I'll give you a call back in a little bit."

"Alright.'

"Love you Hon," Tim says.

"Love you, too.

After they hang up the phone, the young lady speaks. "I apologize for standing so close; I was trying to read the menu."

"You good," Tim answers as he gives her some napkins to wipe her blouse; he then squats down to clean the small spill on the floor.

"Here let me help."

She bends down to help him …… "Awwe!" she says as she grabs her head.

"DAMN! What the fuck is your problem man?" he asks as he holds his lips.

"I'm sorry, I didn't mean…she is interrupted by the blood on his lips.

"Let me get you a paper towel."

"No, back off!" he speaks in a harsh manner.

"It's no problem."

As she turns to go get a napkin, Tim grabs her by the back of her elbow and says, "I said BACK THE FUCK OFF!"

She snatches her elbow out of his arm.

"You ain't gotta be so damn mean!"

"Look lady….You are like some FREAKIN Urkell, so before there be any more mishaps, let's just…"

"Is everything okay, Felicia?" Erica asks as she comes from behind the counter.

"Yea, everything is fine," Felicia answers.

"Are you in a hurry? Do you have to get to work?" Erica asks.

"Yeah, but I'm good."

"Sit over there for a minute and take a breather; you look stressed."

"You okay Tim?" Erica asks.

"You know that clown?" he asks.

"Come on Tim, don't act like that. What happened?"

"I'm getting my coffee, and when I turn around, this bitch is standing right up on me, talking 'bout she was trying to see the menu. I think her ass was smelling me or some shit." They both laugh. "So, of course, before I could put the lid on, some of it spilled on her and the floor; I go get napkins and give her a couple to clean her shirt; I go to clean the spill off the floor and she decides she wants to help. Well it was only a small spill so as she was coming down I was coming up and my lip hit her fat head."

"Well, her name is Felicia, and she actually has a thing for you."

"No the fuck she don't." Tim starts laughing. He notices Erica is serious. "Really?"

"Yeah, so she probably was trying to smell you," Erica says sarcastically and laughs.

"EEwww!"

"What do you mean ewww? She ain't ugly now."

"No she not, but she like some….. Steve Urrrkell, or Med-school Melony type," he responds as he frowns up his face.

"Med-school Melony?"

"Yeah, Melony from *The Game*; she always doing shit," Tim laughs. "Anyhow, let me bounce up out of here. I'll holla at you later. Tell your girl Felicia she owe me coffee."

"Alright Tim," Erica laughs and walks over to Felicia.

"What'd he say?" Felicia asks.

"He said you were standing all up on him like you were trying to smell his ass or something!" Erica laughs.

"Girl I was; he smelled so damn good! But everything went downhill from there."

"Well, I told him you had a thing for him."

"Ericaaa!" She looks with disbelief. "What did he say?"

"He thinks you're a Med-school."

"Well I hope you corrected him and told him I'm in cosmetology school and I work at Café latte' across town."

"Nooo! He thinks you are a Med-school Melony from the TV show *The Game*."

"The one that's married to Derwin, that's always doing shit?" Felicia asks.

"That's the same thing he said."

[122]

"Well that ain't good," Felicia replies as she drops her head.

"And he also said you owe him coffee."

"Okay. He left some hope; that mean I still have a chance then. Let me get to work. I'll talk with you later Erica. Thanks girl!"

"Alright girl."

*****CAFÉLATTE' *****

"Hello," Brittney answers.

"Hey I'm back. What you doing?" Tim asks.

"Sitting here talking to Monet; everything okay?"

"Honey, you have noooo idea of what just happened."

"What happened, hon?"

"When I went to clean up the spill, the broad I was telling you about decides she wants to help me and her head bust my lip."

"Bust your lip? Oh Lawd! You didn't cuss her out did you, Bay?"

"I don't know; Shit!" He starts laughing. "I *know* I was cussing." He continues to laugh.

"Anyway hon, go ahead and finish talking with Monet, I'll holla at you later.

"Alright baby, bye."

"Cuss who out?" Monet asks.

"Some chick over at the Starbucks was standing too close to Tim made him spill his coffee; he goes to clean it up and somehow her head busts his lip. You know how he is."

"Yeah," Monet nodding her head in agreement.

[123]

At this time Felicia walks in the door. "Good morning, Boss lady."

"Morning Felicia. Slow down; you gonna run somebody over," Monet states.

"You okay this morning!?"

"I don't know," Felicia answers. "I don't know if I should be embarrassed, happy or what."

"Well what happened?" Monet asks.

"Nothing." Felicia shakes her head. "I'll tell you later."

She continues to walk to the back to put her purse away.

"A new employee?" Brittney asks.

"Yeah; well she's been here a couple of months--one of Zibra's friends."

"How's she working out? Is she anything like Zi?"

"They are one in the same."

"So is she boochetto too?"

"What the hell is boochetto?" Monet asks.

"Boojee and Ghetto," Brittney answers.

Monet laughs, "Girl you are stupid. Is that what you call it?"

"Umm hmm." Brittney shakes her head yes.

"Well I guess she is, but she is not as bad as Zi. They're good people. They keep me laughing, but you never know what they're gonna say."

"They kind of remind me of a toned down version of Halle Berry and Natalie Desselle, on that movie Baps," Brittney remarks.

Monet looks at Brittney, shakes her head, and laughs. "Girl I don't know what I'm gonna do with you. But so far she's working out fine

[124]

although the heifer had the nerves to tell me she loves Starbuck coffee."

"What!" Brittney answers in disbelief.

"Now that's just disrespectful," Brittney laughs. "That's gonna be her new name: "Disrespectful" with her disrespectful ass." The two of them laugh hysterically.

"You *will* give somebody a name," Monet says as she continues to laugh.

"I mean… how you say some shit like that…excuse me girl; but how do you say some mess like that to someone who owns the coffee shop you work at?" Brittney asks.

Monet imitates her, "She goes: *'I don't mean no harm Boss lady.'* She throws her hand up and rolls her neck. *'Your coffee good and all but I love me some Starbucks.'"* They laugh.

"What did you say?"

"I asked her why she didn't go get a job over there. She said Zi wanted her over here with her so they can trip out. But then she goes on to say: *But don't worry Boss lady, I ain't promoting Starbucks, I'm just letting you know.*"

"Letting you know for what? She coulda kept that shit to herself," Brittney says sarcastically as Monet laughs.

While they are sitting there talking, Ciara walks in the door. Not noticing Monet and Brittney sitting in the back of the shop, she walks to the counter to order an ice Mocha.

"Is that Ciara?" Monet asks.

"Ciara from the church?" Brittney turns around.

[125]

"She's pregnant?" Brittney is shocked. "Did you know this?"

"Umm um," Monet answers with disbelief.

"Ciara!" Monet calls her name.

Ciara turns around. "Heeeeeey!"

She answers with excitement. "I didn't see you guys over here."

She walks over to them and gives them a hug.

"How you been?" Monet asks as they hug.

"I've been doing good," she answers as she hugs Brittney.

"We miss you in church," Monet admits.

"I miss you all, too."

"You know Kim is the praise and worship leader now, and she is a mess," Brittney says.

"I bet," Ciara answers and smiles.

"So how far along are you?" Monet asks.

"Six months," Ciara answers.

"Heifer, why you didn't tell anyone you were pregnant?" Brittney asks.

"I don't know; after Pastor asked me to sit down, I was devastated, hurt, and confused. Things were so messed up at my parents' house that I had to move out. And I was too embarrassed to come to church like this."

"The sin was in the sex not the pregnancy," Monet comments.

"I know, but yall know how much I enjoyed singing for the Lord."

"Yeah, totally different from Kim. She like singing for herself," Brittney smartly remarks.

"Wait a minute, you say you're six months?" Monet asks.

"Yep." Ciara nods her head.

"So you were pregnant while you were still at church."

"I didn't want to tell anybody not even the father because he would have asked me to get another abortion. So when I began to show, Pastor called me and asked was I pregnant and I told him yes and he said he had to ask me to step down from the praise team."

"*Another* abortion? Ciara you had an abortion?" Monet asks.

"Don't sit up here and act like you don't know that shit go on in the church, Monet!" Brittney butts in. "I can name three off the top of my head: Stacy, Trin and Tam."

"Why you telling they business?" Monet says.

"Hell I'm just letting her know she ain't the only one. That mess runs rampant in the church. Don't get me wrong; I'm not condoning it, but I understand."

"What you mean understand? You had one done, too?"

"I said I understand didn't I?"

"Wow! You and I got to talk later."

"Talk about what? That's in the past, God has forgiven me, I've forgiven myself and I've moved on. That's why I can talk about it freely. And neither you nor the devil can hold this over my head. But what you ain't gone do, Monet, is try to condemn me. I'm a firm believer that there is no condemnation for those in Christ Jesus."

"Listen baby…" Brittney says to Ciara. "How old are you?"

"Nineteen," she answers.

"Nineteen? Let me tell you something, don't you let that baby daddy or another man roll up in you without making a commitment to you

[127]

first, and by commitment I mean marriage. And another thing, you have got to get over people; you can't be worried 'bout what them folks in church think. Look, people ain't got a heaven or hell to put you in. But understand this...God has forgiven you. You did ask for forgiveness didn't you?" she asks sarcastically.

"Yeah," she nods.

"Then it's done. God done threw that shit..." She pauses, "excuse me baby, I know you don't know this side of Brittney but I say what's on my mind because I'm so over people and it feels good. But like I was saying, God done threw that crap, mess; it's all the same... in the sea of forgetfulness. Now have you forgiven yourself?"

"I think so."

"No you haven't because you would have been more confident with your answer; but it's okay. Sometimes it takes a while... Now who's the daddy?"

"Wait a minute Brittney. How do you know Stacy, Tam, and Trin all had an abortion? Did they come to the doctor's office you work at?" Monet asks.

"Hell Naw! We don't do abortions and if we did, that would be against company policy for me to tell their business."

"You told it anyway," Monet says.

"Well all I got to say is, it was no longer THEIR business once they told somebody else. Everybody best friend got a best friend and somebody gone tell somebody. But I've talked to all them just like I'm talking with Ciara now. Now who's your baby daddy?" she asks Ciara again.

Ciara hesitantly answers, "You don't know him."

"You sure?" Brittney asks.

"I'm sure."

"Come on let's go get some lunch," Monet says. "Ciara, you wanna join us?"

"No thank you. I think I'll go home and take a nap. Do you guys come here often?"

"Every once in a while," Brittney answers.

"I actually own the place."

"Really? Are you hiring?"

"You need a job?"

"I sure do."

"Get an application and fill it out and I'll see what I can do."

"Okay. Thank you." Ciara gets up from the table and walks to the counter to get her iced mocha and an application.

"Felicia!" Monet yells. "Give her an application for me."

Felicia reaches under the counter to get an application.

"Thank you."

"You're welcome."

"Thanks Monet!" she yells as she walks out the door.

"Okay, you're welcome. Make sure you fill it out and bring it back," Monet yells back.

"Come on lets go, I'm hungry." They get up to leave.

"Come here let me introduce you right quick… Felicia, this is one of my good friends, Brittney. Brittney, this is Felicia."

"Nice to meet you." They both say in unison.

"We're going to lunch; be back shortly," Monet says.

As they walk to the car, Monet asks, "Why you kept asking that girl who her baby daddy is?"

"In due time." Brittney answers.

"What that supposed to mean… In due time?"

Brittney ignores her. "Look." They notice Ciara walking.

"Ciara," Monet yells. "Where are you going?

"Home," she yells back.

"Come on I'll give you a ride. It's hot out this door."

They all get in the car, "Where do you live?" Monet asks.

"Just around the corner; make a right at this next light… Okay, you can slow down; turn right here where these blue apartments are."

"Wow I didn't know you lived this close," Monet says.

"Alright turn up in here… right here… Yeah this where I moved when I left my parents' house."

"Are these based on your income?" Brittney asks.

"Yes and No. I mean they are based on your income but not low income apartments; the most you will pay is five hundred and the least you will pay is two hundred and thirty-five depending on your income."

"So what's your income based on?" Brittney asks.

"Dang you nosy, Brit," Monet interrupts.

"I do hair," Ciara answers.

"Oh really, what you do?" Brittney asks.

"Braids."

"Let me get your number 'cause I definitely been looking for somebody to braid my hair. You got pictures of your work?"

"Yes," she answers.

"That's what's up. Alright I'mma be calling you soon."

"Alright. I'll see you guys later," Ciara says as she gets out of the car.

"Bye baby, take care," Monet responds, "and don't forget to bring the application back."

"Yes ma'am, Thank you."

"Don't 'yes ma'am' me. Make me feel like I'm old."

Ciara chuckles, "okay. See yall later."

They watch as she walks to the second apartment on the top floor. Monet remembers the day she and Kim saw Pastor coming from that same apartment. "Wait a minute," she says out loud.

"What?" Brittney asks.

She hesitantly answers wondering if she should say anything to Brittney. "Nothing," she answers. "I was thinking about something."

"What do you want to eat?" Monet asks.

"Pizza sounds good to me. What do you want?"

"Something light, but pizza is fine. I'll get me a salad."

On the way to GiGi's, Monet can't help but to wonder what Pastor was doing at Ciara's apartment.

"Why you so quiet?" Brittney asks.

"Just thinking."

"I wanna think, too. What's up?"

"I'm straight," she answers. "Just thinking about what I got to do at work."

"You lying; you been quiet ever since you had your 'aha' moment at Ciara's."

They go inside and have a seat.

"What can I get you ladies to drink?" the server asks.

"Water," both of them say.

"Okay and will you ladies need a menu or will you be having the bar?"

"The bar," Monet answers.

"Ooh kay. I'll be right back with your water."

When they come back from the bar Monet blurts out, "I'll bless the food."

"I know what you insinuating but it's okay; go head bless the food 'cause I ain't finna go there with yo' sanctified ass!" she responds laughing.

"Lord, thank you for this food we're about to receive, bless it and let it be a nourishment to our body and help my friend Brittney to stop cussing…"

"And help my friend Monet to see the log in her own eye…In Jesus' name Amen."

Monet gives her a look; "Whatever Britt… Listen, me and you cool right?"

"Yeah, like two box fans sitting in your living room window on a hot day."

"Anyway, do you think I'm judgmental?"

"Judgmental, prejudice, prideful, secret squirrel…."

"Hey!" Monet cuts her off, "I didn't ask you all that."

[132]

"Ain't no need to sugar coat it. I mean seriously, I'm not trying to sound mean, but maybe you hindering your own deliverance from being healed. You need to just fart, let all that out and be healed."

"Brittney, that's mean."

"I'm just saying, you my girl, so I should be able to tell you things that will help you and vice versa. Now I truly think you need to relax a little and stop being so uptight."

"You right, I mean I recognize I have things I need to work on; it's just so hard at times."

"And I recognize I need to work on my cussing; well, I like to call them sentence enhancers... I mean honestly it just sounds better to say ass instead of butt or booty, and shit instead of mess, or crap, and damn instead of dang and it seems like people take you more seriously when you cuss. Think about this... When you were a kid, if you wasn't in the house when them street lights came on, what did your momma yell?"

"You better get your ass in this house," Monet grins.

"See you wouldna took her serious if she said 'Monet, you better get your booty in this house!'" They both laugh.

"But I'm gonna work on it. Pray for me, God already know my name Brittney Renee Elizabeth Brown Johnson; I told Him to add me on his speed dial and make mine number five for grace, 'cause I need plenty of it," Brittney says with a straight face trying not to laugh.

"Girl I don't know what I'm gonna do with you," Monet says laughing.

[133]

"You know I'm telling the truth. And sometimes cussing can be funny, especially when you're telling a story or joke or something." She laughs. "Come on now, you know some stuff just sound better with sentence enhancers." She smiles.

Monet continues to laugh while changing the subject. "I was about to ask you why you had two last names, but I forgot you were married; to Jaylin's father right?"

"Yep, it lasted all about two years."

"You don't talk about him much; why isn't he apart of Jaylin's life?"

"I really don't know. We just haven't talked... I mean after we split, He went his way and I went mine."

"Is that who you were pregnant from when you had the abortion?"

"Nawl, I was fourteen at the time and my mom said I was too young to be somebody momma. Me and Jay's dad met in college, got pregnant then married...."

"Hey yall," Kim interrupts. "Yall heifers didn't have to invite me to lunch."

"We know; that's why we didn't," Brittney responds.

"Brittney, you must think you one of them housewives or basketball wives or something."

"And do why do you say that, Kim?"

"Cause like them, you don't ever have your child with you."

"That's because he's not getting paid to be publicized," she answers.

"That's a good one," Monet says laughing. Kim agrees and laughs as well.

"So are you joining us?" Monet asks.

[134]

"Nawl, Me and Lil Don are having lunch together; I came in here to pick up a pizza and saw yall over here."

"Kim, I still haven't met this Lil Don. When are you gonna let me meet him?"

"Monet interrupts, "We were just talking about having a cookout so you can get a chance to meet him."

"You gonna have a cookout just so I can meet this Lil Don dude? Wow!"

"No silly," Monet answers.

"Well that's what it sound like you said."

"But that's not what I meant."

"Okay, okay, whatever. When is the cookout?" Britt asks.

"We haven't discussed a date yet."

"Well let me know if I need to bring anything. Is Tim invited?"

Kim takes a deep breath and sighs with a fake smile. "Yes, Tim can come."

"Okay great! We will be there."

"Kim, guess who we saw today?"

"Who?"

"Ciara, she is six months pregnant."

"Pregnant? What the hell?"

"Yeah, she came into the coffee shop today and she talked to me and Britt for a little bit. She said Pastor asked her to sit down; she was about four months then. Then she missed those five services that make five months. So, she's six months now."

"What the…." Kim says with disbelief.

[135]

"Yeah, Suze Orman here was giving her some advice," Monet states.

Brittney is looking at Monet confused.

"About finance?" Kim asks.

"No!" Brittney answers in a stern tone.

Monet looks at Brittney confused.

 "Suze Orman is the self-proclaimed financial therapist!" Britt states.

"Oh Yeah that's right!" Monet responds. "Well it sounded good." She laughs.

"It sounded dumb dadumb duummmmb!" Brittney sings.

"Anyway," Monet interrupts. "We were getting ready to go to lunch and I gave her a ride home; she lives in those blue apartments around the corner from the shop."

Kim looks at Monet with a deep thought, "Talking about when you make that right at that light?"

"Yep." The tense look in their eyes causes Brittney to become suspicious. "The second apartment on the top floor…," Monet adds.

"Alright that's enough of that shit," Brittney interrupts. "What's going on with Ciara and them damn blue apartments?"

Kim looks at Brittney with disgust on her face.

"Don't look at me like that; if you didn't want me to know, you should have kept it to yourselves."

"Ooo, I don't like you sometimes!" Kim says to Brit. "But you my girl." She giggles.

"A couple months ago, we saw pastor come out of Ciara's apartment," Monet answers.

"And what does that mean?" He could have been over praying for her or anointing her place," Brittney comments.

"He kissed her," Kim says.

"Did yall see him?"

"Nawl, we just feel like spreading rumors. Of course we did!" Kim answers.

"You better lower your voice, I know that," Brittney replies in a stern voice as she looks away. "So that confirms just what I thought."

"What?" Kim asks.

"I kept asking her who is her baby daddy, and she wouldn't answer; well she said that I wouldn't know him, but I know for a fact, yall, that Pastor done slept with a few of them young ladies in the church."

"What the hell?" Kim asks with disbelief. "The church needs to have a meeting so we can vote his ass up out of…." As she is talking she looks around and sees Mr. Gabriel sitting two tables behind them.

"Hey Mr. Gabriel, where you come from? I didn't see you come in."

"Neither did I," Monet remarks.

"See, his ass be scaring me, popping up every damn where," Kim whispers.

"Hi Kim, Monet, Brittney," he smiles." You ladies doing okay today?"

"Yes!" they all speak.

"That's great," he answers back.

"Now back to what I was saying," Kim says. "What *was* I saying anyway?"

"I think what we should be doing is praying for the man instead of trying to kick him out. God does tell us if any man is over taken in a fault, you who are spiritual should…"

Kim interrupts Brittney…"You who are what?"

Brittney is confused… "Yall, I swear I don't know where that scripture came from. I opened my mouth to say one thing and that's what came out… told yall it's something 'bout that man, I'm telling you; but it's not a bad thing; it's like one of those eerie weird good feelings."

"I know what you mean," Monet comments, "sort of like a peace."

"Yeeeaah!" Brittney agrees.

"Well I'm gonna leave yall with Mr. Peacemaker 'cause Mike is waiting on….Where did he go?" Kim asks.

"Be careful of the strangers you entertain; some have entertained angels unaware," Brittney quotes.

Monet and Kim look at Brittney; and she has this confused look on her face…

"Alright, I'm gone," Kim hollers out.

"Alright see ya," Monet comments.

"Now that was a trip," Brittney comments. "I believe that man Gabriel is an angel. But anyway, what were we talking about before Kim rudely interrupted us?"

"Jaylin's dad," Monet answers.

"Oh yeah. He called a few times after we split to check on Jay but when I moved here I changed my number."

"So why did yall spilt up?"

"It just didn't work. He only married me because I was pregnant; but for the most part he tried to be a good husband and a good dad, but he was holding on to his past. It consumed him to the point where he actually hit me one time, and that was one thing I was not going to tolerate. Then he promised and swore he wouldn't touch me again. So we worked it out, but as the months went by, I can see the frustration and the irritation coming out and I knew something was going on. I would ask him to talk to me and he wouldn't and one day he raised his hand to hit me. I flinched and covered my face and he just fell on the floor crying, apologizing. I got down on the floor and begged him to talk to me and that's when he told me he only married me because I was pregnant and the story about him being in love with somebody else. I was hurt but now I had an understanding where all the frustration and irritation was coming from. And a huge burden was lifted off him. We became roommates and filed for a divorce-- irreconcilable differences. My hurt eventually turned to anger and I knew I had to get away from him to heal, so I left to go stay with my parents for a little while, applied for a job here, met Tim about three years after being here and we've been together almost four years now."

"Wow interesting. And how did you meet Tim?"

"One night I decided it was time for me to get out of the house, so I went to this lounge downtown to listen to some poetry and Tim was there as well. We were both sitting at the bar and he tried to talk to me, and I wouldn't give him the time of day 'cause I thought he was drunk and he thought I was boojee- turns out he doesn't drink; he only had cranberry juice in his glass. After a few laughs and him picking at people in the lounge, we made plans to hang out the next night; we had dinner at Applebee's; we laughed and talked; afterwards we went bowling and that's where we shared our first kiss. He told me he was ready to feel that warm fuzzy feeling he hasn't felt in a long time. It was really romantic; we connected spiritually and physically. The next day he flew back home."

"Flew back home?" Monet asks.

"Yeah, he was here visiting family and two of his kids at the time, but he was also thinking about moving here."

"Really?"

"Yeah, so get this; he called to let me know he made it home safely and the next day when he called he said to me, 'I know this may be too soon, and sound crazy but I love you.' And what was crazy is that I was feeling the same way. He eventually moved back here and we been going strong since."

"Hold up, you said you connected with him spiritually and physically? You slept with the man your first date?"

"Shoot I hadn't had none in three years; it wasn't like it was planned; I was dropping him off at his mom house after our date and we did it in the car behind her house."

"Yall grown behind doing it in a car; that's some high school mess," Monet laughs.

"Girl it was so good, every time I thought of him I puked in my panties. I had to start wearing panty liners. But check this out now; we were so in tuned with one another spiritually; two weeks after he flew

[140]

back home he calls me and says, *'Honey, you're pregnant.'* But the crazy thing is, when my phone rang, I knew what he was about to say."

"Really now?" Monet inquires.

"Yeah, I knew he was my soul mate. After he told me I was pregnant, I asked him how did he know, he said, *'Trust me; I had a vision. Go get a pregnancy test so you will know and call me back.'* He was right. He asked me what I wanted to do. I told him I didn't want any more kids; he didn't either; he told me *don't worry everything is gonna be okay.* He took the next flight down, and we were on our way to the clinic."

Monet looks at Brittney with her eyes wide and mouth open…"Brittney!"

Brittney cuts her off and motions with her hand to close it. "But enough about me; what is Monet's story?"

"Okay, I won't say anything about that other thing but let's back up a little, so Tim has visions?"

"Tim is a very spiritual person. You can't have a conversation about God without him getting so passionate. One thing he loves more than me, his momma, and his kids is God."

"So why doesn't he come to church?"

"I said he loves God, not the church!.... I mean he has his reasons for not coming; frankly, I think it's more of an excuse, but he's a grown ass man; he got to answer to God. Enough about me-- what's your story with men?"

[141]

"Well in a nutshell, I tend to meet all the married men. Where are all the single men? I mean every single guy I meet is married! Why is that Britt?" she asks with tension. "It's like I'm wearing a marriage magnet on my head. This last guy I met Mitchell, I can't stand his tail. He and his wife are both military; she is deployed right now; she started cheating with some guy that's a higher rank than her; he found out about it so he decides to cheat…girl. It's just a whole bunch of mess."

"You slept with him didn't you?" Brittney asks.

"Yes, I did. Oh God I felt so bad! And now when I call him he hardly answer or call me back. He has excuses like he's busy working or he busy taking care of his four year old which by the way looks nothing like him. But anyways he only call me when he wants to do it. And I'm not going for that crap."

"Did you like it?"

"Yeeessss! That's why I got to be strong girl. Dude can lay-it-down with his trifling butt."

"I knew your ass wasn't no saint walking around here like your shit don't stank. See Moni, I know you probably been saved a whole lot longer than me. How long you been saved?"

"Nine years now," Monet answers.

"Dang boo. So I got you by three years. But listen just because we saved, doesn't mean we're devil proof. Things gone happen; we gone fall; we gone make mistakes, but one thing about a child of God, we know how to ask for forgiveness. Now this doesn't give us a license to sin but his grace keeps us. I know it's gonna come a time when I'm gonna have to make a decision about me and Tim's relationship. As much as I love him, it's a battle trying to live right and being with him 'cause he ain't trying to go to nobody's church although he does like to watch Joel Osteen. I mean he says he has his relationship with God, but I don't know. I know he's very passionate about talking about God if you get him on that subject. I think he believes in God; and I also think he believes his gifts are his ticket to heaven. But I said all that to say this, you'll be a much better Christian if you take off your mask and just be real. People looking for realness and they will respect you more. I'm not saying you have to advertise your business to everyone but I'm simply saying don't cut your eyes at me if I tell you I had an abortion, don't condemn Kim if she say a cuss word, when you're round here being a little Rahab."

"I get everything you saying. I do. Look at you trying to give someone advice," Monet says smiling. "I'm usually the one giving out advice."

"Well, it's good to have somebody to pour back in you sometimes, shake you and bring you back to reality," Brittney comments. "So how are you feeling? You know with the MS and all?"

"I'm feeling good today. Sometimes up, sometimes down."

"But you know what? You hide it so well. Nobody ever knows when you have a bad day."

"I try to stay positive and be around positive people that make me laugh. That's why I like being around you. And Kim! Don't ever change Britt. I'm still trusting God. You know...I almost went to one of those spiritual healers; well I did actually go—"

"Realness, that's what I'm talking 'bout," Brittney interrupts.

"Realness doesn't mean it's always right but it frees you and who can accuse you if you're free? But go ahead, I'm sorry to interrupt," Brittney remarks.

"She gave me some stuff to bathe in but when I left, the Holy Spirit arrested me and said, '*Who do you think I am?*' And I answered *God Almighty. 'Then why are you putting a god before me?*' Girl I felt so bad. I apologized, asked God to forgive me and pulled over to the convenient store and threw that mess in the trash. I do believe my day of healing is coming."

"I stand in agreement with you. It's a good thing you did throw it away; there was a good chance you could have opened up that channel to the dark side."

"Thank you for agreeing with me; I appreciate that. So I heard you just passed the state board?"

"Yes, I did. So excited 'bout that."

"So what's next for ya?"

"Well, I got a couple dollars saved up. I think I'm going to open up a salon."

"That would be cool; maybe Ciara can do braids in your place."

"You know what? That might not be such a bad idea 'cause she don't need license to braid in Georgia. I got to check out her work first."

"Hey come to think of it, there is an empty spot on the other side of the coffee shop. I'll show it to you when we get back," Monet says.

[144]

Meanwhile while Brittney and Monet are having lunch on the other side of town, Tim thought he would surprise Brittney by meeting her at Monet's coffee shop. He pulls in the parking lot and didn't see Brittney's' car, so he drives around the plaza to turn around. As he approaches the side of the building, he notices one of them is empty. So he parks his car and looks in the window. As he's looking in the window, he begins to smile and starts to look around for the contact information. "Why the hell they ain't got the information on the window?" He walks around the corner to the coffee shop.

"Excuse me," he says as he walks in.

"Do you know who owns the building around the…." The young lady turns around. "Oh hell nawl, not you again; I'm out!" He turns around to walk back out the door.

"No no no no no no no no, hold up! Please don't go." He stands at the door and turns around. "It's safe! I assure you," she says with a half-smile.

"Look I'm back here…" She stood behind the counter. "…and you're over there, so no mishaps." She gets a smirk out of him. "Let me just first apologize for earlier today. I totally accept all responsibility. Come closer I won't bite." She extends her hand, "Hi my name is…"

"Felicia, I know." He cuts her off as he hesitantly shakes her hand.

"Impressive, you know my name. I'm assuming Erica told you."

"Your assumption is correct." He looks her into her mysterious eyes.

"Did she also inform you I work here?"

[145]

"Please! Don't flatter yourself; you think I came up here to see you?"

He starts laughing.

"Why you got to be so mean?" she asks.

He looks at her and continues laughing.

"You're an ass," she states.

"I know." Still laughing.

He laughs so much 'til she starts laughing.

"Oh yeah, I got your message," she says as she's pouring a small cup of hot coffee.

"What message?"

"You said I owe you a coffee; have you ever had any coffee from here?" She places the small cup in front of him.

"I don't want that!" he states with his face frowned up.

"Why not? Have you even had this before?"

"Yeah," he says with his face still frowned up.

"That shit is nasty." He starts laughing and pushes it aside.

"Felicia leans over the counter to whisper…

"Umm um back your ass up 'fore something fall out the ceiling or something." He continues to laugh. "Whisper yo ass right there."

"Shut up!" She laughs with him.

"You trying to whisper and talk about these people shit and you know how clumsy yo ass is." Umm Um… back the fuck away from me."

He continues to laugh.

"You funny!"

"No yo ass funny!"

[146]

"No, no, no, listen now. I was about to say I don't like this coffee either."

"Get the fuck out of here!" he responds sarcastically. "How you gone work here and not like the coffee? That's foul! What's wrong with the coffee?"

"It's not Starbucks, I can tell you that!"

"I admit, it ain't Starbucks but she's in the top five. Give me a Caramel Macchiato eight shots of espresso, stirred three times not shaken."

Felicia looks at him weird, "I thought you said you didn't like this coffee."

"I don't."

"Sound like you been in here a few times; you got it all down pack of what you want."

"I have," he agrees.

"I never saw you in here before," she states.

"And I never saw you in here before."

"Why you got to be such a smart ass?"

"Cause its funny…. Shit." He starts laughing again.

"Look Sweetheart. Yes, I can be very anal at times, but I love to joke a lot and have fun. Yes I have drank coffee from here from time to time, and yes I do like the coffee here as well as Starbucks. You, on the other hand, was dead ass serious when you said you didn't like it," he laughs, "…and I'm gonna tell the owner."

"She already knows. I told her."

"Get the fuck out of here; you 'bout stupid as me."

"I just told her I'm faithful to my Starbucks. I mean I like the coffee here, too; I was just going along with you."

"No you wasn't!"

"Yes, I was!"

"Was not!"

"Any hoo, so you want to know who owns the building on the side over there? What are you 'bout to do?"

"None of yo damn business, nosy."

"You hiring? I need a part time job?"

"Yep, one of my hoes is M.I.A. and I need somebody to replace her. When can you start?"

"Bitch you done lost yo mutha fuckin' mind! I ain't being nobody's damn hoe."

Tim took a deep breath and put his hand over his mouth trying not to laugh, "You cussed! I'm appalled."

"And I'm Felicia; don't try me like that again."

Tim is dying laughing. "I'm sorry; you should have seen your face. *You done lost yo Mutha fuckin mind," h*e mocks her while trying to remain in his seat laughing.

"Let me get out of here, but do you know who owns it."

"Mr. Thomas owns it. My cousin was looking to get that building. You can find his number in the phone book; Thomas Royce.

"Alright, thanks, hon and thanks for the coffee."

"No problem. By the way, what's your name?"

"Appalled!" he laughs as he is walking out the door dialing 411.

"Yes, do you have a listing for a Thomas Royce?"

[148]

"I'm showing we have two listings for a Thomas Royce and one for a Thomas R," the operator answers.

"Let me get all three," Tim answers as he pulls out of the parking lot. Upon approaching the red light at the intersection, he begins to write the numbers down quickly before the light changes to green. As the light turns green, he proceeds to go through not noticing Brittney's vehicle approaching the light to the left of him.

"That looks like Tim," Brittney says to Monet.

"How can you tell that from way back here?"

"That looks like his car; hold on." She picks up her phone to call him. Just as Tim dials the last digit to the first number of three numbers he has for Mr. T Royce, he is interrupted by ♫*There goes my baby* by Usher coming from his phone. "Awe shit! She musta saw me," he says as he looks around for her vehicle.

"Hello," he answers.

"Hey baby, what you doing?"

"Nothing," he answers. "On my way to finish up this work so I can come see you."

"Oh okay, I thought I just saw you on Arlington crossing over Statenville Hwy.

"Oh okay. Well honey, let me take care of this and I'll hit you back in a few."

"Alright Babe, love you."

"Love you, too, hon."

"Keep straight," Monet tells Brittney after they turned into the parking lot. "This is the building I was telling you about."

Brittney parks the car and looks in the window. "Oh my God, Moni, this is perfect."

She begins to visualize where the reception desk will go, how many stations she will have. "And see right there Moni, that will be my spot."

"Sounds like you got it all worked out."

Brittney looks around for call back info. "How do you know who to get in contact with?"

"I know the owner; I can give you his number."

"How much is the rent?"

"I'm not sure; let me go get the number out my office."

Monet walks around the corner to her office and calls Brittney on the phone.

"Hey, you ready?"

"Yeah," Britt answers.

"678-671-1954."

"Got it! Thanks girl, 'bout to call him right now."

Before she could finish dialing the number, she is interrupted by a phone call. "Uuuugghh!" She let out a sigh of frustration and hit the reject button. Attempting to dial the number again, she is interrupted by the same number. "Hello," she answers.

Meanwhile Tim is dialing the second of three numbers which he has. "Hi, may I speak with Mr. Royce? Thomas Royce."

"He is not in at the moment," the lady replies. "May I take a message for him please?"

"Yes, my name is Roosevelt Brinson and I'm interested in the commercial building he has for rent on Statenville Hwy."

"Oh okay honey, let me give you his cell number. Let me know when you're ready."

"Okay, go ahead."

"It is 678-671-1954."

"678-671-1954?" he repeats back to her. "Alright, I appreciate it. You have yourself a blessed day, ma'am.

"You do the same."

Without hesitation he dials the number. "Hello Mr. Royce. How you doing today?"

"Well, I reckon I'm doing just fine despite this heat, and these old knees of mine. I went to the doctor today and bless the Lord they didn't find anything wrong with my prostate. You know, son, the Lord is still in the blessing business I tell ya."

"He sure is," Tim declares.

"God is great!"

"Yes He is," Tim agrees with a half-smile.

"God is good!"

"He is **vee-ry** good! LeLet me stop you right there reeeal quick before you get too happy," Tim stuttered.

"My bad. I get a lil excited when I think about the goodness of Jesus and aaaall He's done for me…I just…….

"Mr. Royce; LISTEN!" Tim interrupts sternly. My name is Roosevelt Brinson and I'm calling because I'm interested in renting your commercial building on Statenville Hwy.

"Oh ok, Shiiit, I thought you were somebody from the VA office; calling my name like you know me. 'Mr. Royce how are you doing today?'" He imitates Tim.

"I was wondering how they got my cell number."

Tim is laughing his butt off, "We gone get along just fine."

Mr. Royce chuckles. "So you're interested in the building that's in the plaza?"

"Yes sir," Tim answers.

"What you say your name again is?"

"Roosevelt Brinson."

"Okay, let me ask you this Roosevelt. What kind of business are you looking to do in that building?"

"A Salon."

"Oh okay, when would you like to meet me to look in it? And we can go over all the details, rent and whatnots."

"I actually just left from over that way. I got to run and take care of some business and then I can meet you over there say hour, hour and a half?"

"Ok just give me a call when you on your way."

"Alright Mr. Royce."

"Just call me Royce. I'll look for your call in an hour or so."

Meanwhile Brittney is so engaged in her conversation with her best friend from back home, she forgets all about calling Mr. Royce. She gets in her car and heads home. After about two hours of catching up with Sharee, she leaves the house to pick up Jaylin from school. "No I haven't heard nor talked with Jay's father in a long time."

"Mommy, you surprised me. I didn't know you were coming today!" Jaylin says running to the car.

"Yeah, Mommy took the day off to surprise her Jayboodie," she says as she pulls out a bag of gummy bears.

"Yay! You brought me gummy bears my favorite!" he says with excitement.

"Calm down honey. Here, Aunt Sharee is on the phone. Say hi."

"Hi Aunt Ree Ree."

"*Hey baby, did you have a good day in school today?*"

"MMM hmm," he replies stuffing a gummy bear in his mouth. "Aunt Ree Ree when can you bring Caleb and Kai to see me? I miss them and I miss you, too. Momma said she would bring me to visit but her work schedule is crazy, but she said she's getting a salon so we can spend more time together."

"*Awe, we miss you guys, too. But soon honey. We will come visit you soon. I love you.*"

"Love you too. Here mommy."

"Alright Sharee, well I will talk with you soon. I got to make a phone call to check on this building."

"Alright sis, talk with you later. Tell your mom and dad I said hello."

"I sure will. Bye now."

"How was school today?" Brittney asks Jay.

"School was fun."

"Okay, but did you learn anything?" She asks as she dials Mr. Royce's number.

"Yes ma'am."

[153]

"Do you have homework?"

"I did it in class."

"Yes Mr. Royce how are you?"

"Well, I reckon I'm doing just fine despite this heat, and these old knees of mine. I went to the doctor today and bless the Lord they didn't find anything wrong with my prostate."

"That's wonderful. Well listen my name is Brittney and the reason I'm calling is because I want to look in that building you have for rent over on Statenville Hwy."

"Honey, I just rented that out a lil while ago."

"You got to be kidding me? That was like the perfect spot. Don't tell me that; I'm gonna cry."

"Mommy don't cry."

"Mommy's not gonna cry; that's a figure of speech. What did you say Mr. Royce?"

"I said somebody just rented it about an hour ago."

"Well call them back and tell them you changed your mind or something…. I'm gonna cry," she pouts.

"What kind of business are you trying to do?"

"A salon," she answers.

"That's popular today I see, well listen, calm down; I have another one on E. Park if you're interested in taking a look at that one. I can meet you there now, if you like."

"That's fine, but I wanted that one. What's the address?"

"1210," he answers.

"Okay, 1210 E. Park Ave. I'm on my way."

[154]

When she hangs up the phone, she begins to add the numbers in the address together. Brittney tends to relate numbers as another way of God communicating to us. "1+2+1+0= 4. I know this isn't my spot, but I'll check it out anyway."

She pulls up and notices he hasn't made it there yet. She gets out the car. "Be right back Jay, I'm just gonna look in the window."

"Oh my God!"

Mr. Royce pulls up and gets out the car; she turns around and extends her hand. "How you doing? I'm Brittney."

"Royce; nice to meet you."

"Nice to meet you as well."

"Mr. Royce, I don't mean to insult you, but this place is horrible."

"I know but it has potential; come on let's take a look inside," he says as he opens the door.

"Get the keys, Jay, and come on," she yells to him.

"What is this, your storage room?" She frowns.

"Pretty much." He laughs. "I can have all this stuff cleared out of here. It's not a problem."

"It's small and congested."

"See over here you can put a sink."

"For who? Tattoo from Fantasy Island?"

"And over here…"

"Mr. Royce…" she interrupts.

"Please, call me Royce."

"Royce, I almost feel insulted but I understand you don't know me, so let me just tell you. I am a professional woman looking for a professional building," she stresses.

"I done did the kitchen beautician thing and I'm looking for something more spacious, elegant, upscale… get my drift?" she says as she walks back to the door.

"I understand. I have something you definitely might be interested in. Its' not as good as the one on Statenville, but you will like it. Follow me." He locks the door behind them and she starts walking to her car.

"How far is it? I'll follow you; come on Jay get in."

"Not far at all." He walks next door and unlocks the door. She turns around.

"Oh you really meant not far at all. I thought you were talking about another area or something."

As he opens the door, she peeps in.

"Oh my! This is what yo ass shoulda showed me the first time." She looks around in awe.

"You right; it's not like Statenville, but it will do." She walks around imagining where she will put all the equipment.

"Royce I'm upset with you--that you would show me some crap like that next door! Don't you ever show nobody that no more," she laughs, "but you redeemed yourself though. What kind of business was here last?" She asks.

"Transportation," he answers.

"And how long have they been gone?"

"About a month."

"Royce, don't lie to me; that flyer on the door with your contact info is almost faded and crispy which tell me this place been empty for a while."

He looks at her and smiles.

"Me and you ain't building a good relationship starting off," Brittney says. "I think we should start over. Hi, I'm Brittney Johnson and I'm interested in renting your place; let's talk numbers."

"It rents for eight hundred a month," he responds.

"Given that's it's been empty a while, I'll give you five hundred."

"Five hundred?" He answers with unbelief. "Seven seventy- five."

"Five twenty-five and that's my final offer. I'm not going back and forth with you. It will be better for you to make some money than no money at all. You have my number; think about it. Meanwhile I have other places to see." She walks out the door, "Come on Jay!"

"Mommy is your salon going to be right here?"

"I don't know sweetheart," she answers looking for her cell phone in her purse.

"Mommy, where's my daddy?"

She pauses then puts her phone down. "Sweetie what made you ask me a question like that?"

"Well some of the kids be talking about their daddy at school. Brenajah say her daddy is really strong; he is a fire fighter and sometimes she gets to ride on the fire truck. Corey say his daddy is a bum."

"A bum?" she asks.

"Yeah. He said at night time when his mommy and daddy go to bed, he hear his mommy saying, 'you're the bomb.' And Destiny says she doesn't like her daddy very much because he's mean; he touched her in a bad place and now he's in jail. Then they ask me about my daddy and I said I don't know where my daddy is but Mr. Tim has been my daddy since I was three and he plays the PlayStation with me, take me shopping, take me to school and he calls me his lil' man…Mommy I like Mr. Tim. Will you two get married someday?"

"I think we will sweetheart."

"Do you think I'll see my daddy one day? I remember him just a little bit."

"You will see your daddy one day sweetheart."

"Soon?"

"Well I don't know."

"Do you know where he is?"

"I don't, honey."

"Well do you think we can look for him?"

"Jay…. Honey, you are asking a lot of questions; I will see what I can do," Brittney says irritated.

"Yes, Ma'am."

"I love you."

"Love you, too, mommy."

Kim

Kim and Mike are sitting in the living room watching television and finishing up their pizza.

"I really don't feel like going back to work today," Kim states.

"Full huh?" Mike asks.

"Yes and sleepy." She yawns as she crawls off the floor onto the couch and lays her head in Mike's lap.

"Kim, I really appreciate you letting me crash here until I decide what I want to do."

"I wouldn't have it any other way," she answers.

"I've been thinking and I think I'm going to move back home."

"Home? You mean here?" she asks with excitement.

"Yes sweetheart, here in Valdosta." He smiles as he strokes her hair.

"I've been thinking a lot lately about finding my son…I haven't been a good father, Kim; and I know my son needs me right about now."

"When was the last time you talked with his mom?"

"Awe man it's been about five years maybe." I went to her home town looking for her, but she moved."

"What about her parents?"

"They moved, too."

"Any friends? Or best friend?" Kim asks.

"Yea, she has a best friend, but she moved as well."

"Well look, I will be more than happy to help you. I'll just need some names--first and last and I'll see if I can pull some type of records up on the names you give me at work."

"Dang, baby you'll do that for me?"

"Ain't too much I wouldn't do for you. Come on now, you know we go waaay back."

He kisses her on the forehead, "Here hold up a minute; let me reposition myself." He stretches out on the couch and she lies with her back in his chest.

"So me and Monet was talking about having a barbecue and inviting some friends over. And we also want you to meet our friend Brittney. What you think about that?"

"Sounds good. Who's doing the grillin?"

"I am," Kim answers, "unless you want to."

"I'll do it sweetheart. So when were you two talking about having it?"

"Soon, I guess. We'll set a definite date and I'll let you know."

Silence fills the room and the relaxation of their bodies cause them to doze off. Forty- five minutes later, Mike is awakened by a knock at the door. Not wanting to move out of his comfort zone, he ignores it. The knock continues...

"Kim." He taps her to wake her.

"Hmm," she answers lightly.

"Kim, somebody's at the door." He taps her again.

"Mmm" dreading to get up, "Go away!" she yells.

"Kim, it's me. Dino!"

"Dino, I'm sleep; come back later."

"Kim, please open the door." Hesitantly, she gets up to open the door.

"WHAT!" She opens the door irritated. Dino's silence causes her to look him in his eyes and she knows something is wrong. "Dino what's wrong? Come in."

"Kim…" He breaks down and cries. "I'm done."

"Done with what honey; what's going on?"

"I can't live like this anymore." He looks up and notices Mike.

"I'm sorry, I didn't know you had company; I'll come back."

"No, it's okay," Mike says. "I'll go in the room."

"Mike, this is Dino, our neighbor; Dino this is Mike."

"Nice to meet you," Mike says as Dino nods his head. Mike proceeds to the room.

"Come on over here and have a seat. Here wipe your face." She picks up a napkin off the table.

"Now talk to me. What's going on?"

"You remember when we had that talk in the community room and I told you about this dream I had? It was about me stepping on this stick and it snapped, the lights came on and I was at the end of the forest?"

"Yeah."

"I done stepped on that stick," he says wiping his nose.

"What the hell?"

"I had a dream last night me and Mr. Gabriel was having lunch together and in this dream a lady and child came to our table and Gabriel said, *'Thank you for joining us Mrs. Thomas.'* I looked at him and said, *"She ain't no kin to me."*

[161]

"Yes she is, look at her." And when I looked into her eyes as she sat across from me, I got the feeling that this woman was My Wife.

"Hi, honey. Sorry we're late. I had to pick Kayla up from the sitter. Who were you talking to?" she asked.

"Mr Gabriel," I said.

"Oh I'm sorry, I didn't realize you were on the phone. Is that a new client?" she asked.

I'm sitting to the table confused... *"She can't hear nor see me,"* Mr. Gabriel said.

"Is she...."

"Your wife? Yes she is," Gabriel said smiling.

"And whose baby?" I asked.

"That's your little girl," he said.

"Darius are you okay? Why are you looking like that? Are you still on the phone?"

"Yes," I answered and pointed to my blue tooth. Then I told her to excuse me. I had to use the men's room and I grabbed Gabriel's hand and pulled him with me. When we got to the bathroom, I asked him how this could be. I'm gay.

"Yes she's gonna make you very happy." Mr. Gabriel smiled.

"Not gay as in happy." Dino responded,

"Who told you, you were gay?" I looked in his eyes and they were very intense. *"Who told you, you were gay, Darius? You are not what they say you are. That is a lie straight from Satan himself. Look out there and tell me who do you see?"* He opened the bathroom door and

I said, "I see a lady, you say is my wife and a little girl you, say is my daughter."

"*Look again,*" he said.

And when I looked the second time, his arm rested upon my back and it was like scales fell off my eyes. I looked at this woman and I knew she was my wife and that I was in love with her and my daughter Kayla. And he asked, *"What do you see Darius?"* and I said… *"My family; that's my wife and my kid."* And then he said, *"Tonight you have been loosed."* And I turned around and he was gone.

"Oh My God. That was deep," Kim says. "So how did you feel when you woke up?"

"Check this out," he says as he stands up. "The thought of it is about to make me throw up again. But I woke up and looked over next to me and saw Derrick and I gagged. I jumped up out of the bed and ran in the bathroom, threw up and left. I ain't been back since."

"Since when?"

"Since about eight o'clock this morning, and I ain't going back. I don't want Shit out that apartment."

"What about your clothes?"

"NU-THING. He can have all that gay shit!"

Kim starts laughing. "You ain't been delivered twenty-four hours and you already gay bashing?!"

"I know, I know, I know… and I didn't mean for it to come out like that. You just don't know how I feel right about now; Satan had me blind all these years," he says with intensity pounding his fist into his hand with each word.

[163]

"And you sitting over there laughing but I ain't trying to be funny right now. I don't want to go back in that apartment, man."

"Wow!" Kim continues to laugh.

"I'm almost at a loss for words. I mean… I can literally see the change in you. Look at you. You *look* different; you look happy; you look free; hell, you look like a Man."

Kim laughs, "Not to mention your face looks brighter. Your talk is even different. You sound like a MAN!" Kim continues to laugh.

He sits back down on the couch and cups his hand over his mouth and nose. Meditating on how good God has been to him, tears begin to come to his eyes. "I can't change who I was. I've walked that life style proudly, with no shame. Oh my God, I'm about to throw up….But I thank God….." He wipes his tears and silence fills the room for a few minutes as he gathers himself together while Kim watches.

"Alright Dino, you got to stop all that crying, shit now. I mean shoot," she states as she begins to wipe the tears from her eyes.

"Man I am so blessed and thankful…" He takes a deep sigh.

"I'm 'bout to get myself together, and get ready for this wife. I'm telling you Kim…Man it felt so good being in love with a woman again. And she is Gorgeous! And my daughter…..My God…Thank you Jesus. She is so beautiful, long black hair like her mom, pecan tan skin…"

Kim smiles. "I am so happy for you. I really am."

"Me, too; congratulations man!" Mike applauds as he walks in the room and extends his arm out to him and hugs him.

"You see I'm a man, and I know who I am. A lot of men... if they would have heard your testimony they would have shunned you away-'*that nigga gay man, once gay, you always gay!*' But I beg to differ. I listened to your testimony when I was in the room; I wasn't trying to eaves drop but you guys were talking loud enough; but I listened to your testimony and I'm standing here looking you in your face; I don't know you my brother but I know 'Him,'" pointing up towards heaven.

"I know there ain't nothing too hard for Him; I know that He is a mind blower; I know that He can make the impossible possible and I know he can do exceedingly above all we can ask or think," he says with passion.

"Now I never experienced that lifestyle nor had the desire to but I have gotten to know God over the years after my divorce and I have seen him do the extra ordinary, not only in my life but other people that I have encountered. So I want to encourage you to stay strong and the best is yet to come."

"Thanks man….that….that," shaking his head trying to find the right word. "That… I needed that," Dino says.

"Like I was telling Kim, I'm 'bout to get my life together; I'm finna stop cussing, get my credit right, go stay with my mom for a little bit, get me a job at a salon and build my clientele up."

"You have your license?" Kim asks.

"I had my license for six years now."

[165]

"You should have been working in a shop, as good as you are."

"I know but I was trying to be a house…" He starts to gag.

"Yall excuse me; its gonna take some time."

"Gone let it out; but not in here in the bathroom. It's all part of your deliverance. We understand," Kim says.

"Now what were you trying to say?" she asks him again. "House what?"

Dino looks at her and the thought makes him gag again.

"Are you trying to say wife?" Kim asks.

Dino gags some more and Kim points to the bathroom.

"Gone 'cause you been trying to get that out of you since you been here and if it hits my floor, we gone have some problems."

As Kim is talking, Dino is making his way to the bathroom. Kim laughs hysterically.

When Dino comes out the bathroom, Mike asks, "What kind of work you do?"

"I'm a hairstylist and makeup artist."

"Interesting," Mike replies.

"And he is BAD!" Kim vouches.

"Okay, that's what's up?" Mike says.

"Well hey listen, I'm gonna let you two get back to doing whatever you were doing before I interrupted."

"We were sleep Dino," Kim replies.

"I wasn't implying anything."

"Yes you were--heard it in your voice."

"If God did it for me, he gone work on you next," he whispers to her.

[166]

"Dino, this is Mike….My ex."

"Donavan?"

Kim nods her head "yes."

"Lil Don?"

She stretches her eyes and bunches her lips together as she nods her head, "yeah."

"You gonna have to fill me in later. I thought this was just some random guy," he whispers. "Good to finally put a face with the name. I've heard so much about you."

Mike smiles and nods his head.

"God still gone work on you," he whispers again.

"But hey thank yall very much for listening.

Mike, thank you for the words of encouragement.

I'ma get out of here while somebody is still at work, so I don't run into them. Take care."

"That's a cool dude; he gone be alright," Mike states. "So what you want to do now?"

"Lay back down for a few more minutes."

"Alright let's go lay cross the bed," Mike suggests.

"So what are you two talking about up here?" Monet asks Zi and Lisa.

"Felicia was just telling me about her boy crush."

"Boy crush?" Monet asks.

"Yeah some guy she been stalking for 'bout the last two months."

"I have not."

"Boss lady, she goes over to Starbucks to get coffee just to see this dude."

"I do not…. I go over there because I like the coffee, and he just so happen to be there."

Monet looks at her…

"Whaat! Why are you looking at me like that?" Lisa asks.

"You told me you like their coffee, but you also go over there to see this dude; so who is he?"

"Boss lady, He is so fine! He's about five-eleven in height, caramel complexion, shoulder-length locs. He just got this swag about him. He's like this hard thug but yet this funny, comical gentleman."

They both notice how she talks about him with so much passion.

"And guess what?"

"What?" Monet asks.

"He came in here today!"

"Nooo," Monet says as she looks at Zibra.

LaZibra shrugs her shoulders. "She told me the same thing."

"You didn't see him?" Monet asks.

"I was in the back sleep, I…I meant um stocking."

"So he came to see you?" Monet asks.

"Nooo! He came… Well let me back up a little. I ran into him earlier today at Starbucks, literally ran into him. He said a few choice words and that was basically it until he walked in here. He walked in and saw me and turned around. But I stopped him and apologized for earlier and we were cool after that."

"So what did he come in here for?" Monet asks.

"He wanted to know who owned that building on the side over there."

"Really? My girlfriend was thinking about getting that building. What you told him?"

"I told him to look in the phone book for Mr. Royce."

"I better call her and tell her somebody is inquiring about that building so she can go ahead and get it. I'll be back. Aaaahhhh!!" Monet hollers with pain.

"Are you okay, Boss lady? Zibra asks with concern.

"Yeah, I'm okay…This sharp pain just went through my leg; I'll be back."

She limps to her office, sits down and rubs her leg. "Hello," she moans.

"*You okay?*" Brittney asks on the other end.

"Yeah…. I'm okay, my leg is hurting a little. But listen, the reason I called is; Felicia says there was a guy that came in today asking about the building. Did you get a chance to call?"

"*Girl, I did and he had already leased it out an hour before I called. Then he had me to look at some more property he had; one was just plain insulting, the other one will do; and the one that will do, he wants eight hundred dollars for rent for that; I told him I'll give him five twenty-five and left it at that. If he decides to take that he'll call me."*

"What made you say five twenty-five? That's a big jump from eight hundred."

"Cause the place been empty for a long, long time. I wonder what that dude got the building for," Brit asks.

"I have no idea. Well, let me know how everything turns out. Ahhh!" She moans as she hangs up.

Brittney calls right back.

"Hello?" Moni answers.

"Do you have any Tylenol? You don't sound too good."

"I'm going home to take something and lay down for a little bit."

"You make sure you call me if you need me."

"I will....... Bye."

"Okay, Bye."

"Hey Zi, I'm gonna go home for a bit."

"You sure everything is okay with you, Boss lady?"

"All is well."

Before Monet could make it to the door she stops and leans on one of the chairs.

"Unn unn bosslady, I don't think you can drive. Lisa!" She yells.

"I'm OH KAY," Monet reiterates.

"Yeah what's up?" Lisa comes running from the back.

[170]

"Can you give Boss lady a ride home?"

"I told you I'm fine!" She responds anxiously and walks out the door. As soon as she cranks up the car and put it in reverse an excruciating pain shoots up her leg so fast she hollers.

"Felicia runs to the driver's side. "MOVE!"

"Okay, okay," Monet responds frustrated.

"Do you need me to take you to your doctor or the hospital?"

"NO! I need you to take me home."

"Boss lady, I really think…."

"Shhhh! Felicia please! I don't want to hear that now; just take me home. And I probably won't come back tonight so will you guys lock up for me and can you two bring my car when you close up?"

"Not a problem."

They pull up to Monet's house. "Pull in the garage. Alright call me when yall lock up," she says as she tries to get out the car.

"Let me help you." Felicia puts the car in park and opens the door.

"I got it!" Monet yells, "Ooooo God!" she yells again.

Felicia sits back down in the car and just looks at her.

"Oh God! Oh God! Oh God!" She starts to cry. "Why are you just staring at me?"

"Well you told me you had it?" she says sarcastically.

"Well don't listen to me; this crap hurt."

"See here," Felicia states as she gets out the car. "You starting to sound a little bipolar; luckily I know it's the pain talking. Now come on."

She helps her out the car and into the house. "You sure you don't want to go to a doctor?"

"If you ask me that one more time…"

"Okay." Felicia throws both her hands up.

"I'm done and I'm outta here. If you need anything call an ambulance."

"I'mma call YO ass, Smarty. Oh Lord forgive me; see what you made me do?!"

Felicia laughs as she walks out the door.

Monet takes a muscle relaxer and falls to sleep soon after Felicia leaves. At the end of the business day, the girls bring Monet her car and check on her.

"I'm feeling a lot better," she assures them.

As the days and weeks begin to pass, her health begins to take a turn. The pain in her leg becomes so severe she frequently misses work and the doctor soon has her walking with a cane.

"Lord, I am so sorry for anything I have ever done wrong in my life. Please forgive me for my sins, or if I have wronged anybody in any way."

No sooner as she finishes her prayer her doorbell rings.

"Pastor Downs, what a surprise! How are you?"

"I'm good…How you been? I miss you at church."

"I know, I know. I been in a little funk over the weeks but I'm coming tonight."

"Okay good. I'm glad to hear that….. Monet let me say something to you."

[172]

"What's up, Pastor?"

"I've been noticing something is troubling you. I can see it all on your face. You out praise everybody in there; you're constantly at the altar, and now, you come to the door with this limp. Monet what's going on with you? And I'm only asking because I'm your Pastor and I'm concerned."

Monet looks at him clinches her teeth, and puckers her lips to keep from crying. Then she slowly moves her eyes towards the floor.

"Monet, I don't want to pressure you but if we could just pray that will be fine."

"I...I ummm," she swallows, "don't know what's wrong with my leg, Pastor."

He looks at her with a confused look on his face.

"I was diagnosed with MS some time ago; I just been believing that God will heal me."

"And He can sweetie; we already know that the word of God declares by his stripes we are healed, that's the truth... right?" She nods her head in agreement.

"And we can agree the fact is you have been diagnosed with MS."

"Yes sir."

"Well, when the Good Doctor meets the natural doctor, there is no comparison. In other words when Truth meets fact...truth wins all the time."

"I like that," she comments.

"And I like that smile on your face," Pastor compliments her.

"Listen Monet, I ain't gone hold you, but hopefully I'll see you tonight."

"Yes, sir."

"I'll let myself out," Pastor says as he gets up and leaves.

"Truth outweighs the fact… I like that," Monet quotes to herself as she gets up and goes to the restroom. Just as she is about to wash her hands, the doorbell rings.

"Who is it?" she shouts as she limps to the door. She looks through the peep hole and takes a deep sigh before she opens the door.

"What do you want Mitchell?"

"I called and texted you a couple times Monet and you didn't answer my call."

"Oh yeah, Well I called you and texted you more than a few times and I got no answer from you. You know; I'm sick and tired of this crap. You only call me when it's convenient for you or when you want to hunch…"

"That's not true; I can't believe you said that… Look can I come in... I need to talk to you."

She opens the door and limps away… "Baby what happened?"

"Don't baby me Mitchell. If you would have answered your phone, you would have known what's been going on."

"Baby, I'm sorry. I've been so busy…. Listen, sit down I got to talk to you. I know I haven't been the easiest person to deal with; you have been here for me this whole time and you brought me out of my depression. And for that I appreciate everything you have done for me. Nobody, I mean nobody, has ever done for me what you done for me. And nobody has ever made me cry," he says with a smile.

"You remember those two cards you gave me and the words just fit so? How did you or where did you find those cards? The bubble bath with the rose petals, and the tea light candles spread through-out the bedroom and bathroom along with more rose petals covering the floor and the bed…all that meant so much to me and I will never ever forget that. And I got to tell you even though my wife cheated on me, I still love her and I want my marriage to work. I mean, hell, we got a little boy…."

"I understand." She cuts him off.

"Let me ask you this, Mitchell. Even though you said you cheated first because she pushed you away, she forgave you. Then she cheated; yall agreed to counseling. So why is it so hard to push pass what she did?"

"Because she gave him her heart and she continued to lie about it. She was still seeing him when we went through counseling. Then when I told her I had enough I was through, she started to cry and plea, *Don't leave me, I'm sorry…I promise I won't see him again.* I mean that's why I told her I wanted a divorce before she got on that plane for Afghanistan. I just wanted to be done with her when she came back."

"YOU DID WHAT? What were you thinking? Mitchell that was not a good time to tell somebody some news like, especially when they're going over in another country to defend our country."

[175]

He takes a deep sigh… "I know that was wrong. And she's been calling me and Skyping everyday nonstop. She promises to be a better wife."

"I'm confused… you love your wife, you want the marriage to work, now you're talking about divorce…what's going on?"

There was a moment of silence as they both stared in each other eyes.

"If it's not too much to ask, can you come over tonight? I want to finish this conversation and I have something for you."

Monet looks at him with disbelief.

"No I'm not trying to hunch you." He smiles.

"I have church tonight."

"Come after church."

"Where is your son?" Monet asks

"His grandmother came down and picked him up….so will you come?"

Hesitantly she says, "Okay."

He smiles. "Alright sweetheart, let me go, and I'll see you tonight."

He smiles and kisses her on the forehead and lets himself out.

Monet continues to sit on the couch and hold a pillow and smile. "Once again he done day one me…. Let me get ready for church."

After church Monet goes by Mitchell's house as she agreed. She calls him on the phone. "Hey, I'm walking over."

"Come on in; the door is unlocked."

Monet always parks at a vacant lot two houses down from Mitchell's house. As she walks through the neighbor's back yard, she notices something different about Mitchell's house. When she reaches the back door, she notices the patio furniture and the swing is gone. The lawn is well manicured and new shrubs were put down lining the driveway. She opens the back door. "Hey what's going on...?"

She pauses and looks around and notices the house is completely empty.

"I have orders," he says walking up behind her.

Monet turns around... "I didn't know how to tell you." Silence fills the room as she scans the room.

"How long have you known?"

"Two weeks now.... the crazy thing is I have to the end of next month to report."

"Report where?" she asks with sadness.

"Home.... Chicago.... When the military tells you they want you to be somewhere you got to go."

"I understand that but you haven't even been here two years."

"I know baby, and if I could stay, I would."

He takes his right hand and raises her chin so that she makes eye contact with him. "And if I did stay I can almost guarantee we'll be together because I wouldn't stop seeing you."

A momentary silence fills the room once again and Monet's ears began to tune in to music playing in the background.

"Wait here one second." Mitchell goes in the next room and brings out a portable cd player that's playing the music. He gestures for her to come closer.

"I know this may be a little weird dancing in an empty house but, hey, it's memorable; let's create a moment we'll never forget."

She takes his hand and they begin to slow dance to Tony Terri, *With You.* As he is holding her near he begins to sing in ear.... ♫ *When I'm with you, I hear a sound that makes me laugh and smile and sing to you. When I'm with you, I feel so free, I love that love is going to take control of me....*♫

"I can't believe you did all this for me," Monet comments. "These candles, music...

"Why not?" he interrupts.

"Because you're always busy and it seems like the only time you would call is when..."

"Shhhh," he interrupts. "You mean so much more to me than sex, Monet. I really appreciated all the times you've given yourself to me. You've been there for me every time I needed you, no matter what it was. Physically, mentally you listened to me vent as I went through a depression and almost drank myself to death. You made me cry." He smiles "And nobody has ever done that."

"You keep saying that," Monet interrupts.

"It's the truth. When I read those cards, I was like wow! I couldn't do nothing but cry."

She gazes around the room with a sparkle in her eyes.

"I know you couldn't stand me at first but I'm glad you gave me a chance." He starts back singing... ♫ *"Uh-huh (Special touch, a warm embrace)*

A sweet and tender, your smile, whoa

[178]

Body warm my heart, so pure

Chills when I look, look in your eyes

I wonder why

People (Do stop) and stare (And stare and smile at us) and smile at us

When I'm with you, the sun shines my way

Baby, our love reflects its rays of light on everyone in the world"♫

Monet can no longer fight her tears; Mitchell pulls her closer as they continue to dance to the end of the song. He wipes her eyes. "Come on, I have more," he whispers.

As they walk towards the bedroom *I belong to you* by Rome starts to play.

"Wow….you have all the good songs. Can I get a copy of that CD?"

"Baby, you can have that CD."

As they stand in the doorway of the empty bedroom, her eyes light up from the romantic view of red rose petals sprinkled all over the beautiful tan carpet. In the center of the carpet are tea lit candles in a shape of a heart with an arrow going through it.

"Wow… this is beautiful," she says with a lump in her throat.

"Not as beautiful as you, come on." He reaches for her hand and leads her to the bathroom where the rose petals continue to flow.

"Oh my God…... Nobody has ever done anything like this for me before."

"See, that's how I felt when you created that beautiful scenery for me. I couldn't let you out do me." He smiles.

[179]

As Monet stands at the entrance of the bathroom, she finds herself staring at a garden tub filled with a bubble bath; dressed with rose petals, floating candles and tea lit candles all around. She also notices a champagne glass sitting at the back right side of the tub.

"I.....I......I don't know what to say," Monet says.

Mitchell looks at her with his lips folded in with a smile. "I tell you what...I'm going step out and let you get comfortable.

"Is that lavender I smell?" Monet asks.

"Ummm hmm; I want you to be well relaxed....And I know you don't drink so I got you some apple cider."

She smiles as he closes the door behind him. Monet is quite amazed at how romantic Mitchell is. She thinks to herself, *"every time I think I got this joker out of my system, he comes back around and sets me back. I am definitely back at day one."* She takes a deep sigh. *"Be strong Ney,"* she calls herself *"you can't let him see you break. He's about to leave and you won't see him no more; besides he's still in love with his wife."* She leans her head back on tub to relax and notices that the music is no longer at a distance but seems to be near. Mitchell brings the CD player in the bedroom adjoining the bathroom. She hears another one of her favorite songs playing--*You* by Jessie Powell. He taps on the door and pushes it open at the same time.

"You good, baby?"

"Yes," she answers as she sings to the music.

"I have something I want you to hear. It's one of my favorite songs.... Now in the video he's talking about his daughter, but I want to dedicate it to you."

[180]

"What is it?"

"*Joy*" by Blackstreet."

"Oh I love that song. Bring it in here so I can hear the words."

He fast forwards it to the next song and sits the CD player on the His and Her sink. He closes the lid of the toilet and relax his bottom, then leans forward to watch Monet relax with her eyes close.

She begins to think to herself, *this is almost too perfect. God why you playing with me? Be strong girl, be strong... If he starts singing I'm done!*

♫ *"After all the love changes...* He sings.

"I'm Done!" she thinks to herself; she lifts her eyelids and notices he is singing to her.

♫ *My heart had locked the door. Then that girl released her magic and made me love once more, oh.*♫

He smiles at her and she close her eyes and he leans back to rest his head on the wall and continues to sing:

♫ *Goodbye loneliness*
And so long to my heartache
Now that joy has taken over
And decided to stay

Her love lifts me up
Like no other love before
With every beat of my heart
I'm hold, holding on, hey

Just look what she's done for me
She's erased all the sadness away, oh
I can never repay the deed
'Cause she keeps loving me more and more

[181]

She's given me joy, joy, joy

Monet, you bring me joy.♫

She opens her eyes and looks over at him. *"Oh my God, he is dead for real,"* she thinks to herself and turns her head back before he notices she's looking at him.

He leans forward and continues to sing; she opens her eyes again: ♫*"said I love it when your loving me baby, oh girl."*♫ He looks at her and smiles.

She smiles back. As the song fades out, "I didn't know you could sing."

"I do alright," he answers. "I used to sing in a church choir coming up."

"You used to go to church?"

"Man, I grew up in church; my momma didn't play that…. Momma use to say '*as for me and my house we gone serve the Lord.*' So after I graduated, I joined the military and got buck wild. But what she instilled in us, took root. I just wanted to do my own thang. She would love you too, Moni, 'cause you go to church and you're spiritual and all. She used to tell me all the time before I got married *you need to get you a church going spiritual woman.* But then she would say *more so spiritual than church going 'cause you can be close to the truth but not necessarily committed to the truth. But when you are spiritual you are connected to God because God is a spirit and he communicates with your spirit and they that worship him must worship him…."*

"In spirit and in truth," Monet finishes for him.

[182]

"So my momma would say, *make sure your wife is spiritually connected 'cause even the devil comes to church.* Momma say they got to be connected to the Vine!"

"I like your mom." Monet smiles. "Is she still living?"

"Yes," he nods. "She would like you…. I mean don't get me wrong she likes my wife, too; we had been seeing each other for ten years and only been married two but momma say *it's just something 'bout that guh I can't put my finger on.*"

"Do you ever tell your mom what's going on in your marriage or the problems yall having now?"

"Noooo, never! I believe in keeping family out of your personal business… Say we get into it and I run tell my momma or whoever, then I may forgive my wife but the people I told won't be so quick to forgive. I'm just using that as an example but my mom isn't like that; she doesn't get in my business, but if I need advice she will be there."

"Your mom sounds like she is full of wisdom."

"Will you come visit me?" He asks changing the subject.

"Huh?" she asks.

"If I send for you, will you come visit me?"

"Yes."

"Yes?" he asks surprisingly.

She shakes her head in agreement.

"You look surprised," Monet asks.

"I am."

"No, I'm surprised you asked."

"Nay, serious talk, look at me; I don't think you quite understand what you've done for me. Your actions ministered to my soul, my spirit... you were there for me every single time I called you. The little things I can remember meant so much... I'd ask you to bring me something to eat and you would, and remember that time I asked you if you would take my tire to the welding shop to get the rim repaired because I couldn't get off work in time? Oh and this is what did it right here Monet... "That time when I felt like I was at my lowest and you came to hang out with me at the strip bar." He smiles.

"I knew how much you didn't want to go in there but I begged you and you were right there for me as a friend. My ride or die chic." He smiles again.

"It wasn't all that bad" Monet says "I was thinking *these people gone think I'm gay or something.* But it was cool, it was just like being at a sports bar lounge."

"Monet... if I wasn't married..."

"This water is getting cold." She cuts him off and stands up.

"Why you cut me off? You don't want to hear what I got to say?" He asks as he hands her a towel to dry off.

"No.... I don't want to cry anymore."

"Here, let me help you." He takes the towel and dries her back off and kisses her on her neck.

"I don't think you understand, Mitchell. This is a lot to take in all at one time... You're leaving....you're leaving me. How am I supposed to deal with that? Hmm? Tell me? How?"

[184]

Tears begin to form once again and he turns her around to embrace her.

"Listen sweetheart; I don't ever want to lose you. If it was up to me, I wouldn't go anywhere. But you know when Uncle Sam say you got to go then you got to go. I want you to always be a part of my life; you understand?"………….. "Look at me….. I love you."

She looks up at him and he squeezes her tighter.

"I don't ever want to lose you, Monet. Can you promise me we'll stay friends? He asks as he wipes her eyes.

She nods her head, yes.

"I don't know what's going to happen when I get back home to Chicago or when she comes back from TDY, but I want you in my life...Okay? You know you're my baby right?"

She looks up at him and smiles.

"Here put this on." He hands her a robe and steps in the shower.

While sitting on the sink waiting for him to finish, she notices lights flickering from the inside this huge closet that sits off from the bathroom. She hops down off the sink and walks in the closet. To her surprise, she notices more candles lit in the closet surrounding a pallet he had prepared for them.

"I know it's not much, but I'm trying to make the best out the situation," he says as he walks up behind her.

"It's cool," she remarks, "and thoughtful." She kneels down to get on the floor. "Which side do you want to get on?"

"It doesn't matter baby," he answers.

She lays down in a fetal position facing the wall and he lays behind her placing his left arm over her stomach. "You comfortable?" he asks.

"Yes," she answers.

"This is beautiful, Mitchell. I like how you got the candles going and all and the moon is shining through the skylight.....beautiful."

"You're beautiful," he replies.

They blow out the candles and soon doze off to sleep. Sometime in the night they change positions; Mitchell turns toward the door and Monet now has her arm around his stomach. After a few hours, she wakes up to a light sound. *"Did this nigga just poot?"* she thinks to herself. As she lays there in silence with her eyes open staring into the space she hears it again. *"Oh my God, he did just fart; please don't let me smell it.* She lays there frozen anticipating an atrocious smell. She takes a couple of deep breaths not smelling anything as she inhales. "W*ait a min…"* She takes a series of short breath. "*I don't smell anything… that's a good thing. I wonder what time it is.* She gets her cell phone from under her pillow and looks at the time.

"Let me get out of here."

"Mitchell, Mitchell." She shakes him a little to wake him up.

"Mitchell."

"Hmm?" he answers lightly.

"Mitchell!" she calls him again.

"Hmm?"

"Do you love me?" she asks him.

"Umm hmm," he answers.

"Are you in love with me?" she asks.

"Umm hmm," he answers.

She lays there a little while longer for him to fall back to sleep then she attempts to get up and stumbles back down.

"Ahhh," she yells in a whisper.

"Are you okay, baby?" he asks as he turns toward her.

"My leg," she answers.

"Monet, what's going on with your leg?"

"I'm not sure."

"Have you been to the doctor?"

"Nawl, not yet."

"Honey, you need to go get that checked out, seriously. I don't like to see you in pain. What were you trying to do?"

"I was about to leave."

"After you asked me if I loved you... you just gone leave me without saying good- bye?"

"You heard me?" she asks him.

"Of course I did," he answers as he grabs her and pulls her close to him.

"You said, 'yeah.'

"I know what I said," kissing her as he talks. "You asked me if I loved you and I said yeah, then you asked if I was in loved with you and I said yeah."

"Well did you hear when you passed gas?"

"No I did not," he laughs.

"Yes you did… that's what woke me up. You did it twice."

"Tell me you lying, Nay!" he says with a smile.

"I'm dead serious."

"OOOO, I'm sorry, bay! Did it stank?"

"Honestly, it didn't."

He laughs. "What time is it?"

"Like 3:20," she answers.

"Come on hang out just a little longer please and I'll help you get to your car and follow you home and make sure you get there safely."

So she lays back down, staring up at the skylight. "So you leave tomorrow, huh?"

"I do… but I'll be back from time to time. I got to see about my house."

"Are you going to rent it out?"

"I am….It's a military couple coming to move in tomorrow; that's another reason why I had to move quickly."

"Oh, I see."

Silence fills the room once again and Monet starts to doze off.

"Monet." He calls her name.

"Hmm?"

"If I set you up in a place up there, where I am, would you be willing to move to Chicago?"

The room is silent again. "I will pay for all your expenses," he adds.

"Wow! Mitchell."

"Think about it…"

"Yes," she answers before he can finish his sentence.

"You will be willing to give up your business just like that and move to Chicago?"

"I mean… I won't be giving it up; I'll just have somebody to run it for me. I always wanted to open another shop at a new location. And Chi-town just may be the place for me to do that."

"Look at you! You sound like you're ready."

"I'm excited. She turns and throws her arm around him.

"Are you surprise I said yes?"

"I must admit, I am surprised but I'm so looking forward to spending more time with you."

He kiss her on the forehead and the two of them lay there until they both go back to sleep.

Two hours later, Monet begins to lightly move in her sleep. She realizes she's having a dream of her peeing in the toilet. As she jumps up to run to the bathroom, she trips; she clinches her teeth together as the pain shoot through her leg; pee is running down her leg uncontrollably as she tries to get up. *"I can't let this man see me like this, "* she thinks to herself. Monet gets dressed and cleans up the wet spots on the bathroom floor and leaves. She doesn't hear from Mitchell that day nor the next. She figures he needed time to get settled in. After about a month, she still hasn't heard from Mitchell so she decides to send him a text. **Hey Love, thinking about you, hope all is well; give me a call when you can.** Several hours has passed and still no word from him. She decides to call; the phone rings one time before he hits the reject button. She leaves a message… *"Hey, it's me. Just trying to see if you're okay. Give me a call back. "* About an hour later she gets that dose of drug that sends her on a temporary high once again; He texts her, Hey, I'm okay. Just been busy working. I will give you a call later tonight. Relieved to know he is okay she continues on with her daily activities. She comes out of her office, "What are you ladies up to today?" she asks Zi and Felicia.

"You seem to be in a good mood," LaZibra remarks.

"Why you say that?"

"For the past month, you've come in this shop kind of down... I mean you spoke but seem like you had some stuff on your mind."

"Well, you may be right a little bit."

"Was it a man, Boss lady?" Felicia asks.

Monet didn't say anything.

"Was it that military guy?" Zi asks. "I told you he wasn't any good. He probably a drunk and married just like I said...."

As Monet is standing there listening, her vision begins get blurry and the words that are coming out of Zi's mouth seem to be at a distant; she starts seeing spots and everything around her fades to yellow.

"Boss lady...Boss lady? Are you okay?" Felicia asks as she kneels down beside her on the floor.

"Call the ambulance, Zi!"

"No! No! No!" Monet yells. "I'm okay."

"Look, ain't nobody finna go through this with you today. You can be mad with me and fire me later, but you going to the hospital today," Lisa demands.

"You gone learn today...You gone learn what a hospital is today," LaZibra quotes.

[190]

"Look Zi, ain't nobody got time for the Kevin Hart jokes," Felicia says.

"Okay okay, my bad… I couldn't resist. But she's fine."

"Did you call the emergency wagon?"

"They on the way," Zi answers.

"Look, Lisa, I will go to the hospital--just not in the ambulance."

"Boss lady, listen to me. You are going to get in that paddy wagon and me and Zi will make sure everything is okay here. When we close up tonight, we will stop by to check on you."

"But I can't ride in the ambulance!"

"Boss lady, why are you so against the meat wagon?"

"I watched them carry my grandpa off, and he never came home," Monet answers softly.

Felicia looks at her with disbelief. "Boss lady…Where's your faith? Out of all church folk, I expected more from you. "

"Well yeah everybody got flaws, whether they're hidden or not."

"God has sent his angels to take charge over you and He will not let your feet to suffer the ground or touch the ground so you won't hit a stone--you know what I mean." She says mixing up the scripture.

"I didn't think you knew any scriptures," Monet answers with a smirk.

"I know what I need to know; how 'bout that Smarty?" She smiles.

"But I know what you meant; you were trying to quote Psalms 91."

"I know you know what I meant…..Monet God got you," she whispers.

"So you gone learn today." They both smile.

"You gone learn what a hospital wagon is today!" They both laugh.

"You are silly! You done called the ambulance five different names since I been on the floor…. Help me up."

Felicia grabs one arm and Zi grabs the other arm.

"Owwweee" Monet yells.

"What's wrong?" Felicia asks.

"My leg," Monet cries out.

Just as she answers, the ambulance pulls up and two men get out the truck.

"Zi, do you see that?"

"Yeess Girl! You take the fine caramel, with a hint of mocha; you can tell he has a tan. And I'll take the Puerto Rican looking one 'cause I want my children to have good hair," LaZibra answers.

"Hi, we got a dispatch that someone at this address needs medical attention," the Puerto Rican man says.

"Me!" Lazibra says pretending to faint.

"She's only kidding. Hi my name is Felicia and you are?"

"Miguel and this is my partner--"

"William," he answers.

"Nice to meet you," she says to the both of them.

"William this is my boss lady, Monet Johnson; she fainted and she has been complaining about pain in her leg for about three months or so."

"Zi, will you go to the back and get Boss lady purse and phone?"

"Miss Johnson, I'm Will and this is my partner Miguel….how are you?" he shouts.

[192]

"I only fainted; I'm not deaf."

"Are you in any pain right now?"

"Yes my leg."

"And how long have you been experiencing leg pain?"

"About three months now, I guess."

"How severe is the pain on a scale of 1-10 with 1 being mild and 10 being unbearable?"

"Right now with me laying here I'm fine but if you try to move me it's a 10."

"Do you have any of the following or is there a history of diabetes, high blood pressure, cancer, blood clots, arthritis…?"

"MS…I was diagnosed with MS some time ago."

"Any chances you may be pregnant?"

"No!"

"Date of your last cycle?"

Monet stops to think. "I don't remember."

"Oh my God, Boss lady, you done messed around and got yourself pregnant!" Felicia remarks.

"I am not pregnant!"

"Pregnant?" LaZibra yells as she is coming from the back with the purse and cell phone. "It better not be from that military man 'cause you know he ain't no good and he—"

"Dammit, Zi. Shut up! I DON'T WANT TO HEAR THAT CRAP NO MORE!...... MY GOD!

"Sorry, Dang! You ain't got to get all hostile."

[193]

"Miss Johnson, we gonna need to check your blood pressure and your temperature," William says.

"Blood pressure and temperature are normal. Now my question to you is do you want to take a ride in the ambulance today? There is only so much we can do here but the doctors can give you pregnancy test and do an x-ray on your leg. It's totally up to you," William says.

"You mean I don't have to go?"

"Nope, it's totally up to you; we just have you to sign this waiver saying you declined a ride in the ambulance," Miguel answers.

She looks at Felicia, and then looks up at the ceiling; Felicia comes over and kneels down beside her.

"Boss lady, I know you're a strong woman, but you won't be any good to yourself or us if you don't go get yourself seen about. God got you Sweetie."

She looks at Felicia then back at the ceiling.

"Faith without works is dead, Monet," Felicia quotes.

Monet looks at Felicia and smiles. "Thank you."

"You're welcome; now handle your business."

"I'm gone learn Today!" They both laugh.

"She's ready," Felicia tells William.

"Okay, well we're going to go out and get the stretcher."

"Okay Miss Johnson, we're gonna lift you on the count of three; you may feel a little pain but we're going to be as gentle as possible," Miguel says.

After they lift her on the stretcher, Felicia walks up to Monet before they wheel her out.

[194]

"I'm proud of you, Boss lady," she says as she slips her number into William's pocket.

"So am I," LaZibra remarks.

They watch as they wheel Monet to the truck and close the door.

"Zi, do you know Kim's or Brittney number? We need to tell one of them so they can be there with her."

"I'll call Kim," Zi replies.

South Georgia Memorial Hospital

"Kim!" Brittney yells from the parking lot, just as Kim is about to enter the hospital door. Kim waits for Brittney to catch up.

"Thanks for calling me. So what's this about Monet being pregnant?"

"Girl, I didn't know the heifer was sleeping with anybody."

"Me either. Well she did tell me about the military guy, Mitchell, one time."

"Mitchell?" Kim asks with disbelief. "I thought she couldn't stand him?"

"May I help you?" the nurse asks at the window.

"Yes, we're looking for our friend Monet Johnson," Brittney asks.

"Monet Johnson? Monet Johnson? Ahhh, there she is--room 241A," the nurse answers.

"May we go back?" Brittney asks.

"Yes, go right to these double doors and I'll buzz you in."

"Okay, thanks."

"Nurse, can I ask you a question?" Kim asks.

"Yes," the nurse answers politely.

"What is the reason for her coming in?"

"I'm sorry; I'm not allowed to discuss that. But Miss Johnson is up and alert if you want to go back" she answers politely.

"I understand," Kim replies. They turn and walk through the double doors.

"Knock, knock," Brittney says as she knocks and opens the door at the same time.

"Heeey, Nay!!" Brittney smiles.

"Heey you; come on in," she replies back with an even bigger smile.

"Kim is with me."

"Awe, Hey Lady," Monet speaks with a smile.

"How you doing, Hon?" Kim asks.

"I'm fine. Patiently waiting on the doctor to come in with my test results……Who called you guys?"

"Zi called me and I called Britt. Speaking of test results, we got the news you are pregnant…You didn't tell us you were 'round here fornicating… Who the baby daddy?"

"Kim, I'm not pregnant."

"Well that ain't what Zi said… You do know you're the new Secret Squirrel, right?"

"I ain't no secret squirrel; you the secret squirrel; have you told Keith about Lil Don or Butray?"

"Forget you Monet." Kim smiles.

"Anyways, I no longer see Tray and me and Lil Don are just roomies…… that Kut each other every now and then."

"How do yall go from best friends, to lovers, to now Kut buddies?" Monet asks.

"We both realize a lot has changed over the years between us. We talked and talked and talked, and the more I tried to hold on, the more miserable I was becoming; I found myself starting to get attitudes with him and I began to….miss Keith." She speaks hesitantly and softly with a smile.

"Ah ha! The grass wasn't so green on the other side?" Monet quotes.

"Hell nawl, It was Blue." They all laugh.

"But at least now I know. I think the main thing I needed was an apology".

"I understand. And you were blessed to get that. Just think of all the women out there that are waiting to get an apology from their exes. Most of the time an apology is all it takes to put the fire out but some men are just full of pride," Monet comments.

"And then we hurt the ones we love because of our own selfish desire? Like if you desire to be her, then be with her; why you married me, if you knew you weren't over her?" Brittney gets hostile.

"You should never get into a new relationship before you're completely over the last person."

"Calm down Britt," Monet responds.

"Looks like somebody else needs an apology to move on as well"
Monet directs her statement towards Brittney, "I agree with you; you
shouldn't start a new relationship if you're not over the last one, but
sometimes it takes a relationship to get over a relationship."

"But wouldn't that be like a rebound?" Brittney asks.

"Well…not really if you don't jump straight into another commitment
shortly after breaking up," Monet answers.

"Hold up," Kim interrupts. "Enough of the side bar here; why did Zi
tell me you were pregnant?"

"Kim, I'm not pregnant!"

"How do you know?"

"I'm not! Will you stop it already? I think I would know if I was
pregnant?"

"Well how would you know if you never been pregnant before?"

"Dammit, Kim!" Monet yells.

Brittney starts laughing. "Leave her alone, Kim."

"I just asked a question; she the one getting all defensive; that's how
pregnant people do."

"My God, you so durn, nosey! I promise you Zi is fired."

"Wait! Wait! Wait!" Brittney interrupts. "Don't go taking it out on
Zi."

"I know…she's not really fired; just a figure of speech," Monet
reiterates.

"I figure you'll tell us who you been fornicating with," Kim
comments.

"GOD! You better be glad I love you." Monet chuckles. "I swear…"

"Yeah yeah, I love you like a sister too, now talk."

"It's Mitchell," Monet answers.

"The military guy you can't stand?" Kim asks.

"Yes," she answers with a smile.

"I thought you only did him, I meant I thought you two only did it once," Brittney notes.

"How does she know about the one time and I don't?" Kim asks.

"Because you were always spending time with Lil Don and besides I didn't want you to judge me."

"Judge? Monet come on don't go there…You know I'm the last one to judge."

"And I didn't want to hear your sarcastic mouth."

"And you knew it was coming once I found out." Kim smiles. I guess you couldn't **stand** him any longer 'til you decided to **lay** him."

"Shut up, Kim! You stupid!" Monet laughs.

"And I guess you let him make a big deposit in you." Kim continues.

"Britt let me tell you; Me and Moni went to lunch one day and she had the nerve to tell me; *No disrespect, but you need to get saved for real.*" She imitates Monet in her voice. "Then she says; *you know every time you sleep with a man, he makes a deposit in you, cause Men are depositors and women are receivers.* Sounding like Juanita Bynum" They all started laughing hysterically. "I guess you received a big deposit, Secret Squirrel." Kim carries on.

After Monet calm down from laughing she continues; "Ok ok so he got orders to the base in his hometown. The night before he left, we had the most romantic evening…."

"Tell me you did not let him day-one you?" Brittney interrupts.

"Brittney, it was so special; I came in and the house was completely empty."

"What's so special about an empty house?" Kim interrupts.

"If you'll let me finish." She stretches her eyes at Kim.

"The house was completely empty and he had the slow jams playing in the back ground. I was shocked at first because I didn't know what was going on but he walked up behind me and told me he had orders. The music was playing softly in the background; he said he wanted to create some memories, so we danced in an empty house to Tony Terry, *With You*. Yall, he started singing to me.

"Can he sing?" Brittney asks.

"The brother can SANG," Monet answers. "Yall I started crying, then he said there's more and he lead me to the master bathroom and I belong to you by Rome was playing as we were leaving the living room. Yall, check this out… there were rose petals all over the floor and bed, tea light candles everywhere; in the bathroom, floating candles were in the bubble bath more rose petals in the tub. Girl I was back at day- one by then. He told me to get in and relax, and while I was in the tub, he brought the CD player in and *You* by Jessie Powell was playing, then my song came on; Love Train and she starts to sing:

♫ *Warm night, can't sleep, too hurt, too weak, gotta call her up.*

Brittney: *dialed that number, no one answers till two o' clock.*

Kim: *Now if by chance you let me come over. Out on the street, I want to see you baby.*♫

[200]

Kim and Brittney are up dancing to the beat of their rhythm.

♫*And if by chance, you let me just hold ya. I'm down on my knees, I wanna please ya baby, I*

Brit & Moni: *I'll be your righteous lover.*♫

Kim signals for Monet to take the next verse.

Monet: *She said Sugar, Honey, Darlin, I really wanna see you, too. It's just that someone's, over, and baby, I really want be with you.* ♫

Monet points back at Kim.

Kim: *But if by chance you let me just hold ya. I'm calling, I'm free, I wanna see you baby.*♫   Kim points to Britt.

Brit: *When in need, you said you be here. And you hold the key to my very being baby, and I....*

Kim & Monet: *I love you baby.*

All: *If you found that special lover, and love keeps you tied to another, that's the way it goes on love's train.*

Brit: *don't need no, don't need no ticket to ride.*♫

They all laughed hysterically.

"MAN THAT WAS THE JUNK!" Brittney expressed with tension.

"I know right?" Monet agrees.

"Shoot, I would have day-oned myself after that. I'm talking 'bout I would have fell in love with myself all over again," Kim states.

"Kim you stupid," Brittney says.

"I know," she replies. "So what happened after that?"

Joy by Blackstreet came on, and he came in the bathroom and sat on the toilet and sang to me. It was so special. Then we laid down on a pallet he made in his closet; he asked me to move to Chicago, and he told me that he was in love with me…

"Wait! Wait, wait, wait, wait, wait, wait, wait, Speedy Gonzales. Slow yo' ass down. Now back the hell up. You ain't finna just run pass that last sentence like you ain't said nothing," Kim says.

"What?" Monet asks.

"What? What you mean what?" Brittney asks.

"You just said he asked you to move to Chicago!" I hope you told his ass No!"

"Well, I don't know Brit; she gonna need her baby daddy to help her with the baby."

"Kim, I am not.……forget it."

"Hi Monet, I'm Dr. Price and I have your test results; If you all will excuse us."

"No it's okay Doc; they're my sisters."

"Okay. Do you want the good news or the bad first?"

"Give us the good," Kim answers.

"Kim, shut up. Give me the bad Dr. Price," Monet answers.

"The bad news is we can't find anything wrong with your leg on our end; however, we have set you up an appointment with Dr. Neal, a neurologist over on Cranford Avenue. They will be able to do a more extensive research."

Monet shakes her head okay.

[202]

"And the good news is?" she asks with anticipation.

"The good news is you're going to be a mother!"

"I told Yo Ass!" Kim says laughing.

"You're gonna be a Mommy!" Brittney repeats with excitement.

Tim

"Hey baby," she speaks as she walks in the door.

"Hey you!" he stops painting and meets her halfway to give her a kiss.

"How you doing?" she asks.

"I'm fine baby. Just trying to get this room painted."

"I didn't know you were here. I was about to go home and seen your car down here. I miss you."

"Oh yeah, I miss your bighead, too." He smiles.

"So how long are you going to be down here?" she asks.

"I'm not sure I want to finish painting this room."

"You want some help?" she asks.

"Do you want to help?"

"Sure, I don't have anything else to do."

"There's a jumpsuit in that room there." He points in the direction of the room.

As she walks away, *Mr. Wrong,* by Mary J Blige, comes on the radio. She takes her shirt off and Tim notices her in the mirror. He stares as she begins to unzip her pants. As she bends over to take her right leg out of her jeans, he puts his paint brush down. And before she can get the left leg out, he grabs her from behind.

"Augh, you scared me hon." She smiles.

"Damn, baby you sexy as hell," he says as he removes her panties from behind. The chorus of the song begins to play in the background.

"I missed you," he says as he unzips his pants.

"It's only been a week," she responds.

"A week? You sure?" he asks with a smile as he thrusts himself in her.

She lets out a moan… "You really do miss me," she states with a smile.

"You know I do," he answers.

"Damn Felicia, this shit is good."

Hearing those words turned her on even the more. "Asombro mierda papi….. Damn baby, you 'bout to make me--!'"

Before she can finish her sentence they both reach their climaxes.

"I love it when you speak Spanish to me; Hold on baby, let me get something to wipe this up." After examining the room, he finds a cloth and wipes her back. "Here hon."

He hands her the same cloth. Felicia goes in the bathroom to clean herself and Tim walks to his car. When he comes back in and goes to the bathroom, Felicia is coming out.

"I love what you did to the bathroom; the three different shades of purple with that silver is a perfect choice."

"Here." He hands her a morning after pill. "I might have gotten a little bit in you."

She takes the pill out of his hand and he kisses her on the lip. She pops the pill out of the pack as he hands her a water bottle.

"Thanks babe," she says as she puts the pill in her mouth and swallow.

"Open up, let me see."

"Come on, Tim. Damn! Must we go through this every time? I told you I don't want no kids."

"Yeah I see ya mouth moving, but yo ass be saying some slick shit some times."

He kisses her on the forehead. "Now come on, let's get this done." He walks back in the other room and she follows him.

"I may say some slick stuff, but I'm serious babe, I don't want any kids. I'll have to give up my time…

"You don't *do* shit." He interrupts with a smile.

"My money," she adds.

"You definitely don't *make* shit," he says laughing.

"I make enough for me, smarty" she replies and picks up the paint brush.

"I'm just kidding, hon." He continues to laugh.

"I love when you get all worked up and that Puerto Rican side comes out." He smiles and gives her a kiss on the forehead.

They lock eyes on each other. "Where do you want me to start?" she asks.

As she tries to turn away, Tim grabs her hand and she turns back towards him.

"It's funny how we went from you spilling coffee on me at the coffee shop to this," Tim says.

"Yeah then you came in the coffee shop where I work the same day," Felicia adds.

"Do you know from the very first time I saw you in Starbucks, I was attracted to you?"

"Really?"

"Yeah, you didn't see me, but I noticed you and I asked my home girl, Erica, about you and she told me you come in there quite often and you're always alone."

"Oh really?" he responds again.

"So I started going more often just to see if I could catch you there. And the day the coffee was spilled on you, I was going to say something to you but you went from zero to ten just like that." snapping her finger.

He starts laughing.

"I mean you went off on me so bad, my lil' feelings were hurt."

He continues to laugh. "I mean….see that's the thing with what I do as far as my work goes; I have to always keep my guard up and I don't like that….. You should have seen your face." Tim says laughing.

"Shoot, I didn't know what to think; you definitely didn't look like the type that would go off like that especially on a female."

"I'm not," he replies.

"I mean I know that now……And when you came in to where I worked, I figured Erica had told you where I worked and you were coming to apologize."

"Shiiit! I was trying to get the hell up out of there; I didn't want the ceiling to cave in!" he responds laughing.

"And you know you had done pissed me off talking 'bout I could come work for you 'cause one of your hoes quit."

Tim is tickled to death. "Baby, you should have seen your face."

Felicia keeps a straight face while Tim continues to laugh.

"That junk is not funny."

"Yes it is; come on hon."

Tim is laughing until tears form in his eyes. Felicia cracks a smile.

"Man if you could have seen your face and the way you went off," Tim comments.

"It was kind of cute, and your ass went to talking so fast I thought you were speaking in Spanish. Come to find out you part Puerto Rican which yo ass don't look. I believe you took Spanish or something and just telling my ass that." He laughs.

"And how does a Puerto Rican look?"

"Hell, medium tan with long wavy hair, big booty; Well you got the booty." He pats her on the butt.

She shakes her head, "Culo ignorantes!"

"I don't know what the hell you said but it better not be something slick."

She smiles. "Shouldn't we be working while we talk?" Felicia asks.

"Do you have some where to be?" he asks.

"No, not really. I mean I was going over to the hospital to see my boss lady."

"Monet is in the hospital? For what?"

"She's pregnant."

"Pregnant? Get the fuck out of here!"

"When did this happen?"

"I don't know. It hasn't been confirmed yet; I'm just speculating."

"No, when did she go in the hospital?"

"Today, she fainted at the shop and on top of that she's been having problems with her leg."

"Yeah, Britt mentioned something like that." He stares out the window with a blank look on his face.

"Can I ask you a question?" Felicia asks.

"Yeah what's up?" He looks at her.

"Why?"

"Why what?"

"She seems like a nice girl, the one time I met her. I mean we didn't talk or anything but I'm sure if she and Monet are tight then she got to be into church, so what's the deal with you two?"

"In a nutshell, when I met Brittney, she reminded me so much of my mom. She gives me that balance… you know. When I'm out working, collecting my money or checking on my girls that's a whole nother lifestyle and Britt would be my safety net to come home to; she lets me be me and she has never tried to change me."

"You said *would* as in past tense. Is there a problem?" Felicia asks.

"I mean she cool people; that's my girl and I love her. But I think we are growing apart."

"Is it you or her?"

"I mean, it could very well be me. I'm always grinding, but, too, she has some unresolved issues with her ex-husband. She never talks about it, but every now and then her actions show it."

"You think she still love him?"

"Nawl, I think it's more so him not being in their son's life."

"So let me ask you this," Tim says.

"What made you start coming down here to talk to me, after I was being an ass?"

"Honestly, your rudeness kind of turned me on." She smiles. "…and after I kept seeing your car pass by the coffee shop, I wanted to come down and see what kind of business you had going on."

"You know you tried to seduce me the second time you came!"

"I did not!" she declares.

"Yes you did! You came in here with them tight skinny jeans on, ass all in my face--teasing me and shit. They both laugh.

"And the third time you came, you took advantage of me. You wore that nice fitted, not too tight dress with the animal print."

"I took advantage of you? No! You took advantage of me!" she retorts.

"You wanted me too with yo fast behind!" He starts laughing. His laugh turns into a smile as their eyes fix on one another.

"I love you," he says in a soft tone. Felicia, is astonished and doesn't know what to say.

"I know it sounds crazy and I know it may be too soon to be saying those words, but I know what I feel and you give me that warm fuzzy feeling I've been longing for, for some time now."

"No it's not crazy 'cause I feel the same way."

"Now, don't think you have to say it just because I said it," Tim says.

"I'm not, potato head," she replies with a smile as she picks up the paint brush and puts paint on his nose.

"Where do you want me to start?"

"Let's start over here," he answers.

After a few hours it is now four a.m. and the two of them are laughing and having fun not noticing the time.

"Thank God, we are finish with this room," Felicia states.

"I know, right. I appreciate you helping me….Here." He pulls out some money.

"You don't have to pay me."

"You should at least get paid for your time. Always remember, time is valuable and you should never let anyone waste your time nor should you waste anybody time….Now take it." He hands her two crisp bills.

"Two hundred dollars? You need some help tomorrow?" she asks sarcastically. "Thank you."

"No thank you, Hon."

"Now come on let's get out of here; I need to get some rest," Tim says.

He locks the salon door. "Get in; I'll give you a ride up front to your car."

"Alright I'll see you later honey," she says as he pulls up to her car; he gives her a kiss.

"I love you."

"I Love you too," she says.

"All right give me a call or text me and let me know you made it home."

"Will do. Bye," she replies.

Tim goes to Brittney house to get cleaned up and shower. When he walks in the room, he gives Brittney a kiss on the cheek and turns the shower on.

"Hey babe," she mutters.

"Hey honey. I didn't want to wake you but I need to get this paint off me."

"Paint? What paint?" she asks squinting her eyes to see him.

"Yeah I was doing some painting today," he answers putting his phone on the counter near the sink before he gets into the shower.

"Since when did you get into the painting business?"

"Since I took on this project," he answers from the shower.

"What project?" she asks as she gets out the bed and stands in the bathroom doorway.

"Will had offered to paint his dad's house and I told him I would help him."

"Since when do you care about helping somebody do manual labor? You'll normally pay somebody first."

Tim's phone is on silent and Brittney notices that it is lighting up. She glances at it and saw "Licia."

Brittney doesn't get upset nor dismayed about the phone call because she knows "Licia" could very well be either a client or a worker; however, she is a little leery about Tim painting. But she thinks to herself that he has always been straight up with her and she shouldn't let the enemy play with her mind.

"Will's my homeboy; I don't mind helping him," he answers.

"The phone buzzes and it is a text message from "Licia": "Made it home" comes across the screen.

"Licia said she made it home."

"You screening my text now?" he asks as he steps out the shower.

"Come on now….don't go there…It just popped up," she replies.

"I'm kidding, hon."

Because Tim has never made a comment like that before, Brittney is now a little suspicious.

"Really Tim? You never said anything like that before. So who is Licia?"

"Licia is Will's girl," he says as he walks pass her and climbs in the bed naked.

"Will's girl? Then why is she calling and texting you letting you know she made it home? Shouldn't she be calling Will?

"Damn, he thinks to himself. *Shit! Why the fuck did you say Will's girl? Think nigga, Think."* "She works for me, but Will doesn't know it; so will you please don't say anything to him?"

"Why is your homeboy girlfriend working for you?"

"Because she needed some extra cash and she asked me if I could help her out."

"Then why didn't you just loan her the money for crying out loud; she's your homeboy girlfriend!"

"I know and you're right hon but it's only going to be for a little while, so please don't say anything."

"I ain't gone say nothing, but I think if she is having financial problems, she should have communicated that with him."

"Britt, honey, please! I am tired!" Tim cries.

Britt gets quiet long enough for Tim to fall off into a deep sleep; shortly, thereafter, she falls asleep as well. A few hours later she wakes up to get Jaylin ready for school and makes breakfast. As Jaylin sits to the table to eat his breakfast, she fixes Tim a plate and takes it to him in the room. Upon entering the room she notice him on the phone which isn't unusual because he handles a lot of business by phone but what goes unnoticeable is the tone of his voice. "Alright, let me call you back," he says.

"Good morning, hon," he says as he stretches.

"Good morning, babe," she replies back.

"So what's on your agenda today?" she asks.

"Adrian called; he and his mom are not getting along so he wants to come down here and finish his senior year."

"He's already in the second semester; that doesn't make any sense," Brittney replies.

"I know--that's what I said. But he's saying he needs to get out of her house or he won't finish school."

"You're his dad; you need to make him stay."

"I tried honey, but I haven't really been there for him like I have for the others; so now he needs me. I hear it in his voice."

"So what are his plans? And does he know graduation requirements may be different down here? He might not be able to graduate this year," Brittney inquires.

"He wants to go to college, and I'm gonna do everything I can to get him there. And if he has to graduate next year, then that's his ass, but he is going to graduate," he says sternly.

"So what's the deal with him? Why is it so unbearable now?"

"I really don't know, hon. something 'bout he feels like he's being treated like the outcast. I really don't have all the details but I have to go over here to the house and get this room ready for him."

"How soon is he talking about coming?" Brittney asks.

"His mom is putting him on the bus today."

"Do you need me to help you with anything?"

"No honey, but thanks. What are you doing today?"

"I have a couple of clients coming this morning, and then I'm going to look at a building."

"You seem a lot happier, doing what you like to do," Tim says.

"Thanks to you having my back and letting me quit my job... I love you." She whispers.

"I love you more," he responds.

"What do you mean you love me more?" Brittney replies.

"This ain't no competition…. I love you and you love me," Brittney says.

"You right," he answers. "…but I still love you more."

[214]

As he's laughing his phone chimes, and he notices another text from Felicia: **Hello,** the text reads. He ignores it and continues to converse with Britt. Not even five seconds later he receives two more text back to back: **You must be busy?**.....the second text... **Well holla at me later.**

Hold on, he texts back.

Brittney looks at him as he stares at the phone.

"My homeboy just text me letting me know my package just arrived." He lies.

"Aaah I better get up from here; I got a lot of things to do today," he continues.

"You're not going to eat?"

"Yes, I'm going to eat honey. Thanks."

Brittney pretends to head to the kitchen. Tim sits up to eat and at the same time he leans over to peep out the room door.

"Honey!" he calls trying to identify her whereabouts.

She is close enough to the room door to hear a phone conversation if he makes a phone call but out of sight from his view if he peeps out in the hallway. *Dang!* She thinks to herself as she scurries to the kitchen.

"Yes, love?" she answers from in the kitchen.

"I love you!" he yells.

"Love you more!" she answers in return.

Tim's activities are slightly abnormal to Brittney which plants a suspicious seed in her. Thinking she could be wrong, hoping she is wrong, she eases back to the corner where she can hear his conversation if he does make a personal call.

"All the years we've been together, I never had a reason not to trust him. He has always kept it one hundred with me, and he has always made me number one. The devil must be messing with my mind," she thinks to herself as she sits on the couch. *"But God did give me common sense. I don't want to confront him with just an accusation; I need proof."*

So she stood back up to listen.

"Hey honey?" he calls.

With frustration she runs back to the kitchen. "Yes!" she yells back.

"Can you bring me something to drink?"

She brings a glass of orange juice in the room.

"That was fast," he states.

"I had already fixed it and forgot to bring it," she replies.

"What are you doing in there?" he asks.

"Washing the dishes," she answers and leaves back out the room.

Internally she knows something is up; she just has no proof.

"Come here!" He calls her back.

She stands in the doorway with a fake half smile.

"Give me a kiss," he says.

She leans down to give him a kiss as he sits on the side of the bed.

"What's wrong?" he asks.

"Nothing, why you ask?"

"Britt, I know you. Something is on your mind." Just as he says this, his cell phone chimes.

The two of them look down at the phone. Within, Tim is a little nervous of not knowing who just text him and in some weird way, even though Brittney has never screened any of his calls or text before, he feels this is the day she is about to do it.

Brittney sighs and rolls her eyes and storms out the room.

"Brit come here," he calls.

In between him calling her name he looks at his text real quick; relieved to see it's his homeboy he calls for her again, "Honey come here!"

She comes to the doorway in distress.

"What's wrong? And don't tell me it's nothing," he asks.

"It's nothing. I'm just feeling some type of way."

"What type of way? Come on baby, keep it one hundred!"

"Honestly," she replies. "I'm feeling your business is a little personal."

"Why you say that?" he asks defensively.

"The phone calls, the texting… you seem slightly different today; I can't really describe it."

"You talking 'bout the fuckin' text Britt? It was my homeboy. Look!" He shows her the text:

Yo Scoop, man where you at? The text reads. "Mutha fuckin' Will, man!" he says sternly. "Why you getting all defensive?" she asks. "I'm not, but yo ass trippin!"

"I'm trippin? Last night you came in here with paint all over yo' ass. You got this weird ass look on your face every time yo' phone go off… and lately you have distanced yourself from me and I'm trippin? You must got something to hide."

"What the fuck ever man. You know what--?"

"What the fuck ever?" she interrupts him.

"I'm not your homeboy! What the fuck is wrong with you talking to me like that?"

Tim doesn't feel the need to respond; he knows he has already messed up so he gets up, puts his clothes and shoes on, grabs his keys, kisses her on the forehead and leaves.

"So you just gone leave? Is that how we doing it now?"

He is so in a hurry he forgets his phone but Brittney notices it still laying on the bed and she lets him walk out the door because she knows the evidence she needs is in that phone. As soon as he closes the door she locks it behind him. She knows she has to move fast because it's only a matter of seconds before he realizes he left it. She opens the inbox text: It feels good being in love again.

"Britt, open the door!" Tim yells knocking on the door.

She throws the phone on the bed without hesitation.

"Britt open the...."

"Did you forget something?" She asks sarcastically as she opens the door.

"My phone!" He states as he walks pass her into the bedroom.

"Should I confront him now or later?" She thinks to herself.

"Wait!" She says as she stands in front of him not knowing what to say; she found herself staring at him and fighting back the tears.

"What Britt?" he asks.

"Nothing." She shakes her head.

Tim proceeds to walk pass her and out the door. Still holding back the tears, she sits on her couch.

"Mommy are you okay?" Jaylin asks.

"Mommy's okay; go get your book bag so I can take you to school."

He walks away slowly. "Mommy are you sure you okay?" He turns around and asks.

"Mommy is fine--now go!" She motions her hand for him to scurry along. *"How did I get here?"* She thinks to herself. *"Lord, could you just show me what I need to know; I don't want to be nobody's fool."*

Jaylin returns to the living room. "Mommy, I think I want to stay home today and take care of you."

"Oh no you're not mister!" She gets up to tickle him.

"You're going to school and Mommy has a couple clients coming by this morning to get their hair done, then I'm going to look for a building so I don't have to keep doing hair at the house."

"Is Nina picking me up?"

"No, I am. Now let's go."

After she drops Jaylin off to school, she drives pass Tim's house.

"He's not here," she thinks to herself. Her cell phone rings: "Hello?"

"What are you doing today?" Kim asks.

"I have a couple of clients this morning; then I'm going to look for a building. Why? What's up?"

"I'm going over to Moni's house later to check on her; you want to come?"

"Sure, just give me a call."

[219]

Monet

Later on that evening, Brittney takes Jaylin to her parents' house and goes over to Monet's.

"Knock, knock," Brittney says.

"Come on in," Monet answers as she unlocks the screen door.

"I just came by to check on you. How are you feeling?" Brittney asks.

"I'm feeling okay. I go see the neurologist tomorrow."

"Oh good, do you need me to go with you?

"That will be nice, thank you."

"So are you feeling pregnant?"

"No. I mean I never been pregnant before, so I wouldn't know what it feels like."

"Changes in your hormones, your appetite, tired, moody, emotional, cravings…. Stop me when the description fits you."

"Nope. None of that." She smiles.

"I talked to Pastor."

"Really? What did he say?"

"He told me to let him know what the doctors say about my leg and he prayed for me."

"What about the pregnancy?"

"He basically encouraged me and told me the sin was in the sex not the pregnancy, don't be discourage, continue to come to church, don't worry 'bout what people say….blah blah blah."

Blah, blah, blah' is literally what Brittney heard; her mind is on Tim.

"Britt?" Monet calls.

"Yeah," she answers.

"You checked out! Where did you go?"

"Tim is cheating on me," she answers swiftly.

"Well, Dang! I didn't see that coming."

"Me either, I just need to catch his ass."

"Knock Knock!"

"That's Kim," Brittney says. "She told me she was coming by."

"It's open!" Monet yells.

"What yall doing?" Kim asks.

"Nothing much. Brittney was just telling me—

"…that I would go with her to the doctor tomorrow." She cuts Monet off.

Brittney looks back at Monet and Monet shrugs her shoulders.

"So are you feeling very pregnant yet?" Kim laughs. "I told yo' ass you were pregnant!"

"Whatever! I am not pregnant; that was somebody else test result," Monet replies with a laugh.

"Child boo, what you got in here to eat?" Kim asks as she walks toward the refrigerator.

"Nothing but some barbecue," Monet answers.

"Speaking of Barbecue, wasn't the two of yall supposed to be having a barbecue?" Brittney asks.

"We are!" Kim yells from the kitchen.

"You were about to tell that heifer my business," Brittney whispers.

"I didn't think you would mind," Monet whispers back.

"You know she don't like Tim; she will have a field day with that."

"I'm sorry."

"So what day you guys want to do this?" Kim asks when she comes back in the room.

"How 'bout the third weekend of next month?" Britt suggests.

"Sounds good," Monet agrees.

"Okay, so what's going to be on the menu or should we hire a caterer?" Kim asks.

"Hell nawl!" Britt replies. "We gone cook this ourselves…I'll bring the pasta salad, seven layer salad, and potato salad."

"And I'll do the meatballs, baked beans and corn," Monet adds.

"I'll get the chicken and hamburger," Kim says. "…but yall heifers gonna help me clean the chicken."

"That ain't no problem," Brittney responds.

"Okay so we all agree, next month on the sixteenth?" Kim asks looking at her calendar.

Everyone nods their head in agreement.

The next day Brittney accompanies Monet to the doctor.

"You walking fine today," Brittney comments.

"It comes and goes, but I tell you the truth, I decree and declare that under the mighty name of the most High, one that died for me! For my sin! For my sickness… the Prince of Peace! My Comforter…

"Come on now!" Brittney butts in.

"THE ALMIGHTY GOD! .... I am HEALED!"

"You betta say that! Girl, you 'bout to get something started early this morning," Brittney remarks.

When they walked in the doctor's office the waiting area was very warm and inviting. The colors on the wall were more of fall colors; burnt orange and brown. There was also a beautiful floral center piece on the circular table that sat in the middle of the floor. "This place is beautiful" Brittney says.

"Yes it is. Monet agrees, It's also relaxing, I can go to sleep in here." After thirty minutes of waiting Monet starts to become fidgety. She picks up one magazine flips through it put it down, pick up another one, she does this about eight times before Brittney says something. "Monet are you ok?"

"I'm fine, no I'm not. I'm nervous as heck."

"What are you afraid of Moni?"

"The unknown." She answers.

"Look everything is gonna be alright, I'm here for you."

"Monet Johnson?" The nurse calls.

"Can she come back with me?" Monet asks the nurse.

"Sure, yeah come on." She answers "Are you guys sisters?"

"You can say that." Monet says.

After going through a series of tests at the doctor's office, he gives her some not so good news...

"Monet, from what we gathered from the testing, it looks like the MS is attacking the nerve in your leg," Dr. Neal says.

"It's a possibility you may lose your ability to walk."

She hesitantly speaks, "When I came to you over a year ago and you diagnosed me with this MS, I didn't really take it seriously; I was trusting that God and still is trusting that He is going to heal me…. Can you refresh my memory, what exactly is this disease?"

"Yeah and is there a cure?" Brittney asks.

"Multiple sclerosis is a neurologic disease that affects women more often than men. It is most common in the 20s and 30s. It is a chronic, often disabling, disease that attacks the central nervous system which is made up of the brain, spinal cord, and optic nerves. Some symptoms may be mild, such as numbness in the limbs, or severe, such as paralysis or loss of vision. The progress, severity, and specific symptoms of MS are unpredictable and vary from one person to another."

"What causes it?" Monet asks.

"No one knows what causes it, and at this time there is no known cure for it," Dr. Neal replies.

"So you mean to tell me this can get worse? What about my baby?"

"You should be able to carry the baby to full term with close monitoring. Your doctor may want you on bed rest if your symptoms progress. Meanwhile I'm gonna suggest you use a cane. I can write you a prescription for one and you can pick it up from the pharmacy."

"No thank you, doctor. I won't be needing that," Monet replies sorrowfully and gets up from the table.

"Is there anything else?"

"Monet it will be wise if you take my advice and use the cane. If your leg gives out on you and fall, you can very well cause harm or miscarry."

"Will there be anything else?" she asks again.

"We will need to see you in a month."

"I'll be in touch," she says and walks out.

Brittney and Dr. Neal are left standing in the room.

"Listen, if you don't mind, I'll take that prescription for her. This is too much for her to take in at once."

"Believe me I understand. I love my job but most time it is not the easiest coming back telling patients a negative report."

He writes the prescription and hands it to her. "Are you a relative or friend?"

"We're close friends--almost like sisters. I'm gonna need one more."

He looks at her strange. "Trust me I know my friend."

"Well good because she's going to need plenty of support."

"Thank you Dr. Neal; we'll be in touch."

Brittney gets in the car and starts it up. "Are you okay?"

 "I'm good. It was just too much for me to take in at once."

"That's what I told Dr. Neal. I got this for you anyway." She hands her the prescription.

"You know how I feel about stuff like this." She tore up the prescription

"I know you have the faith of Abraham, but…"

"No buts! I don't want to hear it," Monet interrupts.

"When you say but, you cancel out everything just said."

"Okay, okay," Brittney says.

"Give me that other prescription you got as well."

"What other prescription?" Brittney asks.

"Come on Britt; you know me as well as I know you. I know you told that doctor to give you two prescriptions 'cause you knew I would tear the first one up. So give it to me."

"I don't know what you're talking about!"

"Brittney, come on, you know I don't like negativity in my circle, especially at a time like this. I don't want to be one of those people the minute they hear bad news their health starts deteriorating because it sets in their mind. I need to stay positive, think positive, laugh, be in good spirits and all that stuff.

"Well, hey you know I got your back," Brittney assures.

"Thanks."

"Now let's pray," Brittney says.

"Not before you give me that prescription for that cane," Monet states.

Brittney shakes her head and gives her the prescription. "Fine, who writes a prescription for a cane anyways?"

"Come on now, if you got my back I need you to have my back! I don't need you to be like one of the ten spies in the bible that brought back the bad report. You feel me? I know this situation may appear to be a giant but my God, your God, our God is bigger than some MS.

"I feel you," Britt replies.

"I need a Caleb on my team; you feel me? I'm Joshua and you Caleb." She stressed.

[226]

"I got you!" Brittney reassures her.

"Now let's pray."

Monet begins to pray, not only for her situation, but everyone in her circle--her baby, Kim, Britt, Tim and the doctors. The prayer is touching so much to the point where one of Britt's eyes begin to tear up. She clenches her teeth together and try hard not to blink because she doesn't want the people in the cars coming in the opposite direction to see her crying. Just as Monet finishes praying Brittney bursts out, "Shit! You stupid idiot!"

Monet looks at her and takes a deep breath.

"I am so sorry, Mousha…. I meant Joshua. I'm Caleb and you Joshua right?" She asks with a big smile, being sarcastic.

Monet shakes her head. "YOU THINK IT'S A GAME?" She asks sternly.

"I SAID I WAS SORRY! THAT IDIOT ALMOST HIT US!"

"But damn, Britt! We just got finish praying. You need deliverance from all that cussing," Monet replies, frustrated.

"You right. I'mma do better."

Brittney

Brittney drops Monet off by the house and calls Tim's phone. *"You have reached the voice mailbox of..."* She hangs up the phone before the recording can end and decides to ride by his house before she makes her way home. Needless to say he is not home. Several days has passed by and the relationship seems to have taken a turn; there has been little to no conversation from Tim. The very sound of Brittney's voice is now beginning to irritate him. The thing that use to comfort him has now become a nuisance and it's not because of something she's done but because he has begun to dance to another sound that appears to be more soothing than the rhythm he already knows the moves to. Every time the two of them converse, he has an attitude or he's short with her. This goes on for the next few weeks so much to the point that Brittney decides to call the girls to postpone the barbecue. She explains the situation to Monet but cannot bring herself to tell Kim. She makes up some lie about her getting things in order for the salon and going to a local hair show.

While sitting at home one day, Brittney begins thinking about one of their conversations... *"Tim, I'm not happy."*

"What do you mean you're not happy?"

"Tim you treating me like I'm some stranger, like you can't stand me, like I'm getting on your nerves, or like I'm the other woman! Am I the other woman Tim? Are you seeing somebody else? Who is she?"

"Whatever! Ain't nobody seeing nobody."

"You are acting like this over one fucking disagreement? Come on man what the fuck?" She stated.

"It ain't like that; I just been working out a lot lately and this new protein shake I'm taking makes me irritable and moody… Look I'll talk with you later." He hung up the phone.

Tears begin to race down her face as she remembered that phone call. "Lord, I know he seeing somebody else, please show me. I don't know how much more of this I can take. Four years and I ain't ever seen him act like this." She says to herself.

The weeks turn to months and still there is no change in Tim's mood. This thing has really taken a toll on Brittney, but she's a strong individual and refuses to let this break her, but like most of us when we want something really really bad, we find ourselves praying for something God don't intend for us to keep.

Brittney found herself praying for keeps: *"Lord please bring my baby back to me. Touch his mind, touch his heart, I don't know what I'm gonna do, I love him so much. Lord Please bring him back to me."*

One morning Britt awakes to her favorite televangelist on TV.

"Sometimes God will give you what you ask for just to show you, you don't need it." Just as he finishes saying this, her phone rings. She receives the phone call she had longed to hear for months.

"Listen honey, I want to apologize for being so mean to you. I love you and I know you love me. We been going strong for the last four years and this new protein shake I'm on got me acting an ass. Baby

I'm sorry; you have still treated me kind when I was mean and rude to you. Can you forgive me?"

Brittney is lost without words, she don't know how to answer, doesn't know if she should answer. But this is what she prayed for.

"Hon, are you there?"

"I'm here," she spoke softly.

"I love you honey," he says.

"Love you too," she mutters.

"Talk to you later," he says.

Just as she is about to shout *Thank you Jesus*, she is immediately arrested in her spirit; *"He had a fight with the other woman."* The Holy Spirit rings in her spirit.

Disappointment sets in once again. *"Lord I cannot believe this; you have got to show me what's really going on!"*

One evening, after picking Jaylin up from her parents' house she stops by McDonald's to get them something to eat. While placing an order at the drive thru, Tim calls her phone but she doesn't answer because she is in the midst of ordering. She drives around to pick up her food; just as she was about to call Tim back, her phone rings; It's Niecy, Tim's sister.

"Hello?" she answers.

"Hey sis," Niecy speaks.

"What's up?"

"I apologize, I've been busy, and my phone's been acting up, but I got all ten of your messages. What's going on?"

[230]

"I was wondering if you had spoken to Tim and if so if he said anything to you about us?"

"I talked with him earlier. He told me he had to go back home to take care of some business."

"Oh okay, then, I'll just go by there, thanks."

"Nooo; back home," she stresses.

"Back home? Virginia?" Brittney asks in shock.

"So he just gone leave and not say nothing?"

"Well, you ain't heard it from me. I thought you already knew."

"He's cheating on me, Niecy," she blurts out.

"What makes you say that?"

"He has changed! A few months ago we had an argument; he left out of the house and forgot his phone. I went through it and saw these texts this girl sent him; I didn't confront him but soon after that it became more obvious. It's to the point where sometimes he doesn't answer my calls; and if he does, he act like I'm getting on his nerves. I'm sick of this and I ain't gonna put up with this too much longer."

"You know my brother..."

"That's the problem, I know your brother but I don't know who this is!"

"Look... You know how to pray. Just keep praying to God and he'll come around."

"I have been praying," she says in a soft tone.

"Maybe I've been praying the wrong thing."

"Well if his butt can't appreciate you, then leave him. That's my brother and all, but wrong is wrong...... men are crazy, they think they

[231]

can just do anything they want and get away with it. Robert butt thought he could talk to me any kind of way... shoot I showed his butt, I went and gave Joe some."

"Yeah, you really showed him," Britt remarks sarcastically.

Niecy laughed. "I know, right? I wanted to do him anyway. He called me and said—"

"Niecy! Niecyl! Please not today!"

"I see you're feeling some type of way."

"I am," Britt agrees. "And I know you; you like to give every little detail from what he said... to what you said, line upon line precept upon precept and, sweetie, I cannot do this today!"

"You trying to say I talk too much?"

"I'm saying you have diarrhea at the mouth!"

"You know.... You almost hurt my feelings; but I'll take that from you 'cause you my sista in law and you feeling some type of way right now. But I need to make an appointment with you; I need my hair done. When can you do it?"

"Ummm.... maybe tomorrow or Friday, I'll have to check my schedule when I get back home."

"Alright girl, I'll talk to you later. Call me now."

"I will," Britt replies.

She calls Tim back and his phone picks up "Hello....Hello" she calls out. "Helloooo…"

She realizes his phone automatically answered on its own. She is just about to hang up when she hears a female voice in the background.

"Honey, where's the mayo?"

"It's in the fridge hon," he answers.

"Honey what movie you want to watch?" he asks.

"Nothing scary," she replies. *"...a suspense maybe."*

When Brittney pulls up in her driveway she tells Jaylin to get out and go to his room to finish eating as she continues to listen in on Tim and this female converse. Some of the words are distorted but she has heard enough to know that this is what she has been asking the Lord to show her. She pays attention to every detail and jots down little things so she wouldn't forget, even the minute he goes to the bathroom and flushes the toilet. After about forty- five minutes she had had enough.

She thinks to herself.... *"I wonder if he has an answering machine or voice mail on his home phone. I hope it's the answering machine so If I can leave him a message and she hear it. But if he has a voice mail....* she took a deep sigh. *"Fuck it!"*

She dials his home number; she hears the home phone saying, *"Call from Georgia......call from Georgia."*.... *"Call from Georgia!"*

"But It used to ring call from Brittney." She thinks to herself.

Now she is more furious. Apparently, his son, Adrian is looking at the caller ID because he says, "Dad, its Brittney."

"Brittney!" He thinks to himself. *"What the... why she calling the house phone?"*

At that instant he looks down and notices she has been on his cell phone for the last forty-eight minutes. He immediately hangs up. She calls back several times and he refuses to answer the phone; then she texts him: **What thefuckisyourproblem**

She gets no response. **So it's like that now**

Yes he replies.

Wow! You a coward ass nigga!.... You not man enough to pick up the phone and talk to me She dials his number again and he picks up and hangs up. **Oh, you trying to be funny! Well i got something for you Mr. Funny Man,** she texts. She throws the phone down on the couch, closes her eyes and takes a deep breath; she begins to rock back and forth as the tears begin to form in her eyes. She wipes them as they flow to her cheek. Trying to be strong, she puts the palm of her hands on her thighs and rocks back and forth as if she is massaging her thighs. Negative thoughts begin to replay in her mind. She recalls the time when they had plans to move up north; he purchased the house without her which was not too long ago. *"Don't you think I should go with you to look for a house since we're gonna be living together?"* Brittney asked. *"I'm getting this house for me and my kids."* He responded.

Speechless and bothered by the comment, she was now getting the hint that she is not a part of his future. She begins to think about all the times he wouldn't answer the phone or when he did answer the phone he would hang up and call back because he thought she was working with the police to set him up. As she sits on the couch rocking back and forth she is pondering the thought, 'when did the relationship take a turn?' Then she recalls the day in the restaurant when she heard, *"No man can serve two masters."*

I'm not serving him LORD, I LOVE HIM!" she blurts out with tears running down her face nonstop.

"You asked for this." That quiet still voice; some relates to as a conscience others may call it the Holy Spirit; reminds her.

"I know; but it hurts so bad…. I love him so much. What am I supposed to do?" she talks back.

She gets up and walks in the kitchen, not giving it a second thought to hear if God would speak back to her. She grabs a Styrofoam cup and pours some wine. Even though she drinks wine, she has never wanted her son to actually see her consume it, so whenever she would partake, she would pour it in a cup instead of a glass. She takes the whole bottle in her room and sits it on her dresser. She then goes to double check her front door to make sure it is locked and proceeds towards Jaylin's room. She wipes the tears from her eyes before she opens his door. "Are you done eating?"

"Yes ma'am."

"Okay, put your jammies on and get in the bed; you can bathe in the morning. Give me a kiss. I love you."

"Love you, too, mommy."

"Mommy is going to bed."

"Are you okay, Mommy?"

"Mommy is fine," she states with her lips folded in.

"But it looks like you're about to cry. What's wrong? Did Mr. Tim do something wrong?"

"Honey, I'm okay. I just have some stuff on my mind. Now get to bed."

She gives him another kiss and leaves out the room.

Unhappy about the way Tim's been treating her, she drinks the whole bottle and goes to sleep. The next morning she awakes with an arm wrapped around her. When she turns over, she realizes it is Jaylin.

"Jay...honey, wake up," she calls.

"What are you doing in mommy's bed?" She asks rubbing her forehead.

"I wanted to comfort you mommy."

"Awe, honey that was sweet of you!" She kisses him on the cheek.

"Now go shower and get ready for school."

Amazed by his thoughtfulness, she promises him they would do something special after school today. After dropping Jaylin off to school, she goes by the fish market.

"Yes ma'am, what can I do for you this morning?" The gentleman behind the counter asks.

"Do you have live crabs?"

"Yes ma'am we do."

"What about crawfish?"

"Yes."

"Squid?" she asks.

"We have one left."

"Okay, let me get those three and some fish."

"What kind of fish?"

She put her nose down to smell each individual container. "Oh god what is that?" she asks with a disgruntled look.

"That is mud fish," he answers.

"Let me get all four of them and some other stuff. I'm having a seafood broil." She smiles.

After leaving the fish market, she drives across town to Tim's place; she tries to use her key to unlock the door, but he has changed the locks. She checks the two places he would normally hide a spare key and nothing is there. She remembers she has a garage door opener in her car; she tries to use that and it doesn't work. Her hurt is now turning to anger because he has gone through great lengths to rid her from his life instead of letting her know upfront.

"He want to act like that? I got something for him," she thinks to herself.

She takes the bucket of fish out of her car so she doesn't have to ride around with the scent. She sits the bucket on his back porch and googles a locksmith on her phone and drives away. "Yes, my name is Sheila Greene and I locked myself out of my house. My address is 1442 Pin Cir.....yes, I'll hold."

As she waits on hold, she walks into the stationary store. "May I have a lease please?"

"Will that be all for you?"

"Yes," she answers.

"Sorry to cut you off Ma'am, But I have your address as 1442 Pin Circle you said?"

"Yes, that's correct." She answers the lady on the phone.

"I have somebody in the area; he can be there in ten minutes," she answers.

"Perfect."

[237]

"That will be seventy-five cents," the cashier says.

She fills the lease out giving a fake name for the landlord and a fake signature for herself; she then crumbles the paper to take away its newness. She pulls back up in the yard, gets out and waits on the locksmith. Within a few minutes of her pulling up; he pulls up and parks on the side of the road. He gets out the car and they greet one another.

"Mrs. Greene?" he asks.

"It's Miss Greene but you can call me Sheila."

"Okay, Sheila is this your house?" he asks.

Brittney looks at him stunned even though she knew it was a possibility of him asking her that, but she had to play it off

"It's standard procedure. We just have to ask that to make sure you're not breaking in your boyfriends' house or anything." He states sarcastically.

"Yes, this is my house." She lies uncomfortably.

"Do you have any proof, like mail or lease?"

"I think I have a copy of my lease in the car."

She goes to her car and pretends to go through some papers in her glove compartment; she also finds an old piece of mail that once came for her at this address which really works in her favor. He looks over the info. "Do you have your driver's license or ID?"

"It's in the house," she answers.

"Miss Greene, our company policy requires us to see ID before we unlock the door."

"Well how am I supposed to show you if I can't get in the hose to get them?" she asked smartly.

He looks at her

"Look Mr...

"Stanley" he answers

"Look Mr. Stanley, I am a mother and a professional business woman, I took my son to school this morning and locked myself out of my house because I couldn't find my keys so I used my spare car key." She holds up the single key.

Brittney has the evidence and convincing story but something in Mr. Stanley was not quite buying it, however looking in her hypnotizing eyes made him go against company policy.

"Sheila I'm gonna let you in. I hope to God this is your house and if it's not I pray I don't read about you in the paper."

"Oh you won't Stanley, I meant Mr. Stanley."

He gives her a firm look.

And she gives him an innocent but sneaky smile.

"Thank you so much." She smiles as she walks in the door.

"You have a good day," she adds.

He looks at her, raises one eyebrow and turns and walks away. She closes the door behind her and scurries along to the back door to grab the bucket of fish. She begins to perfume the entire house by saturating the hardwood floors with fish juice; not neglecting any room except Adrian's. After she wet the floors she took the mop and began to mop the floor.

"Oh my God, I'm 'bout to throw up," she says as she gags and runs to the back door to get a breath of fresh air. She continues where she left off, racing against time because she doesn't want anyone to be able to pinpoint her car being in the driveway at this time. As she mops, her thoughts are raging on about all the negative stuff he has done.

"You wanna play games with me and take me on an emotional roller coaster?? Well here's a free trip to fucking Sea World, Bitch! I brought all your cousins to visit you, Fucking Shamu, Nemo and his absent minded ass friend Dory!" She adds with anger as she mops the last little bit into the floor. She quickly departs and goes straight home.

As soon as she pulls up in her driveway, Kim pulls up behind her.

"Where have you been?" Kim asks as she jumps out the car to meet Brittney getting out of hers.

"Oh My god! What the hell is that? You need to bathe; you smell like fish! Where you been? I've been calling you all morning?"

"What do you want Kim?" Brittney asks walking past her.

"I want to go to lunch and talk. Where you been smelling like that? Are you okay? Do you need to change your pad?"

"I'll be out in a sec."

She proceeds to go in the house.

"A second? No hell you won't," Kim remarks as she grabs the screen door before it closes and goes in.

"Yo ass better soak in some lemon juice and Febreze. Where the hell you been? For the third time!"

"Fishing," she answers as she walks past Kim to go in the bathroom.

"Fishing? With who? You smell like you were the bait."

"Whatever, I'll be out in a minute."

"Yeah, gone in there and bathe your stankin' tail 'cause you have some explaining to do."

After about twenty minutes, Brittney comes in the living room fully dressed and ready to go. "So where do you want to go eat?" Brittney asks.

"Look at you; done went in there and did a Clark Kent. All cleaned up, smelling good, looking good, done washed them spirits off, come out here with a new attitude, Looking all housewife-ish. Girl you look clean!"

Brittney starts twirling. "You 'gone with the wind fabulous. Now that I gave you all your accolades, let's go eat."

"You get on my nerves," Brittney says laughing.

"So where do you want to go? Kim asks.

"Let's go to the Salad Bar."

Upon entering the salad bar, they run into Keith coming out.

"Ladies, how are you?" He asks holding the door open for them to go in.

"Keith, how are you?" Brittney asks with surprise.

"I'm blessed."

"Kim," he acknowledges. "Good to see you."

"You, too, Keith," she replies.

"You ladies take care and enjoy the rest of your day."

"…so yeah, that's why I smell like fish."

[241]

Brittney continues from where she left off in the car.

"Is this table fine?"

"Yeah, it's cool." Kim answers faintly.

"What's wrong?" Brittney asks.

"Nothing. I'm cool."

"No you're not. Did seeing Keith bother you?"

"It did something…. More like confirmation I think."

"What did it confirm?"

"What will you ladies be drinking today?"

"White or Red wine, Kim?" Brittney asks.

"White."

"Good deal. Bring us a bottle of white wine."

"What kind?" The waitress asks.

"Moscato," Brittney answers.

"Okay, be right back," the waitress states.

"I wanted to have lunch with you today to talk about Keith."

"Really now?" Brittney is surprised. "Okay I'm listening."

"I miss Keith. I miss what we had; I miss who we were together…… I mean Lil Don is cool and all and we gone always be friends but it's nothing there anymore. Sometimes the grass isn't always greener on the other side; you know?"

"I beg to differ; sometimes it is actually greener, but if you dig under that pretty green grass you'll see that it's full of shit."

Kim starts laughing.

"I'm serious," Britt continues.

"What is used to grow the pretty green grass?"

[242]

"Cow manure," Kim answers laughing.

"Shit! My point exactly; so although the grass maybe greener on the other side, under that pretty grass is something that smells really horrible. Everything that looks good doesn't always smell good."

Kim is killing herself laughing.

"See I'm glad I called you 'cause even though I don't like your ass sometime, I knew you would make me laugh."

"I'm serious, you got to get to the core; you got to get inside a person to see what's really going on," she preaches.

"The outside package may be looking all fine and good but if the inside is messed up, My God…."

"So I need to take that to the altar?" Kim interrupts laughing.

"Hell Nawl! God don't want that stankin' shit. He wants a nice sweet aroma. You gone mess around, and that same shit that's on him gone hop on you; trust me I know

Kim is laughing hysterically especially at the seriousness and the different expressions on Brittney's face.

"I'm telling you what I know, not something I heard. I wish somebody would have told me this shit I'm telling you; this some good stuff." She continues to preach.

"Look at me and my situation. I got pregnant in college, my baby daddy felt obligated to marry me, he really didn't give a damn 'bout me 'cause he was still in love with his ex. You know the story; I told you right?"

"Go ahead; I'm listening."

"Oh okay, I don't want to sound like Niecy, repeating myself. But yeah, Dude became abusive because he really didn't want to be with me. It had nothing to do with me as a person but with everything going on inside him; prime example of the outside looking good but inside tore up; but anyway we divorced; he went his way, I got a job here and I met Tim which brings me to my second example of the outside not matching the inside. Tim was the sweetest person in the world, not only to me but to Jaylin as well. I knew he was hard core. I knew he sold drugs, I knew he was a part time pimp but I overlooked all that. Now look at me; hard core, cuss like a sailor, done turned the man house into Joe's Crab Shack. There's a battle going on in me lady, and it ain't cool, but the good thing is, I'm not too far out there where I don't see what's going on in me. Thank God for Jesus! I'm sorry girl, I had got caught up in me, but my point to all that is I chose to be with Tim, the things that were in him, have now attached itself to me. And when you're in this place, it's so easy to do wrong because your flesh wants to do wrong. It's like Paul say *I really don't understand myself; I want to do what is right, but I don't; instead, I do what I hate.* But all that is about to change."

"And how is that?"

"Well it starts with a better me. I will just take one day at a time. As for you, your situation reminds me of my ex. It's not that you thought the grass was greener on the other side, you needed closure. See Kim...."

Brittney realizes that she is monopolizing the conversation. "I'm sorry I'm talking too much; you wanted to talk about Keith."

[244]

"No! Go ahead; preach."

See Kim, we can never understand the mind of God because His ways are not our ways and His thoughts are not our thoughts. And it's impossible for our finite minds to understand someone who is infinite. You never went back to Lil Don because in reality you never moved forward. You been stuck in that same place for so many years. It's like that man that sat by the pool of Bethesda for thirty eight years. You know the story. God sent you a good man and you couldn't receive him because you were holding on to what God separated from you. You tried to fill the void by sleeping around, going to church, playing patty cake with God. But God see you as much more than that; he aligned it where you can meet back with your ex, so you can receive your healing. You kept praying asking God to bring him back to you, so He did, only for you to see it's not what you really want. So all you need to do now is to take up your bed and walk!"

"I agree with you one hundred percent. See that's why I was led to talk to you." She smiles.

"I want Keith back," she says quickly.

"Brittney, I did him so wrong, but I realize after going back to Donavan ain't nothing more satisfying than being with Keith. I'm through with all that trying to fill a void with this person and that person sleeping with every Tom, Dick, and Butray. I'm tired of the devil tormenting me at night. The thing that really got me to thinking about my life is, one night recently, the enemy began to torment me while I was sleep. I tossed and turned and couldn't get any rest. When I finally dozed off, I heard a voice say *I got you just where I want you in your mind, your spirit. You gave me the power to control you. Why do you think I wake you up for church? Because I know you can do more damage inside the church than outside the church."* I jumped up and began to plead the blood. But that's not the first time that happened."

"That's some scary shit right there. I meant mess, I'm' bout to work on this cussing starting today… A Better Me." Britt nods her head. "But go 'head."

"But yeah, if Keith was there he would just roll over and lay his hand on me, rebuke the devil and go back to sleep. Even though his job kept him going a lot, that was a praying man. And nothing turns me on more than a man who knows how to pray. He be like *'Bay, you gone give me some?' I be like, 'Talk to Jesus.'* Girl halfway through the prayer I be like *'Amen, let's go!'"*

"Girl you are stupid!" Brittney is killing herself laughing.

"I'm so serious; I miss my man, girl. We had fun together. I'mma get him back and we gone create some new memories after we get married."

"You think he gone want to do that? Remember that was his problem before, scared because of what Sonya did to him."

"Oh baby that is not going to be an issue because I'mma put it on him so good…"

"Come on now!" Brittney high-fives her.

"See it's my job as his woman to make him feel secure. He shouldn't ever have to wonder if I got his back. He should have no doubt that I'm doing the right thing if he isn't around. He should know without a shadow of a doubt that if a rumor comes his way, he knows it's not true. As his woman he should have so much faith in me that there will be NO DOUBT ABOUT IT!"

"Touch your neighbor and say No Doubt About It!"

"I like that Kim. So how are you going to get things started with Keith?"

"I'm'ma call him."

"Just like that; pick up the phone and call him; even though you haven't talked to him in months; what about six months or more?

"Yep."

"You a bad bitch!" She high-fives her with a smile.

"I mean, I'mma be subtle and see what's going on with him."

"What if he has a girlfriend? Or somebody he talking to?"

"Then all I can say is *move over bacon, now there's something meatier.*"

They both start laughing.

"Kim you done lost some weight," Britt comments.

"Yeah a little."

"More than a little, your face is slimming down."

"Thank you girl. So tell me what are you going to do about Tim?" Do you think you're done with him for real?"

"Realistically, I don't want to be one of them dumb broads that say, *I ain't never going back. Or I'm done! But* I can say this, where I'm at right now, I don't want him back. My mind is so done with him but my heart wants to know what I did wrong... you know what I mean? So that's where I'm at."

"Well even though I never really cared for him—"

"Yeah, why didn't you like him?" Brittney interrupts taking a drink.

"I don't know. You know how when you meet somebody, it's just something 'bout them that you don't like. I mean for what I seen, he treated you and Jaylin good, so I really don't know." Kim laughs.

"…but for what it's worth you are a good person, a great mother and you deserve the best."

"Well, well, well, is it the wine talking or you?"

"It's me. I'm relaxed not drunk."

"Well, Kim, I'm actually glad we had lunch today. I saw a different side of you and you saw a different side of me."

"Yeah that man gone kick yo ass when he find out you fished his house." Kim says with a smile.

"Here, here." Brittney lifts her glass and drinks with a smile.

"So let's talk about this cookout. Do you still want to do it? Kim asks.

"I mean it will be good, just to get everybody together and maybe Monet can meet a man… Her baby daddy is married. Did you know that Mitchell is married?"

"Yes, I know. I just hate she's going through this pregnancy alone. And what's going on with her leg?"

"Please don't say anything Kim, but the doctor, think it could be the MS."

"Oh noo!"

"Please Kim, don't go around her feeling sorry for her. That will put a damper in her spirit. And let her tell you. You didn't hear it from me.

[248]

But she been doing great overall. She met a young lady at one of her doctor visits name Traci. They have been strengthening each other. I think it's therapeutic for the both of them."

"So Traci has MS, too?"

"No Traci has breast cancer. Real nice lady--very sweet and beautiful. She found out about her cancer a few months ago. You gonna have to meet her Kim; you'll love her. I'll invite her to the cook out… So let's set another date and stick with it."

"Okay this time if you cancel, we are having it without you."

"I know, I know, I was going through. Tim had my mind gone, girl."

"Thought you were going to a hair show?' Kim asks.

"Child that was a lie; I couldn't tell you at the time."

"So we straight now; Tim gone and we moving forward?"

"Right," Britt nods her head.

"So how about the third weekend of the month after next? This gives us a little over a month and gives people time to make plans to attend," Kim asks.

"Alright sounds good, so let's shoot for the fourteenth of June."

"Let's get out of here. I have something I want to show you."

"Where are we going?" Brittney asks.

"You'll see."

Kim takes Brittney to an office plaza on the east side of town about twenty minutes away from where they ate lunch and about ten minutes away from Brittney's house. Kim stops in front of a vacant spot.

"Get out."

"What is this?"

"Could be your potential business; go check it out."

Brittney gets out the car and looks in the window. She notices that it was previously a salon, kind of small, but she can make it do what it do.

"Kim, this is okay. I really think I can do something with this, kind of small but it will work," she says as she looks in the window.

"I saw the previous owners moving out one night and stopped and asked them 'bout the building and who can I contact, and they were really nice about."

"So did you get…?" As she turns around, Kim is holding the paper to give to her.

"That's what I'm talking 'bout. Let me call them right now."

"Hello…Hello, Hey how are you? My name is Brittney and I'm over here in the Brookview Plaza. I'm interested In this Salon, how much is it?... Oh really?... When can I take a look in it? Okay… Okay.. That's not a problem at all. I'll be here…..Okay see you soon.

"What did they say?" Kim asks.

"He said if I would like, I can see it today. Just give him a few minutes; he has to make a couple of stops and he'll be right over…. Kim, thank you so much girl."

"Hey, it's no problem at all."

While Kim and Britt sit in the parking lot waiting for the owner to come show them the inside of the building, Kim notices Monet and another lady walking up to the Jamaican Restaurant a few doors down.

"Isn't that Monet?" Kim asks.

"Yeah, that's her. Look at that belly getting out there a little bit." Brittney smiles.

"Who is that she's with?"

"That's Traci, the young lady I was telling you about. Naaay!" Brittney calls her name.

Monet turns around and notices Britt standing next to Kim's car.

"Heeey!" Monet yells from a distance. She and Traci start walking towards Brittney.

Brittney is so excited to see her friend she starts to sing and dance walking towards them.

"Heeey Ma!" Brittney says with a big smile then she starts to sing a jingle and move her shoulders.

"Wobble wobble, shake shake shake shakey, wobble wobble."

Monet entertains her by doing a little wobbling and shaking.

"You didn't know, but I use to love to dance," Monet says.

They both laugh and hug.

"Hey Traci! How you doing?" Brittney asks as she gives her a hug as well.

"I'm doing well, thanks for asking."

"I was just telling Kim…"

"Kim? Is Kim over there?" Monet asks as she starts walking towards the car.

"Yeah, she's in the car; we had lunch today and she wanted me to see this building she found, so now we're waiting on the owner to let us look in it."

"Kiiiimmm! Hey honey, I missed you," Monet says as she gives her a hug.

"Seem like we both be missing each other in church. One week you there and I'm not or I'm there and you not."

"I know child; we got to get it together." Kim smiles.

"Well this is our new friend Traci. You haven't had a chance to meet her—"

"I was just telling Kim about her over lunch," Brittney interrupts.

"Good things I hope?" Traci asks.

"Yes, I gave her all your accolades…you nasty, mean, you pretty but your spirit ain't right - I said to Kim, *'yep, she fits right in with us,'*" Brittney says with a smile.

Monet and Traci smile.

"I'm just kidding," Brittney says.

"Pleased to meet you." Traci extends her hand to Kim.

"Pleased to meet you, too. Brittney has told me so many good things about you," she smiles.

"So which one of these buildings were you looking at?" Monet asks.

"This one right here; come here let me show you."

The three of them walk over to the window. "I love it Britt. You like it?" Monet asks.

"I like it. It's kinda smaller than what I wanted but I can make it work."

"Oh yeah, you can definitely make this work."

The owner of the building pulls up.

"Hey that's Mr. Thomas," Monet says.

"Royce Thomas?" Brittney asks.

"Yeah, he owns that building over by the café. The one I told you about a while ago and somebody got it?"

"Yeah, I remember. Is somebody still in it?"

"Nobody ever moved in it. They put paper up to the window so you can't look on the inside," Monet answers.

"How you pretty ladies doing?" Mr. Thomas asks.

Fine and great they answer.

"Hey Mr. Thomas," Monet speaks.

"Hey Monet, what you doing over here?'

"I came over here to eat, and I saw my friends over here; this is Brittney, Kim and this is Traci." Monet introduces them.

"Brittney is the one that's interested in looking at the building."

"How you doing, young lady?" He speaks as he opens the door.

"I'm good, Royce; do you remember me? I met you a while ago, you showed me another building you have on E .Park?"

"Yes I remember you; you're a feisty lil something." He smiles.

"Yall come on in." He holds the door open for them to enter.

"So Brittney what kind of business are you wanting to do again?"

"A salon," she answers.

"Oh okay, Well this will be perfect," he answers.

"I was telling her about the building over by me. Is somebody in it? 'Cause nobody is ever over there."

"Yeah, well I don't know what the young fellow is actually doing with the building, but he paid me seven months advance."

"I tried to be nosey and peep in the window one day, but I couldn't see anything because he has paper covering the windows." Monet states.

"Yeah, well again, I haven't inquired about it," Mr. Thomas answers.

"One of the girls that work for me, Zibra, said it is a salon."

"This here was a salon, too; as you can see. The people here just ran out on me in the middle of the night--didn't wanna pay me no rent. Lord I tell you, they ain't gone have no good luck. Well any hoo, do you think you're interested in this one, Brittney?"

"How much is it?"

"Four hundred a month."

"I'll take it."

"Go on through and take a look at the rest of it," He says.

"Oh there's more?" Britt asks.

"You thought this was it? Go on through that door there."

Britt opens the door and the others follow behind her.

"Wow, Okay! Now this makes all the difference. I like this. And I like the combination of the two purples they have on the wall in here, it's so relaxing. And look at this big ole wall mirror….love it, love it, love it. This can be the shampoo area, dryers can go here and maybe I can take this door down right there, if you don't mind, Mr. Thomas."

"Do whatever you want to accommodate you, but don't throw the door away."

"Oh no, sir. I won't do that."

"Britt, this is you hon!" Monet comments.

"Really nice," Traci says shaking her head.

"And really all you need is styling chairs 'cause they left everything else," Kim comments.

"Well if you want to take it as is, just give me last month rent and I'll waive the first month if you do the cleaning."

"Really? You girls got my back?"

"Go for it!" Monet says shaking her head.

"You can do it!" Traci says.

"Ain't none of yall heifers say you got my back."

"We got you!" They answer collectively.

"Okay how 'bout this?" Kim says. "How 'bout we pray about it?"

"Pray about it?" Monet asks surprisingly.

"It's cool, Monet; she's in good standing now; she'll get through. God won't hit the reject button," Brittney answers with sarcasm.

"I'm just saying, it's something about the way she said it--matter fact it's something about your whole demeanor; you haven't really been saying much. Are you okay?"

"I'm fine; anyways, like I was saying, let's pray about it and go home sleep on it and see what God has to say about it."

Kim extends both of her arms out to pray and the three of them look at each other and grab hands.

"You, too, Mr. Thomas; this is your building and even if God say no, it's still gonna be blessed.

"Well I suppose so."

"You suppose so? Mr. Thomas is your first name Doubting? 'Cause you sound like you ain't got no belief. Do you go to church, Mr. Thomas?"

"Well yes I do."

"What's the name of it?"

"Hold My Mule Down by the River Missionary Baptist Church," he answers.

"Hold My Mule Down by the River? What the… I ain't never heard of that. It sounds dead."

"Kim!" Monet yells.

Traci and Brittney try not to laugh.

"I'm sorry. He still working on me; but I'm just saying, look at him…. Mr. Thomas, I just have to speak my mind sometime and be honest with you, but you look like you ain't got no life in you. How long you been going to this church?"

"All my life."

"All your life? So this church been around for a while? I ain't never heard of it."

"I have," Monet says. "Actually Zibra go to that church. It's out in the country. Way out in the woods."

"That's the problem; you can't see the forest for trees--literally!" Kim remarks.

The three of them try not to laugh at her.

"It's a family church and they only have church on second and fourth Sundays," Monet adds.

"Well Mr. Doubting Thomas, you gone have to come visit our church on yall Sunday off."

He looks at her with nothing to say.

"I'm serious, we got to get some motivation in you and feed that little faith so that doubt can starve to death."

"I here you, young lady. I'll come check you out."

"I'm serious. 'Round here looking like an old man, I bet you younger than you look. How old are you?"

"I'm forty-seven."

"I knew it," Kim says. "Round here looking like you sixty-seven… I see the potential behind all that. You a nice looking fella." Kim rambles on.

Mr. Thomas begins to smile.

"Why thank you young lady. And Zibra is my niece."

"Well I'll be…. small world. And that smile made a big difference. Now we 'bout to pray and see what the Lord got to say about this building. Does anybody have anything they want to pray about? I'm being serious now."

"Healing," Traci states.

"Healing as well," Monet agrees.

"Direction," Brittney answers.

"And you Mr. Thomas?" Kim asks.

"God help my unbelief."

"Okay all hearts and mind are clear."

Kim begins to pray and as she prays the anointing rests so beautifully on her. Everybody is in tuned and on one accord. There is not one dry eye in the building. After she finishes she begins to sing and everybody joins in to worship.

"Monet, I'm feeling weak; I need to get something to eat," Traci says.

"Okay. Listen yall, I really enjoyed this prayer session….," she says as she hugs everybody. "But we got to go eat. The baby is hungry and Traci is feeling a little weak."

"You okay?" Britt and Kim asks at the same time.

"I'm okay; I just need to eat something," Traci answers.

"Well if yall church is anything like this, I'll be to visit," Mr. Thomas comments.

"Okay we look forward to seeing you," Monet states as she starts to walk to the door.

"Alright, see you guys!!! Love yall!! Bye. And Kim come by and see me… we need to talk," Monet continues as she walks out the door.

"Okay, love you too," Kim and Brittney remarks.

"See you guys," Traci says.

"Well, Mr. Thomas. We will be seeing you around, hopefully sooner than later," Kim quotes.

"Where is yall church located and what's the name of it?"

"Friendly Freewill over on John Road."

"I know exactly where you at."

"Okay, Well It's been a pleasure meeting you," Kim says.

"Yeah, thanks for coming by showing us the property."

"My pleasure; you ladies take care."

"You too!"

Kim turns to Brittney. "Where to now?"

"I guess you can take me to get my fish tank; it's time for me to get Jay. Hopefully the smell will be gone."

"Girl that scent is gonna be in your car for a few days." She smiles.

"Come on I'll take you to get Jaylin." They get in the car.

Jaylin was standing in front of the school with friends when Britt and Kim pulled up.

"Jay!" Britt calls his name as she gets out the car to meet him.

"Hey mom! See you later guys," he turns and says to his friends.

"Mom where's our car?"

"We're riding with Aunt Kim."

"Momma don't take this the wrong way, but since when did she become Aunt Kim?"

"Since today."

"Are you sure 'cause I thought she wasn't one of your favorite people."

"Yeah, well…. She's pretty cool now. It's amazing how God can change people."

"Really now? Well do you think he can change Kayla?"

"Who is Kayla?"

"She's in my class. She is the one in the pink shirt that's behind us. But don't look now mom. Play it off."

"Play it off? What do you know about playing something off?" She begins tickling him and then picks him up and spins him around.

"She's pretty," Brittney comments.

"You're good mom!" He smiles.

"I know 'cause I'm the queen of playing things off." She smiles back at him.

"So what do you want God to change about her?"

"Her attitude! She's pretty, but her attitude sometimes, makes her reeeeaaaal ugly!"

"I know how that goes. But yeah God can definitely change that. Pray for her," she says as they get in the car.

"Hey Miss Kim," Jay speaks.

"Aunt Kim!" She corrects him.

"What happened today?" Jaylin asks with sarcasm as he flops back in the seat.

"And what does that supposed to mean?" Kim asks.

"I just told him we were riding with Aunt Kim and he can't believe we're getting along to the point where you're aunt," Brittney answers.

"Anyway." Kim shakes her head smiling.

"Hey baby," she speaks back.

"That little boy is beyond his years," Kim says as she pulls off.

"You got that right," Britt agrees.

"So who are we praying for? Do I need to go get some straightening about my nephew? Who bothering you?" She asks looking into the rearview mirror.

"It's this girl in his class," Britt answers.

"I fight children, too." Kim looks at Jay in the mirror and smiles. He smiles back at her. "Miss Kim, I meant Aunt Kim. I don't want nothing bad to happen to her--I actually like her, but I don't like her attitude most of the time."

"Well what kind of attitude does she have?" Kim asks.

"She acts boojee…."

"That's your momma," Kim interrupts with a laugh.

"…kind of stuck up sometime…"

"That's your aunt Kim," Brittney smiles.

"…and bossy."

"That's Aunt Monet!" They both say as they look at each other.

"And she always wants to be in control of things."

"That's all of us!" Brittney comments.

"Yep, sounds like your little friend is definitely an Aries," Kim suggests.

"What's an Aries?" Jaylin asks.

"Your smart ass just held what seemed to be an intellectual conversation and you don't know what an Aries is?"

"Kim!"

"Excuse me baby. I'm just saying… I swear God is sending these kids here with some extra shi…I meant stuff."

"I know, right? They ain't nothing like we used to be. Remember back in the day a baby wouldn't open their eyes for about two to four weeks? Now these nosey things come out with their eyes open."

"Ummm hmm, and remember when—"

"Will somebody just answer my question?" Jaylin interrupts.

[261]

"JAYLIN JERROD!" His mom calls. "I will hit you in your damn mouth if you ever disrespect your elder again!"

"Sorry Aunt Kim."

"Umm hmm; didn't I just tell you I fight kids? Don't let it happen again. See back then children didn't be in grown folk conversation; hell we wasn't even allowed to be in the same room with the adults."

"You got that right," Brittney agrees.

"Shoot, when company came over, we either had to take our tails in the room or outside. Oooh! I used to be so mad when somebody came over 'cause I'll be watching my USA Cartoon Express and my momma would say '*Britt go in the room or go outside and play.*' And we didn't have a TV in the room like these kids today with these flat screens. But when my parents did get me one, I had a small thirteen inch with the rabbit ears," Brittney says.

"Shoot when my momma got me one, it didn't have cable on it. Matter fact, the knobs were missing." She laughs.

"We had to use pliers to turn the TV and it only got three channels-- six, ten, and thirteen." Kim continues to laugh.

"Girl, thanks for the ride; tell Aunt Kim bye, Jay."

"See you later Aunt Kim."

"Okay Sweetie."

"Here honey." She hands Jaylin the key to open the door. "So what are you 'bout to get into?" She leans in the car door.

"I'mma go figure out a way to get my man back," Kim smiles.

"I hear ya; and you will figure it out, that I know," Brittney responds with a smile.

[262]

"Hey, I was thinking; maybe Donavan can hang out with Jay sometime since Tim's not around. I mean I think it will be good for him and it might even be good for Don as well 'cause he got a son somewhere he been looking for."

"Sounds like a plan; set something up and let me know," Britt says.

"Okay, I will." Before she could pull off, her phone rings; its Lil Don. She motions to Britt to show her the name on the ID.

"Hello?" She answers…... *"We were just talking about you....My friend I go to church with.....No silly she doesn't know you....She has a son, and I was telling her that you can probably hang out with him sometime... He's……. Six? Seven?"* She asks looking at Brittney.

"Seven," Brittney says

"He's seven" Kim answers.

"Mike this isn't your average seven year old. We picked the lil boy up from school today and he started to talking 'bout some chick he like, but he don't like her attitude; she pretty but her attitude makes her look ugly..... yeah really!" Kim answers back. *"Mike I cannot make this up--no lie; this baby knows how to hold a conversation, little smart mouth, but he got it honest, so we won't hold it against him."* Kim looks at Brittney and smiles.

*"So let me know when Uncle Mike have time.... Yes Uncle Mike....Yes I am....*she laughs. *"Well this is a new Kim and I have officially adopted my first nephew."* She continues to laugh. *"Okay, I'll text you her number so the two of you can set something up. Alright talk to you later"*

"So what I'll do is text him your number and he'll give you a call."

[263]

"Alright girl, let me go in here and fix him a snack; call me later."

"Okay, bye."

Kim puts the car in reverse and hears her song playing faintly on the radio. She turns it up and begins to sing along: ♫ *"Nobody greater...nobody greater than you. Searched all over, couldn't find nobody, I looked high and looow, still couldn't find nobody, Nobody greater, nobody greater Jesus, Nobody greater than yoouu."* ♫

Just as she is getting into the song bobbing her head and swaying to the melody, her phone rings. She looks at it and thinks to herself, *that's just like the enemy to try to distract your worship;* and she continues to sing until the very end and her phone rings again.

Kim / Patricia

"Hello?" she answers in her islander accent because she doesn't recognize the number.

"I'm sorry I have the wrong number," the female answers.

""Who are you lookin' fa?" she continues in her foreign voice.

"My name is Patricia, and I am looking for Kim."

"How you doing Patricia?" she asks in her regular voice.

"Is this Kim?"

[264]

"Yeah this me, I didn't recognize your number and I had to make sure it wasn't anybody I didn't won't to be bothered with," she smirks.
"Listen, I don't won't to take up too much of your time, but are you busy?"
"Not particularly, just headed to the house. Why? What's up?"
"I want to speak with you concerning my husband, Butray?"
Kim gets quiet; she is unsure where this conversation is going.
"Lord I hope she hasn't heard anything," she thinks to herself.
"Kim? Kim? Are you still there?"
"Yes, I'm here, I'm sorry, my cheek accidently hit the mute button." She lies.
"So what's on your mind Patricia?" as she prepares for the worst.
"I know you haven't seen me in church in a while and I know we don't talk like that, but for some strange reason it was laid upon my heart to call you. Can we meet somewhere?"
"Well...I..."
"Please Kim, I promise not to take up too much of your time."
"Okay sure, what's good for you?"
"Can you meet me at Orange Park?"
"Yeah what time?"
"I'm actually here now."
"Okay I'll be there in a few." Kim answers.
Kim begins to talk to herself on the way to Orange Park "Lord Jesus, what does this lady want? And why is she calling me out of all people? She must of heard something, but how would she know, I hope stupid ass, Tray didn't say anything." Her pressure starts to rise.

"Ok calm down Kim, she didn't sound upset but she did sound troubled. Ok Kim, You got this, if she ask just be honest. Just answer the questions she ask but don't volunteer no information."

As Kim arrives in Orange Park she gazes around for Patricia's car.

"Where is she? I thought she told me she was already here," Kim says as she dials her number. *"Hey where are you? I'm here……. Oh okay I see you; I was looking for your car…..ooh I see it…..niiiicce; I like it. You fancy, huh? Okay here I come."*

Patricia greets Kim. "Thanks for meeting up with me."

"Oh, it's no problem. So when did you get your new car?"

"A few days ago." Patricia answers.

"That's nice there, I was looking for the Camry. Do you want to sit or walk?"

"Let's walk," Tricia answers.

"So what's on your mind?"

"I know we don't know each other that well and we only speak in passing. And I know you probably thinking: Why does she want to talk to me? I know I don't come to church that often like I used to, and I have my reasons; it's not an excuse but… that's neither here nor there right now. But when I would see you in church, I would say to myself, *'that sister got it together! If anybody gonna make it in, she is.'* The anointing of God would fall on you and not a dry eye would be in the church. You can tell the glory of God be in the building every time. And I would think to myself, *'Lord I want that. I want what she got. I want to be where she is.'"*

"Really?" Kim asks.

[266]

"Yep and I would pray, 'Lord don't let me leave out of here the same'. And Kim….. nothing changed. Every time I tried to do right, I found myself doing wrong……. My marriage is over…"

"Why do you say that?"

"My husband is a good man; he may not be the best lookin' thang but he is a very good man. And he tried so hard to please me in every way he could but my own selfish desire got in the way and I only thought about me, myself, and I.. I stopped cooking for him, I wouldn't clean, I wouldn't sleep with him.

"What brought all this on?"

"I got a new job and I ain't gone lie Kim, I went on this high horse…. Me and my husband been together going on nineteen years and he has always been there for me, giving me everything I wanted. He's been there emotionally, spiritually and I can honestly say I never questioned him cheating on me until now."

"He's cheating on you?"

"I don't know, I think he is; if he is, it's my fault because I pushed him away."

"Don't say that Tricia."

"I did Kim; I cussed him out… I mean you don't know the half of it. It's like I turned into this person that I don't even know. I called him names, cursed him out, and called him ugly….Ugly?" She smirks.

"I married the man and called him ugly." She smiles shaking her head.

"Who does that? I don't know what the hell got in me?"

"You just answered your on question."

"What's that?" Patricia asks.

"Hell… Hell is what got in you. Some way, somehow you allowed the enemy to creep in and kill your character, steal your identity, and destroy your marriage. He's doing his job, but what are you going to do about it in return?"

"I want my husband back! I want things the way they used to be."

"So what are you gonna do about it?"

"First, I'm going to work on me which I've already started doing…. I've been praying and God has been revealing to me who I am. I have started developing a one on one relationship with Him; baby steps, you know. I've tried to go back to church but every time I go, I'm worst off coming out than I went in. I thought the church is supposed to be like a hospital for the sick…"

"It is."

"But how come I feel contaminated with a virus or something whenever I leave? I can go in feeling good, clean, redeemed and all that good stuff but when I come out, I'm feeling like I brought some bacteria out with me and I need to go sanitize. You know what I mean? Does it make sense?"

Kim checks out of the conversation and begins to remember when she and Monet saw Pastor and Tricia eating lunch.

Kim stops walking and looks at Patricia and asks, "So how long have you been sleeping with him?"

How long have you been sleeping with my husband? Kim hears as she stares at Patricia waiting for an answer.

"Excuse me?" Kim asks

"Sleeping with who? My husband?" Patricia asks.

Kim takes a sigh of relief. Her guilt has started to get to her to the point where she is hallucinating. She thought Patricia was answering her question with a question.

"Kim are you okay? Sleeping with who?" she asks again.

Kim thinks to herself once again, *"I can't believe I just blurted that out like that. What was I thinking? I wasn't thinking, shoot!"*

"Look, I'm sorry if I over stepped my bounds, but I saw you and pastor having what appeared to be an intimate lunch one day."

"Wow!.......Well since we're talking, I might as well put it all on the table; you might want to sit down for this one." The two of them sit down on the park bench.

"You ready?"

"I'm ready."

"I went in to see Pastor one day concerning my marriage. This was before we started having church in your living room. I was feeling a little bad because my husband had been pulling all the weight by himself while I went to school. Well once I got my degree, I started sending in my resume to different companies and nobody was calling me back. One place told me I needed experience, so I went to talk to Pastor. He told me to keep the faith and that God would surely work it out. He started telling me about his marriage and how being so involved in the church and not spending enough at home caused his wife to leave. Next thing I know he walks around the back of my chair and he begins to massage my neck. I was shocked--didn't see

[269]

that coming. I didn't know what to think or how to react; then he started kissing me on my neck, Kim." She sighs.

"I have never been with anyone in nineteen years besides my husband and a part of me wanted him to stop but another part of me wanted him to keep going; not to mention he was smelling sooo good. Anyway, we did it, *and I felt so horrible afterwards. I felt really really bad. But it was really really good.*

"YOU AND PASTOR?"

"I know it Kim. I feel so bad now, but I didn't then because I was too caught up in him. It was like I was in a trance or something."

"So what happened?" What's different now?"

"Well to make a long story tolerable. We spent a lot of time together; he was quite a gentleman, very romantic and full of surprises. He even helped me get this job. We started sleeping together without condoms and I ended up getting pregnant."

Kim looks at her surprised. "Pregnant?"

"Yeah, I got pregnant," she says with tears in her eyes.

Kim looks down at Tricia's stomach. "You pregnant now?"

"No, I'm not. He talked me into having an abortion."

"An abortion? Are you okay?" Kim asks with sympathy.

"Yeah…well, I will be," Patricia says wiping the tears from her eyes. "For years me and Tray tried to get pregnant but couldn't. I really wanted that baby but after he said we need to get rid of it, something in me just turned sour towards him. I went home and I prayed on it. I prayed and prayed and prayed."

"About an abortion Patricia? Really? Did you really think God was gonna give you the okay?"

"I know! I'm so ashamed of what I done."

"So did you get an answer?" Kim asks being funny.

"Actually, I did. The night before I was to go have the procedure done, I had a dream and in this dream a very tall man dressed in all white--I assume it was a man, but he was very, very tall-- anyway he extended both his arms out to me to give me a baby boy. It was the most beautiful baby I've ever seen--skin smooth with a bronze complexion, head full of black hair. He was lying in the man's arms sleeping so peacefully with his baby blue onesie on. I extended both my arms to receive him; I looked at him and woke up. I know I disappointed God and I know He's punishing me right about now." Patricia cuffs her face in her arms as she begins to cry; Kim puts one arm around her and begins to console her. "You know Patricia; you're not the first and you're definitely not going to be the last person to terminate a pregnancy. Quiet as it's kept, the abortion rate is just as high in the church as it is in the world. Now I'm not saying it's right nor excusing it, neither am I condoning nor condemning it. But we, as Christians, are taught since we know better, we are to do better. That's one of the sins in the church people hide because they feel that's *the big ULTIMATE sin; people can't find out about this or I'll be ostracized.* Nobody wants that feeling of being cast to the side. You already feel bad enough. The word of God tells us there ain't one sin greater than the other, sin is sin. Somebody ought to be able to say; I been there and done that…. Testimonies help people!

Testimonies heal people! Testimonies free people! And the bible states that '*they overcame* him because of the blood of the Lamb and because of the word of their testimony.'"

Patricia looks up at Kim and cuffs her face back into her hands. She is feeling ashamed about what she done

Kim continues, "When you do something like that; you begin to question whether God forgives you or not…… He does… I know. Look, look at me…"

Patricia wipes her eyes and looks at Kim. "God is so full of love, matter fact He is Love. If you ask God to forgive you, He will and he won't hold it against you."

"Why does it feel like I'm being punished? Why can't I get this out of my head? Why can't I let it go?"

"Number one, you kept this balled up in you with no one to share it with--except the baby daddy and it began to torture you. The bible tells us to confess your faults one to another, that you may be healed… Now your healing can begin because the devil, I mean the enemy, no longer can hold this over your head… let me ask you this. When you opened up to me, didn't you feel a little better?"

"I honestly felt like a weight was lifted off me."

"That's what I'm talking about! Now that you have taken that mask off, forgive yourself and take up your bed and walk."

"What do you mean take up my bed and walk?"

"In the book of John there is this pool; people with all kinds of issues would come to this pool to get healed. There is this man that laid by this pool for thirty-eight years with an issue until Jesus came along

[272]

one day and asked him did he want to get well. The man started having a pity party and said, '*I have no one to put me in; everybody just walk over me and they not trying to help me,*' mocking the man in a pitiful voice. You know how we do. We start complaining and making excuses, blaming other people; so Jesus said, '*Just get up and take your bed and go; ain't nobody got time for this!*' And instantly he was healed. Thirty-eight years that man lied there; he probably didn't open his mouth and ask nobody for help, that's why he carried that issue for so long- nobody knew what he was going through. They thought he was chilling. And just like you he kept that balled up in him, he probably sat there and complained to himself, but when Jesus came along within thirty-eight seconds he was healed."

"Okay. Yeah I remember that story," Patricia says.

"Jesus asked that man one simple question and he wanted somebody to feel sorry for him. Then Jesus thought, '*Lord have mercy;* Jesus talked to himself, he said, *Lord have mercy; aint nobody got time for this today; do you know how many more people I got to see today and he come wanting to have a pity party; I tell you what's pitiful; he sat his behind here for thirty-eight years waddling in his mess and didn't even try to scoot in the pool.*' This is the Kim's version," she says as she hands her a tissue out of her purse.

"But I believe that's when God came up with the scripture, 'Faith without works is dead', but anyway like I was saying, after Jesus thought that in his head, he said, *'just get up…get your bed, your matt, your pallet, whatever you laying on and get out of here, but leave them issues right here.*' See Patricia, you something like that man

[273]

with the issue and I'm something like that pool. God sent you to me to get your healing today."

"I appreciate that," she smirks "you're comical."

"You're welcome; it's good to laugh; laughter is good for the soul and it's good to cry, too; it's purifying." She hands her another tissue to wipe her nose.

"So how long has this thing been marinating in you?"

"About nine months," she answers.

"And because you opened up your mouth and confessed to me within nine seconds you were healed."

Kim begins to pretend shout, "Wooo, somebody ought to give God some praise! Ain't He awesome?" She looks at Patricia. "I said ain't He awesome? Girl, I'm 'bout to have church out here all by myself!"

Patricia smiles and claps her hands. "I wish I had your spirit."

"You do!" Kim remarks smartly.

"No I don't. You're all bubbly, funny, you know your bible… and your Christian walk…. If I could just be where you at, I'd be okay."

"No! You gone be okay where you at! Tricia let me help you a lil bit. Everybody has their own levels of anointing. You can't possibly wish you were me, and not know what I had to go through to get here. It didn't come by night, honey. I had to tread over some water, girl. I was once in that same place you're in now. You have to understand, you got to go through things in order to gain wisdom." Kim stresses. "The bible tells us 'if you want Wisdom ask, and He'll give it to you.' I used to ask all the time before I understood--every time I asked God for wisdom, I went through something. That might not be the case

[274]

with you, but as you're growing spiritually and if your world starts spinning out of control, don't think it's the devil. God can very well be taking you through something to give you knowledge and wisdom on that situation. Selah…. Think about it….. My Bishop from my old church use to say that all the time, '*Selah…think about it.*'" She smiles as she remembers.

"I understand…. Okay let me ask you this; the bible says He chastens those He loves. You think I'm being punished?"

"That is true. He does whoops those He loves but in Psalms 103 I believe…. it says that He doesn't punish us for all our sins. To me I believe, and this is just my opinion, I believe sometimes we can feel so bad and remorseful about a situation, to where God say that's your punishment right there. I ain't gone whoop you 'cause your conscience is already beating you up." Kim shrugs her shoulders. "However, you know how you can look at somebody's life and it seems like they get away with everything?… Well I heard this one Pastor say, *God don't whoop other people children."*

"Ooh, that's a good one, I like how that was put." Patricia comments. "But why do I feel so bad Kim?"

"Because you're human and because you are in this flesh, you will experience emotions. The enemy will remind you, condemn you and accuse you daily if you allow him to, but the bible say there is no condemnation for those who belong to Christ Jesus. He will forgive you as far as the east is from the west; He will throw your sin in the Sea of Forgetfulness. Read your bible sometime; it will bless ya," she says in her Madea voice.

Patricia smiles. "Kim this isn't what I called you for, I called you to talk about my—"

"Oh but God had a divine plan." She cuts her off.

"Let me share this with you. Why do you think out of all people, God put it in your spirit to call me?"

"I don't know Kim. Why?"

"Because I done been through what you been through," she answers.

"YOU WERE WITH THE PASTOR, TOO!?"

"No, No, No, No, Noooo. Hell No! I'm talking about the abortion."

"You had an abortion, too!?" Tricia asks.

"I did when I was younger, from my childhood boyfriend. My momma felt I was too young so she took me to get rid of it."

"Are you serious?"

"Yep!"

"I was fourteen when I had mine; no one in my family ever knew."

"Do you want children, Kim?"

"Not really. Kids are expensive and high maintenance."

"Kim? Are you serious? You don't want kids because they are high maintenance?"

"Child they're high maintenance and then some," Kim begins to quickly run down a list, "such as doctor visits, Wic appoiontments, weaning them off the bottle, the pacifier, potty training, not to mention it takes forever to get out the house cause not only do you have to get you dress but now you have to get this baby dress and if they're a toddler they want to do everything themselves; put on their own clothes, their own shoes and you standing there like 'will you

[276]

pleeease hurry up'. And my god you can't just run in the store and grab something ….you got to get them out the car seat, strap them in the car seat and God forbid you take them in Wal-Mart, the moment you get to the back of the store… here they lil ass go, *'I gotta use the bathroom.'* Ain't nobody got time for that!"

"Oh my!" Patricia says.

"I mean everybody got a right to feel how they feel, and that's how I feel. I'm still somewhat selfish and I'm not ready to share my time with a baby." Kim says as her speech slows down while she has a flashback. "Maybe one day my mindset will change but not now, honey!"

"Yeah, that did sound a little selfish, but I didn't want to come out and say it." Patricia smiles. "For somebody who doesn't have any kids, you sure know a lot."

"I use to hang around people with kids but I had to cut them loose, 'cause they were holding me back. I be trying to get somewhere and they got to get the kids ready, strap them in, take them to the bathroom…

"Kim!" She cuts her off, "I get it!" She cackles. "Please don't get stirred up again." Patricia continues to smile "I know one thing, I feel a whole lot better talking to you… Kim I want my husband back," Patricia blurts out.

"Well go get him!"

"How?"

"By being a Wife! Everything you used to do in the beginning, you got to start back doing it, but first I suggest you have a conversation with him and see if he even wants the marriage to work."

"You right, you are absolutely right! And I have taken up too much of your time. Let me go; Thank you so much." She gives her a hug swiftly and says, "I'll be talking with ya."

"Okay, be good," Kim responds.

Patricia and Kim walk away in opposite directions. Kim pulls out her phone and contemplates on calling Keith. As she was talking to Patricia she realized she needed to take her own advice.

"Hello….Hey Keith. How are you?"

"I'm blessed, and yourself?"

"I'm doing good," she answers.

Silence covers the phone only momentarily.

"So what's up Kim?"

"Listen I was wondering……First of all are you busy?"

"No, what's up love?

"I was wondering if you have any plans for this evening?"

"This evennnning?" He begins to think.

"Naw, I don't. What's up? You need anything?"

"I need to see you!"

"See me? Is everything okay? I mean I haven't spoken with you in months and all of sudden we run into each other earlier and now you want to see me? What's going on Kim?"

"I want to talk to you; what time can I come over?"

"Kim I don't know if that's a good--"

[278]

"I won't take up too much of your time." She cuts him off.

"Look, I..I...I.. I, ummm…

I'll be there, say about six?"

"That's not good."

"Well what time is good?"

"Kim, I uummm…"

"You what? Look I'll be there at seven o clock."

"That's only a few more hours!"

"I know, See ya then."

Kim hangs up her phone and gets into her car. When she arrives home, she notices Mike's truck in the driveway.

"Hey Kim," Mike speaks when she walks in the house."

"Hey hon. I'm surprised to see you're off this early."

"Well we finished up with the church early."

"Finished? As in finished finished? Kim asks.

"Yes, we are finally done. People were filling this living room up so I had to get it done in order to get our privacy back."

"Privacy?"

"Calm down!" He gets two glasses down from the cabinet.

"What I mean is we don't have to worry about people being in all up in our home."

"Home?"

"Look Kim, you and I both realize that what we HAD is exactly what it is--had! Past tense!" He pours the two of them juice.

"It was good that we came back together because neither one of us were able to move on and I know this is your home but it was your idea that I stay here until I figured out what I was going to do, so you don't have to keep making lil' slick comments like that. I have been looking at some places and I think it's time for me to move on so you can have your space."

Kim sits down at the islander in the kitchen.

"You right and I'm sorry. Listen, we gone always be besties; I guess I've had a lot of stuff on my mind lately."

"Like what?"

Kim shrugs her shoulders.

"Listen… let's make a pack right now as friends or besties, as you put it, that we'll be an open book. So whateva is bothering you or me we can talk to each other without passing judgment on one another. How 'bout that?" Mike suggests.

"I like that," she answers.

"So you gonna tell me what's been on your mind lately?"

"Keith," she speaks softly.

"Keith? What about Keith?"

"I kinda miss him. Me and Brittney ran into him today and I sort of gave him a call."

"What did he say?"

"He really didn't say much--stuttered a bit."

"Stuttered? Why did he stutter?"

"I asked him did he have plans for tonight. He said no then I told him I'll be stopping by."

"YOU TOLD HIM? Kim you can't just tell this man you coming over! You don't know if—"

"If what?"

"Nothing."

"If what, Mike? If he still has feelings for me? Or if I'm wasting my time?"

"Or if he has someone else, KIM!" He cuts her off.

Kim looks surprised.

"What do you mean if he has someone else? Is there something that I should know?"

Mike thinks back to the time he saw Keith coming out of the store with a young lady; he looks at Kim. Not wanting to disappoint her he answers, "No. But you shouldn't just debo your way over the man house without him inviting you. I mean if I hadn't spoken with you in months, I wouldn't appreciate you inviting yourself over."

"You right, but I already told him I'm coming and I doubt if he's seeing anyone; now with that being said, I better go get ready."

She scurries out of the kitchen like a teenager.

"Kim!" He yells. Mike takes a deep sigh and thinks to himself *I should have told her*.

Mike listens to his Pandora while he starts dinner. When he finishes, he calls Kim in the kitchen to eat.

"Look at you, looking all fancy, huh? Here, I fixed your plate."

"Thank you!" She twirls around.

The two of them sit down and eat dinner.

"So what are you gonna do the rest of the evening?" Kim asks.

"Umm, I don't know, probably relax and watch a couple movies or something."

"Well, I'll fill you in when I get back tonight if I get back tonight. Don't wait up."

"Kim!" He stops her before she makes it out the door-- "I love you, be careful."

"See ya in a lil' bit." She smiles and turns to walk out the door.

Kim arrives at Keith's place a few minutes early. Just as she is about to knock on the door, it flings open from the opposite side. Kim finds herself in a stare down with a young lady; average in size, approximately about 5'5 in height, wavy two-toned hair which appears to be all natural, and caramel in complexion. She has on a coral pink baby doll dress with black leggings that stop at her calves. Her sandals are unique--suede with a peep toe, thin straps in the front starting from the toe up to where the shoe ends just above her ankle. The straps seem to be covered in pearls. After Kim does her quick overview, she focuses in on the one thing that almost gives her an anxiety attack; she notices this young lady appears to be very pregnant.

"You must be Kim?" The young lady asks.

"Yes, I'm Kim," She hesitantly answers with a disordered look.

"Hi, I'm Alexis."

"Alexis, who are you talking to?" Keith asks as he comes to the door and sees Kim.

"Oh."

He takes a deep breath and roll his eyes anticipating what Kim will do or say next.

Alexis breaks the silence.

"I'll see you later, hon," she says to Keith.

Just as Alexis leaves, Kim steps in the door and goes ham on Keith.

"Who the….." She stops and takes a deep breath.

"Keith, I'mma ask you this one time. Who is that bitch?"

"Look Kim, you can't just run up in my house demanding answers. You left me a long time ago. What are you doing here?"

"I asked you a question?" Kim responds.

"It's complicated!"

"It's complicated? Its fuckin' complicated? What's so complicated about you getting another bitch pregnant, Keith?"

"IT'S NOT LIKE THAT!"

"WHAT THE FUCK YOU MEAN IT'S NOT LIKE THAT? THE BITCH IS OBVIOUSLY PREGNANT!" He looks at her speechless.

"How far along is she? Huh? Huh? Answer me. Dammit?"

Keith stares at her with frustration because he cannot believe she has the audacity to come over to his place questioning him.

"Answer me. Dammit!!!" Kim begins to break down and cry.

"You owe me!" She sobs.

"Owe you? Owe you, Kim? I can't believe you just said that. Get the fuck up out of my house!" He grabs her arm and walks her towards the door.

"NO! I'm not going anywhere!" She snatches her arm and moves towards the couch.

[283]

"How you gonna say I owe you Kim; you left me a long time ago. You took your heart from me years ago, Kim," Keith spurts as he pounds his fist in his hand. "When I was out on the road working, you were working other men."

"That's not true!"

"Come on baby, let's keep it one hundred."

"Well since you want to keep it one hundred, you never gave me yours." She continues to cry.

"Gave you what, Kim? I gave you everything you asked for. You wanted a man of God; you had that. A praying man--had that, too. And everything you spoke of, I gave you, baby." He begins to cry.

"…and you left me. You left me Kim! You let some other nigga move in *my* space, *my* territory—"

"YOU GAVE ME EVERYTHING BUT YOUR HEART!!!!" she interrupts in frustration. "Why, Keith? I don't understand. Why would you go get another bitch pregnant?" she asks in a calm tone. At this time Kim is on an emotional roller coaster. One minute she's crying uncontrollably the next she calm.

"I love you Keith, so much. I wouldn't have done you like that!" She cries.

"KIM! YOU LEFT ME FOR ANOTHER MAN! YOU LET YOUR EX MOVE IN ON WHAT I THOUGHT WAS MINE! YOU DON'T THINK THAT SHIT HURTS? THAT SHIT HURT, KIM!!! MEN HURT, TOO!!!" Pounding his fist in his hand.

"I'm sorry," she whispers. Worn out from the outpour of emotion she sits down on the couch and suddenly realizes that her being stuck in the past also played a role in the demise of their relationship.

"Keeping it one-hundred, I held this in for years….. when you came into my life, it was like pouring new wine into old wine. I wanted so bad to be free of him but the "what if," and the "shoulda-coulda-wouldas" kept coming into play. And it didn't help that you kept telling me you don't ever want to get married again because of what Sonya did to you. Yes, I thought I still loved him and I loved you, too, but I realized you can't mix old wine with new wine; I needed closure."

Keith stares at her with tears rolling down his face and his left fist to his mouth. "Is that all you holding in?"

"Yeah, what do you mean?"

"Just asking." He shrugs his shoulders.

"Who is she Keith?"

He doesn't say a word; he just looks at her.

"Answer me, WHO THE FUCK IS THAT BITCH?" she demands.

"THAT BITCH IS…..You know what it's time for you to go." He grabs her arm again.

"No Keith don't do this. I need you." He puts her on the other side of the door and closes it without looking at her. "Keith I love you!" she says banging on the door. She quickly gathers herself and runs outside of the complex before she draws attention to herself from the neighbors.

Alexis sits in her car watching as Kim gets in her car and leaves. She goes back in the house and finds Keith sitting on the couch with his elbows resting on his legs and his fingers intertwined like in a prayer position. She notices he has been crying.

"Is everything okay? Did you tell her?" Alexis asks.

"No I did not, but you gotta fix this and fix it fast!"

"I will and thank you for not saying anything. I'll make this right soon." Alexis walks in the room and closes the door.

Meanwhile, Kim walks in her front door and goes straight to her bedroom without saying a word. Mike is lying on the couch watching TV and notices she has been crying. He follows her to her room and knocks on her door. "Kim? Kim, honey, open the door!" He can hear running water. "Kim? Will you please open the door?" Kim continues to wash her face. "I guess you found out?" Kim raises her face from the rag and begins to listen. "About his pregnant girlfriend?" He continues.

Kim opens her door. "You knew?"

"I saw them coming out of the mini mart one day."

"You knew?" She raises her eyebrow. "And you let me take my happy ass over there and embarrass myself!"

"Kim you were gonna go anyway. And me telling you would not have made a difference. I knew you; you would have wanted to see it for yourself."

Kim cuffs her face into her hands and begins to cry again. Mike pulls her closer to hold her. "I know it hurts babe, but Kim you have got to stop being selfish; you can't expect this man to sit around and wait on you while you do what you want to do."

"But you don't understand; A baby, Mike? We talking about you bringing another child in the world with another female. Not to mention she looks pretty big which means he had to be seeing her when we were together." She buries her head in his chest and continues to cry.

"Listen, honey… come on, I know it doesn't feel good right now, and it's gonna take some time getting past this but Lil Don is here for you okay?" I couldn't be there before, but we gonna get through this okay?"

She nods her head in agreement. "Now come on; I have something that will make you laugh a little." They walk in the living room… "Sit here while I fix you a glass of wine to relax." After he fixes the wine, he sits the glass on a coaster and changes the DVD. "Your favorite movie, *Hangover*, and a glass of Moscata Rose'….. Here come lay next to me." He scoots over and as she lays down, he puts the blanket over the two of them. She scoots back towards him and he puts his arms around her. She drinks her wine and laughs a little bit and half way through the movie she falls to sleep. Mike looks at her and kisses the back of her neck and holds her tighter.

My poor baby. He thinks to himself. *You will rise above this. One thing I know for sure, you gone always be my girl, my homie, my Ace, my Bestie as you would say.* He smiles. *I love you Kim. Look at you sleeping all peacefully. I don't know if you're exhausted from all the crying or the relaxation from the wine. Or it could be a combination*

[287]

of the two. You're so adorable. He thinks as he strokes her hair. *Even though destiny didn't see us together, I feel a strong connection with you.* He closes his eyes and falls asleep holding her all night.

Over the next couple of weeks, Mike keeps his word and stays devoted to his friend Kim. When she comes in from work he has dinner cooked and a nice hot bubble bath waiting for her. One night she had been so tired, she came home and went straight to the tub to relax. "Kim!" Mike calls her name as he knocks on her door. "Kim honey, the food is ready." After waiting a few seconds for a response he taps on the door again only this time he turns the knob to open at the same time. "Kim, Honey. The food is done." He repeats himself. Upon slowly gazing in he sees she is sound asleep. "Kim, honey wake up," she is so tired she doesn't hear him come in. Mike takes the towel from behind the door and lifts her from the tub and dries her off, he then put her robe around her and place her in her bed. The next morning while Kim is getting dress Mike comes and taps on the door. "Come in."

"Good morning," Mike speaks.

"Good morning."

"You were very tired last night, huh?"

"I don't remember anything from the time I walked in the door. I remember getting off work and I made a detour. I road by Keith's house and I saw his lil' pregnant girlfriend going in the building. She can't be from here 'cause I never saw her before; however, she does have a familiar face. But, anyway, the heifer can dress; she had on

[288]

blue skinny jeans with a long grey top and these bangin' sandle boots. But she can't be no more than eighteen, nineteen….

"We are not doing this today," he interjects. "Do not start your day like this, hon."

"You're right…… moving forward; so how did I end up in my robe?"

"You came in and went straight to the room; I knocked on the door to tell you dinner was ready, you didn't answer so I went in and found you fast asleep in the tub; I took you out and put you in the bed."

Kim looks him in his eye and softly speaks, "Mike, thank you….. I don't know what I would do without you. I mean all my life it's been one disappointment after another. I'm so tired of getting hurt or hurting other people, I just wanna scream."

"I'm proud of you Mommie; listen you have done well for yourself, Miss Independent. You have your own condo, your own business-- successful business, I may add. No kids. You struggled a long time to get here and you did it….. Enjoy it! Every moment of it, enjoy it. Don't let any man offset your mind to where you can't enjoy the things God has blessed you with. Everything you went through happened for a reason….. God takes you places you never been, strange places, unfamiliar territory, and the unknown scares you, but if He takes you there, you got to know he will bring you through. Though it may not feel good to be in unfamiliar territory, just know that your trials and tests come to make you strong…… See you've been hurt before, but each time was a different type hurt, am I right?" She nods her head. And see this hurt is a new hurt an unfamiliar hurt and when God gets through perfecting this thing in you, you gone be able to recognize all the hurts by name; ain't nobody gonna be able to tell you about hurt. You gone have hurt down to the tee. But I believe God is building you and setting you up for where He's taking you. And where He's taking you, He needs you to be solid as a brick wall because when things start to come at you, He don't need you to be easily offended….. I'm just saying." He throws up both his hands. "Food for thought."

"You always had a way with words… Encouragement, that's your gift," she smiles.

"That may be one of them," he answers back. "Say, how about we get away from here for a little while; take a mini vacation. You need it and I can use it as well."

"What do you have in mind?"

"Anywhere you wanna go?" he answers.

"How 'bout to the beach?"

"I said anywhere and you say the beach, Kim? Really?"

She smiles, "Okay then well surprise me. When are we leaving?"

"I'll let you know when you get in from work."

Brittney

Brittney is on her way to her new salon, H.B.I.C., listening to *How Can I Ease the Pain* by Lisa Fischer. Just as she is about to hit the high note, her phone rings.

"Hello," she answers.

"Brittney, Devin's in the hospital."

"What you callin' me for? Call his momma."

Tim takes a deep sigh. "Look I'm sorry, I need you right now."

"No what you need to do is call that bitch you been hanging out with."

"Look, I'm done with that Honey.

"And I'm done with you!" She hangs up the phone.

The phone rings again and she looks at it and ignores it. She pulls up at the salon and gets out. As she walks in the door, a spirit of peace overcomes her. The earth tone contrast on the walls, and the décor really makes the place feel cozy and inviting. The Water fall cascade down the wall to the left makes the ambiance warm and relaxing. The smell of the Fruiti Tutti scent embellishes the whole building.

"Lord I couldn't have made it this far without you. Thank you so much for all you have done for me. Thank you for covering this place. Let every chair be filled with returning clients and let every booth be filled with faithful, loyal, dedicated, and passionate stylists," she prays. "Now all I have to do is paint this back room and redo these floors then I'll be ready to open. Thank God."

Brittney works the next few hours painting the back area of the salon. When she finishes, she sits back and marvels at the beautiful work she had done. "Wow I can't believe I'm almost done. Whew! It's time to get out of here now, I'll come back later and put the second coat on and have the floors done on Wednesday and I'll be ready for business." She smiles.

Brittney looks at her watch and notices that it is getting later and later. She locks up the salon and heads towards the door. Just as she is getting in the car, her phone stops ringing. When she looks at it, she notices she has twenty missed calls; nineteen of them were from Tim. The last one was from Kim.

She calls Kim back, "hello, you just called me?" she asks.

"Yes, what you doing?"

"Just finished painting the back room at the salon."

"Oh cool, how's it coming along?"

"Girl I'm 'bout ready to open these doors!"

"Really? You done that much? How come you haven't called me, I would have helped?"

"I know but I wanted it to be a project I did on my own. I just repainted all the rooms, took the carpet up, now all I have left to do is go over one more wall with another coat of paint, then have the tile put down on Wednesday."

"Ooo Britt, I bet it looks nice, I want to see it."

"You'll see it soon."

"So listen, guess who called my phone today?" Kim says

"Who?" Brittney responds.

"Tim!"

"Girl bye," she says in her Ne Ne Leaks voice "I don't want to hear that foolishness. He called me earlier talking 'bout his son Devin is in the hospital."

"What's wrong with him?"

"The hell if I know; I said what the fuck you callin' me for? Call his momma."

"Britt, you did not say that?" Kim laughs.

"Yes I did to….Girl ain't nobody got time for his games. He thought the grass was greener on the other side 'til he started smelling that manure."

"Britt, you know I don't care for the man, but he sounded really sincere. He wants to talk to you."

"Kim, think about it. If your son is in the hospital, would you be more concerned about your son or your ex, who you done wrong and ain't studdin yo ass?"

"So you trying to say his son ain't in the hospital?"

"I don't know, but his priorities are backwards."

"Maybe he just need you there with him," Kim suggests.

"Hell, what about when I needed his tail?"

"Britt, you did fish the man house. You can kinda say yall even; just hear what he has to say."

"Whatever! I don't want to talk about him no more. What's going on with you? Did you ever call Keith?"

"Girl let me tell you, I've been so depressed these past few weeks, but thank God, Donanvan has been a true friend. Girl he has been taking care of me. You hear me? Well to make a long story tolerable, I went over to Keith house and some teenie bopper was there; she was cute, I'll give her that, but she looks like she couldn't be no more than eighteen or nineteen."

"Whaaat?"

"Um um hold on get this, she was pregnant."

"Shut the Mutha fuckin' front door, Kim!... Are you serious?"

"No lie."

"What did he say?"

Kim braces herself so that she can relive the moment once again for Brittney. "We got into it; it was very intense but he didn't deny it."

"Did he admit it?"

"No Britt, but his ass didn't deny it either; listen, I don't want to talk about it anymore. I'm still not over that shit."

"Okay cool, you should of called me; I woulda came by and got you out the house and we could of hung out, and perhaps caused a slip and fall accident."

"Cause who to slip and fall?"

"Don't you still have the key to Keith's apartment or you gave it back?"

"I have it. Why?"

"I mean we could have waxed his floor with some Crisco, Wesson, Canola, Peanut, Olive or even coconut oil."

[294]

Kim starts laughing. "Girl you are Gone with the wind Stupid; with a capital 'S'!"

"I know; pray for my mind, child. What are you doing now?"

"Nothing at the moment, just finished packing."

"Packing? Where are you going?"

"Don is taking me away from here for a few days."

"Well I'm coming by to get you. You need to get out the house for a lil' bit."

"Okay, where are you now?" Kim asks.

"Right around the corner. I'll be there in two minutes."

"Okay, let me throw on some clothes."

When Brittney hangs up the phone she notices she has five voice messages on her phone. She dials the number, *you have five new messages and seventeen saved messages, you have two messages which are due for automatic deletion, the messages must be resaved…. Save message due for automatic deletion…*She hits the number nine twice *message saved, message saved……New message…. "Britt, honey. Look, we need to talk. I'm out here to the hospital…" Message deleted. New message… "Britt honey…."* *Message deleted. New message… "I fucked up…" Message deleted…New message… Message deleted… New message "Britt, I don't know what else to say, I miss you girl. Can we talk? Hit me back." Message deleted.* When she pull up outside the complex, she calls Kim back, "hey Kim, I'm outside."

"Okay I'm coming." She hangs up the phone. "Hey Don, I'll be back in a little bit."

"Where you going?"

"I'm gonna hang with Britt for a little while; we'll probably go by and visit Monet or something."

"I still haven't met this Brittney…."

"I'll have her to come in when we get back."

"Sounds good. Hey you make sure you have yourself some fun. Lord knows you need it."

"I will - see ya in a little bit."

"So where are we going?" Kim asks Britt when she gets in the car.

"I don't know; what do you want to do?" Britt asks.

"Let's go see what Monet is doing," Kim suggests.

"When was the last time you spoke with her?" Britt asks.

"The day we all met at the salon. She should be home; it's after five. What about you?"

"She called me one day, telling me Traci wasn't feeling her best."

"Yeah, let's go see her. Then the three of us can ride over to Traci's house," Kim suggests.

"Should we call her?" Brittney asks.

"Nawl... let's just go over there. Hey speaking of salon, did you come up with a name?"

"Yep. HBIC."

"I like that... Head Bitch In Charge." She smiles, "…but I don't know if I like that for a salon name though."

"Girl, HBIC stands for Hair Braiding In Cutz."

"That's the best you can come up with?" Kim laughs.

"You got something better?"

"We gone pray about that one. And why are you going this way?"

"I'm taking a short cut to Monet's house."

"No you taking a short cut to Keith's house. Look Britt for real for real. I can't do this. I don't want to see him, her, his car, his house…."

"Shh, shh, shh! Is that him leaving?"

"Follow him," Kim remarks.

"I thought you didn't want anything to do with him."

"I don't," she says looking sad. "Let's go on to Moni's. So what's going on with Tim? Did you call him back?"

"Nope. And I'm not."

"Britt, just hear what he has to say. Yall been together just as long as me and Keith were."

Britt saw the sincerity in Kim's eyes and thought about what she was saying. She begins to replay in her mind the games he played and how she had to investigate to find out for herself because he wasn't man enough to tell her on his own. She thought their relationship was worth more than that.

"He hurt me, Kim."

"Don't let the spirit of Pride overtake you, Britt. You know you have to forgive."

"I'll forgive him," she responds hurtfully.

"Seriously, Britt."

"I want to so bad, I really do, but I don't know how. One day I will, but not just now."

"You have to now because tomorrow is not promised. It's a hard thing to do, but it's a command from the Lord….. Britt you know this, I don't have to tell you… The bible say if you have an aught against your brother, you need to lay your gift down and go reconcile with him or her."

"Good thing I don't have a gift," Britt says sarcastically

"OMG! What am I gonna do with you?" Kim laughs. "You are too much like me! Let me ask you this….Other than this, has he ever done anything else that was so unforgivable?"

"Nawl, He has never given me a reason to think otherwise, but Kim he *cheated* on me!"

"Talk to him," Kim whispers. "…and why are you still following Him?"

"Why does it look like he's going to your house?"

"Girl SHUT-UP! Why is he riding by my apartments?"

"Maybe he misses you."

"BULLSHIT!" Let's go over to Monet's house; you done pissed me off, talking 'bout maybe he miss me. If he missed me he wouldn't of got that chick pregnant. If he missed me he shoulda called, texted, put a message in a bottle or something!"

"Maybe he wanted to but he doesn't know what's going on with you and Don or maybe…."

"Enough with the speculations. I'm getting sick."

"That's that unforgiveness," Brittney laughs.

When they make it to Mone't house, they notice a new model navy blue Cadillac Escalade truck in her yard with an out of town tag.

"This heifa got company," Kim says.

"I knew we should have called," Britt remarks.

[298]

"Well we here now." Kim comments.

They get out the car and knock on the door. She doesn't answer.

"Knock! Knock!" Kim yells.

"Mooni, Moni Moni, Mooooni," Brittney sings.

"God must you two always be so rachet!" Monet says as she opens the door.

"We sorry, you should of came to the door the first five times we knocked and rang the doorbell," Kim says.

"What 'cha doing? You have company? Brittney asks as they walk in.

"What yall want and why didn't you call before yall came over?"

"I told Kim we need to call, but she said, 'nawl, we'll just bust up in there like Hancock.'" Brittney does a karate kick to demonstrate.

"Hi ladies." Kim and Brittney look up.

"Well well well, looka whose here… Babydaddy!" Brittney comments.

"How are you Mitchell?" Kim asks.

"I'm good."

"We haven't been formally introduced but I've seen a picture and heard about you,- I'm Brittney."

"Nice to meet you Brittney. – Look I'mma get outta yall way. Monet, I'll see you later. Take care of my baby" He rubs her stomach, then kisses her on the forehead. "Alright, you ladies take it easy."

When he walks out the door Brittney comments, "Dang, that mutha…."

"Unn unn," Kim interrupts.

"Sorry, my bad." Britt breaks out of her trance. "…but dude got it going on--voice of Keith Sweat and the looks of Rick Fox. Dang! Can we share baby daddies?"

"Everything that glitter ain't gold," Monet comments.

"What is he doing here? " Kim asks.

"He came back to check on me and guess what? He found out his lil boy wasn't his. His wife lied to him." She showed them a picture of the lil boy on her phone.

"She knew better than that," Kim comments.

"Nawl, *he* knew better than that," Brittney comments. "He knew damn well that boy didn't look nothing like him."

"He's talking 'bout me moving up there and being a family--and stuff."

"No Moni. That's some rebound type shit? Brittney says.

"Yeah you better think, well, pray about that," Kim adds.

"I am. So what yall two doing today?"

"Nothing much. Britt came to get me out the house; I was depressed about Keith and I really don't want to talk about it right now."

"Keith?" Monet asks.

"Another time Monet?" Brittney pleads.

"So what's going on with Traci?" Kim asks.

"I talked to her earlier today and she was doing well," Monet answers.

"I was thinking we could go by and see her. Are you feeling up to it?" Kim asks.

"That's cool. I'll give her a call and let her know, unlike some people I know," Monet sarcastically retorts.

"So how have you been feeling?" Brittney asks Monet.

"I've been doing good."

"If you wasn't, would you tell us?" Kim asks.

"No!" Monet smiles. "I'll be right back." Monet goes to her room…

"Okay I'm ready."

"Did you call her?" Kim asks.

"Oh yeah; she said it would be okay."

"Okay, you guys fill me in on what's been going on in yall life. Wait! Wait! Wait! You guys remember the Barbecue is the Saturday after next."

"Awe Shit!" Kim and Brittney say at the same time.

"Yall forgot?"

"Not really," Brittney says.

"Uuugh….. I did," Kim replies.

"Okay, I did too," Brittney admits.

"But it's cool, though. We can still do it; we just need to figure out the place and start letting everybody know now," Kim says.

"We can have it at my place," Monet offers.

Kim picks up her phone to dial Butrays' number… *Nawl, I better text him cause he gonna want to talk.* She thinks to herself. "Oooh yall guess what? Guess who called me and wanted to talk to me about her husband?"

"That can be anybody Kim." Monet says; she and Britt laugh.

"Ha Ha. So funny," Kim says sarcastically. "I'm so done with that life. Anyways, it was Patricia."

"SHUT THE FRONT DOOR!" Brittney exclaims.

[301]

Monet couldn't say a word; she just held her mouth open.

"So what did she say?" Brittney asks.

"It was crazy 'cause she called me to talk about Tray but ended up talking 'bout her affair with Pastor."

Brittney slams on the brakes and looks over at Kim. "Say what now Bitch?" Kim bursts out laughing.

"KIM! SHE'S SLEEPING WITH THE PASTOR?" Monet leans towards the front seat.

"Monet, you knew that," Kim says. "I told you that when we saw them together at that restaurant."

Monet thinks back, "Yep, you right, I forgot all about that."

"KIM?" Brittney calls her name with disbelief.

"What? Will you drive?" Kim answers still tickled.

"I'm saying…"

"I know…will you just go!" Kim cuts her off. When Brittney pulls off, Kim stops laughing long enough to continue. "It's been going on for a while now and get this; she got pregnant…"

"Oh I can't take no more," Monet says.

"But he told her to get an abortion," Kim continues.

"Okay let's talk about something else!" Monet shouts.

"No hold up," Brittney interrupts. "…so what does Butray have to do with this?"

"Well, she doesn't want to be with Pastor anymore and she wants her husband back. I think she just wanted someone to talk to."

"So she doesn't know about you and…"

Kim shakes her head.

[302]

"So she chose you to talk to, out of all people, the one that's been screwing her husband?" Monet asks.

"We were bartering, for God's sake!" Kim says with a smile.

"Bartering? Brittney laughs. "I've heard enough; get out," she says as she pulls up to Traci's house.

Tracy comes to the door, "Heeey!" She greets them with a hug. "Yall come on in. I'm in here preparing dinner for the kids; Robbie has to work late. – You guys can come in the kitchen. Have yall eaten anything?"

"What you cookin'?" Brittney asks. Walking through the front door. "Tracy I love the hardwood flooring and this chocolate and cream is really pretty. How do you keep it clean with two small kids?"

"Oh honey, they do not come in here. They know Momma don't play that.

"Now that chocolate wall sets it off in here, I wouldn't have thought of that." Brittney says as she continues to follow Traci in the kitchen. Kim and Monet slowly follows behind.

"Who is Robbie?" Kim whispers to Monet.

"Robbie is her husband."

"He sounds white," Kim remarks.

"Close," Monet answers back. "He's black and Columbian or black and Dominican. I can't remember."

"Oh is this him?" Kim asks as she picks up a family portrait with a white back drop. The whole family had on a red shirt, blue jeans and they all had their shoes off.

"Yep." Monet answers.

[303]

"He almost looks like your baby daddy," she says to Monet. "No wonder you and Traci hit it off. Yall both like light skin men with wavy hair." She notices more family pictures as she gazes around the living room.

"Hey are you two coming?" Brittney peeps into the living room. "She asked if we want anything to eat."

"Dang, he looks good!" Kim continues to look around the room and back at the family portrait.

"Give me that!" Monet snatches the picture out of her hand. "My friend husband better not become one of your victims!"

Kim steps back and looks at her; "You must think I'm some hoe or something?"

Monet steps back and gives her a look.

"Ummm, excuse me. I hate to interrupt yall hoedown but do you guys want something to eat; she's waiting on an answer?" Brittney diverts.

Monet steps away and goes into the kitchen; Kim proceeds to walk behind her with Brittney.

"Did you just hear her call me a hoe?" She asks Brittney.

"She didn't call you a hoe, Kim," Brittney laughs.

"She might as well, you seen the way she looked at me? She better be glad she pregnant or I would kick her in the back of her knee," Kim whispers.

"Sorry girl, we were looking at your pictures up front," Monet says.

"Yeah I was telling Monet, you have a good looking husband and she seems to think that I want him because I gave him a compliment."

"He Is Fine!" Traci reiterates with a smile and gives Kim a high-five.

"I told her he better not become a victim." Monet rolls her eyes.

"Traci…I **met** you, I **know** you and I **like** you; therefore, I wouldn't **do** you," Kim comments.

"Traci smiles, "I know you wouldn't and she know you wouldn't either, Monet. Leave her alone. You guys want something to eat?"

"What you cooked Kim asked?"

"Lasagna. Come on yall get a plate. I cooked two pans," she insists and hands Kim the spatula.

Kim took the spatula and a plate and the others fell in line behind her. Traci takes out three glasses and begins to pour some wine and she refills her glass as well.

"Yeah like I was saying, Kim, Monet knows you wouldn't do anything like that. She talks about you all the time. She's quite fond of you actually. If she had an alter ego, I think it would be you."

"Really now!" Kim asks surprisingly.

"Traci?" Monet calls her name in disbelief.

"Monet, come on; you always talking about Kim and her men and how she does this and that but you also talk about her sweet side, how thoughtful and fun she is and how she makes you laugh."

Monet takes a sip of wine. "Kim knows she's my girl, I Lylas her…. Yall remember that from back in the day, Lylas? We use to write them on notes in middle school. L.y.l.a.s, Love you like a sister.

"I Lylas yo ass too but you better not start that damn crying and shit. And when did you start back drinking? Matter fact why are you drinking and you pregnant?"

[305]

"I'll have a glass of wine to relax every now and then. Most doctors don't recommend it but some do. Mine just happen to be one of the ones that do. She says it will help keep my stress level down. And especially in my condition, I don't need to be stressed or worried 'bout nothing."

"You all come with me; we're going to eat out on the patio. The wind is blowing and it's nice and cool.

"Heeey" Kim says captivated by the center fireplace shaped like a huge bowl in the middle of the patio. "I love this, when you said patio I was thinking we were coming to sit on those plastic beach chairs or something." She smiles. "But this is really really nice Traci."

"Thank you, Kim. I think this patio is why I fell in love with this house. Sometimes me and Robbie come out here just to relax and we find ourselves out here talking for hours."

"Britt," Traci continues. "Monet talks about you as well."

"Traci, if I knew you had a big mouth…." Monet jumps in.

"Too late now; yall done messed around and let me in the wolf pack. There was one of us then there was two," mocking Allen from the movie *Hangover*. Kim starts laughing.

"I love that movie! That is my favorite movie," Kim says. "What about this *he's like a fucking gremlin and shit, he comes with instructions.*" Everybody laughs.

Then Monet says, "What about this--*is there a payphone around here? I might get a beep on my beeper.*"

"No, no, no! *Does Caesar live here?*" Brittney puts her two cents in.

Everybody is laughing hysterically. "That movie is the best," Traci says. They continue to quote other parts of the movie for the next twenty minutes; then on to reality shows such as *Basketball Wives, Atlanta Housewives*, and *Hip Hop Atlanta*. While they continue to talk, Traci grabs another bottle of wine out the fridge.

"Hi hon," she kiss her husband. "How was work today?"

"I had a pretty good day at the office today." He says as he pulls her close to embrace her. "How was your day?"

"I had a good day, the ladies came over. We're having dinner and wine out back. Your plate is in the microwave." She sets the timer to one minute to heat up his food. "Come on back." She takes his hand, "I want you to meet everybody." They walk out to the patio area.

"Everybody this is my husband, Robbie."

"Hi hubbie," Kim says.

"Hi," Brittney speaks.

"That's Kim and that's Brittney and, of course, you know Monet.

"Yeah I know Moni. How you ladies doing tonight?"

"We are quite lovely," Kim speaks properly and everyone laughs.

"How much wine did you guys have?" Robbie asks smiling.

"We're good," Kim answers.

"I see, feeling REEAAL GOOD!" He quotes

"Hey thanks for the hospitality, and I want you to know, you have a very beautiful wife; inside and out," Kim says.

"Thank you." He turns and looks at Traci, "This is my baby, the apple to my martini, the sun in my morning, the moon in my night. I love this woman unconditionally. She is strong, vibrant, thoughtful and caring. She also keeps me laughing. She makes me happy."

"We make each other happy, babe." Traci chimes in and kisses him as well, "Now go get your food, with your romantic self." She smacks him on the butt when he turns around.

"Dang, that was some romantic shit right there. I was trying to think of who can I call and love on," Kim says jokingly.

"Me too, then I thought, I ain't got nobody," Britt comments.

"I was thinking the same thing as well," Monet speaks properly with a tear streaming down her face.

"Monet I told your ass, don't start that crying and shit. What's wrong with you?"

"I don't know…" she bursts into tears.

"She's backed up; she need to get some," Brittney says.

"I'm just thankful to have friends like yall. And Traci I'm thankful that God had us to meet. You guys are the funniest people I know; yall keep me in good spirits. And Britt… Traci was right. I do talk about you; I say how you are such a good friend, and you have been there for me. I love all yall like a sister. Let's toast to that, Lylas. They all throw up their glasses and say, "*LYLAS!*"

"Monet, the baby drunk," Kim says in a joking manner and everybody is rolling on the floor laughing their butts off.

"I only had one and a half glass, thank you." Monet comments with a smile.

"And I'll like to say," Brittney interrupts laughing. "I know we been drinking but I'm not drunk. I have a high tolerance; I'm just relaxed, but I'll like to say, Monet, Kim and my new found sista Traci, I love you all…"

"It's **Yall** not **you all**. You are drunk," Kim interjects smiling.

"And Monet," Brittney continues with her speech ignoring Kim's comment. "…you try to keep me level headed. Kim, you bring out that bull dog in me. Traci, what can I say...? Nothing but love for you; you are a strong woman, mother, wife, you're patient, caring, I see you are about unity and you're family oriented. And I love the chemistry between you and Robbie. That's some real love type shit--I meant stuff there."

They all are laying back in their chairs gazing at the stars in the sky.

"It's so beautiful out here." Monet breaks the silence.

"Traci, I must say you have inspired me," Kim remarks. "You have been through so much, the chemo, radiation, and for you to be in good spirits… and let me say that you look good, too, lady."

"Thank you girls so much for coming by today; you can't begin to imagine what you have done for me. Sometimes I do have meltdowns. I have good days and bad days. Some days I'm so weak I can't get out of bed and some days I have a burst of energy. I feel like I inherited a bipolar spirit." She laughs a little. "This has been a very humbling journey; my husband is there for me every single time. He tells me I'm beautiful, we take walks together; we have even talked about if I don't make it…"

"Traci, No don't do this," Monet gets up and gives her a hug. Traci begins to tear up. Brittney and Kim join Monet.

"Traci, honey, no, don't talk like that!" Brittney says.

"Tracy, honey, listen to me. I sympathize with you, I know this can't be easy; you shall live and not die to declare the works of the Lord. I'm speaking that, and I want you to believe that. You have faith, right?" Kim says.

Traci nods her head. "Thank yall so much, I love yall… We got to plan a girls' trip. I would say a family trip but yall got to get a man first." They all laugh.

"We definitely need to do that." Everybody agrees.

"Well I'm leaving tomorrow for a mini getaway," Kim says.

"Where are you going?" Traci asks.

"I'm not sure. Mike said I need to get out of town to get my mind off Keith. He asked me where I wanted to go, and I said the beach."

"He gave you the option to go anywhere and you said the beach?" Traci asks.

"That's the same thing he said." Kim smiles. "I just told him to surprise me."

"Well good," Traci comments. Yall know what I've been thinking about lately?"

"What's that?" They ask.

"We need to start back going to church more often."

"We need a new pastor," Kim comments.

"I believe we need to do more outreach now that the new building is ready. At least we have a stable place to have worship service." Traci directs to Kim.

"I know, right? 'Cause there will be times if Kim don't want to be bothered, she'll tell Pastor, 'yall take that somewhere else or Monet house, I won't be in town'; she love to holla she going out of town."

"Girl, I be tired. I need a break from all that foolishness," Kim comments.

"So you saying church is foolishness?" Traci asks.

"NOOO! The people with their foolishness. All that carrying on, talking 'bout folks, tearing up people chairs, and cussing….just being totally disrespectful."

"Who be cussing?" Brittney asks.

"Derrick and them, I had to get on them one time. I told them just because we're not in a church building, does not mean we're not having church. And see I don't have time for all that playing and shit."

"Okay, let's make a pact," Traci suggests. "Let's be the change we want to see in others. Let's make a difference in other people lives. We need to get with Pastor and the other members and have a meeting. Kim, you seem to be good at managing things and so are you Monet, maybe you two can work on the people in the church and me and Brittney can work outside, doing street ministry or something and help bring more people in. Everybody is not called to do ministry inside the church…"

"I know mine is outside the church," Brittney interrupts.

"Mine too," Traci says. "…so we can get with Pastor and start delegating and creating some ministries and things for the people.

"What type ministries you have in mine?" Monet asks.

"Women's, Men's, children, clothing, food, street team, whateva is going to help build up God's kingdom. But first we need to make changes within ourselves because we want what we do to be pure. Kim and Brittney, I love you. Please don't curse at me," she says hesitantly," but you two have got to stop cussing…"

"See Traci it's like this, I look at cursing like a sentence enhancer…" Kim says.

"Yeah, it makes your words more colorful!" Brittney agrees with a smile.

"You twoooooo!" Traci smiles clenching her teeth together.

"Traci, hon, we know… We talk about it all the time. And actually, I was doing good," Kim says.

"She was. She really was," Brittney cosigns.

"But we are working on it, right Brittney?" Kim asks and Brittney responds with a "yes."

"But on a side bar; we are having a big Bar B Chu the Saturday after next and we will love for you, Robbie, and the kids to come. What's their names?"

"Jada and Jalen," Traci answers.

"Oh you have a Jalen too!" Kim says.

"Yep, but mine is spelled with an 'e' and I believe you spell yours with an 'i', Brittney?"

Brittney nods her head.

"Are they twins?" Kim asks.

"Yes, they are."

"Beautiful," Kim answers. "But hey please come, it's going to be at Monet's."

"You know I will. Do we need to bring anything?"

"Nope just yourselves," Kim answers. "Well, it's getting kind of late and I got to make sure I have everything for my trip tomorrow. Thanks so much for feeding me, and the wine, you got to tell me where you get it from, so I can get some for the Chu."

"Girl I'll bring some."

"And I'll pay you. Where is your bathroom?" Kim asks. She points in the direction. "Monet, you know you better let some of that out before your baby be drunk .Mitchell gone kick your tail; he ain't fallin' for *'my doctor said it helps me relax'* shit--I meant stuff. Don't trip he ain't through with me yet," she smiles.

"Girl take yo' crazy tail to the bathroom so I can use it," Monet says.

"No, you can go first, I can wait. You the one got the extra body in you."

"Kim does it ever stop?" Traci asks with a smile.

"Nope," Monet answers as she walks pass Kim to go to the bathroom. After everybody uses the restroom, they all say their good byes and go home.

Monet is the first to get dropped off. "Moni, does Mitchell have a key? How did he get back in the house?" Brittney asks.

"He thinks he has a key. I gave him an old one and I just leave the door unlocked." She smiles.

"Kim, we have taught her well…. High-five bitch I meant sis," she says to Monet.

"Kim walk her up there and do ding dong ditch," Britt laughs.

"I am not drunk!" Monet shouts with a smile.

"Then why are you yelling?" Brittney asks.

"Because you guys are clowning me."

"That's because we love you, now let me help you."

"Love you guys," Monet says.

"Love you too," they both answer.

Brittney remains in the car while Kim walks her to the door. "Kim, you and Mike have a safe trip and I'll see you when you get back. Let me get my keys." Kim rings the doorbell and takes off running to the car laughing. Brittney sits in the car cheering her on. "Come on, come on!" Monet turns around and smiles. "Yall too old for that crap!" She yells.

Mitchell comes to the door, "Why are they driving off so fast?"

"They old behinds playing ding dong ditch."

"Oh!" Mitchell smiles. "Sound like you guys had fun."

While driving to Kim's house, Britt asks Kim is she excited about her vacation. Kim answers that she was very excited and anxious. "But I will be even more excited when the four of us go on vacation," Kim says.

"Well when you get back, we'll get together and make some arrangements."

"So are you gonna at least talk to Tim and hear what he has to say, Britt?"

Britt takes a deep sigh.

"Swallow that pride, Britt!"

"I guess I'll listen to him." She pulls up to the complex. "Listen have fun, be safe, I love ya…"

"Oh Donavan wants to meet you."

"Girl it is super late; I'll meet him when you guys come back."

"It's only eleven o clock!" Kim responds.

"Girl, get out of my car!"

"Alright see ya….. Call me when you get home; let me know you made it."

"Okay," Brittney responds and watches Kim until she makes it in her apartment.

Meanwhile Tim is passing by Brittney's house for the tenth time tonight. He picks up his phone to call her and once again she doesn't answer. *Damn I fucked up!* He thinks to himself. He turns the radio up and Lyfe Jennings, *Must Be Nice* is playing. He begins to head back towards his hotel room and as he's riding vibing to the music. He passes Brittney going in the opposite direction. He takes his feet off the gas, "that look like my cupcake right there," he says looking through the rearview mirror. "I think that is her." He turns around and head in the same direction as the car he assumes is Brittney. When she pulls up in her driveway, he pulls on the side of the road in front of the house, gets out the car, and leaves his door open with the music playing. He walks up to the window and taps on it.

"Shoot, you scared me, boy!" She lets down her window; he notices she is listening to the same station. He starts to speak, but doesn't quite know how to articulate the words at the moment; he gets caught up in the lyrics of the song and as the two of them stare at one another; the chorus comes on….. ♫*Even when those hustlin' days are gone, she'll be by your side still holding on and even when those twenties stop spinning and all those gold diggin' women disappear, you'll still be here.*♫ – He leans his forearm on her door while his forehead rests on his arm. As she sits in her car she look straight ahead with an deaf ear because at the point she can careless for any explanation he has to give.

 "I love you girl," he whispers in a soft succulent voice. Brittney doesn't flinch, but she begins to think to herself; *love? love?* Then the words of *Love don't live here anymore* by Rose Royce begin to ring in her head.

"I'm sorry I hurt you. I'm sorry I disrespected you. Girl, you mean so much…get out the car." Tim opens the door. She jumps at the sound of the door opening because she was still in a zone listening to the Rose Royce song in her head. "Britt get out! Come on we're better than this."

Her pride doesn't want her to break however he continues to stand there with the door open waiting for her to get out. "Britt?"

 After the song on the radio goes off, she exits the car and tries to walk pass him to go in the house. He grabs her hand and tears began to flow down her face, he pulls her back to the car. With her back against the car door, she holds her head down so he won't see the tears. He stands in front of her and raises her head by cuffing his hand on her chin; "Babe, please don't cry." He wipes her tears. As he's pulling her close to embrace her and she goes off into a rage and push him.

[316]

"Don't touch me!" she yells. "You promised me, you promised me. Tim. And I trusted you to always be honest with me. We had a pack to always keep it one hundred!"

"I know babe and I…I…I.." He tries to pull her close.

"Don't you fuckin' touch me! Who is she? How long have you been seeing her? Where did you meet her? Is she one of your hoes?"

"ALRIGHT! ALRIGHT! ALRIGHT! I MESSED UP! SHIT! I MESSED UP!" He's yelling as he spends around cuffing his nose and mouth with his hand. "AND I'M SORRY DAMMIT!

"SORRY FOR WHAT, TIM?"

"FOR HURTING YOU!"

"SORRY FOR WHAT MUTHA FUCKA?"

"FOR HURTING YOU!"

"HOW DID YOU HURT ME? I want to hear you say it!"

Tim looks at her with tears falling from his eyes; she stares back with a strong face waiting for an answer.

"Damn, Brittney." He drops his head.

Even though they both know he cheated, she wants him to acknowledge verbally what he did wrong. She wants him to understand why she is so hurt. Tim doesn't want to verbally admit it because as a man he's thinking he wants to spare her feelings, and he doesn't want to hurt her. But what he fails to internalize is that she is already hurt. And at his point all she wants to hear is the truth no matter what. And the truth she desires to hear will actually set her free; free to forgive and move forward in the relationship or free to move on without him. *Men, what you have to realize is that your rebuilding can start right here with your honesty....Selah.*

"Just what I thought, get the fuck out of my yard!" She walks off towards the house.

"I'm sorry, I cheated!" He yells.

Britt stops and takes a deep sigh. Tim begins walking up behind her.

"I cheated and I'm sorry. Look, babe, we been together four almost five years and I have NEVER, NEVER, cheated on you or even given you a reason to think there was somebody else. I never disrespected you; I love you, Britt--you and Jay. I was tricked and I admit I let the devil use me, and I want to do whateva it takes to make this right." She turns around and looks at him. "Will you forgive me?"

She takes a deep breath, and thinks about the things Kim said to her.

"You have a lot of explaining to do," she answers angrily.

He swallows and shakes his head while looking into her eyes. "Can I come in?"

"You stink."

"Yeah it's my clothes," he says smelling them. "I may have to get a whole new wardrobe. I've been staying in a hotel 'cause my place smells like a fish market or oyster bar or something."

"Where do you think it's coming from?" she asks.

"I don't know, I think maybe from under the house. A cat might have crawled under there and died."

Brittney squints her eyes and raises one eyebrow. "Well I guess you can come in, but you gonna have to leave them clothes on the outside."

[318]

"Britt!"

"What? You ain't about to stink up my place."

"I'm not about to get undressed on the porch."

She looks at him with her brows frowned and lips puckered. "Well take yo ass back to the hotel then, your cheating ass."

"Listen, am I gonna have to hear this all the time?"

"Maybe, but you the one fucked up not me."

"Do I still have some clothes in there or did you throw them away?"

"There is nothing of yours in there. Get undressed and I'll bring you something." She walks off.

"Can you turn the light off? This some bull shit, I want you to know that!"

She smiles and continues to walk in the house. She comes back with a pair of tights.

"What the hell is this?"

"Yoga pants," she answers.

"What the hell am I supposed to do with this?

"Put them on."

"Britt quit playing, you know damn well I can't fit these!"

"Well stay out here until you put them on or take your butt back to the fish aquarium." She closes the door and stands behind it laughing.

He attempts to put the pants on to amuse her only to find out they only came to his knees. "Briiiittt!" he calls her name. She opens the door and looks down and starts laughing. He is happy 'bout the fact that she is laughing and he starts to laugh. "Glad you find it funny. Now can I come in?"

[319]

"Yeah," she hands him a pair of sweats that belongs to him.

Tim and Britt had reached a crossroad. She understood if she took him back and forgave him, she would have to forget as well and Tim knew once he had been forgiven he had to do whatever it would take to reestablish the trust he had broken. They both realized that building a relationship back up wasn't easy, but it all begins with Tim being honest.

Kim / Mike's Vacation

The next morning Kim and Mike got up at 3 a.m. to catch their 5:45 flight. The drive to the airport was quiet but Kim didn't think much of it because it's still early morning. Mike didn't say too much while they were waiting on their flight neither. "Would you like some coffee," Kim asks.

"I'm good," he answers in a choppy tone.

"So are you gonna tell me where we're going?"

"You'll find out soon enough," he answers in a low tone.

"Well, I'll be back. I'm going to get me a cup of coffee. You sure you don't want any?"

He looks at her and takes a deep sigh, raises his eye brows, cut his eyes and shakes his head.

[320]

"Alright then, I'll be right back."

As soon as she walks off, pre-boarding announcements are announced: *Flight 5227 is now boarding for Bora Bora at gate 17c.*

"Uumm Kim," he calls her back. "We gotta go, hon."

She turns around with her eyes stretched wide. "We're going to Bora Bora?" She runs and grabs his neck. Mike has a smirk on his face.

"Yes we're going to Bora Bora. " He grabs her bags and the two of them go stand in line. Kim could not stop smiling, "I can not believe you are taking me to Bora Bora.

"Ever since we were kids, that's all you would talk about, *I wanna go to Bora Bora. I wanna go to Bora Bora."*

"Yep, in fourth grade, I met Contessa Nelson and she told me her dad took her and her sister Shanna over the summer; and she bragged about how beautiful it was and how the water was so blue and they slept in this hut looking thing. And ever since then I said I wanted to go. And you….."

 Kim becomes speechless, her throat begins to clog and water forms in her eyes.

"Don't cry." He puts his arm around the back of her head and buries her face in his chest. He holds her for a few minutes. "Come on," he whispers. "They're boarding now."

After twelve hours of flying, they finally reach their destination.

"OMG! I can't believe I'm here. "CONTESSA BABY, I MADE IT GIRL!" she yells with excitement. Mike looks at her and smiles.

They were greeted with a lei around their neck and after they got their luggage, a limo driver waited next the limo with the door open patiently awaiting their arrival. "Welcome back Mr. Johnson" the limo driver greets them as he holds the door for them to get in.

"Back? What does he mean back?"

"I don't know. Maybe they have the same slogan as Wendy's, Taco Bell, one of them." As they are driving along to get to their room, the limo drive is kind of quiet. Kim is on one side of the window and Mike is on the other.

"Would you like to have some champagne?" Kim asks.

"Na," he answers.

"What is wrong with you?"

"You know what? Yeah, pour me a glass." He changes his mind.

"I'm saying… you don't seem like yourself. Come to think about it. You've been acting different ever since I came in last night. Did something happen?"

He takes a sip and rubs his nose with his thumb and pointer finger, "Nawl everything cool."

"No it's not! I can tell."

"How can you tell?"

"The way you rub your nose; you use to do that all the time when something was on your mind."

Mike looks at her but doesn't say anything.

When they arrive at their destination, the driver takes the bags to the room while they waited in the limo. When he comes back, he opens the door and nods to Mike, signifying everything was good.

"This is unbelievable!" She looks all around gazing at the water and the huts; they were just as they were described to her.

[322]

Mike waits by the door as he looks at her he signals with his head for her to open the door and go in first. When she opens the door, her eyes light up. Candles and rose pedals are everywhere. The candles light up the room and the fresh rose pedals fragrance the room. Kim sits down on the edge of the bed with her forehead buried in her hand. She begins to cry and Mike stands in the door looking at her with something heavy on his mind. He walks over to her and kneels down in front of her. "Why are you crying?"

"I'm just so thankful for you being here with me at this time in my life; you don't know how much this means to me. Keith and I……….. *Wonk wonk wonk wonk wonk wonk wonk* is the next thing he hears; he has a flashback to last night. *"Hello….. Yeah cool, man."*

"Don….. Don," Kim calls his name. "Are you listening to me? What's on your mind?"

Mike begins kissing Kim on her thigh. "What are you doing?" Kim asks. He continues to kiss her on her inner thigh; she grabs his face with both her hands, "Don, what are you doing?"

He continues to work his way to her stomach. He picks up the remote to turn the satellite radio on. *Let's Make Love* by Silk comes on. He hits the Up button to change the song. *Mr. Wrong* by Mary J Blige featuring Drake plays. The passion between the two becomes tense as Mike works his way up to her breast and begins to kiss her left one then moves to the right one. He then begins to kiss her lips with passion; she holds him tight as he slides her shirt up and moves her panties to the side. He unzips his pants as they continue to kiss, then he thrusts himself inside of her with a moan and slight force. Kim is a little confused because she doesn't know if he is making love to her or sexing her. She has never experienced this rough side of him; however, she likes it. As he continues to stroke, he begins to have flashbacks again from last night. *"Who is it?"* He asked as he walked towards the door.

"It's me." The voice from the other side of the door answered.

"Come in have a seat," Mike invited.

"Look I don't want to take up too much of your time; I was a little hesitant about coming over, so that's why I called first."

Kim begins to moan and he snaps back to reality. "You good baby?" he asks as he strokes. "You like that? Come on, baby." While Kim continues to moan, Mike flashes back to last night again. Kim's moans are getting louder and he begins to grunt; pictures of him conversing last night kept flashing in his head. With each scene he strokes harder until he was about to reach his climax. "Kim I want you to have my baby," he says as he made one last thrust.

"What are you doing?" She pushes him off her and runs to the bathroom to pee, hoping the myth of going to the bathroom right after sex would decrease your chances of getting pregnant would work. She turns the shower on and sit on the toilet with her hand propped up on the sink holding her chin up. Mike comes and stands to the door. "What were you thinking?" she asks him.

Without hesitation he puts his face between her legs and Kim tries to push his head up. "Mike Stop! What is wrong with you?" She can't resist any longer so she gives in. He pulls her panties down, stands her up and turns her around and he thrusts himself in her again. Kim begins to moan and curse, telling him how good it feels and after about seven strokes, Mike pulls out and the semen hits the floor. Kim turns around, "Did you cum in me?"

"No," he answers.

"I'm talking 'bout when we were in the bed?"

"No, Kim, I did not."

"What's with the attitude and why are you being so damn short with me?"

"I'm not."

"Donavan, this me you talking to; you can talk to me. You can tell me anything."

He looks at her and gets in the shower. "So you brought me all the way out here to act like an ass? Talk to me dammit!" He steps out the shower when he finishes and he leaves the water running. Kim is so confused about what's going on but she knows something is bothering him. After she gets out the shower, she notices he has left; she looks out the window and sees him standing on the beach with linen pants and no shirt on. She thinks to herself, *should I go comfort him or should I let him deal with it on his own?* She gets dressed and goes on the beach; she walks up behind him and gathers her arms around his waist. She rests her head on his back while she holds him. She steps in front of him and notices he has tears rolling down his cheek. "Don, honey, we have three days on this trip."

"Five," he corrects her.

"Okay, so I'll have to do some shopping, but, listen, whatever it is, we can deal with it. Talk to me."

After about twenty minutes and many deep sighs, "Why didn't you tell me?" he asks.

"Tell you what?" Kim asks confused.

"About the baby, Kim!"

Kim hesitates because she's trying to figure out how he found this out… "I had an abortion. Who told you?"

"You didn't have an abortion Kim, Don't lie to me." He turns around and looks at her

"Yes, I did."

"YOU – DID- NOT- HAVE- AN- ABORTION- KIM!" he yells.

"I DID!" she tries to plead her case with tears.

"YOU DID NOT; WANT ME TO TELL YOU HOW I KNOW?"

Kim looks waiting for an answer. "Because I *saw* our daughter! You never once told me I had a fuckin' child, Kim. And here I go marrying some stranger I had a one night stand with in college because I wanted to do the right thing for my child. I'm trying to make that shit work and all along I wish it was you! Kiiimm, baby why?"

She holds her hand to her mouth shakes her head and cries. He walks off. She breaks down and moments later she goes back in the room to lay down. She falls asleep and Mike comes in later and lie beside her. He stares at the ceiling for a long time, thinking of the shouldas, coulda's and what if's. Kim wakes up and rolls over. "I'm sorry. The first time we had sex behind your house in the utility room, I got pregnant. I didn't know what was going on with my body. I would wake up in the mornings and try to eat something and would get sick.

The smell of food would make me nauseous. Momma noticed I started saying everything stinks and she asked me have I had sex with anybody. Quite naturally I was embarrassed but I told her what had happened between us and she told me I was pregnant. I took a pregnancy test and it came back positive. Momma made me an appointment to go see this doctor. We traveled a long way. I remember falling asleep going there and back. But she told me the doctor was gonna take care of me and that I was too young to have a baby right now so the doctor was gonna make sure the baby went back to heaven. So then after that, Momma took me to see this doctor which gave me some birth control pills, and I can remember that day well. Me and you had been hanging out all day, playing ball, marbles, command, BB, left hand give it up; we even played hop scotch that day." She laughs a little. "That evening we were watching TV at your house and your mother went to the store and we went in your room and had sex. I forgot to take my pill that day. But with that pregnancy I didn't get sick, nor did I notice my periods had stopped; well, to make a long story tolerable remember that summer my mom was telling everybody I went to go help take care of my aunt?"

"Yes," he answers.

"And I didn't come back until after Christmas holidays? Well I was starting to show and momma told me not to tell anybody, because she didn't want to be embarrassed and she made me give the baby up for adoption to a family friend. She said a child would ruin my life and if I wanted to come back home I had to forget that ever happened and not make mention of it to nobody, not even you. So as time went on I tried to put it out of my mind, I often thought about it until I was able to suppress it.

"So you had an abortion, too? FUCK!!!" He yells, "Do you know how much I loved you, girl? We had two kids, two babies together. Kim do you not know how that would of change things, I wish you would have said something!"

"If I would have brought it up, momma would have shipped me back off so fast. I wouldn't have been able to see you anymore. Years later, momma saw how much you loved me and that you wasn't going anywhere, she said, *'no need to bring up the baby 'cause she's doing good and we don't want to disturb her life'.* Don, you've got to believe me when I say, if I can go back and do things differently, I would. We were kids doing grown folks things, I was ignorant--didn't know any better. What momma said, I did! Please forgive me, I'm sorry."

"I forgive you Kim 'cause we were so young back then; I'm just so hurt right now." He takes a pause. "After I left my wife, I had a scholarship to play ball over seas, so I left." He gets out of bed and walks over to the dresser. "I played ball for a long time. God had to build me up and make me into a man. I had so much anger in me and I sure didn't know how to be a father. So by me praying and asking God to guide me, He began to show me who I was and taught me to be a better man. I would often come here as a vacation spot. I liked it so much I bought it because I knew you always wanted to come here. I would imagine you being here." He smiles and opens the top drawer and pulls out a picture of the two of them taken before he went off to college. He sits it on the dresser. I brought you here a long time ago right here." He pats his heart. "And I prayed God would allow me to bring you here in the flesh one day." She smiles.

"And I would like to apologize to you as well," Mike says. "It was not my intentions to get you here to make love to you. I just wanted you to get away, relax and enjoy yourself. I didn't mean to bring any confusion to you. I know you're dealing with your feelings with Keith and I respect that. It won't happen again."

"I…I... I really don't know what to say. Like…. where do we go from here?"

"We can't go anywhere until you resolve your issue with Keith. And if you choose to stay with him, I'll still be here."

"Stay with him? Why would I do that? He clearly has somebody and you know that. A pregnant somebody!" she remarks smartly.

"It's not like that honey," He comes and sits next to her on the bed.

"What do you mean it's not like that?"

"Alexis, that's her name…"

"Yeah, I know her name," she interrupts with agitation in her voice.

"Look why are we even talking 'bout them anyway? You bought me over her to relax and get my mind off them," she says as she gets up to go to the bathroom.

"Alexis is our daughter," he blurts out.

Kim stops just before she even makes it to the restroom and turns around with a confused look. "What did you say?"

"I said Alexis is our daughter."

"Well that can't be 'cause I didn't name her Alexis."

"They changed her name; they thought she looked more like an Alexis than a Ruby Ann," he smiles.

"Well I wanted to name her after your mom."

"I see that; thanks for thinking of me but I'm kinda glad they did change it."

"So you mean to tell me Keith is sleeping with our daughter and she's pregnant from him? Oh God I'm 'bout to be sick!" She runs to the bathroom gagging.

"Kim, honey, come here. He is not seeing her."

"He's not?" she asks bent over.

"No, he's not. He called the house yesterday evening and asked if he could stop by; he wanted to talk to me. So when he got there he started telling me how 'Lexis had found out she was adopted and found out where you lived and worked, saved some money came here. Apparently she had been following you for quite some time. After she noticed you and Keith split, she went to Keith for help, needed a place to stay until she found a job because her money was running low. She told Keith who she was and made him promise not to say anything right now. But after you went by there and he saw how hurt you was, he came to explain the whole story to me. And asked me not to say anything until 'Lexis came to you."

"Poor thing! My baby, she needs me, she needs us, we got to go back."

"No! I promised Keith I would not say *nothing*! So *you're* not going to say nothing! She is fine. Keith has been doing a good job watching over her and we are gonna let her come to us. Okay?"

[330]

"Does she know who you are?"

He nods his head. "So we are going to relax and enjoy ourselves and have fun."

"How can I relax when you done told me something like this?"

"Sweetie, this is Bora Bora, the place you always dreamed of coming. And you can come here as often as you like for now on." Mi Casa is Su Casa," he smiles.

"Let me ask you this," Kim says. "Why did you make love to me knowing Keith felt the same way I felt about him."

"I honestly don't know... Confused... A part of me doesn't want to let you go. I mean I'm not gone lie Kim, I will always love you. But I have to let you do your thing with Him. That's why I fell back because you couldn't completely give me your all with your unresolved issues. I think we both knew it. So what do you want to do while we're here?"

"I don't know. I just always wanted to come here; I don't know anything about this place." She smiles.

"I tell you what, let's get some rest and I'll be your tour guide in the morning."

"Sounds like a plan." They both climb in the bed and fall asleep.

The next morning Brittney wakes up to Tim cooking breakfast, "Good morning, love."

"Good morning," she replies.

"Uh uh! Come give me some." He turns his cheek to the side so she can give him a kiss. "After breakfast I want you to get dressed. I have something to show you.

"What time is my lil' man coming home?"

"Momma took him to school, so I'll pick him up."

"We'll pick him up," Tim corrects her.

"Okay, whatever."

"Brittney, I'm trying honey."

"I know…. So what is it you want to show me?"

"I can't tell you; it's a surprise. Matter fact I been…. Well I don't want to say too much."

After breakfast, they both take a shower and get dressed; just as she steps outside, she feels a cool breeze rush pass her. "It is hot as hell out this door; did you just feel that cool breeze?"

"I did," he answers.

As they begin to get close to their destination, Tim reaches over to the glove compartment and opens it. He takes out this blind fold. "Here put this on please ma'am."

She goes along with him and puts it on. "No peeping."

When they pull up in front of the building, he park and walks around to the passenger side to open her door. "Be careful babe," he says as he closes the door behind her. He guides her to the door "No peeping."

When he unlocks the door, she comments, "It smells really good in here. Well, I know we're not at your place." She smiles.

"Ha ha, you got jokes." Okay we gone play a little game and I want you to guess what the item is. This is the first one." He sits her under the dryer and turns it on.

"It's a dryer," she answers.

"Okay next one." He walks her to the sink and lets her feel the shampoo bowl then he turns the water on.

"It's a shampoo bowl."

"Okay that's two. You have three more to get correct.

He takes her and sits her in a chair and spins it around. "It's a chair," she answers.

He put the cape around her, "What's this," he asks.

"It's a cape, silly."

Then he picks up the blow dryer and comb and turns the blower on and starts combing her hair "What is this?" he asks.

"Which one? The blow dryer or comb?" she answers. And that's six items, not five."

"I know… had to give you a bonus, to try to throw you off."

He stands her up and takes the blind fold off.

"Oh my freakin' god!" She is amazed. "This is beautiful! Where's everybody and where is the owner? What you doing with a key? You work here now?"

"There's nobody here now except the owner and no, I do not work here and the reason I have a key is because I got this place for you." He opens a small box with two keys on the inside.

Her eyes light up like stars. "I don't understand, when did you do all this? Remember, when I came home to your place and I said I was helping my homeboy, Will, paint?"

She nods.

"Well I couldn't really tell you what I was doing; it would of ruined the surprise, you feel me? I actually got the building a while ago and worked on it. I been done with it, but, of course…"

"Awe maan, I'm speechless."

"It's right around the corner from your home girl's café."

"Seriously," she looks to the window but she can't see because paper is covering the windows, so she steps outside the salon… "Tim? This is the one I wanted. But Mr. Royce told me, somebody had just got it, like minutes or an hour before I called, I can't remember. I'm so excited. Now I don't know what I'mma do with the other salon."

"What other salon?" Tim asks.

"I got a building from Royce; it's smaller than this but cozy. I haven't even opened yet. Shoot I haven't even quite finished it yet. So I guess what I'll do is call Royce and tell him what's up, and put a post on Craiglist to sell the equipment." She walks around checking out the whole salon. "I cannot believe this."

[334]

"Believe it baby, so am I scoring some points or, like they say in prison, am I getting gain time?

"You are getting Gain time babe," she smiles and kisses him.

"Will you come to the hospital with me to see Devin?"

"You know I will babe," she smiles.

"Yesterday it was *"What the...."* He was just about to mock her when she puts her finger over his lips,

"Shhh," she interrupts "yesterday was yesterday. Today is a new day."

"Just as she says that, her phone rings, "Hello...   I can't understand you honey, where are you? Are you okay?... Moni honey, please calm down you're scaring me. Where are you?..... Hospital?" Tim touches her elbow for her to come on. "Honey, what happened?"

"Monet you have got to calm down, SWEETIE WHAT HAPPENED?!" Brittney yells hysterically. Tim helps her in the car and they drive to the hospital. "What happened to Traci; Monet?" Brittney drops the phone and has a blank stare on her face. Tim picks up the phone out of her lap.

"Monet listen, this is Tim; we are on the way. Calm down sweetie. We'll see you in a few minutes, bye-bye."

When they arrive at the hospital they run quickly in the building.

"Excuse me, can you tell me what floor Traci...honey did you say Traci?" he asks Britt.

"Yes." she nods through tears.

"Traci...What's her last name, hon?" Britt walks up to the counter.

"Welch," Brittney answers.

"Traci Welch," Tim reiterates.

"She's on the third floor," the receptionist answers.

Britt wiped her face in the elevator. Upon reaching the third floor they see Monet is crying hysterically. Brittney runs up to her and holds her tight. "He can't take my friend," Monet yells. "God please don't take my friend!" Seeing Monet cry, cause Britt to cry again. "She is too young to die. Oh God don't do me like this! I know you able to heal, I know you able to bring her through, turn this around Lord Jesus," Monet prays as she falls down to the floor.

 Brittney settles down long enough to get Monet to settle down. "Honey, Calm down and tell us what happened."

Monet tries to gain her composure and catch her breath. "Robbie called me and said Traci started feeling real bad about five this morning and she began throwing up and couldn't stop; he rushed her to the emergency room, they ran tests and did x-rays only to find out they needed to do emergency surgery. She wasn't strong enough to recover." She starts to cry again.

"Let's pray," Tim suggests. "Spirit of the Living True God, fall fresh on us right now, Lord. We ask that you forgive us of our sins, known as well as unknown. We need you like never before. We need you to show up Lord, Jehovah Rophi we ask that you reign down on Traci right now, heal her body right now in the name of Jesus…"

As they are praying Gabriel and Traci's spirit are sitting in the waiting area listening.

"They are praying for me" Tracy says to Gabriel.

"Yes they are, but it's time to go."

[336]

"Can I just say good-bye?"

"I'm sorry, we must leave Tracy."

"Oh, Please," she stares at him.

Gabriel looks at her and tells her he'll be back.

Traci jumps back in her body and her heart monitor starts beeping again. Robbie comes out in the hallway and tells them she's breathing; he then signals the nurse to come here. The nurse gets the doctor and they have no explanation to what's going on. "The only thing I can tell you is that we will monitor her closely," the doctor says and they both leave out the room.

"Traci, Mummie, can you hear me? I love you," Robbie says. She begins to open her eyes. "I hear you, Poppy," she answers in a low raspy voice, "and I love you too. Where are the kids?"

"Downstairs, I'll get them." He leaves to go get them.

"Thank yall so much for praying for me. I appreciate that, Tim." Everyone looks confused. I saw yall; I was sitting in the waiting area. Matter fact I saw all of you all earlier. Monet, when you peeped out the blinds because you heard your chimes ringing, that was me," she smiles. "And Britt, when you stepped on the porch and you felt the cool breeze go pass you…" They both smile. "I saw Kim, too, yall. By the way, she has a daughter."

"A daughter?" they all reply at the same time.

"Yep, listen, I want you guys to be happy for me. Don't be sad. If you guys want to do anything for me, just help Robbie out with the twins every now and then."

"We got you sis," Brittney answers.

[337]

"But God answered our prayers and you came back; everything is gonna be okay, don't talk like that," Monet states.

"Monet, honey, you've been there for me and I thank you and love you so much, but whether God intends for me to stay or go, don't you dare lose your faith. I know you will miss me, but don't you shed one sad tear, if you cry, it better be tears of joy."

Robbie comes back in the room with the kids. "Mommie, Mommie!" they yell coming in the room. She smiles slightly.

"There's my pumpkin and bumpkin, Mommie loves you so much, come a little closer so I can feel you."

"Mommy guess what?"

"What honey?"

"I was praying to God, and this man came up to me. He said, *"Jalen your mother wants to see you.* "And I asked him how he knew my name. He said he knows everybody name. Then I asked him if he was God? And he started laughing and said, *"Oh nooo, I work for God."* He said his name is Mr Gabriel. Then daddy came down to get us. When I turned around, the man was gone.

"Well you know what honey? I've had the pleasure of meeting Mr. Gabriel myself."

"You diiiiid Mommie? Jalen asks with excitement. "How does he know everybody name?" he asks.

"He's an angel," she answers.

"Woooowww! So angels are real."

"They sure are honey."

"I wanna see him too!" Jada states sadly.

[338]

"We'll see honey. Oooh I love you guys so much," she smiles. "Can someone snap a picture of us? Come on you guys hop up here; be careful."

Brittney pulls out her phone and snaps a picture of the three of them.

"Now with daddy," Jalen says. She snaps a picture of the four of them.

Monet takes the kids out to the waiting room to give Robbie time to be alone with Traci.

"Monet, are you gonna be okay?" We got to go up here to the 4th floor to see Devin, Tim's son.

"Is everything okay?"

"I hope so," Tim answers. "The doctors don't know what is wrong with him."

"Well I pray all is well."

"Thanks Monet."

"We'll be back," Brittney says.

When they get upstairs they are told Devin has been moved to the 5th floor to the ICU unit.

When they get to ICU, they ask the nurse what is wrong and the nurse says that the doctor is still running tests. She also says that his breathing had become irregular that's why they moved him to ICU. Tim takes a deep sigh and closes his eyes.

"Let's pray, babe," Britt says. They walk in the room and hold his hand; Britt begins to pray. And just as she finishes, Devin's mom comes in.

"I'll let you two talk; I'll be out in the waiting area."

"Brittney," she calls her name.

Brittney stops just before she opens the door.

"Thank you for the prayer."

She turns around and smiles, "You're welcome."

After being at the hospital all day, Tim and Brittney are exhausted. Monet agrees to feed the kids and put them to bed. "Monet, let me have your keys. I'll take your car home and you can ride with Mitchell. Tim will follow me to your house and we will see you tomorrow," Brittney states.

"Babe, awe man I forgot about lil man," Tim mentions.

"I told daddy to go get him."

"Oh, thank God. We can go get him on the way home. He walks Britt to Monet's car, gives her a kiss. "I love you," he says and closes the door.

When he gets in his car, Lil Wayne *How to Love* is playing; he turns the radio off. He was not in the mood to hear any rap or hip hop; the only thing he desires to hear at this time is something inspirational. He pulls up Kirk Franklin on his Mp3 and listens to *How It Used to Be.* As much as he has listened to this song, it is something about the lyrics that really pierces his soul this time.

After dropping Monet's car off and picking up Jaylin, the two of them head home. "Are you okay?" Britt asks Tim.

"I'm okay, just a little worn out," he yawns.

"What do you want to eat?" she asks.

"Let's pick up something… say a sub maybe?"

"That sounds good," Britt agrees. "Hey Jayboodie, you want a sub sandwich?"

"It doesn't matter."

At the end of the night everybody is drained. A prayer from every household begins to go up before they close their eyes:

Dear God, please don't take my son from me – **Renee**
Lord, please heal my son and touch Traci as well – **Tim**
God, we are asking for your healing anointing to fall on
Devin, Traci, and Monet. Lord strengthen Traci's family,
Robbie, Jalen, and Jada – **Brittney**
God, please don't take my mommy away – **Jada**
Lord, heal my mommy please, I'll do anything – **Jalen**
God, please don't take my Traci from me – **Robbie**
God, Traci is such a good friend, loving mother, and
devoted wife; I'm asking you to touch her body and
little Devin's body – **Monet**

Over the next couple of days, both families and Monet were back and forth to the hospital. Neither Traci nor Devin seems to be making any progress. When Kim comes back in town, she is filled in on everything that has been going on. They all meet up in Traci's room one day. "Traci?" Monet calls her name as she steps in the room. "Honey, look whose back?" Traci barely opens her eyes.

"Kim," she says softly, "it's so good to see you. How was your trip?"

[341]

"You should know; I heard you were there. I can't leave one day without you dying on me, Traci. If you wanted to go, you should of said something," Kim remarks smartly.

Traci smiles. "You know I couldn't leave without telling you good-bye."

Kim takes a sigh, "listen, don't talk like that." Kim holds her hand. "You are gonna be up out of here in no time. We have a girl's trip we have to go on." Kim begins to tear up. We have the barbecue on Saturday. Well we can always have it another day--when you come home."

Traci squeezes her hand and a tear rolls down her cheek, "No! You guys go on and have the barbecue; have fun matter fact let Robbie cook, he's good on the grill."

"Look at this heifer," Monet says. "All this time you been strong and encouraging me and telling me not to cry and I haven't seen you shed one tear, Kim gets here and you cry," Monet says sarcastically.

"My tears are tears of joy. I am happy, really I am. You are my girls and I feel I can be myself around yall. Robbie and I have known for quite some time…" she pauses.

"Known what?" Monet asks.

"I have had stage four, for quite some time." Monet and Britt hold her other hand. "I'm not afraid, I have seen heaven and it's Beautiful." Traci starts to doze off because of the medication.

"Traci honey, we're gonna pray for you," Kim says.

As soon as Kim finished praying Monet wipes Traci's tears and Robbie comes in the room.

[342]

"Robbie, I was telling them to go on and have the barbecue and that you are good with the grill."

"Oh yeah, I got you, just tell me the time and place."

"You two are so calm," Britt says.

"We've had our ugly days," Robbie assures them. "We didn't get here over night. We've been battling…" He pauses. "Honey did you tell them?" he asks Traci.

She nods her head.

"We've been battling this off and on for quite some time. And we've known for a while that she's at stage four. We decided to live for the kids and let God's will be done. So what do you say; are we having a barbecue Saturday or what?" Robbie changes the subject.

Kim looks at Traci and wipes her eyes, "Yes," she answers hesitantly while looking at the girls for confirmation. Britt and Monet nods their heads yes in agreement and Kim smiles.

"One condition, you stay your butt in your body and don't you go dying on us." Traci smiles and dozes off to sleep.

I guess we'll leave now. Robbie, how are the kids?" Monet asks.

"They are well," he answers.

"Okay, we'll call you later with the details," Monet says.

Just as they arrive at the elevator, Monet asks, "Do you think Tim would mind if we went by and saw Devin?"

"Of course not."

When they get up to his room Brittney taps on the door, "Knock knock."

"Come on in," his mom says.

"Hi Renee."

"Hi Brittney," she smiles.

"This is Kim and Monet; and this is Renee', Devin's mom," she introduces. "We were out here seeing a friend of ours and wanted to come by and check on Devin."

"Oh, Yeah, Tim told me about your friend; Traci, right?"

Brittney nods yes.

"How is she doing?"

"All is well," she answers.

"Well, hey, thank you ladies for coming by to check on Devin. Brittney do you mind waiting here while I go down stairs and get me something to eat?"

"Sure go ahead."

"Poor baby," Kim comments. "So he's just been lying here?"

"Comatose," Brittney answers.

"How many children do they have together?'

"Two; Devin and Di'jonae," Brittney answers.

"Oh this the one you got into with about her daughter hair that time."

Brittney smiles and shakes her head.

"She's pretty," Monet comments. "And nice."

"I guess she realized that Tim wasn't coming back, so she started dating somebody else. Now everything is kosher between us."

"Well, that's real good," Kim comments. "I would like to pray for Devin," she says as she stares at his helpless body. "You mean to tell me, the doctors can't figure out what's wrong with him? Well what happened for him to come in here?"

[344]

"Tim said he kept complaining about his stomach, then his head, then one day he went to go outside to play and he collapsed when he touched the door knob."

"And I'm sure they ran tests," Kim states.

"They did and they couldn't find anything."

"I think God is trying to get somebody attention." Kim says

"I was thinking the same thing, Monet states.

Renee comes back in the room. "Renee, we gonna get ready to get out of here; before we go, we want to pray for Devin."

"That will be no problem at all."

Just as they are getting ready to pray Tim walks in, "I'm just in time." Kim begins to pray. As she is praying, Tim feels as if God is speaking to him. For some reason he is feeling a sense of responsibility for his son being there. When she finishes, he thanks them for coming and hugs each one of them beginning with Monet. "Kim, thank you so much for the prayer, it touched me; God bless you Britt," he hugs and smacks her on the lips. "Thank you so much, hon. I love you. See you when I get home."

When they get outside of the hospital, they are standing around. Kim asks, "so what are you guys about to do?"

"I'm going to see Mitchell off. He's leaving today."

He's not going to be here for Saturday?" Brittney asks.

"Nawl, He has to get back to work."

"What about you Britt?" Kim asks.

"I'm probably gonna go to the house until it's time for me to pick up Jay."

[345]

"What about you?" Brittney asks Kim.

"I'm probably gonna go unpack."

"Alright well, I'll see you guys later, I'll be here tomorrow same time if anybody wants to meet me here," Monet says.

Monet starts to walk to her car and notices Felicia's car parked next to hers. *Wonder what she doing out here?* She thinks to herself. She calls her cell phone; *you have reached the sprint voicemail box...* she hangs up. *She probably don't have service, I'll send her a text.* Hey girl, is everything okay? I see your vehicle parked next to mine at the hospital.

Brittney looks at her watch and thinks; *I have a minute before its time for me to get Jay, so s*he turns around and goes back in the hospital to be with Tim. As she steps off the elevator, she sees Tim walking back towards Devin's room and just as she is about to yell his name, a female walking in the opposite direction states, "Oh you just gone walk pass me and not say nothing?" He keeps walking. "I'm talking to you, Roosevelt!" she says with an attitude. He turns around and Brittney quickly hides behind a pillar.

"Look, I don't have time for your shit today, Lisa. My son is in that fuckin' room fighting for his life."

"Well what about this child!" she argues.

He grabs her by her throat and slowly pushes her up against the wall, "That is not my baby!" He whispers in a stern voice.

"You think I swallowed every Plan B pill?" She comes back at him. By this time Brittney is walking up the hall; Tim is so distracted he hasn't even noticed.

"Tim, what's going on? Is this true?"

[346]

He looks down into Brittney's eyes and lets Felicia go. "I'll explain everything to you later, let's go." He grabs Brittney by the waist and proceeds to walk away.

"So who is this? One of your hoes?" Felicia asks; not recognizing Brittney because her hair is different from the time she met her in the café'.

Brittney starts counting in her head; *1, 2, 3…*

Felicia keeps talking, "Did he tell you I was pregnant?…. You'll be back," she yells with confidence.

Brittney turns around to walk back towards her. Tim tries to grab her hand but she is too quick. Brittney walks up to her and smoothly says, "I am your worst fuckin' nightmare."

"Bitch, you don't scare me," Felicia interrupts.

Brittney then grabs her by her throat and place her in the same position Tim had her in and looks her in her eyes, "Lil girl, I will mop the floor with yo ass and use that so called baby as the Mop n Glo. I assume you must be the hoe my husband cheated with." Felicia is looking confused. "Yeah you heard me, HUSBAND! That means I have Seniority 'round this mutha fucka; so I could never be the hoe; that's your job. Now I tried to refrain from getting in yo ass but your disrespectful ass keep flappin' off at the mouth…"

"Britt honey, let's go." He tries to pull her away, "It's not about her today, this bitch crazy."

Brittney lets her neck go and Felicia proceeds to pop off at the mouth, "Crazy huh? Funny you wasn't saying that when you was getting it."

Brittney begins her count again in her head, *1, 2, 3, 4, 5….*

"Come on baby," Tim convinces her to be the bigger person. Just as Brittney is about to step away, Felicia asks sarcastically, "Is this the bitch you got the salon for?"

Brittney stops and looks at her with curiosity; Felicia has this evil smile on her face. "We made love in your chair. Yeah that's right… that middle chair in front of the fancy custom made station. It's amazing what that chair can do. Do you know it reclines back to a 150 degree angle?"

One more thing and she about to get a bitch slap at a 45 degree angle, Brittney thinks to herself as she continues to count.

"Matter of fact, that's where this baby was conceived."

"Forty-five!" Brittney counts aloud and slaps her across the face at the same time.

"Did you know if you're standing this close to someone talking shit, you can get slapped at a 45 degree angle?" Brittney says sarcastically with a smile. She then leans in to whisper in Felicia's ear, "You can never be me; continue to do what you do best, make coffee!" And walks away.

Tim grabs her by the waist and they walk towards Devin's room. Tim opens the door and walk in first. "Honey did you bring me a --," Renee stops as soon as she sees Brittney walk in behind him.

"Brittney, Hi, I didn't know you were here," she says surprisingly. Brittney unknowingly speaks back; she is still bothered by some of the things that Felicia said.

"Renee, do you need to go anywhere or run any errands?" Tim asks. "I can stay here with Devin."

"As a matter of fact I do. It shouldn't take me too long."

When Renee leaves the room the tension becomes thick between Brittney and Tim; he is sitting in the recliner and she's sitting in a regular chair, quiet. "Go ahead, ask me anything," Tim encourages her.

"Is it your baby?"

"Nawl," he answers.

"How do you know? Obviously you slept with that bitch without a condom."

"I had a vasectomy."

"When?" She looks confused.

"Shortly after you had the abortion," he answers. "Remember right after we met, I went back home to Virginia, and I told you I got really sick?"

She looks at him, "Yeah."

"And you sent me that get- well gift basket from 1800 flowers.com?"

"Yeah," she answers.

"I was home recovering for a couple days. You said you didn't want any more kids, I already have four and I didn't want any more…"

"But then we talked about possibly having one together one day." She says

No, you talked about having one, he thinks to himself "It can always be reversed if we decide," he answers.

"Tim, is this where you want to be?"

"Baby, I love you with everything that's in me. Of course this is where I want to be."

"Then, don't ever lie to me again." Brittney had a look that was so serious he dared not challenge her. "How does she know about the salon?"

"I went into Monet's café one day, and she was there, we got to talking and I asked her about a building; she told me it was a vacant one in the same plaza around the corner. She gave me Royce's info.

"So you just walked in and got some coffee and started talking to her?"

"No, no, I'm lying." He says as he remembers what really happened. "I went over there to Monet's to try to catch you… remember a while back you called and said I thought I just saw you crossing Arlington and Statenville?" Brittney nodded yeah. "That was the day." I went over there to surprise you, wanted to have lunch and you wasn't there so I drove through the plaza and saw the building, I was going in the café and she was there and I asked who owned the building and she told me she knew who owned it but didn't know the number. She told me her cousin was looking to get the building at one time that's how she knew. She gave me Royce's name, I dialed 411 and got three listings and it went from there."

"I'm not even gonna ask you the next question 'cause I'm not sure if I really want to know the answer."

Tim is not saying anything because he really doesn't want to volunteer any information nor encourage her to ask anything. "So did you sleep with her in my chair?" Curiosity wouldn't let her not ask. Tim looks at her and takes a deep sigh, "Britt?"

"Answer the fuckin' question!"

"Yes!"

Silence fills the room very quickly.

"Do you want me to throw it out? I'll get rid of it!"

"No! It's fine. I'm not about to let your infidelity nor her trifling ass ruin what I feel is a blessing to me."

Tim is surprised by her response.

"Are you sleeping with Renee?"

"Noooo! Where did that come from?"

"Roosevelt Timothy Brinson, don't lie to me! I shouldn't have to keep reminding you NOT to lie to me! You see when I ask you these questions 9 times out of 10 I already know the answer so just answer the fuckin' question truthfully! Now do you want to work this out or not?"

"Is that a trick question? Of course I want to work this out!"

"Now let's try this again…ARE YOU SLEEPING WITH RENEE?"

"NO!"

"I don't believe you, when was the last time?"

"What the fuck do you mean when was the last time?"

"When we walked in this room, she said Honey did you get…"

"She probably thought I was Koy, her boyfriend."

"No because she stopped once she saw me come in behind you; and she had this stupid ass look on her face. Then she said, '*Hi Brittney, I didn't know you were here*'; she never once said to you; '*oh I thought you were Koy*' when you walked in the door."

"Britt, Listen," He gets out of his chair and walk over to her. "I wouldn't do that to you babe."

"But you did!"

"Not with Renee, honey, I know you...I meant we been through a lot with her and I wouldn't take you there." Brittney looks at him with nothing to say. "I'm willing… No I want to work this out, Babe. I know you've just forgiven me but hon, this is it… No more secrets." Renee comes back in the room. "Renee?" Tim calls. "Brittney seems to think there is something going on with us, Will you tell her nothing is going on."

"Oh come on Brittney!" Renee gets a little agitated. "Are you serious right now? Devin is fighting for his life and you here with this B.S.?"

"RENEE!" Tim yells with frustration.

"I'm sorry; I'm just a little frustrated."

"No I'm sorry, Brittney says, it's cool. You're right, another time. Tim, I'll see you later," Brittney responds.

"Renee!" Tim looks at her disappointed

"Really Tim? Really?"

"No, Tim, it's cool, she don't have to answer," she looks at Renee and opens the door.

Tim signals Renee to say something and Renee shrugs her shoulders. She takes a deep breath "Brittney?" she stops at the door without turning around "FYI, we're not sleeping together." Brittney proceeds to walk out the door and stops on the other side of it to listen...

"Renee what the hell is wrong with you?"

"What the hell is wrong with you?" she answers.

"You know what; I'm not doing this with you today, I'll see you later."

Brittney hears this and scurries down the hall.

"Aye Britt honey wait up." The two of them leave the hospital together.

The Barbecue

"Hello?" Monet answers the phone.

"Wake uuup!" Kim yells on the other end of the phone.

"Kim, its 6:30 in the morning! Have you lost your mind?"

"Yes, now get up! We got so much to do today."

"Girl I am so tired."

"Tired? Me and Brittney should be tired. You fell asleep on us."

" I am so sorry, did yall finish cleaning the meat?

"Yeah we did."

"Girl, hold on; Britt is beeping in…. "Hello?"

"You up?"

"Not really, Kim just called yelling in my ear. She's on the other line; hold on let me click her on."

"Hello?" Monet says.

"Hello?" Kim answers.

"Britt you there?" Monet asks.

"Yeah I'm here."

"So what time is Robbie coming over to start the grill?" Kim asks.

"Giiirl, he came at five; I got up to let him and the kids in and I went back to sleep."

"Where are the kids?" Brittney asks.

"Asleep in the guest room."

"I'mma get up in a little bit and take them to go see their mom and by the time we get back Robbie should be done cooking and he can go out there to see her."

"What time are you going?" Kim asks. "I'll meet you out there."

"Me too." Brittney says.

"Probably about 8:30."

"Okay good; I'm about to bring the rest of this stuff over and start setting up," Brittney says.

"It's 6:45, you guys; Oh my god! Can yall wait a little bit? I'm so tired.

"How you tired and you went to sleep before us?" Kim asks.

"Monet, I hope you don't mind but I got a bounce house for the kids," Brittney says.

"That's fine girl. But hey, I'm 'bout to get a little more sleep and I will see you guys in a little bit."

"Alright," Kim says.

"Well, I'll be over there in a minute. I'll just get Robbie to let me in."

"Okay, yall. Whateva." Monet puts the phone down without hanging it up.

A few hours later Kim arrives to the hospital; when she makes it upstairs she realizes she has beat Monet there.

"Hey, Traci, how are you today."

"I'm so tired," Traci responds.

"That seems to be going around this morning. Did you get any rest?"

"Kim, I'm tired!" The expression in her voice leads Kim to look into her eyes and what she sees is her being more than just physically tired but mentally tired.

"No, honey, don't say that. You don't mean that."

"Yes, I do and I'm only saying this to you because I know you're the strong one in the group; I believe Britt can handle it, too, but Moni, she would have a fit; then she'll think I don't have faith which I do Kim, but I'm drained. I can barely keep my eyes open with all this medication they keep giving me."

"Let's talk about something positive that will help lift your spirits… We can start with this wig I brought for you; you'll love it and I bought my makeup bag."

She lifts the bed up and walk over to get the bag off the counter. "So you know Monet will be bringing the kids shortly. She said Robbie came over about five to start grilling. He's gonna come by…."

Kim turns around and sees that Traci has fallen asleep and at the same time the kids come running in the room,

"Mommy! Mommy!" they both yell.

"Shhhh! Mommy is very tired today, so let's not make too much noise," Kim explains.

"Now very quietly, using your inside voice let's wake her up." While the twins call their mom's name, Kim taps her arm to wake her up. Brittney walks in the room.

"Where's Monet?" Kim asks.

"She was too tired to get up," Brittney says. She said when she tries to get up, she feels really dizzy and just want to sleep. So I brought the kids over."

"Mommy," Jada calls.

Kim taps her on her arm again, then leans down to her ear to whisper, "Traci, the kids are here," she sings.

"Jada?" she calls her name faintly. "Jalen?" she calls his name as well.

"Mommy, are you tired?" Jada asks.

"Mommy is very tired, honey," she answers.

"CJ said when his mom was in the hospital she was tired and she went to sleep and she never woke up. Mommy will you wake up if you go to sleep?" Jalen asks.

"Mommy will always be with you right here." She points to his heart.

"But mommy, if you go to sleep and don't wake up will you be with the angels?"

She looks at the twins and tears begin to form, "Yes honey."

"But will you be cold?" Jalen asks.

"No sweetie. Mommy will be just fine. I promise you."

"But mommy, I want you to wake up, so you can come to my school field trip. Mommy will you please wake up! Please mommy! Everybody else's mommy will be there; Mommy!" He jumps down off the bed and runs outside the door. Traci extends her arm a little to reach for him as tears flow down her face. Jada hops down and runs behind him to console him. Brittney follows her.

"Miss Brittney, if you don't mind I'd like to speak with my brother alone, please," Jada requests.

While Jada speaks to her brother, Brittney goes back in the room and sees Kim wiping tears from her eyes. "This is hard," Brittney states.

"I know, right?" Kim agrees as she continue to wipe her eyes. "She told me right before you guys got here that she was tired."

"Awe man; so she doesn't want to fight anymore? Jesus Christ!"

"Where are the kids?"

"Jada asked me if she could speak to Jalen alone for a minute."

"She seems to be handling it well. I must say she is quite a lil' lady for a seven year old," Kim comments.

"Let me step back out here and check on them.

Mr. Gabriel is walking up the hall "Hi Mr. Gabriel."

"Hello Brittney."

"How are you?" She asks.

"All is well," he answers.

"Are you here to visit someone?" She asks.

"Yes; well actually I'm here to escort someone home."

"I know they're excited to be leaving this place."

"Yeah, well it's kind of a bitter sweet moment."

"My friend Traci here has been fighting breast cancer and these are her children, Jada and Jalen."

"Jada is very strong, like her mom," Gabriel answers.

"How do you know that?" Brittney asks curiously.

"Just observing how she's consoling her brother."

"Oh," Brittney states. "My step son is on the fifth floor fighting for his life as well."

"He's gonna be okay," Gabriel answers.

"Mr. Gabriel, don't take this the wrong way, but you be freakin' me out at times; I mean you seem a little weird…." she pauses and remembers Jalen saying something about Mr. Gabriel working for God.

"Brittney, are you okay?"

"Mr. Gabriel can I ask you a question?" She looks suspiciously into his eyes.

"What's that Brittney?"

She hesitates. "Are you… **The Gabriel?** Jalen told us the conversation you had with him."

He smiles.

"I knew it!" she says with excitement. "Every time you came around, I would feel a sense of peace, like a calm feeling. You understand what I'm saying?"

"Well, I'm glad you feel that way; if you will excuse me….." He pauses….. "Do you mind if I step in to see your friend, Traci?"

"No, go ahead" She answers still excited. It quickly hits her; Wait! You're not here to take her away, are you?" she asks.

Gabriel doesn't answer the question; He looks at her and turns to walk towards the room.

"Gabriel please!" Brittney pleads.

He stops then proceeds to walk in the room, "Hello?"

"Hello, Mr. Gabby, how are you?"

"All is well. How are you Kim?"

"I've been better."

"I was talking to Brittney in the hall and she said it was okay to come in."

"Oh sure, sure, sure, by all means, come in."

He stands at the foot of the bed as Kim continues to talk, "Are you out here visiting someone?"

"In a sense…. I'm taking somebody home."

The kids and Brittney come back in the room. "Mommy!" Jalen calls.

"Mommy! Mommy, I'm sorry I ran out on you; please wake up, I have something to tell you," he whimpers.

"Here let me try," Kim says. She whispers in Traci's ear again; and Traci squints her eyes.

"Mommy!" Jalen calls her again. This time she opens her eyes and the first person she sees is Mr. Gabriel.

"Have you come to take me home?" she asks looking at Gabriel.

"Honey, nobody is taking you anywhere; Jalen has something to tell you," Kim replies.

"Mommy, can you hear me?"

"Yes, baby. I can hear you. Come up here so I can see that handsome face." He climbs on the bed. Where's sissy?"

"I'm here, Mommy."

"Come up here so I can see your beautiful face too."

"Mommy, I love you," Jalen says.

"I love you too; the both of you." She squeezes them with the little strength she has.

[359]

"Mommy, I just want to tell you that sissy talked to me and its okay with me if you go to sleep."

Traci clenches her lips tight together and begins to weep. So much emotion fills the room nobody seems to notice Gabriel has disappeared and not one dry eye is in the room except Jada. She is trying to be strong for her brother.

"Mommy, I love you, so much," Jada says as she buries her head in her mom's chest to hide the tears that are coming.

"I love you too, baby," she says softly as she drifts back off to sleep.

"Jada, honey, are you okay?" Brittney asks. "Come here." When she picks her up, Jada tries to cover her face. "Listen honey, it's okay to cry; Aunt Brittney is right here.....Listen, come here Jalen." She stands the two of them in front of her side by side. "Jalen that was very brave of you to say that; it made your mother very happy. And Jada, I know you're trying to be strong for your brother but honey, it's okay to show some emotion, crying helps bring the hurt out and you'll feel better. You understand?"

"Yes ma'am," she answers.

"Now myself, Aunt Monet, and Aunt Kim, are going to be here for you guys whenever you need us; ain't that right Kim?"

"Yeah, umm hmm," she says nodding her head.

"We have a big day planned for you guys and I rented a bounce house and a waterslide for you..."

"You didn't say anything about a water slide; you only told Monet about the bounce house," Kim butts in.

[360]

"That's because I didn't want to risk the chance of her fussing 'bout water being all over her yard. But, any hoo, you guys stay here with Aunt Kim I'm going to run up stairs to see my son."

"Jaylin is here?" Jalen asks.

"No, honey, Devin is actually my stepson. You guys haven't met him yet."

"Is he sick?" Jada asks.

"Yes he is sweetie."

"Can I come with you?" she asks.

"Hummm, I don't think that would be—"

"Pleeeeaaassse! Can I? Pretty please?"

Britt looks at Kim and Kim shrugs her shoulders. "Jalen, do you want to come too?" Brittney asks.

"No ma'am. "

"Come on Jada."

Jalen decides to sit by his mom's side until Brittney and his sister came back.

"Knock, knock; Hey yall," Robbie speaks as he walks in the door.

"Daddy!" They run up to him.

"Monet isn't feeling very well. She wanted to come but every time she tried to get up, she felt real dizzy. She told me as long as her head was down on the pillow she was fine. I told her I was coming here and I would be right back."

"We better get back to the house; her blood pressure may be low," Britt says.

"Yeah, let's go."

"Okay. I'll see you guys in a lil bit," Robbie says.

"Bye, Daddy," Jalen says.

"Okay, see you later buddy, come here and give daddy a hug; you, too, Jadaboo."

Once they make it back to Monet's place, Brittney grabs her blood pressure monitor out of the car and checks Monet's pressure. "Your pressure is normal," Brittney answers.

"So you only feel bad when you try to stand up?" Brittney asks.

"Yeah," Monet answers. "It started last night."

"Do you want to go to the hospital; do you think it's related to the MS?" Kim asks.

"No, I don't want to go to the hospital and no I don't think it's related to the MS."

"Kim, why did you ask her a dumb question like that; does she want to go to the hospital? You know she was going to say no."

"Monet, I have something to tell you; remember earlier I said I had a bounce house?"

"Yeah."

"I also got a water slide."

"That's fine Brittney; let the kids enjoy themselves."

"Okay, I have everything set up; Kim is gonna finish the rest…Right, Kim?"

"What are you about to do?" Kim asks.

"I got to go back to the house and get my girlfriend, Sharee, and her kids. They came in this morning."

"Where's Jaylin?" Kim asks.

"He's home too. Okay, so let me run, so I can get back and check on you."

"Alright girl. Kim can you close the door behind you?" Monet asks.

"Is that your nice way of saying get out?"

"Yes, I'm going back to sleep. It's still kinda early for me."

"It ain't no damn early. If yo ass wasn't sick, I'd push you out that bed."

Monet smiles. "How's Traci?"

"She's well." She answers; not wanting Monet to worry. "Robbie came just as we were about to leave."

"Hopefully, I can get out this bed to go see her, today, if not, then tomorrow."

"Well if you don't go today, I'll drive you tomorrow. Alright get some rest and I'll check on you later." Kim closes the door behind her and goes to finish setting things up. The bounce houses are delivered and set up. Mike brings the music. Brittney, Tim, Sharee and the kids arrive. The kids join the twins, Jada and Jalen, on the bounce houses and the women were sitting at the patio table laughing and talking.

"What yall got to drink with all this food?" Tim asks.

"Mike is about to go to the store and get some beer, daiquiris', and whateva anybody want. You can ride with him," Kim says.

"Mike?" Tim looks at Britt confused. "Britt do we know Mike?"

"Naw, we never met him. Mike is Keith's replacement."

"Really? You want to go there?" Kim interrupts.

"I'm just kidding; Mike is Don."

"Let me go check dude out…get inside his head and all; make sure you didn't get a lemon. You probably just looked at the body and didn't check under the hood. I cannot believe you traded my boy in."

"We're just friends!" Kim cuts him off.

"Still man! How you gone break-up the home team like that?"

"Tim; I-did-not-like-you," Kim cuts him off again.

"But still…"

"Tim, Go!" Brittney points, "…before he leaves you."

"Alright, alright, alright." He walks in the house and looks around and doesn't see Mike. He opens the front door and sees a dude getting in a car, "Yo man, you Mike? Or Don?"

"Yeah man, what's up?"

"I'm Tim, Brittney's dude. Kim said you were going to get drinks; you mind if I roll with ya?"

"Yeah yeah, sure, hop in."

As they were pulling out, people were pulling in.

"I am sorry. Where are my manners?" Brittney states. "Kim this is my best friend, Sharee, from back home and Sharee, this Kim."

"Nice to meet you," they both say at the same time.

At that moment, a gentleman walks around back; six foot two, bald head, dark complexion, well-built and very good looking. "Kim who is that?" Brittney asks.

"That's Carlos."

"Is he one of your victims?"

"Yes, he is; brother can put it down, put it down!" Brittney looks at Sharee and Sharee smiles. "I had to leave him alone, he like to do it

[364]

too much. Child, one day, I had a yeast infection and we were doing it and he thought I was really happy to see him." She laughs.

"Eeewww, yo ass is *nasty*!" Brittney yells and Sharee falls out laughing.

"Girl that day he thought I was doing all that moaning because of him; Shoot I was itching real bad!" Kim says.

Sharee had just taken a sip of drink and spits it out everywhere.

Brittney can't stay in her seat she is laughing so hard.

"Girl you are stupid!" Brittney shouts laughing.

"Yeah, Monet probably invited him," Kim says with a straight face.

Carlos notices them laughing and walk over to them. "How yall ladies doing?"

"Fine!" Brittney and Sharee answer still laughing.

"Hey Carlos," Kim speaks.

"What yall laughing at over here?" He smiles.

"Actually when I saw you come around the corner, I made a comment; you know me."

"Oh yeah; was it a good comment?" he asks looking at her in a seductive way.

Disgusted by his looks she holds her tongue from embarrassing him, "I gave you a compliment."

"Really now? Do you have an itch that needs to be scratch? "He asks.

Brittney and Sharee bust out laughing again while Kim keeps a straight face.

"Nawl, not today," she answers.

"Where's Nay?" he asks.

"She's not feeling well right now; she'll join us later.

"Well, I'll let you ladies continue and I'm going to mingle a bit."

"Okay" Kim answers.

"Nice meeting you Carlos!" Brittney says.

He smiles and walks off.

"Girl, it's gonna be a long day; we just getting started and you already trippin'," Brittney says.

"She really is like you described her," Sharee says. "I thought you were over exaggerating."

"Now you see! You see it for yourself," Brittney assures Sharee.

"That's why we couldn't get along at first because we too much alike," Brittney says.

"And that's why yall do get along because yall too much alike," Sharee comments.

"You know what the best natural cure for a yeast infection is, right?" Brittney asks.

"Plain yogurt," Sharee answers.

"Yogurt?" Kim asks.

"It has to be plain," Brittney answers.

"And what you do with it?"

"You can eat it or its quicker if you just insert it," Britt answers.

"You never told me this Brittney," Kim says.

"I thought everybody knew that," Brittney responds.

"And it works?" Kim asks.

"Yeah," Sharee answers.

"You tried it?"

"Yes, I have! It works."

"Did you also know you can take a fresh garlic clove and insert it, you do that before you go to bed at night, and it works, too," Britt says.

"Okay, I didn't know that one," Sharee says.

"Yeah, I've done both at the same time," Brittney answers distracted. "Kim, who is that girl with Butray? It ain't Patricia that's for sho."

"Girl, I don't know, I invited him but I didn't know he was going to bring somebody; I invited Tricia, too."

"You did what?" Brittney asks.

"I didn't know he was gonna be bold enough to bring his Lolita," Kim states.

"YOU KNOW HER!" Brittney asks.

"No!"

"Well how do you know her name is Lolita?"

"Lolita is a term for a young sexual or seductive girl," Kim answers.

"I was being sarcastic."

"Oh my bad; did you know that Sharee?" Sharee shakes her head no.

"Good, well I don't feel so bad."

"Tray!" Kim calls his name. He looks and she signals for him to come here. He starts walking towards Kim leaving his date behind.

"What's going on everybody?" He speaks.

"Who is that? Your daughter?" Kim asks.

"Really Kim?"

"She looks young enough to be your daughter."

"That's my lil' friend, Tiara."

"Tiara, now I really know she's young. Tiara's, Ciara's, Kiara's and Diara's all came out in the late eighties. You need to be ashamed of yourself."

"Come on now she's grown, she twenty-one."

"I just want to give you heads up that I invited Patricia."

"Well this is going to be an interesting day." He turns and walks off.

"Tray!" Kim gets up and follows him. He stops and turns around. "I had a talk with Tricia; she called me one day and wanted to talk to me about you."

Tray looks confused. "I know. I was nervous too when she said that; but she doesn't know about me and you, I mean what we use to do; she just needed somebody to talk to and God laid it on her heart to call me."

"So God really does have a sense of humor; reeaal funny God!" He looks up to the sky.

"She misses you and she wants the marriage to work."

"You couldn't have told me this when you invited me?"

"I thought she would have talked to you by now."

"Shit! I meant shoot, excuse me. What am I gonna do?" he asks.

"Take her home."

"I can't she doesn't live here," he says whispering as they approach his date.

"Hi how are you? I'm Kim."

"Nice to meet you. I'm Tiara."

"Did you know,he was married?" Kim asks.

"Kim! What are you doing?" Tray asks with disbelief

"Helping you out," she whispers.

"NO I DIDN'T KNOW!" she looks at him angrily. "You have some nerves bringing me to a barbecue where your wife is!"

"Oh no, I'm not his wife; she hasn't got here yet."

Ciara arrives and walk over to speak to everybody, "Hi Kim, Butray; Tiara what are you doing here?"

"You know her?" Tray asks.

"Yeah, we're roommates."

"I thought you told me you didn't live here?"

"And I thought you told me you were single."

"I never told you that, however, I am separated."

"I bet. You wasn't nothing but a sugar daddy anyway."

"You didn't say that last night, Lolita!"

As Ciara pushes Tiara away, Butray comments, "Ciara, take her over there and play somewhere; yall go get in the bounce house or something."

"What is wrong with you, stooping to her level? You a grown ass man. And you smashed her?" Kim chastises him.

"Tray come on, man, I hope you wore a condom 'cause if she lied about her not living here, I'm sure she sleeping with somebody else as well. The fellows should be back any minute now with some drinks."

"You know I don't drink Kim."

"YOU GONE LEARN TODAY! You gone learn what a bud light is today!" She says as she walks off.

"Where Sharee?" Kim asks when she walks back over to the patio.

"She went to use the restroom."

Mike and Tim make it back from the liquor store with the drinks.

"Tim hollers out the back door, "Aye, babe what yall want to drink?"

"Did you bring me Smirnoff apple flavor?"

"Yeah."

"Bring me one; Kim you want one?"

"I'll try it."

"Bring Kim one too, babe."

Tim pops the bottle and takes the two of them their drinks; just as he turns to go back in the house, they hear a loud scream coming from the kitchen.

Brittney takes off running fast with her bottle in her hand; Kim and Tim follow her speed walking. "Sharee are you okay?" she asks as she opens the door. Mike turns around, Brittney drops her bottle on the floor and at the same time Mike drop his cup of Grey Goose and cranberry he just mixed.

"Aye man, what's going on?" Tim asks. He walks in and notices the drinks spilled on the floor. "Somebody gonna pay for this shit! Yall just dropping drinks on the floor… What's up?"

Mike and Brittney literally just stare at each other without words to say. "What's up? You two know each other or something?" Tim asks. Sharee, Mike, and Brittney are too shocked to say anything.

"Mike?" Kim calls his name. "Sharee? Somebody say something?" Kim demands.

"Somebody better open up their mutha fuckin mouths and say something; shit; cat, dog, something!" By this time everybody from the outside has made their way in the door.

"Everybody, this is Jaylin's father." Brittney breaks the trance.

"Father?" Tim asks.

"Father?" Kim asks.

"Yes, this is the Michael Johnson I was married to."

"But I thought you said he abused you; this Michael wouldn't do that," Kim comments.

"You put your hands on my girl?" Tim asks with anger.

"It wasn't like that; I was a different man back then; we talked about that and you know I had to deal with my feeling for my ex, which is Kim by the way."

"You're Donavan?" Brittney asks. "This is too much, excuse me."

"Mommy, are you okay?" Jaylin asks as she walks past him. Tim and Sharee proceed to follow behind her.

"Tim, with all due respect; If you don't mind, I'd like to talk with her," Mike says. Tim looks him in the eye and gives him the okay.

"Okay people show is over; anybody hungry? Let's eat. And somebody, put some turn- up music on before I get to singing gospel around this mug," Tim yells.

♫*"Throw it up, throw it up;* that's what I'm talking 'bout!"♫ Kim throws her hands in the air as she continues to sing along with Rihanna: ♫*Watch it all fall out.*

Pour it up, pour it up; That's how we ball out
Throw it up, throw it up
Watch it all fall out; Pour it up, pour it up
That's how we ball out. Strip clubs and dollar bills…♫

Kim walks back outside, "Pastor, heeeey! I didn't know you were coming."

"I hope it's not a problem; Butray invited me."

"No, no. It's not a problem; I hope you're not bothered by the music."

"It's okay. Where's Monet?" he asks.

"She's in the house resting."

"How's she feeling?"

"She's just tired," Kim answers. "Well, we have food in the kitchen, everyone is eating now. I must forewarn you," she begins to give him the run-down. "…the red cooler is a danger zone. Red equals stop. The blue cooler has the water and the green cooler has…well it's okay to have whatever is in the green cooler. Ciara is here." She looks at him to see his expression. "You do remember Ciara that use to lead the praise team?"

"Of course I remember Ciara, I haven't seen her…"

Kim cuts him off by clearing her throat. "Wouldn't want you to shorten your days," she murmurs under her breath.

"Excuse me?"

She grabs him by the hand. "I said let's take a walk through this maze," and leads him through the crowd standing at the door. "Tray is right over here and I think he can use a friend right about now." She leaves the two of them to talk.

As she is walking back over to her table where Ciara and Tiara is sitting, she notices Robbie entering the back yard.

"Robbie!" she calls his name as they meet half way. The two of them put one arm around each other and begin to walk and talk. "How is she?" Kim asks.

"Well, she's the same. I don't know how much longer…" Kim cuts him off by making some weird noises.

"Today, we celebrate her. We celebrate life- her life!"

Robbie looks at Kim and smiles, "How is Monet?"

"She was still resting earlier; I better go check on her. Come let me introduce you to some of the fellas. This is Tim, Brittney's boyfriend."

"How you doing?" Rob greets.

"What's up?" Tim says at the same time.

"You'll meet Mike shortly; we just found out that he's Brittney's baby daddy." Robbie looks at Kim confused.

"Don't worry 'bout it, I'm sure you'll hear all different type of rumors today, and you can put your own pieces together to make your own story. Follow me… And over here we have Pastor Downs, and Butray. I think you met them at the church."

"Yeah we met," Rob answers.

"What's good man?" Butray asks.

"Chillin."

"Call me DeAngelo," Pastor corrects.

"Alright nice meeting you again, look like you guys were in a middle of something, I'll get with you later."

"Yeah, man just give us a lil' bit."

He walks back over to Tim while Kim goes to check on Monet; and just as she is knocking on the door, Monet opens it dressed and ready to go outside.

"I'm glad you feeling better," Kim states.

"Giirl me too. I don't know what that was. Every time I tried to get up, I felt so dizzy like I was doped up on morphine or something, and as long as I was laying down I was good. But honey, I think that was a spiritual attack; I prayed and prayed and prayed until I fell asleep and after I woke up, I tried to get up and I feel good! Thank you Jesus!"

"I know that's right! Now let's go get a drink."

Monet looks at her.

"I'm just playing child. But girl, you have missed the drama!"

"What drama? Please don't tell me yall been showing out at my house. You know, these white folks in this neighborhood ain't with that ghetto mess."

"Forget them white folks! But listen; let me fill you in real quick. Butray brought his teenybopper with him; she lied and told him she lived out of town come to find out, she is Ciara's roommate.

"Ciara Ciara?" Monet asks.

"Yes, Pregnant Ciara…. And she didn't know he was married…. And I invited Patricia."

"Patricia is here?"

"Not yet. I really don't know if she is coming but I invited her."

"Wow!"

"Oh that's not it! How 'bout Mike is Jaylin's Dad!"

[374]

Monet is confused.

"You heard right; Britt was the one he met in college, slept with, got pregnant, left me for and married her."

"Cut my legs off and call me Shawty!" Monet comments. "All this time, both of them been here in the same town and same circle of friends."

"I know. Right?"

"How do you feel?" Monet asks.

"I really haven't had the time to feel anything. I guess it hasn't soaked in yet."

"So what happened?" Monet asks.

"Sharee, Brittney's best friend from back home, went to the bathroom and when she came out, she saw Mike in the kitchen and screamed."

"That's what woke me up," Monet interrupts.

"So Britt went running in the house and she and Mike dropping glasses and shit, I meant stuff."

"Wow! This is an interesting day and it's really just getting started," Monet replies. "Girl, let's get out of here; they playing my song; she throws her arms in the air and starts singing Tina Marie, *Square Biz*:

♫ So *don't you have no doubt, I'm gonna spell it out*

I'll hip you to the Tee that is

I got the best, the most, baby, from coast to coast

And I don't wanna boast, but I love you Square Biz ♫

They both joined in on the chorus:

♫*I'm talkin' Square Biz to you, baby*

Square, Square Biz

[375]

I'm talkin' love that it

Square, Square Biz♫

They dance their way into the kitchen. "Girl how do you know them lyrics?" Kim asks rhetorically. "Don't nobody know what she be saying."

Kim laughs and fix Monet a plate. "Girl that's my song," Monet replies.

"I see… You done threw your hands up, shaking that belly." They both laugh as they walk outside to the patio and at the same time Patricia comes up.

"Hi ladies," she speaks to everyone upon approaching the table. Everyone speaks back and Kim formally introduces her to everyone sitting at the table.

Everybody is sitting around in their cliques chatting and sipping on drinks; Tim has even taken it upon himself to offer Pastor and Butray a beer. At first they both decline but somehow, as convincing as Tim can be, he talks them into having one which in turn leads to about three.

Butray has had enough liquid courage to build up the nerves to pull Patricia away from the table. "Tricia, can I speak with you a minute?" He turns and walks off.

"Dang! He just Jim Jones'd your ass!" Kim laughs.

"I know and it kind of turned me on!" Patricia gets up and walks behind him.

Tiara is just about to say something smart when Kim gives her an evil look and shakes her head. "Let me tell you something lil' girl; does the term barter system mean anything to you?" Tiara stares back at Kim. "You do realize that's what the two of you had right? You got something from him and he treated you good, reeal good," Kim stresses. Tiara couldn't argue with the fact that she is right. "Now see what you're not about do is ruin any chances of them two getting back together; am I making myself clear? You wasn't even invited, matter of fact, why are you still here?"

"Miss Kim, chill, she's here with me now," Ciara intervenes.

Tiara rolls her eyes at Kim. "You can roll your eyes, you can stomp your feet but this one black girl, you sho can't beat!"

Monet bust out laughing. "Girl, shut the hell up! And leave that girl alone."

"I'm just trying to break her in that's all."

"You went waaay back!" Monet continues to laugh.

Kim turns around and looks at Patricia. "Look at her, she looks so happy; Now how you gone come between that?" Kim asks Tiara.

"You got to learn to pick your battles, sweetheart."

Tiara takes a deep breath and begins to meditate on the things Kim said.

"Kim? What did you mean by he "Jim Jones'd" her?" Monet asks.

"Child you got to start watching TV; but on this one episode of *Love and Hip Hop*, Chrissy goes to Miami to get away, and Jim, her boyfriend, shows up unexpectedly to the restaurant where she is eating. He pretends to have an attitude but actually proposes to her. The attitude he had when he stepped to her was a complete turn on; you should of seen it," Kim smiles.

"Should of seen what?" Brittney asks as she walks back to the table. "You telling my business already? Did you go get her out of the bed for this?" she asks as she sits down. "My God do yall know how crazy this is? Mike has been here all this time; and my baby has been asking 'bout his father. I don't know how we didn't run into each other all this time. And Kim how crazy is it for you and me to have bumped heads. How you feeling?" she asks Kim.

"What you mean bumped heads?" Kim asks

"Bumped heads; You never heard that term? "Brittney asks

Kim shakes her head No

"Bump heads meaning we slept with the same guy."

"Oh ok" Kim says

"So how does this whole thing make you feel?" Britt ask again

"I'm cool, I mean I really haven't had time for it to marinate."

"Well before it does, let me say this, I know how you felt about Mike and I know how he felt about you. For whatever reason, I happened to be the one that came between yall; whether God designed it or the enemy had a hand in it, I don't know but what I do know is what the devil meant for bad God turns it around for our good. And even though we only tolerated each other for a long time, we have come a long way; you are like one of my besties now and I love you. I would like to keep our friendship; I don't want anything to change between us. I didn't know you back then; I didn't even know he had a girlfriend until after we were married. I remember that last heated argument we had." She begins to tell them, *"Mike raised his hand to hit me... 'You promised!'* I looked him in his eyes. I can tell he was

[378]

not himself but he withdrew his hand and fell to the ground and began to weep. I knelt down to comfort him. *'Please help me understand! Are you on drugs?'* I asked.

'I can't do this anymore; you deserve so much more,' he answered. *'Do what honey? Talk to me.' 'I only married you because you got pregnant; I'm not in love with you.'* The more and more he spoke, the more he sliced my heart. He told me he couldn't pretend anymore and that he was taking his frustrations out on me. *'I've hurt you, I've hurt her,'* he said. I pulled back off of him trying not to go in panic mode because I literally saw my whole world coming down, but at the same time everything was beginning to make sense. *'Who is she?'*

He told me he had an ex from back home he had been with for as long as he could remember. He said the two of you grew up together and were supposed to get married after college and start a life, but he messed it up. He beat himself up for a long time about that. He told me the hardest thing he had to do was to break up with you and he wasn't able to forgive himself, but he wanted to be there for his child. So we tried the co-parent thing for a while but it just didn't work out. I knew he really didn't want to be there and I didn't want him there, so we parted ways and haven't heard or spoke in about five years and here we are." Everybody sat quietly at the table until Kim broke the silence

"Brittney, me and Mike had our time and it just didn't work out. I'm so over that right now. I'm cool; we're cool; let's keep it moving." She gets up and gives her a hug.

"Dino!" Monet yells.

Kim turns around and Dino is running up to everybody, "Heeey everybody!" He hugs them.

"I missed you!" Kim states.

"I missed yall, too."

"What you been up to? You just disappeared from the face of the earth," Brittney asks.

"Look at you!" Monet says. "You looking good; all manly and stuff; what's really going on?"

"I been good; Just been working and building my clientele up."

"Clientele for what?" Monet asks.

"Hair?" he answers.

"You do hair?" Brittney asks.

"Yep, I've had my license for six years now."

Brittney high-fives him. "Shut the front door; I did not know!"

"You know Brittney has a salon?" Monet mentions.

"Shut-Up!" He high-fives her again. "I need to talk to you because I'm tired of doing hair at my place."

"So who invited you?" Monet asks.

"Kim!"

"Kim you didn't tell us Dino was coming. Any more surprises?" Monet asks.

She smiles. "So Dino, sit down and tell us what's been going on; we really haven't talked since you moved out the building."

"Well, you know I moved back in with my parents. I started doing some soul searching and working on me then God led me to go back to school.

[380]

"That's good Dino," Kim praises him. "Why are you smiling?"

"I met someone!"

"You did!?" Kim asks. "I hope he ain't like that pyscho freaky Jason, you lived with."

"Oh noo no no! I brought them with me. I hope its okay."

"Yeah yeah, that's fine. Where is he?" Kim asks. About the same time a person they had never seen before comes walking in the back yard.

"Dino takes notice, smiles and stands up, "He is a She." Dino corrects her.

"DINO, YOU GOT A GIRLFRIEND!?" Kim yells. "YEESSS! I'm so proud of you"

Everybody screams at the same time they began to celebrate him by clapping and when she approach it to the table, Dino puts his arm around her and kiss her on her cheek. "Everybody this Tacara. Babe, these are my friends Kim, Monet, Brittney, and I don't know…"

Kim interrupts, "Oh I'm sorry, this is Ciara and Tiara," Kim introduces them to Dino.

"Twins?" he asks.

"Dino, you know damn well, they don't look alike; she pregnant and she ain't." Everybody simply smile and shake their heads. "Nawl seriously they're not twins."

"I didn't know; they could have been fraternal," Dino says.

"But anyway, I am so happy for you!" Kim states.

"Me too," Monet and Brittney agrees.

"Dino! The Dream?"

"I was just about to ask you do you remember that dream I told you about."

"Wow! That's awesome, Dino."

"Excuse me," Tacara interrupts. "May I use the restroom?"

"Sure can, go through that door and make a left, it's the second door on the right."

"Darius, honey, I'll be right back," Tacara says. He admires her backside as she walks off.

"Wow she used your government name," Kim remarks. "That's funny, I never actually heard anyone call you Darius."

Dino shakes his head and smiles, "Girl, I'm in love."

"I can tell. Is she the same one from the dream?"

"Yep, and when I saw her, Kim, the Holy Spirit said that's your wife."

"Where did yall meet?"

"At school."

"She seems to be good people," Brittney says.

"Does she know 'bout your past?" Kim asks.

"Yes she does. Ain't no shame in where God has bought me from."

"Well I'm happy for you," Kim says and the others agree. "We already started eating so you guys can go fix a plate."

As Tacara comes back outside, *Adorn* by Miguel is playing, "That's our song right there!"

He meets her half way as she comes across the yard and takes her hand and the two of them begin to dance.

"Awww, that is so cute," Kim comments. "He really likes her."

[382]

"He has definitely done a 180," Brittney comments.

"Girl, look who is here," Monet says to Kim.

Keith walks up to Tim and Robbie and joins their conversation. Mike walks over to Keith and greets him. "What's up man; glad you can make it. What you drinking on?" Mike asks him.

"I'm good, man," Keith responds.

"I'm sorry, but we have a minimum of one drink policy," Mike responds. Some crazy stuff went down and we just want everybody to be in relax mode and enjoy; ain't no telling what might pop off next. Check out the Pastor and the deacon over there; they're feeling good right about now."

"Okay, okay. I'll take one beer. You got any Coronas with lime?"

"Yes siirr!"

Mike walks over to the cooler and gets Keith a beer. "Hey Jaylin," Keith speaks to him as he is holding on to Mike's leg.

"You know my boy?" Mike asks. "Well, of course you would know him; his momma and Kim are friends.

"Of course I know Jay; he's my boy too." He gives him some pound.

"No, he's my boy as in my SON," Mike explains.

Keith begins to look a little confused, "You're Jaylin's father? Like for real, for real?"

"I just told you some crazy stuff just went down and it's still early." Mike responds. "Yeah, me and Brittney were married 'bout seven ago."

"Small world," Keith comments.

"You think?" Mike says. He looks over to Pastor. "Looks like Tray left the Pastor over there by himself while he over there selling cakes to that lady," Mike chuckles.

"That's his wife," Keith answers.

"Oh really! But he came in with that young lady sitting at the table with Kim and them."

"WHAT?" Keith asks with disbelief.

"The man just told you, some crazy stuff going on!" Tim intervenes.

"Let's go over and sit with Pastor," Mike suggests.

"I think he wants to be called Deangelo," Robbie says "…at least that's what he told me."

"Well yeah that would seem kind of awkward calling the man Pastor and we all drinking," Tim says. They all laugh as they walk towards him.

"You look a lil lonely," Mike says to Pastor.

"Just chillin', taking in the fresh air."

"Daddy, I'm going to play with my friends," Jaylin says.

"Okay buddy, I'll see you in a bit. Love you."

"Love you too, daddy," he says as he runs off.

"So what's going on Pastor or do you want us to call you, Lo?" Mike asks.

"Call me Lo, that's cool."

"How are things going with the new building?"

"Man I appreciate the work you put in; you did an excellent job. When are you coming to visit?"

"I don't know, I reckon I'll come one day."

"What about you Tim? When are you coming back?"

"I don't know man, feels kind of awkward, drinking a beer with you then coming to hear you preach."

"That's the excuse you going with? The bible says know no man after the flesh but after the spirit."

"I know but I'm looking at you chugging down the spirits over here, and it ain't the Holy Spirit," Tim laughs. "How many you done had so far?"

"Alright, alright, Mr. Funny man," Pastor laughs it off. "What about you, Keith? Haven't seen you in a while."

"I had to work on me, get myself together; you know?"

"Well did you get YOU together?" Pastor asks.

"Nope, not yet," Keith answers.

"Do you know how you sound? If we could do it ourselves we wouldn't need God."

"I know, but I'd rather have myself together before I come back. I'm either in all the way or I'm out."

"I feel you, bro," Tim agrees. "…'cause the bible does states, you need to be hot or cold, God don't want you warm; trying to play both sides ain't good. So I feel you, Keith, man; I'mma be either in all the way or out doing my thang."

"You are right," Pastor agrees but I would rather be in- in my sin; than

than out in my mess. At least if I'm in, something may jump on me to make me wanna stay in. That's what my daddy use to tell us."

"I kind of like that," Mike says. "Okay, you said *I'd rather be In-in my sin (meaning going to church) than out in my mess (not going to church) At least* if I'm in, something (which is the Holy Spirit) may jump on me to make me wanna stay in. That was a good one," Mike smirks.

 "Yall excuse me I'm going to talk to Kim for a minute," Keith says.

"Hold on! Let me holla at you for one second," Mike says to Keith. The two of them walk away from everybody else. "Where is Alexis?"

"She didn't want to come. I think the baby has her tired or sick or something," Keith answers.

"Man, I'm sorry to hear that. Maybe me and Kim can stop by later and check on her?"

"Cool, I'll holla at you in a minute." Keith intentionally brush him off and walks away because he had only one thing on his mind at this time.

Tricia comes back to the table from talking with Tray just as Keith approaches; he speaks to everyone. "Kim can I holla at you a second." As she is getting up from the table Tricia hollers out, "Jim Jonesss!" They all start laughing. "What's that about?" Keith asks Kim.

"Inside joke," she answers.

"Am I the butt of the joke?"

"Oh noo! What's up?"

"I don't know if Mike has told you already, but the young lady you saw at the house that day--her name is Alexis. And Alexis is....."

"My daughter; I know. He told me."

"Kim, I miss you so much and when you walked out of my apartment that day, I knew I didn't want to be with anybody else but you. You hurt me when you left me and started seeing Mike. I know it probably wasn't intentional but you had to do what you had to do in order to get closure. I realize you were hurting too and what do hurting people do? They hurt other people. Same with me; I carried that hurt of my ex-wife leaving me for another woman; do you know what that can do to a man's ego? I know you felt rejected by Mike when he abandoned you, then that same spirit of rejection revisited you when I wouldn't commit to you because I was afraid. I let the spirit of fear dictate my life for a loong time. But not anymore; I've closed that chapter. See, Kim, you leaving me was the best thing you could have done because I didn't appreciate you nor could I see that woman of God in you. I know we all have flaws but we will not succumb to the devil and his tricks anymore. He will NOT tear us apart again. See baby, I had to realize every relationship is not the same and I can't hold my past or the way she treated me against you.... Baby I'm so over that and ready to move forward." He gets down on his knee.

"What the hell?" Tim says admiring from a distant.

"Is he...?" Monet sputters.

Mike looks up and notices a young lady coming up behind Kim. Everybody's attention is now on the two of them and the young lady walking up behind Kim.

"Will you marry me?" Keith asks. Kim is shocked. "Turn around," he tells her.

When she turns around, Alexis is standing there holding an engagement ring. Kim doesn't know whether to take the ring or hug Alexis. She looks back at Keith, then turns back to look at Alexis. "Well?" Keith asks.

She nods her head with tears in her eyes. While everyone begins to clap, he introduces them, "Kim, this is your daughter Alexis. Alexis this is your mother, Kimberly." Kim hesitates for a moment holding her fist under her nose sobbing.

"It's okay, Momma," Alexis assures her and gives her a hug. By this time, Mike comes over to embrace the two of them and the crowd gathers around to celebrate the good news and to also find out who this girl is.

They hug for a long time; then, finally, Kim pulls back to take a good look at her. Then she hugs her again. "Kim who is this?" Brittney asks.

"Our daughter," Mike responds.

"Daughter?" everybody says together.

"Look we just found out right before we went on our trip. We, well, I was just as surprised as you guys are" Mike says.

"Kim, when were you pregnant? I don't remember you ever having a baby," Monet says.

Kim is too emotional to answer. "Remember when she left and went out of town?" Mike asks Monet.

"You were pregnant and you never told me?"

"Make you wonder what else is she hiding, huh?" Brittney smiles.

"Congratulations Girl! I'm happy for you."

"Yeah, we got the same baby daddy," Kim says sarcastically. "This will be a story to tell my grandchild!" Kim rubs Lexis' stomach.

"Mike you went from having one child to two children and grandfather in one day, and Kim you went from having no kids to a daughter and a grandchild in one day," Brittney comments.

"Talking about God doing exceedingly and abundantly above all we can ask or think," Monet says.

"Aye Mike man…I couldn't tell you she was here I wanted to surprise both of you." Keith says.

Everybody laughs and *Candy* by Cameo comes on.

"Uh oh! Yall remember this song at the end of *Best Man*," Tim yells out. Come on yall, I always wanted to do this ever since I saw that movie." Everybody joins Tim in the electric slide; Renee walks in the back yard and Brittney signals for her to come join in. She is a little hesitant so Brittney steps out the dance line and pulls her in. When Tim spins around, he is very surprised to see her there. "What are you doing here?"

"Brittney invited me."

"Who's at the hospital with Devin?"

"My mom."

"How is he?"

"He was the same when I left. Look, Brittney invited me and I needed to clear my mind. If this is gonna be a problem, I'll leave."

"It's cool, enjoy yourself." He continues to dance.

Brittney, Kim and Alexis join Monet back at the table.

"Kim, I cannot believe you have a daughter. How old are you?" Monet asks.

"I'm 17," she answers.

"How do you know Keith?" Monet inquires.

"Monet, if you don't mind, I'd like to talk with her at a later time, please," Kim interrupts.

"No problem," she responds. "Britt, isn't that Tim's baby momma?"

"Yep."

"Why is she here?"

"I invited her."

"Then why were you looking at her side-ways when yall were out there dancing?" Monet asks.

"I wasn't."

"Yes you were, Britt," Kim agrees.

"I was not."

"Then why are you looking at them now?" Monet asks.

"Because what's done in the dark will come to the light!"

"Britt, come on. You can't possibly think he has something going on with her? Hell, yall just got back together," Kim says.

"WHAT THE…..Ooooo I almost cussed Lord Jesus, and I said I wasn't gonna cuss no more, but what hell is she doing here?"

"Who?" Kim and Moni ask simultaneously

"That bitch walking back here with Will, Tim's best friend."

"Lisa?" Monet asks. And at the same time Kim says Felicia.

"YES!"

"She works at the café," Monet says.

[390]

"I remember; oh, she got some nerve!"

Brittney attempts to get up but Kim grabs her. "Hold up, what's the beef with Felicia?" Kim asks. "She the one Tim was fuckin with!" Kim turns her loose and in that moment Monet reverts to the conversation she, Zi, and Felicia had at the Café one day about Lisa's boy crush. His height, his build, his complexion and locs all were the same characteristics of Tim.

Tim spots Brittney walking firm in his direction like a bull charging red but her focus is not on him. He turns to see where she is looking and runs over to grab her.

"What the fuck you grabbing me for? What she doing here?"

"Brittney chill….. SHIT! Kids are out here."

"Tim ain't nobody thinking 'bout them damn kids right now; I said what is she doing here?"

Will is walking towards them with a confused look on his face. "Yo yo yo," he yells holding his arm out trying to prevent Brittney from getting closer. "Scoop man what's going on?" he asks Tim.

"I'll tell you what's going on," Brittney answers.

"Brittney, I said CHILL! Shit!"

"Obviously, yall know each other. What's going on baby?" Will asks Felicia.

"This the bitch Tim cheated with," Britt answers.

"What? When?" Will asks looking confused.

"Oh it's been going on for a minute now!" Brittney assures Will. "Did she disappear for a few days or a weekend?"

Will starts thinking back to a time when she said she was going out of town to visit family.

"She and Tim went up to Virginia. And the bitch claim to be pregnant from him."

"Okay wait, wait, wait! This is too much," Will says. "So when you told me you were going to visit your family in Virginia; you were with him? My dog, my homie, my best mutha fuckin friend?"

"I didn't know yall were friends," she answers.

"So you think it would have been okay if it wasn't a friend. You lied. You flat out lied to me, and I told your ass how I felt about liars. I told yo ass, I don't care what…. just keep it one-hundred with me…Did we not talk about that? So you saying he supposed to be the daddy?"

"Yo Will man, you know we go way back, I didn't know man. You know I wouldn't have went there; she told me she was single."

"I was single when we met," Felicia admits.

"So this the Mutha Fucka you want to be with?" Will asks.

"No!"

"Obviously, you saying it's his mutha fuckin baby. Whose baby is it Felicia?" Will asks.

"Quit yelling at me; I'm not your child!"

"But you supposed to be carrying my child….. Right?"

"YEAH! ….. I DON'T KNOW! Take me home!" she yells.

"Which one is it?"

"Come on Will, man; we both know it ain't mine."

Hurt by his words, Felicia attempts to walk off, but he grabs her hand.

"No ma'am; you know how we do. We face problems head on; we don't run away," Will says.

"Let me go, Will!" She snatches her arm and walks off.

"Let her go; stupid ho," Brittney yells.

"Stay out of it Britt, It's over!" Tim yells.

Will walks behind her. "Felicia! Felicia!" he calls.

She stops on the side of the house. "Why did you walk off? You know we don't walk away from our problems, we face them head on…."

"We, we, we, you and your stupid rules! I'm not your child, Will, and I'm sick of you and these stupid rules you make up every time you want something to go your way. Well you see what your stupid rules did? They caused me to cheat!"

"No! You did that; it had nothing to do with my…. I meant the rules."

"No! You and your control issues, you cannot control me, Will; I'm a person not an animal. I can't help that your last relationship failed and you think you can control this one with some dumb rules…"

"They're not dumb and they seem to be working just fine!"

"For who? For you? 'Cause they damn sho' 'nough ain't working for me."

"Baby, don't look at it as rules, look at it as structure," he tries to stress.

"Dress it up and put a bow tie on it but underneath all that, it's still control. And let me tell you another thing, I didn't appreciate you trying to handle me in front of your lil' friends. What about that rule, RESPECT!"

"What fuckin respect? Felicia, how you think I felt, I'm expecting to come here and introduce you to my peeps and I'm blindsided by this bull!"

"You've changed, Will. When I first met you, that day you came into the Café, I thought you were the finest thing in that EMT uniform. I slipped my number into your pocket just before yall took my boss lady away. We started dating and you were the perfect gentleman. We would talk about the Lord and sometimes go to church together; I could even go for your "STRUCTURE" then because it made sense. But somewhere along the way, you got on this power trip, I gave you an inch and you took a mile; you kept adding and adding and adding. Whenever you didn't like something here come another "structure" to accommodate you. I'm sick of you and your stupid ass rules." She turns and walks away. "And by the way, I pray this is Tim baby; he treated me kind and with respect and he loved me."

"Well, you can stop praying 'cause Tim went and got himself fixed a long time ago. And he don't love you boo boo; you were just a piece of ass to him."

Felicia is so upset with him, she walks off. Tim is coming around the corner to check on them and sees Felicia walking off and Will standing there.

"Will, you alright man? "He asks as he walks up to him

"Get the fuck off me, man!"

"Really! You gone trip on me over some fuckin' broad I didn't even know you were dating?"

[394]

"Will man…. just leave 'cause you upset right now!" Tim asks calmly.

"Upset? Would Brittney feel upset if she knew you were still fuckin' Renee?" Just as he says this, he looks up and realizes Brittney is standing behind Tim; he drops his head in sorrow. "Dang!" Tim feels as if his eyes are going to roll in the back of his head as he slowly turns around, fearing the worst; Brittney standing behind him was the last thing he needed. As he completes a partial turn, he notices what he feared he is now facing. To look in Britt's eyes is unbearable.

"I'm sorry man," Will mutters as he walks off.

"Britt, let me explain."

Before he can completely get it out she takes off running. Hell hath no fury like a woman scorned and Renee is completely blindsided to what would happen next. Brittney grabs Renee from behind and throws her down while she is still sitting in her chair. Everyone quickly moves from the table. She jumps on top of her and begins punching her in the face. "I knew yall were still messing around, that's why I invited yo ass!"

It seem as if she spoke a word for each hit; Kim rushes around the table to pull her off but Mike actually picks her up and carries her away; at the same time Tim is walking towards them. "Britt?" he calls her name as the three of them walk towards the house.

"I'm finna beat you ass, too!" She's kicking and tussling trying to get free from Mike.

Kim helps Renee up. "I'm pressing charges," Renee yells.

[395]

"No you're not!" Kim responds softly. Renee looks at Kim as she continues to speak. "Number one--you didn't have any business messing with that girl man and coming over here amongst her friends trying to be buddy buddy. And number two--you gone have to deal with me." By this time Tim makes it to the table. "Help her to her car, Tim," Kim says.

"I'm pressing charges," Renee tells Tim as they walk off.

Meanwhile Mike takes Brittney in the house and sits her on the couch.

"Renee?"

"Don't call me that; don't you fuckin' call me that right now Mike!"

"But I have always called you by your middle name."

"Not today, Okay?"

"Okay….. Now what's going on? From what I seen today, you've become so hostile. You use to be this sweet, loving and caring girl..."

"I'm sick of him cheating on me." She interrupts

"Renee, I meant… Brittney; it feels funny calling you Brittney; Listen, who are you? This not the person I married--the sweet, loving, and caring person I knew I met back then; why are you acting like this? How long the two of you been together? Four years? You have lost yourself, Renee. You cannot let a man change who you are. A relationship is about coming together, finding a common ground, conforming as one and letting God be the pilot. Do you guys pray together?" Brittney's anger won't allow her to answer.

"I tell you what I feel like, Mike….I feel like taking his ass to the zoo."

Mike is confused, "the zoo?" He asks.

[396]

"Yes the fuckin' zoo; where there's a lot of shit, literally," she states. "I took his ass to Sea World a little while ago."

Mike is totally confused; he thinks Brittney is talking out of her head. "I have no idea what you're talking about," he says. "Do you guys go to church together or read together?" He continues, "Do you even have a conversation about God? Hell, Renee, does Tim even know God?"

"Mike, No disrespect to you or God, but I don't want to hear that shit right now; I'm trying to think!"

"You're no different than him you know? What I have observed is that he has made you a mini me… I'm not saying the man don't care 'bout you. I'm not even saying he doesn't love you but what I am saying is you need to find You! Go back to who you know, that's where your heart truly lies…. with God" Brittney starts to tear up. "If he loves you Renee, he'll follow you. The bible says a man who finds a wife finds a good thing." He looks at her and smiles. "And this I know first-hand, you are a Good Thang." He wipes her tears.

Kim, Monet, Patricia, Ciara and Tiara are sitting at one table while Butray, Pastor and Robbie are sitting at a table next to them. Just as Tim is walking up, his phone rings. *"Hello…. No she's not with me; she just left….. …Is something wrong? Miss Diane, calm down. I can't hear you! Whaat! I'm on my way."*

"Tim is everything okay?" Monet asks.

"Tell Britt they just called a code blue on Devin," he answers as he runs away.

[397]

"Oh my God!" Monet responds.

"Yall let's pray and send forth some angels ahead of him," Kim says anxiously. "Pastor, would you lead us in prayer?"

"What is he praying for?" Tiara asks.

"Tiara, SHUT UP!" Ciara says.

"Honey, you need to upgrade your friends," Kim tells Ciara.

Pastor begins to pray: "*Most gracious heavenly Father, we come before you asking you to forgive each and every one of us for our sins; known and unknown. You said where two or three are gathered in your name you will be in the mist, Jehovah Rapha, God of healing; we need you right now. Send forth your angels right now to little Devin. We decree and declare that all is well. Comfort the family and give them peace which surpasses all understanding. And we'll be careful to give you all the praise and glory. In Jesus name and everybody say.....Amen*"

Every one says Amen and immediately after prayer Tiara says, "*And Lord please let the pastor stop creeping over to our apartment, using my friend for sex and don't won't to acknowledge her in public, made her leave the church because he didn't want it to be exposed that she is having his baby.*" Kim spits out her drink; everyone is shocked; nobody knows what to say or do. "*Lord, you said what's done in the dark will surely come to the light and today, Lord, we, I meant I can no longer pass judgment on this man because his sins have been exposed. Amen!!!*"

"TIARA, WHAT IS YOUR PROBLEM!!!" Ciara yells and runs off.

Pastor drops his head and claps his hands, "And the Stella award goes to…" Tiara stares him in his eyes boldly. "My grandmother used to tell us, "Son if you assume something, you make an ass out of yourself."

"You're the Ass! And you call yourself a Pastor," Tiara says.

"Little girl, you just mad because I wouldn't sleep with you."

"Alright that's enough," Kim interrupts. "Butray, can you take the 'Aras, Tiara and Ciara, home?"

Patricia is furious; even though she broke it off with Pastor, the thought of him bringing a child in the world after he suggested that they get rid of theirs is upsetting her.

After Tray escorts Tiara to the front, Patricia gets up from the table and slaps Pastor Lo. "You were sleeping with her while you were sleeping with me? You knew how bad I wanted that baby and you made..."

"Traaaay!" Kim interrupts. "What are you doing back here?"

"I forgot my phone. Patricia, what's going on here; why are you in his face? What baby are you talking 'bout?"

Everybody gets quiet waiting on an answer. "Somebody better tell me something." He turns to Pastor, "DeAngelo?"

Pastor looks at Tray. While he stares him down waiting on an answer, Patricia takes a deep breath and says, "I had an affair with DeAngelo and I got pregnant."

"Come on maaan, my wife?" Butray says.

"You were sleeping with Kim," he strikes back.

Tray punches Pastor Lo in the face and walks off.

Kim turns and looks at Tricia. "It wasn't like that."

"I trusted you!?"

"Patricia, it wasn't like that. I'm sorry."

"Then what was it like? Hmm, did you enjoy making fun of me when I came to spill my heart out to you, knowing you were sleeping with my husband?"

"I wasn't sleeping with your husband then; it happened a while ago. I barely knew you."

"So that makes it right?"

"No, it was more like us doing each other a favor. He said you were neglecting him at home and my business was slow and I needed the extra money."

"So you were sleeping with him for money?" Keith interrupts. "I was your Man! How do you think that makes me look as a man? My lady going to some other nigga for money! ...... I'm out of here!"

"What's going on?" Britt asks Monet.

"Giirrrl, you thought you had drama! I'm officially declaring this day National Drama Day. It all started with prayer, girl."

"Prayer?" Britt asks.

"By the way Tim received a phone call that Devin was code blue."

"Oh my God!" Brittney holds her mouth.

"We prayed for him already; but listen, this is what happened. So after Tim got the phone call Pastor prayed and when he finished, Tiara said her own little prayer, disclosing personal information about Pastor sleeping with Ciara and being pregnant from him. Ciara left walking and Kim asked Tray to take Tiara and Ciara home. He left his phone, came back to get it and overheard Patricia fussing at Pastor about her having to get rid of their baby. Butray confronts Pastor and Pastor turns around and says you were sleeping with Kim. Butray punches Pastor in the face…. and here we are."

"Shut the front door!!!"

"Girl ALL these doors need to be shut around here! Who in the hell left the gate open! That's all I'm asking, that's all I'm asking." Monet states.

Everyone at the barbecue is feeling some type of way; each begins to reflect on a significant moment in his or her life, and the one thing or person they have in common—Gabriel.

Keith is so angry and once again disappointed to the point he can no longer deal with Kim so he leaves. Butray and Tricia part ways and Pastor leaves soon after.

So much commotion is happening all at once; Monet almost doesn't hear her phone ring.

"Monet, is this your phone ringing?" Brittney asks.

"Yes," she answers.

Brittney passes her the phone, "Hello?"

"Yes, I'm looking for a Monet Johnson, please."

"This is Monet."

"I'm Dr. Peterson; I've been trying to get a hold of Robbie…"

"YES, hold on please," she cuts him off.

Robbie is standing out in the yard with Mike observing everything that is going on

"Robbie!" she calls. "Telephone!" she points to the phone

Robbie thinks to himself, *who could be asking for me?* At that moment he takes his phone out his pocket and realizes he had eight missed calls; his phone had been on silent and he hadn't the slightest idea how that could have happened because he never puts his phone on silent. He immediately jogs over to Monet and answers the phone, "Hello?"

"Robbie, hey how are you? Listen we need you over at the hospital right away."

"Is something wrong?" he asks.

"There's something you should see."

"I'll be right over." He hangs up the phone.

"Is everything okay?" Monet asks.

"I don't know; the doctor didn't say. He said there's something I should see."

"We should go with you?" Monet suggests.

"Okay that's fine."

"I'll go too," Brittney says. "Sharee, do you mind getting Jaylin and Di'jonae dressed along with your two and bring them to the hospital? I'm gonna ride with Robbie and Monet. And I'll tell Kim to get Jada and Jalen dressed and that you'll follow her."

"Okay, that's fine." Sharee answers.

As soon as Monet gets up, she screams from the sharp pain she felt and falls back to her seat.

"Are you okay?" Britt asks.

Kim and Mike rush over to find out why she screamed.

"I'm okay, I think…..," she answers.

"Just sit here for a second," Mike suggests.

"Robbie, you can go ahead, we'll be right behind you," Brittney states. "Sharee, can you get the kids and tell them to get dressed?" Brittney explains to Kim and Mike about the phone call. Kim goes to help Sharee with the kids.

"Is it your leg that's cramping?"

"No it's is my stomach; it felt like a menstrual cramp."

"It's probably Braxton Hicks."

"What is that?"

"It feels like labor pain but its false labor. It comes and goes. How are you feeling now?"

"I feel better now."

"Do you want to try to get up again?"

"Yeah."

"Mike can you stand on the other side just in case."

"Yall, I'm okay… Brittney what did I tell you about…"

"Moni, don't start that faith talk with me; you didn't even have enough to keep your butt standing a second ago."

Monet limps all the way to the car with Britt on one side and Mike on the other and Alexis behind her.

[404]

"Alexis, you come walk on this side by me; me and your daddy got this. I don't need her falling back on you and sending you into labor," Kim says.

South Georgia Memorial Hospital

Meanwhile Robbie makes it to the hospital and walks up to the nurses' station.

"Is Dr. Peterson in?" he asks.

"Ummmm," when she looks up, she sees it's Traci's husband. "Yes; Mr. Welch, he's been expecting you." Just as she's about to page him, he walks out of the office from behind the station.

"Dr. Peterson, is everything okay?"

Dr. Peterson didn't know how to answer. He stares at him, folds his lips in and drops his head looking at his clipboard.

"Dr. Peterson please tell me….," Robbie turns around and starts walking towards Traci's room.

"Wait! I think you should read this first." He hands him an envelope.

"What is this?" He turns back around, "Traci!" He yells as he turns and walks towards her room again. Upon opening the door he notices all the machines turned off and Traci's lifeless body lying there as if she were sleep. "Traci," he begins to sob. "I'm sorry I wasn't here for you." He grabs her and holds her; "Traci, honey I love you!" he continues. He lays her down gently on the pillow and lays across her stomach and cries for the next twenty minutes. The doctor walks in and overhears him saying, "*if only my phone wasn't on silent, I would have been here sooner.*"

"She was already gone," the doctor answers him.

"Soon after you left, she asked for pen and paper. She was too weak to write so she asked one of the nurses to write for her. When she was done, she told the nurse to place the pen in her hand and step out the room. Five minutes later the nurse taps on the door to check on her. When she didn't get a response she walked in and found her non responsive...... I think she knew she was about to pass on.

"Yeah, she did." Robbie responds wiping his tears. I'm just sorry I wasn't here for her. Is the nurse here that wrote the letter?"

"Yes, I'll get her."

When the nurse comes in the room, he asks, "How was she? Was she happy, sad, did she ask for me?"

"Mr. Welch, your wife was very happy. She told me to tell you, you and the kids were the best thing that ever happened to her and she loves y'all very much. I think if you read the letter, it will answer a lot of your questions."

Meanwhile, Tim is upstairs kneeling down at Devin's bedside praying to God while Miss Diane, Devin's grandmother, stand on the opposite side of the bed.

"I don't won't this life no more!" Tim cries out to God. "I want my son to be okay, Please God I give it all up; I don't want to do this no more!"

[406]

Miss Diane walks over to the other side of the bed and rubs Tim on the back to calm him.

Renee walks in the room and sees Tim on the floor and gets furious all over again. "Get your punk ass up and get out!"

Tim didn't move; he didn't even look up. "Don't come in here with that foolishness!" her mom yells at her. "Where have you been? I've been calling and calling you!"

"I've been to the police station pressing charges on HIS girlfriend," she stresses. "She jumped me from behind."

"I told you not to take your ass over there in the first place. What have I always told you, Renee? Stop with all the lying and trying to manipulate people. This baby had done stopped breathing for eight minutes while you got your ass down at the police station filing a false report."

"FALSE REPORT? Momma she assaulted me!"

"No, she whooped your ass; Back in the day when we fought, you took your ass whooping like a champ and kept it moving…….. and you come in here calling him a punk ass…Huh," she smirks. "That's like the pot calling the kettle black. I swear child you need to get it together and get it together fast. You don't know when your time gone be up from here. Tomorrow is not promised."

"I know tomorrow is not promised, Ma!"

"You don't act like it; you act just like the devil sometimes, I don't understand you; you wasn't raised this way Renee. And look at this man; he loves his son, he loves his kids and you do all you can to keep him away from them if you can't have your way. Renee honey I'm telling you, you need to start coming back to church."

Renee stands there with nothing to say; she is angry and slightly remorseful.

"Can't you see God is trying to get yall attention through Devin?"

Tim gets up, wipes his face and proceeds to walk by Renee to leave.

"I don't think I want the kids around Brittney anymore," she states.

He stops and looks at her. "I'm done," he answers softly.

"You're done when I say you're done," she responds cunningly.

"You no longer have power over me," he responds and walks out the door.

Renee knows there is something different, something different in his tone, something about his calmness that lets her know it is really over. Renee sits down in the recliner with a blank stare on her face.

Downstairs, Monet, Britt, Sharee, Kim, Mike, Alexis and the kids show up at the hospital. Monet stops by the gift store in the hospital to purchase a Teddy Bear dressed in a pink breast cancer T-shirt. When they get off the elevator, Alexis volunteers to keep the kids with her in the waiting area.

Monet taps on the door as she opens it; she has a big smile on her face because she's excited to see her friend but the smile quickly dwindles away when she sees Robbie laying across the bed with his head on her stomach holding a letter. "Robbie," she calls. "Is everything okay?"

He turns his head towards them and everyone knows by the look on his face that this was going to be far from good news. Mike drops his

[408]

head and holds onto Kim. Brittney knows this is not about to be easy for Monet so she holds her as she asks the question again. "Robbie," she begins to get choked up. "Is she....?" Tears begin to form in her eyes.

"She's gone," Robbie answers.

"Monet cannot contain her emotions. She begins to cry as she runs over to Traci and hugs her- "Lord Nooooo; how could this happen to someone like her, Lord no, no, no...."

No one in the room is untouched by Traci's passing. Monet takes it the hardest. She cries so much until she is about to faint. Brittney tries to hold her up as she is going down, but Monet's weight is a little much for Brittney to hold up on her own; Mike notices she is headed south and quickly grabs her from the other side and holds her up. "Traci!!!" she shouts. "Ooouch! Ouch ouch ouch!" she screams immediately afterward.

"Monet, you okay?" Britt asks.

"Ouch!" Monet yells again.

"Here, let's sit her over here; Kim, can you get somebody in here?" When they sit Monet on the chair, Britt notices blood on the floor and Monet's leg. "Monet honey, you need to calm down," Britt states.

"OUCH!" She bends over and holds her stomach.

"Honey; listen you are bleeding pretty heavy; I'm pretty sure you're in labor."

Just as soon as she says this, a nurse comes rushing in the room. "I think she's in labor!" Britt tells the nurse.

The nurse sees the blood. "Let me get a wheelchair." She rushes out the room.

The nurse yells for a doctor in the hallway. They soon return with a stretcher; Mike and Robbie help her onto it.

"We're right here for you, Moni," Brittney states.

"Do you know how to get in touch with Mitchell?" Kim asks Britt.

"Ummm yeah; He gave me his number a while ago in case of an emergency. Here can you give him a call?" She hands Kim her phone. Shortly afterwards, they all went into the waiting room with Alexis and the kids. Robbie comes out of the room about thirty minutes later.

"Any word on Monet?" he asks.

"Not yet," Brittney answers.

"You okay, Man?" Mike asks.

"I'm okay," he answers. "I knew this day was coming I just thought I would be by her side.

"We here for you man."

"Yeah," Kim agrees; "and the children as well; whatever you need just let us know."

"She put my phone on silent," he said holding the letter up. "She wanted me to enjoy my day with friends without me worrying about her."

"That was thoughtful of her," Britt speaks softly.

"That's the kind of person she was, thoughtful, caring, full of energy and witty," he smiles a little.

"Guess that's why she fitted right in with us," Kim smiles.

"How did she manage to put your phone on silent?" Britt asks.

"She said in the letter she did it right before I left when she asked me to hold my phone."

"I'll be back; I'm going to see if I can find out anything," Britt states. As she walks up the hall and makes a left turn; she sees Tiara coming through a set of double doors. When they get within speaking distance, Brittney asks, "What are you doing here?"

"Ciara just had her baby."

"Really? What did she have?"

"She had a boy; they're cleaning him up now."

Oh my God, Well tell her congratulations and we will come back by later to check on her.

"I sure will," Tiara says with a big smile.

"You seem to be in a good mood," Brittney comments.

"I am.... I was in the delivery room with her and seeing the baby being born did something to me. I mean… it is such a blessing to be able to give life and then you have this little person that's so helpless to depend on you for everything. I don't know Miss uumm…"

"Brittney," Britt answers.

"Miss Brittney…," she continues. "I suddenly felt it's not all about me anymore; I guess I'm turning over a new leaf. God is so good." Tiara smiles.

Brittney stares at her with a smile and thinks to herself; *it's so funny how God works. This girl was so ratchet a few hours ago and now it's like she's a whole new person.*

"Yes, God is VERY good," Britt agrees.

"And guess what? I'm the godmother."

"That's awesome, Tiara; I'm so happy for you. Keep it up honey, and whatever you do, don't lose that what you got."

"Lose what?"

"That joy. I'll talk with you later." She turns around to go in the opposite direction because she realizes she went the wrong way. When she makes it to the opposite end of the hall she makes a right and bumps into Tim.

"Brittney, look, for what it's worth I'm sorry. I never meant to hurt you…"

"You never meant for me to find out," she interrupts.

"Please let me explain."

"How is Devin?" She changes the subject.

"Still waiting; His grandmother called and said he had a code blue; he stopped breathing for eight minutes; the doctors managed to resuscitate him and right now he's stable; he's stable but still in a coma." He takes her hand. "I'm glad you came out here to support me. Again baby I'm…"

"I can't do this no more." She cuts him off

"Britt honey, what are you saying?"

"Living for God and you is just not pleasing God. My spirit is confused and my soul is vexed. I have lost myself, compromised myself and took on this spirit of a lil thuggette so to speak. I have become a female you! You said it yourself it was my spirit and my love for God that attracted you the most! You told me I reminded you of your mom, but I don't know who the hell I've become and I can't do this, I'm not gonna do this anymore!" she stress with tension.

[412]

"Brittney please don't do this, I don't think I can do this without you!" He grabs her hand.

"I'm sorry." She turns and walks away.

Still holding her by the hand, he tugs it a little. "Brittney, please baby don't do this," with tears in his eyes, "I'll do whateva you want honey; whateva you want."

She walks away.

"Noooo!" He falls to the ground. God I can't take no more of this!!!! What kind of God are you to have me suffer like this? I need you; if you are real, I need you to send her back to me. Lord I'm sorry I hurt her, Britt please come back."

Brittney walks away feeling sad and at the same time can't believe she just ended her four year relationship. *Lord I need your strength. And I need you to keep me because I desire to be kept*, she thought to herself. She stops by the nurses' station to check on the status of Monet.

"She's in room 205, she's resting now but you can go and see her if you like."

Brittney sticks her head in the door; "Knock knock," Brittney says.

The doctor comes right in behind her. "Miss Johnson, how are you?"

"I don't know, a little groggy but I'm not in pain anymore so I guess that's a good thing," she answers.

"I think you got a little anxious and over exerted yourself," the doctor states.

"What are you talking about?" Monet asks.

"Is this a family member?" the doctor asks.

"Yeah, whatever you have to say, she can hear."

"Miss Johnson I'm sorry to tell you; your baby girl didn't make it."

"Didn't make it?" Monet feels her stomach. "What happened?"

"You fainted and you were bleeding so much we had to do an emergency C section. The baby wasn't breathing and she was just too little to pull through. I'm sorry."

Monet thought she didn't have any tears left, but once again they start flowing like a river. The doctor leaves out of the room and Brittney holds her hand.

Once Monet pulled it together, Brittney tells her she's going to go get the others that were waiting in the waiting area.

"Britt can you give me a moment alone," she asks. "You guys can come back in about an hour."

"No problem," she answers. "Love you girl!"

"Love you too."

Brittney goes back and gives the report to the others. Kim informs Britt that Mitchell is going to take an emergency leave and take the next flight out. Everyone keeps looking at their watches anxiously waiting for an hour to pass. "Let's all go walk to the nursery to see Ciara's baby. That will give us something to do to help pass the time," Britt suggests.

Everyone but Robbie gets up. "Robbie you come on too. We in this together, you're family now," Britt says.

When they reach the nursery, Britt pulls Mike and Robbie to the side. "I need you guys to do me a favor; Tim and I broke up and as much as

I want to be with him right now, I can't. His little boy Devin is in a coma upstairs and he can really use you guys to talk to."

"No problem at all," Mike says.

"Yeah, we'll go now," Robbie agrees.

After being at the hospital all day everyone grows weary and decides to go home. Monet stays in the hospital for the next three days with Mitchell by her side to take her home and after speaking with Robbie, it becomes clear to her why she wasn't able to make it to the hospital the day of Traci's passing. The reason she had been so weak is because she was actually feeling Traci's sickness. With all the morphine going in Traci's system, it was apparent to Monet that was the reason she could not stand, but when she would lie down she would feel just fine. Traci knew it was time for her to leave and she also understood to be absent from the body is to be present with the Lord. She had no worries, only a concern for her friend who once had the faith of Abraham. A friend that use to say *send me Lord and I'll go, or I can handle anything.* She did not want her friend to lose faith but she understood how easily a sickness can come as a distraction and cause you to take your eyes off the promises of God. Robbie had also informed Monet of the time of death which was around the same time Monet began to feel better. In her letter she left these words for Monet:

> *"Monet, this little time I have had the pleasure of knowing you, I have enjoyed every moment of it. We would talk for hours, laughing and encouraging one another. It has been an honor to have you as a friend. Don't look at this as a lost but*

[415]

as a gain. I have gained a sister; you have gained a sister. You may feel that you lost me, but I am not lost, I am hidden or shall I say concealed in your heart and I love you dearly. I couldn't let you come see me because you would have been too emotional but I need you to understand, this is my destiny. My destiny doesn't determine your faith. You use to tell me how you once had the faith of Abraham, or you'll say "send me Lord I'll go." You even told me one time you spoke "I can handle anything." Well here it is! Can you handle this MS? Can you handle me going home? Trials come to make you not break you; Never lose Faith, Monet. Go get your Abraham faith back. God is not through with you yet; He has so much more in store for you; however, my journey has come to an end and I'm going home to my daddy. Don't cry for me but celebrate me. Until we meet again, Lylas. Ps. I saw your daughter, she is so beautiful and she is okay.

After hearing that, Monet had a speedy recovery; her health took a turn to what appeared to be better. She hadn't had any pain in her leg for quite some time now.

Kim, Mike and Alexis went home and bonded. Alexis told them all about the family that raised her; her upbringing and even the time she was sexually molested. Sharee and the kids went back home. Brittney spent time with Jaylin and worked on getting ready for her grand opening at the Salon which she has not revealed the new name to anyone just yet. And Robbie made funeral arrangements.

Tim / Brittney

One night Brittney was sitting at home listening to the Sweat Hotel on the radio as she sometimes did to relax. Just as she was about to walk into the kitchen to get a refill on coffee, she heard a man's voice:

"Welcome to the Sweat Hotel."

"I normally don't do this but Keith man, I messed up. My name is Tim and I need my girl, Britt, to know that I'm sorry. I never meant to hurt her again; and I love her."

"Again?"

"Yeah man, this the second time… And I know she's listening.

"Well talk to her man."

"Brittney honey, I'm sorry, Remember the love we had…"

Brittney looks out her living room window and see Tim parked in her driveway. She stares as he continues to talk.

He looks up and notices Britt is looking out the window; as he continues to talk on the radio, he made eye contact with her as if he were talking with her face to face.

"You're my everything….. Forgive me….I love you."

"Well I hope she's listening, Man," Keith comments.

"She is."

"What would you like for me to play tonight?"

"Why Would You Stay by Kem."

"Alright man, you take care and hope everything works out for you."

[417]

They continue to look at one another as the song come on

♫ *There's a light shining on you.*

And baby I'm trembling inside.

Loved a woman that I barely knew,

I must've been outta mind.

Ohhh I

I ll never hurt you again

Girl I

I know you deserve a better man

Hey I

I was a fool to ever let you down

So why would you stay?

Woman I beg your forgiveness

And I'll do whatever it takes

And may the Lord be my witness

Honey I never meant to treat you this way

Sugar your heart has been broken

But I could still see true love shine in your eyes

When every word has been spoken

Woman I'll love you for the rest of my life.♫

Brittney can't help the way she feels; she is still in love with Tim and she wants so bad to run to his arms; she closes the curtains and goes to open the door. Upon touching the door knob she remembers she cannot go back down that same road. Her heart was torn between God and Tim who she both loved dearly; however, Tim had no desire to compromise on his life style and she could no longer be a part of that. She closes the curtain and Tim lays his head back on his seat listening to the rest of the song praying she would come outside.

Brittney, holding onto the door knob, slid down to the floor crying as the song continued to play:

♫ *You're my baby*

Hey girl

Yeahhhh I

I'll never hurt you again

Girl I

I know you deserve a better man

Girl IIIIIIIIIII

I was a fool to ever let you down

But I want you to staaaaay

Girl I

I'll never hurt you again

Baby

I know you deserve a better man

Girl I

Girl I

I was a fool to ever let you down

But I want yooooou... to stay.♫

As the weeks went by, members stopped attending Friendly Freewill regular. The weeks turn into a month then two; Members started visiting other churches and some joined bedside Baptists; the church role was down to two attendants and one or two visitors on Sundays and no one attended Wednesday night Bible study any more. Deacon Butray resigned, nevertheless, he and Patricia were able to work past her infidelity with Pastor and she forgave him for cheating with Kim and now their marriage is stronger than ever.

Pastor is sitting in his office praying on the fourteenth day of his twenty- one day fast when he receives a visit.

"Knock knock."

"Come in; how may I help you? Do you have an appointment?"

"Yes I do."

"Really," he looks at the schedule on his desk.

"It's not on your schedule," he answers.

Pastor looks up and tells the man he can have a seat.

"How can I help you?" Pastor asks

"The question is how may I help you? You called." The man states

Pastor is really confused now, "Look Mister, I don't know what kind of games you're playing but I was in the middle of something…"

"Praying I know," the man interrupts, "…and your prayers are being answered."

"Is this some kind of joke?"

"Pastor Down, De'Angelo Downs, we haven't officially met; allow me to introduce myself; my name is Gabriel. And I've been watching you for the past three years…"

"Watching me? What are you stalking me? I ain't with that gay stuff."

"PASTOR DOWNS!" He over talks him. "You have been tainting and raping your congregation, misusing your gifts to manipulate the women, tippin and dippin, and and making babies and what-nots. You have lived up to your name LO Down; truth be told you have lived up to your other name Down Lo."

"I want you out of my office right now!"

"A hit dog will holler; but I'm not here to judge you; that's not my job. I'm here to help you. I was sent here on an assignment three years ago by God. God found favor with your grandmother Willie Mae Jones and let me tell you, she has a lot of prayers stored up for you in her bank account."

"So are you THE GABRIEL?"

"The one and only; I was sent here to help guide, but I couldn't impose on your freewill. So when you began to cry out with a contrite heart, I was able to come in and here I am."

"But I'm only on day fourteen of my twenty-one day fast. I thought God would answer on my last day."

"God can do whatever he wants, whenever he wants to do it, besides this is your day of Grace."

"Day 14" Pastor says, "1+4=5; Wow! I'm just lost for words right now."

"Yeah I notice you like to relate things to numbers," he smiles. "One thing you got to do is right the wrong you've done. You have some apologizing to do."

"You're right." He drops his head.

"No, no, don't drop your head. Hold your head up; today is a new day for you; by the way God wants to change your name."

"My name? To what?" He has a curious look on his face.

"Yes, to something more meaningful…….Harun al Rashid which translates to Aaron the upright."

"You don't say? Aaron huh?" Pastor repeats the name.

"Aaron is a leader who takes responsibility." Gabriel says

"I got you," Pastor answers. "Aaron," he says again proud… "I like that; I can roll with that. That other name sounds Arabic or something."

"It is……. Now it's time for me to be getting out of here."

"Thanks Man."

"Aye don't thank me, thank Him." Gabriel looks up. "You take care yourself and by the way; Go eat!"

"Will do!" Pastor smiles.

The first thing he did was call up Stacy and Trin; he apologizes to the both of them and admits he overstepped his bounds as their Pastor. After two weeks of tracking Tam down in another city, she informs him that she never went through with the abortion and that they have a daughter. He couldn't deny the fact that he had indeed been with her, however, in a respectful manner he asked her for a DNA test

[422]

which she agreed to. The test confirmed that he is the father; and he has accepted his responsibility.

He then contacts Ciara and apologize to her as well, and respectfully asked her for a DNA test also. When those results came back, he accepted his responsibility of his son.

Now it's was time to put out his biggest fire. He makes an attempt to contact Butray but he got no response. After several attempts and numerous voice and text messages he then tries calling Patricia. Neither one of them would take his calls. So one day with influence of the Holy Spirit, he drives by their house and to his surprise he sees Butray getting out of the vehicle so he stops.

"Tray, can I talk with you a minute, please?"

Tray continues to walk in the house.

"Man to man, I was wrong.... I was wrong for what I done."

Tray keeps walking.

"I betrayed you and I'm sorry. The word of God says if we have an aught with our brothers and sisters to go get it right, man. Come on Tray I'm sorry... If you see your brother overtaken in a fault, pray man," Pastor quoted scriptures and pleaded.

Tray stops and drops his head to the ground. He turns around and walks up to Pastor and without a second thought he punches him in the jaw.

"I can take that; I deserve that," he says opening and closing his mouth. He turns his other cheek. "Go ahead." He invites him to take another shot.

Tray looks at him and turns to walk away. Pastor grabs his hand.

"Don't touch me man."

"Look man I'm sorry. I was wrong, dead wrong….. Look I'm in a different place right now…. Look at me."

Tray didn't want to look.

"Look at me, Tray."

When Tray looked at him, he knew this wasn't the same man.

"I know I hurt you man….."

"So you repay me by going after my wife, sleeping with my wife and impregnating my wife!"

"Tray, it wasn't like that man!"

"Oh really, then what was it like because I recall a certain someone being really bitter after I no longer wanted to be with him."

"Tray, you not wanting to be with me had nothing to do with me being with Patricia. I was sick. Mentally sick. That was a spirit that I wasn't aware of or shall I say a spirit I wasn't ready to address--that sexual, seductive, homo spirit was a stronghold. And even though you pulled away a long time ago, I apologize for imposing my demons on you."

"I am not gay man, don't you ever make mention of this ever again!"

"I didn't say you were gay. I know you straight…. I just wanted to come over and apologize to you and Patricia and ask for your forgiveness."

Patricia came to the door. "Tray," she calls.

"I'll be there in a minute," he answers.

"Do you mind if I talk to her?" Pastor asks.

"Yes, I do. Stay the hell away from my wife."

[424]

"I just want to apologize to her; what is the harm in that?"

"You were able to give her the one thing I couldn't--a baby."

"Look I'm sorry, truly I am and I'm not gonna keep apologizing for the same thing but this ain't about you, right now, I got to make things right."

"You Low-down dirty..."

"That is no longer my name." Pastor cut him off.

"Okay, Mr. Down Lo," Butray looks him in the eyes.

"Does your wife know you carried that title as well? Now excuse me."

He leaves Butray standing in the yard and made his way to the door where Patricia was standing.

"Honey?" she calls Tray as if she were asking for his permission.

"It's okay," he answers.

She opens the door to let him in as Tray follows behind him.

Before he leaves, Patricia was able to get the closure she needed and was quickly loosed from the unforgiveness that was harvesting in her. Butray, however, still had some reservations.

Once leaving their house he stops by his wife, Michelle's house and after hours of conversing she no longer felt bitter towards him. She actually felt kind of bad for him but she understood the power of forgiveness. They agreed to continue to be friends but staying married was no longer an option. They both realize they are on two different paths right now.

It has now been three months and Pastor needs to reach out to the members of Friendly Freewill. He calls Kim and asks if she can round everybody up to meet at the church Wednesday night for a meeting. Kim asks Monet to assist her.

The first person Kim call is Butray and he respectfully declines; Monet asks Patricia and she agrees to be there. Monet also had heard from Felicia who heard from Erica that works at Starbucks that Tim has turned over a new leaf and he is now saved, so she sends him a text message inviting him to the meeting on Wednesday. She also invites Keith.

It is now Wednesday evening and God has laid it on Pastor's heart to preach instead of just meet. As the church begins to fill, he lays in his office on his face for a receiving spirit and not a responding spirit from the people.

When he comes out, he is in awe because he sees that God has multiplied the people. As he steps up to the podium, he clears his throat and begins to speak. He lets everyone know it was his intentions to meet, but God said preach.

> "I can say this; I have made mistakes, I have asked for forgiveness and I have been forgiven. We all have some type of issue. We all have that thorn that Paul talked about. We are imperfect people, living in an imperfect world. We are Spirits having a Human experience. But thanks be to God that said *my grace is sufficient.* And in our weakness is when he is strong. Count it all joy when you fall into divers temptation; if

[426]

you see your brother overtaken in a fault, you that are spiritual, should pray, lest you be tempted….. Do I have any spiritual folks in the house? And many are the affliction of the righteous but… somebody say but,"

"But" they say in unison.

"…the Lord delivers him out of the all. Today I want to talk to from the subject *Take up Your Bed and Walk*. But first I would like Ciara…. And the rest of the praise team to come forth and sing a selection.

Ciara begins to sing *Can't nobody do me like Jesus,* James Cleveland's version:

♫*Can't nobody do me like like Jesus.*

Can't nobody do me like like the Lord.

Can't nobody do me like like Jesus.

He's my friend.

He picked me up and turned me around.

He picked me up and turned me around.

He picked me up and turned me around.

He's my friend.

Healed my body, told me to run on

Healed my body, told me to run on

Healed my body, told me to run on

He's my friend ♫

"Hold up, hold up, hold up," Kim interrupts. "How many of yall believe can't nobody do you like Jesus? How many of yall know, can't nobody do you like the Lord? See I know can't nobody do me like Jesus 'cause when I was in my mess, he kept me. I could have been dead, I could have had HIV or AIDS'…you see God is going to love you even when you leave him. Let me tell you how the enemy used to do me."

Butray walks in and sits in the back of the church.

"The devil made sure I came to church; he made sure he woke me up every Sunday morning to be in service; you wanna know why?.... Go ahead and ask me, Say why,"

"Why" They ask.

"… because he knew I could do more damage in the church than outside the church. But how many of you know if we confess our sins, God is faithful and just to forgive us of them all? That's why I know

♫*Can't nobody do me like like Jesus.*
Can't nobody do me like like the Lord.
Can't nobody do me like like Jesus.
He's my friend.
Can't nobody do me like Jesus

Picked me up and turned me around
Healed my body and told me to run on

He's my friend.♫

Everybody in the building is on their feet--including Tray.

After that one selection that lasted about eleven minutes, the praise team takes a seat but the people in the congregation cannot sit down; they are running and shouting everywhere. Sister Shirley no longer

[428]

has a shout ministry; however, the Holy Spirit moves on her as well. She shouts herself free of that arrogant spirit.

And after about twenty minutes of praising the people begin to contain themselves and Pastor takes a stand back at the podium…. "I got a phone call earlier today and I was surprised that this person had given his life to Christ; he broke down and told me his testimony and now ladies and gentleman the brother is on fye.- F.Y.E. for God. Yall help me welcome Brother Roosevelt."

Tim comes out and hand his CD to the minister of music and ask him to play number eight.

Brittney is still on the floor worshipping so she didn't hear anything Pastor said because she tuned him out. Upon getting up off the floor she goes straight to the bathroom to wipe her face. The music begins to play and Tim begins to do a hip hop praise dance off Kirk Franklin's, *The Way It Used to Be:*

♫ I ain't gonna lie, I can't even count the days
Or the many nights I tried living here alone
A heart full of pride, you couldn't see the enemy was me
I was blind and thought my second chance was gone

A ship without a sail, battered by a raging sea
Taking any love I can to try and stop the rain
While waiting to exhale, I finally got on my knees
I know it's been a long time, do You still remember my name?♫

Brittney is completely stunned when she walks back in the church and sees Tim dancing and not only that, he cut his locs off. She sits down and continues to watch.

♫ *Can I go back in time? Can I have another try?*
But I can't change yesterday

Oh, I can't take another day without You
Cause this heart don't beat the same without You
I forgot who I was, got caught up in this world
Jesus, I apologize

I should've lost my mind without You
Not another sleepless night without You, Jesus
I'm sorry and I'm asking please
Make us how we used to be

I try and try to keep my mind on You
But trouble keeps calling me
Every time a wound heals
Something else takes the healing away

But even when I've gone too far
You don't even call my name
Mama said, "If you love let it go
And if it comes back then it's back to stay"

You already know I belong to only You
I run to Your arms and say

Oh, I can't take another day without You
Cause this heart don't beat the same without You
I forgot who I was, got caught up in this world
Jesus, I apologize

I should've lost my mind without You
Not another sleepless night without You, Jesus
I'm sorry and I'm asking please

Never knew a life so cold
Thought that things could fulfill my soul
Tried to find love on my own
It was hard to admit I was wrong

[430]

No money, no cars, no fame, no lies, no games
My life is taken

Now we've come to the break
Tell me what You gonna say, I know
I give my life right, but You know
You ain't promised tonight, baby girl

Without You, I can't breathe
Without You, I can't exist
Without You, this world ain't got nothing for me

I'm coming home

Oh, I can't take another day without You
Cause this heart don't beat the same without You
I forgot who I was, got caught up in this world
Jesus, I apologize♪

At the end of the song Tim falls to his knees and everyone that wasn't already standing, stands up and applauds. The song he chose was perfect for him, the words fit just right. Church seems to be back to *the way it used to be.* Literally.

When Tim stands up he goes over to whisper in Pastors ear; Pastor then nods and gives him the microphone.

"Thank you Pastor, I know this isn't a part of the service but when I was coming up in church we had a sign that read: "Services are subject to change according to the Holy Spirit.""

"Amen," the congregation agrees.

"But ummm, I need to say something to a certain someone I hurt dearly, and I want to ask her for forgiveness. Brittney, I know I have not been that Godly man you need. But baby, I've changed; I have a job now that pays me more than I was making in the streets; I restored my relationship with God and I just want to do right by you and Jaylin. As I stand here before you, God, and all these people; I wanna know one thing…"

She looks at him with anticipation.

"…Brittney Renee Elizabeth Brown Johnson…"

"NOT THE WHOLE GOVERNMENT NAME!" Someone remarks smartly and the whole congregation laughs.

"…Brittney baby, Will you marry me?"

She answers "yes" with tears in her eyes and every one claps with excitement. Tim gives the microphone back and sits next to Brittney.

"Let the church say amen."

"Amen!"

"Let the church say amen again."

"Amen!"

"One more time for the Holy Spirit."

"Amen!"

"Brother Roosevelt said something tonight….he said he's a changed man. And that's so profound because some time ago, I had a visitation from an angel by the name of Gabriel."

Everyone that knew Gabriel began to look around at each other.

"I was on day fourteen of a twenty-one day fast in my office, on my face praying to God and I had what I call my Jacob experience. To make a long story tolerable, God sent Gabriel here on an assignment. And for three years he has been amongst us. I'm just so grateful to God that he thought enough of me, he thought enough of Friendly Freewill to send one of his Angels here to see about us .And what I mean by a Jacob experience is, He told me God wants to change my name. He said no longer will you be known as Lo-Down or Down- Lo but you will be called Haran al Rashid which translates to Aaron, a leader with responsibility. So Brother Tim, that's why I referred to you by your first name Roosevelt because it is apparent to us, you have had your Jacob experience as well."

Everyone begins to give God praise by clapping.

"If you have your bibles and I pray that you do, turn with me to John, chapter five." He begins to read verses one through eight. "And as I said earlier my subject is: "Take up your Bed and Walk."

We see here that there are a great number of people with all kinds of issues; impotent folks, blind folks, crippled folks, and people with all kinds of diseases came and waited by this pool called Bethesda waiting for the angels to come down and trouble the water. For when the water was stirred you could get in and be made whole. There lies a man paralyzed for thirty-eight years because he had no one to help him in the pool. I come here tonight to tell you it's time for us to "Git it Rite" church. It's time for us to stop acting like we're on that lil' yellow bus church, I'm here to tell you that even with your issues, God loves you. He loves you just the way you are but He loves you too much to leave you that way. So whatever your issues maybe, whether you're a drug addict, prostitute, homosexual, bisexual, bi-curious, adulterer, whether you were molested….."

Gabriel appears in the pulpit, unseen by the people, and begins to pour fire onto Pastor which represents the anointing being poured on him.

"Oooh, I feel my help coming on…"

Some people were starting to get delivered as they began to get out their seats some clapped, screamed and others cried.

"…or you may have been the molester; you may be dealing with HIV, AIDS, cancer, kidney disease, liver disease, MS, High blood pressure, sugar diabetes, hepatitis ABC and D. You may have been abused or you may be the abuser. You may not have always been a good parent and you feel I'm the reason my child turned out the way he or she did. You may be in a gang, you may be a murderer, wronged somebody, adultery, done your best friend wrong, hurt somebody you really loved, your parents may have wronged you, you may have been adopted, in foster care, victim of rape, hate crime…… E shoda do ba sa ta…." He speaks in tongues.

"Folks talked about you, they lied on you, church folk done you wrong….listen, listen, listen; verse 6 Jesus asked a question…..this man had been with this issue for thirty-eight years and within thirty-eight seconds he was made whole. Jesus said *Wilt thou be made whole?"* Verse 8 *"Take up your bed and walk."* I'm here tonight to ask you, will you be made whole? The doors of the church are open………

One person went to the altar followed by another.

"OOOOOh if I was you, I'd step in this water while it's being troubled! Will you be whole? It's according to your faith… If you need prayer…Come…. There's an angel, an angel right here people in this aisle….. Come!"

The people begin to move to the altar; healing, deliverance, and restoration takes place on this night; relationships are mended and most importantly Friendly Freewill is restored and God is pleased.